# 2016 YOUNG EXPLORER'S ADVENTURE GUIDE

dreaming robot press

quality middle grade and young adult
science fiction and fantasy stories

The 2016 Young Explorer's Adventure Guide
Edited by Sean and Corie Weaver
© 2016 by Corie J. Weaver. All Rights Reserved
First Print Edition: December 2015

ISBN: 978-1-940924-11-3

Published by Dreaming Robot Press
1214 San Francisco Avenue
Las Vegas, NM 87701
www.dreamingrobotpress.com

# Contents

## Permissions

Red Dust and Dancing Horse *has been published previously in* Stupefying Stories *and was republished and podcast on* Escape Pod.

The Rum Cake Runner *has been published previously at* Crossed Genres Magazine *and podcasted at* Cast of Wonders. *Reprinted by permission of the author.*

Lunar Camp *has been published previously in* Athena's Daughters. *Reprinted by permission of the author.*

# The Aliens and Me
## Nancy Kress

*Nancy Kress is the author of thirty-two books, including twenty-five novels, four collections of short stories, and three books on writing. Her work has won six Nebulas, two Hugos, a Sturgeon, and the John W. Campbell Memorial Award. Most recent works are the Nebula-nominated* Yesterday's Kin *(Tachyon, 2014) and the forthcoming* Best of Nancy Kress *(Subterranean, September, 2015). In addition to writing, Kress often teaches at various venues around the country and abroad; in 2008 she was the Picador visiting lecturer at the University of Leipzig. Kress lives in Seattle with her husband, writer Jack Skillingstead, and Cosette, the world's most spoiled toy poodle.*

What do you say to an alien?

I looked at the alien and all I could think of was "Hi." But what was in my mind was: *This meeting is really stupid.* Maybe the alien thought so too, because he didn't say anything at all. Both of us just stared past each other, out the clear dome, at the stars shining in a black sky, while the cameras recorded on and on like something was actually happening here.

But I should back up and tell you how I got to be standing on the moon staring at a silent alien in the first place.

•••

My name is Nia. I'm ten years old. I used to live on Alpha Colony on the moon, and then Mom, Dad, and I moved to Earth, which I hated at first, only then I made friends and got to like it. I had a new school and we got a new dog and my bratty little cousin moved in with us for a year while his parents were on an expedition to some asteroid someplace. The point here is that I was *settled*. Alice and Kezia and Maria and I built a clubhouse in the woods. I joined a soccer league. I won the fourth-grade spelling bee, spelling "assertive." It was a sort of lucky guess because I never heard of "assertive" and didn't know what it meant, but I spelled it right and so I won. A-S-S-E-R-T-I-V-E. After that everybody came to me to spell hard words for them. Sometimes at night I studied the dictionary on my tablet, so I could be ready. Life was good.

Then aliens landed on the moon.

For months, from January till June, everybody got hysterical about the aliens. What did they want? Were they going to hurt Earth? How weird did they look?

It turned out they looked a little weird but not too much. Pictures were on the TV and Internet. They were kind of blueish and bald, but they had a head and legs and arms and stuff, like humans, although they also had long skinny tails, and their hands ended in six tentacles. They didn't hurt anybody, they just wanted to be friends, which sounded reasonable to me. Adults, though, aren't always reasonable. A whole lot of them kept thinking that the aliens were just pretending to be friends so they could think up some nasty plot later on.

That's called "duplicity." D-U-P-L-I-C-I-T-Y.

My parents didn't think the aliens had duplicity. Mom and Dad are both scientists so they were in on a lot of high-level talks about the aliens, like with the president and stuff. Well, Mom was. She's really important. Dad stayed home to work on his science, which he could do on computers and which something to do with math. To be honest. I get along a lot better with Dad, which was probably why he was the one to tell me about the plan to unsettle my life. *Again.*

"Nia," he said while I was looking hopelessly around my bedroom. I was supposed to be cleaning it before I was allowed to go hiking with Alice. Cleaning isn't really my thing. It all just gets dirty again anyway. My plan was to shove everything under the bed, but it was already full of stuff I'd shoved under there the last time I'd cleaned.

Dad said, "A great opportunity has opened up for you. For our whole family, but especially for you."

"What?" I said.

"How would you like us to move back to the moon?"

That hit me so hard I had to sit down. Move back to the moon! That was all I'd wanted when we first came to Earth. But now I'd made friends and summer vacation was just starting and three of my best friends on Alpha Colony no longer lived there. Katie had moved to China and Jack to Argentina. Rosa's family had gone really far away, to the new colony on Mars.

I blurted out, "But I'm settled here!"

"I know. But you always loved Alpha Colony."

"There are aliens on the moon now!"

"Well, yes. That's the point, actually." Dad ran his fingers through his hair, which was getting really thin on top. He only does that when he's agitated.

A-G-I-T-A-T-E-D. It means "upset."

"You already know that the United Nations has sent a lot of scientists up to the moon to talk to the aliens. We're making a dictionary of their language and learning to speak it. Sort of. But it's hard because it uses both sounds and hand signals, so that if you say a word with one tentacle raised it means one thing, but if you raise a different tentacle, it means something else."

"But," I pointed out reasonably, "humans don't have tentacles."

"Well, that's part of the problem. We're using fingers but they have one more tentacle than we have fingers."

"What's the rest of the problem?" I asked. A strange feeling had started to grow in my belly, part excitement and part fear. Somehow, this was going to involve me.

"The aliens have made a request. Nia, do you know what a 'window of opportunity' is?"

"No." How could a window have an opportunity? Opportunities

meant you got to do something, and windows pretty much don't do anything. They just sit there.

Dad said, "A window of opportunity means a time when you can do something, and after that, you can't. You're too old or it's too late."

"Oh," I said. "Like ballet. If you don't start when you're a kid, you can't get your feet up on toe." Kezia takes ballet. She told me.

"Yes! That's it exactly. The aliens—they never ask for anything, but now they have. They want some human children to play with their children, to learn to speak their language and understand their culture in a natural way. There's a window of opportunity for learning language fluently and without an accent, and it closes around twelve years old. That's why Maria's mother speaks English with a Spanish accent; she didn't come to the United States until she was a grown-up."

"No," I said. And then, desperately, "I'm too old! Get some younger kids. Get Jordan!" Jordan is my bratty cousin, and he's only seven.

"Jordan is too young. The human kids have to be old enough to not be afraid, to report on what they learn, and to understand the mission here. But still be under twelve."

I said, "Do I have to?"

"Of course not, Nia. Nobody is going to make you play with aliens if you don't want to. This is completely your choice."

Really? Usually nobody gives me a choice about anything. It was always: *Clean your room, Nia. Do your homework, Nia. Move to Earth, Nia.*

But…

"Mission" sounded cool—sort of important. I'd be a girl with a mission.

Still…

I said, "How long would we go for?"

"Six months. Then back to Earth."

"How many kids are going with me?"

"That's not clear yet."

"How many alien kids are there?"

"I don't know, really."

Dad didn't have a lot of information. I said, "Will you be there?"

"Of course. Are you worried about safety? There will be adults present every minute, and cameras will record everything. You'll be safe."

"Well… can I talk it over with Alice and Kezia and Maria?"

"Are you really proposing that a mission of interstellar significance be decided by a group of ten-year-old girls?"

"Yes," I said, to see what he would answer. Dad ran his hand through his hair again. He should stop doing that. I think that's why his hair getting so thin.

He said, "Tell me your answer tomorrow, at the latest,"

Wow! I really do get to decide!

"Assertive" means "in charge."

•••

Alice and Kezia and Maria all said that of course I should go talk to alien kids on the moon, as long as I came back in six months because they would miss me. We all hugged and Alice, who gets emotional, cried a little. We all promised to be best friends forever. Then we went for ice cream.

•••

So now I was standing in the park under the moon dome. The sky above the dome was black, thick with stars. Alpha Colony lay underground, beneath my feet. Adults and cameras were off to one side behind some benches—like that was supposed to make them invisible. On the other side of the little park stood some aliens. Maybe they were the alien kid's parents. Nobody told me. The alien kid, whose name is H'raf, or something like that (you blow out air through your lips real fast, say "raf," and raise up your left pinkie) and I stared at each other through the faceplates of our space suits.

Nobody told me I'd have to wear a space suit. Actually, I didn't have to, because the air inside the dome is just like Earth's. But H'raf and the other aliens breathe some different air, and it wouldn't be fair if humans were out of s-suits while aliens had to be in theirs. So I wore the stupid s-suit, which wasn't uncomfortable except for the big tank of oxygen on my back like a backpack full of rocks.

Actually, there was a lot of stuff nobody told me. Like: There was only *one* alien kid. Like: There was only one human kid too—me. Nobody else's parents would let them go first. What did they think the aliens would do now that they didn't do before? Blow us all up because now Nia Philips was there? Sometimes adults just don't *think*.

So there I was, feeling dumb because all the cameras and watching people made "playing" impossible. So I said, "Hi." I said it first in English and then in alien, which sounds sort of like blowing your nose and jumping up and down at the same time. There was a dictionary of alien words we humans had learned so far, and I memorized part of it on the way up to the moon.

H'raf smiled. At least I hoped it was a smile and not a snarl. He kind of twisted his blue lips, showing some teeth. Then he said nothing.

"How are you?" I asked, first in English and then in alien. Another memorized sentence.

He smiled again and still said nothing. Did nothing. Just stood there like a blue moon rock with teeth.

And it went on and on like that. I asked if he liked the moon. I asked if he liked to jump. I jumped, to show him. I whistled for Luna, and my robodog came running from where Mom was holding her. I made Luna sit and roll over and I said "This is my dog" in English. I asked if H'raf had a dog. I brought over a soccer ball and showed him how I can kick it. You can kick a ball really, really high and far on the moon, and I managed to hit one of the cameras, which wasn't good because it broke.

Mom said, "Never mind the camera, Nia. Just keep playing."

This was *not* playing. This was not anything. H'raf didn't answer my questions. He didn't kick the soccer ball. He ignored Luna, which got me mad. Luna is adorable!

Mom saw that I was getting mad and she ended the "play date" before I could ask my next question to H'raf, which was, "What the devil is *wrong* with you?"

That would not be a tactful thing to say.

T-A-C-T-F-U-L. It means being careful not to upset other people.

•••

"It was awful," I said to Jordan, my bratty little cousin. I was talking to him only because my last two friends on Alpha Colony, Jillian and Ben, were in school, which is where I wish I was. Jordan was home from school because he had a cold, or was faking a cold. Only this wasn't "home" and Jordan was no good to talk to.

He had brought his ant farm with him from Earth. Mom wasn't going to let him because animals brought up to the moon are supposed to be approved by a committee, which takes forever. We couldn't bring Bandit, Dad's dog, but Mom got special permission for the ant farm because the ants are sealed inside a box of unbreakable plastic. Although *I* think she got permission because Jordan threw one of his horrible temper tantrums, lying on the floor and kicking his heels in the air and screaming until his face turned bright red. If I behaved that way, I would get the longest time-out in the history of the universe. But Jordan? Nooo… he got to bring his ant farm because his parents were gone for six months and he used that same excuse to get away with murder.

The ant farm, however, *was* kind of interesting. The plastic box was long and thin so you can see the tunnels the ants make. The box was filled with colored sand that shifted into different patterns when the worker ants dug. The feeder ants scurried along the tunnels, carrying bits of the food that Dad and Jordan put in the top of the box twice a day. At the bottom was a nest where the queen ant laid eggs. Jordan could watch it for hours, which was a good thing because, otherwise he's a pain in the butt.

"Jordan," I said. "Did you hear me?"

"No," he said, which made no sense. If he answered, he must have heard me.

I didn't like my cousin. I didn't like H'raf either. Why couldn't he at least answer me when I spoke to him? He was not tactful. And it wasn't fair that I had to be.

Then it got even more unfair, because Mom and Dad came into my room, looking upset. Mom said, "Nia, did you say anything to H'raf that the microphones didn't pick up?"

"No. And didn't you tell me that the microphones are so sensitive they pick up everything?"

"Yes, that's true. Did you *do* anything, then? Make a nasty face or anything?"

"No! You saw—I was nice! More nice than H'raf deserved. He was so rude."

"Well, he told his parents that you were rude."

*What?* "I was not rude! You saw!"

Dad stepped in. "Yes, we did and you were fine, Nia. We don't understand this at all, honey. But the aliens are pretty upset. So tomorrow, try to be extra nice to H'raf, okay?"

"Tomorrow? I have to go again tomorrow?"

"Yes," Mom said, her voice softer now. "They've requested another play date. It's so important, Nia. Please try."

"I was trying!"

"I know. Let's come up with a plan to interest H'raf tomorrow."

When Mom and Dad finally left the room, Jordan looked up from his ant farm. "Rude," he said. "Nia was rude, rude, rude!"

"Shut up," I said. I wanted to say a bad word, but he would only tell Mom, so I didn't. Little brat.

●●●

The "plan" for the next day's play date was for me to bring different stuff to show H'raf. So I did.

I brought the programmable holo drone that you can make fly around the dome while it projects 3-D pictures of anything. I have a lot of software for it. I projected a jungle, a pair of baby elephants, a ballet dancer. I programmed the ballerina myself, doing leaps and twirls. "You like, H'raf?"

H'raf smiled and said nothing.

I showed him my fighting robots. They're really fun. One

person works one robot and the other person works the other, and the first robot to fall down, loses. I acted out for him how his robot would work and I held out the remote.

H'raf smiled and did nothing.

I unpacked my building set. It had light, strong bricks and motors and you can make awesome stuff. I started on a car we could ride around the dome in. I showed him how the bricks fit together and handed him one.

H'raf smiled and didn't take it.

That was the last straw—I mean, the last brick! It really was! The stupid kid wouldn't do anything, and all the alien adults were doing something with their feet, shifting around on the rocky moon like they were feeling something, but I didn't know what. And everybody looked at me making a fool of myself. And the cameras went on recording. And I lost it.

"I hate this!" I ripped off my s-suit and stomped toward the elevator. Dad rushed toward me. The alien adults shifted their feet even harder. I didn't care. Over my shoulder, I called, "Go home, H'raf! Just go back where you came from!"

•••

Mom was really mad. She stormed into our apartment where Dad had been trying to calm me down for half an hour. Jordan sat on the floor with his ant farm, his mouth hanging open while he listened.

"Nia! What was *that*?"

Dad's calming down hadn't worked very well. I jumped up from my chair and faced her. "*That* was me leaving! H'raf wouldn't do anything! I was trying, you know I was, so don't get all upset with me!"

Mom doesn't calm down easily either. We're alike that way. She said, "Don't take that tone with me, young lady! I've just spent half an hour trying to apologize to the alien leader. That's his son you insulted. Actually, you insulted all of them! Didn't you see them making angry gestures with their feet?"

"I didn't know their stupid feet moves meant they were angry!

And I don't care if the aliens were angry or not. They're the ones who should apologize! I tried and tried…"

Mom's voice softened. "I know you did. But, Nia, you can't tell visitors to go back where they came from. It's rude. Remember when we first moved to Earth and those mean kids called you 'Moony' and told you to go back to where *you* came from? How did you like it?"

Jordan finally said something. He grinned and said, "Nia's in trouble. Heh heh."

That really was the last straw, or brick, or something. I burst into tears, ran into my room, and slammed the door. I wasn't coming out ever, not even if I starved to death. No, I wasn't! What I said to H'raf was justified!

J-U-S-T-I-F-I-E-D. It means you were right.

•••

I wasn't justified.

This came to me in the middle of the night. I couldn't sleep. I kept remembering how bad the bullying felt when I first moved to Earth, and Ellen and David and their jerky friends kept telling me to go back to the moon. Did H'raf feel bad like that?

Also, I remembered that when I showed him the fighting robots, his eyes got sort of brighter. Maybe he did like them—although if he did, why didn't he take the remote I tried to hand him so he could work one of the robots? I didn't know. But I didn't want him to feel bad because of me. I also did not want to apologize to him in front of a whole bunch of people and cameras.

I could do it right now, alone.

I put on my clothes in the dark bedroom and slipped out of my room. A night light glowed dim in the big room. I had just reached the door to the outside corridor when Jordan's bedroom door opened. His bedroom used to be a closet because, since the aliens arrived, we have all these important people from Earth crammed into Alpha Colony and nobody gets much space. Jordan stumbled out in his babyish pajamas with stars and planets all over them. "Where are you going?"

"Shhhhh! You'll wake Mom and Dad!"

"I want to go, too!"

"No, you don't. I'm going someplace really scary."

It was the wrong thing to say. I forgot what a lunatic Jordan can be. "I want to go someplace scary!"

"No. Go back to bed."

"If you don't take me, I'll scream real loud and Aunt Julia and Uncle Wayne will wake up and then you won't be allowed to go."

He was such a brat. But I saw from his grinning face that he would do it. I would have to take him. "Oh, all right! But don't blame me if you die."

It didn't bother him at all. He picked up his ant farm—why was he bringing that? But on second thought, maybe it was a good idea. Maybe H'raf would like it. He hadn't liked anything else I'd brought him, but maybe he was interested in bugs. I was feeling desperate.

Alpha Colony doesn't have security cameras in the corridors around the living areas. There were so few of us living here before, only a hundred and fifty people, and everybody knew everybody and trusted them, or they wouldn't be here. There are security cameras other places in Alpha Colony, but I used to live here. I know all the back routes and old tunnels and even some of the e-codes to open doors. Jordan and I made our way to the s-suit room with no problem. There were cameras on the ceiling, but we wouldn't be here very long. I hurried both of us into s-suits, ignoring Jordan's dumb comments ("Cool!" "Maybe we'll see a moon monster!" Like there really were such things.)

Alarms sounded; we ignored them. The aliens' shuttle was in the shuttle bay, right next to the s-suit chamber, and before any guards could run in to stop us, I was knocking on the bay door. I think the aliens were watching because the airlock opened instantly. We went into the airlock and it shut just as the first guard raced toward us.

"Cool!" Jordan said, still holding his ant farm

All of a sudden, I wasn't so sure. The shuttle bay would be

filled with the aliens' air. The aliens controlled the air lock. What if they decided to puncture our s-suits because I had insulted them? Mom said we didn't understand their culture yet. Maybe I was doing a really stupid thing. Maybe I would get both me and Jordan killed.

It was too late to change my mind. The air lock opened on the other side.

Four aliens stood outside their shuttle, waiting for us. Three adults and H'raf. Before anybody could kill us, I yelled, "I'm sorry! H'raf, I'm sorry! I didn't mean it. I don't want you to go back home. Stay here forever. I'm really sorry."

The aliens didn't say a word or lift a tentacle. But at least they weren't making angry-moves with their feet. Out of their space suits, they looked smaller. Also bluer, and more alien. Their tails were visible, about two feet long and strong-looking.

I said again, "I'm sorry. You see, I—"

Jordan screamed.

I whirled around to face him. He wasn't hurt, but his face was red. He yelled, "My ants are dead!"

I peered through the glass. Some of the ants did look dead. Others twitched, and then they stopped and they looked dead too. All at once I knew what had happened. The s-suits kept the alien air away from Jordan and me, but the ant farm had teeny holes in it so the ants could breathe. The alien air was poison to them.

Jordan cried, "You killed my ants!" and threw the ant farm at H'raf.

Luckily, it missed. The thing fell onto the rock floor of the shuttle bay and the wooden frame shattered. Dirt, plastic, and ants flew everywhere. It was a mess and…oh, what if there was something in the ant farm that was poisonous to the aliens? What if it killed them?

They must have thought so too, because they all jumped into their shuttle and slammed the door. Jordan lay on the deck, yelling and kicking his legs and turning red. The alarms sounded and a really angry voice said over the sound system, "Nia Philips!

Open this airlock door right now!"

But it was like I couldn't move at all, I was so miserable. I'd wrecked the mission. I'd killed aliens (maybe). I was a terrible, terrible person. And it was all my own fault.

No—*some* of it was Jordan's fault. He threw the ant farm, not me. I yelled at him, "Help me clean up this mess!"

Behind me, the shuttle door must have opened because H'raf and his father stood there, both wearing s-suits. H'raf said, "Okay."

I whirled around. "What?"

"I'll help," H'raf said. "I'm sorry the small creatures are not living more."

I stared at him. He smiled, bent, and started using a small vacuum-like-thingie to suck up the dirt and ants.

I blurted, "You're talking! To me! You're cooperating!"

"Of course," he said. "You are now polite. But that one—" He pointed with s-suited finger at Jordan—"must stop making so much noise."

I said, "Good luck with that," and bent to help sweep up dead ants.

•••

It turned out there was an explanation for all this. The aliens have not just a different language but a different culture and do things much different than we do. Whenever someone is a guest, you're supposed to start a visit by ordering them to do something. That shows that you are willing to accept them like members of the family, because family members order each other around all the time. Then the guests feel welcome and everything can go on from there. When I yelled at Jordan to help clean up the ant farm, H'raf thought I was yelling at him, so he felt welcome on Alpha Colony. Up till then, nobody had ordered the aliens to do anything.

Like I said: weird. But it did sort of make sense. My family orders me around all the time.

So now, it's a few weeks later. Jordan got shipped back to his other cousin back on Earth, where he can have all the ants he wants. H'raf and I, plus Jillian and Ben and two other alien kids spend a lot of time together.

I was right about the fighting robots, they're H'raf's favorite. I like a thing he has, a b'b'cal (blow out twice and twist both thumbs to the left). Before you use it, it looks like just a lump of green plastic. But when you talk to it, it responds to your voice by changing shape, and you can make really cool things out of it. The alien kids and we are learning each other's tech, culture, and language.

About the language. H'raf is a lot better at English than I am at alien. So are B'h'pril and T'june. When I ordered Jordan to clean up the dead ants, H'raf and the other aliens already understood most of what humans said. We don't understand as much, partly because we're short a finger to make all the words. Also, I think they're smarter than us.

That's okay as long as I can still spell better. So everything is copacetic.

That means good.

C-O-P-A-C-E-T-I-C.

# Red Dust and Dancing Horses
## Beth Cato

*Beth Cato hails from Hanford, California, but currently writes and bakes cookies in a lair west of Phoenix, Arizona. She's the author of steampunk fantasy novels such as* The Clockwork Dagger *(a 2015 finalist for the Locus Award for First Novel) and* The Clockwork Crown *from Harper Voyager, with a new series called* Breath of Earth *starting in 2016. Follow her at BethCato.com and on Twitter at @BethCato.*

No horses existed on Mars. Nara could change that.

She stared out the thick-paned window. Tinted dirt sprawled to the horizon, mesas and rock-lipped craters cutting the mottled sky. It almost looked like a scene from somewhere out of the Old West on Earth, like in the two-dimensional movies she studied on her tablet.

Mama thought that $20^{th}$-century films were the ultimate brain-rotting waste of time, so Nara made sure to see at least two a week. Silver, Trigger, Buttermilk, Rex, Champion — she knew them all. She had spent months picturing just how their hooves would sink into that soft dirt, how their manes would lash in the wind. How her feet needed to rest in the stirrups, heels down, and how the hot curve of a muzzle would fit between her cupped hands.

The terraforming process had come a long way in the two hundred years since mechs established the Martian colonies. Nara didn't need a pressure suit to walk outside, but in her lifetime she'd never breathed on her own outside of her house or the Corcoran

Dome. There would never be real horses here. Not for hundreds of years, if ever.

But a mechanical horse could find its way home in a dust storm or handle the boggy sand without breaking a leg. She could ride it. Explore. It was better than nothing. Her forehead bumped against the glass. But to have a real horse with hot skin and silky mane…

"Nara, you're moping again." Mama held a monitor to each window, following the seal along the glass. "No matter how long you stare out the window and sulk, we can't afford to fly you back to Earth just to see those animals. They're hard to find as it is. Besides, you know what happened when that simulator came through last year."

Yeah. She did.

Each Martian-borne eleven-year-old child had sat in a booth strung with wires and sensors so that they could feel the patter of rain and touch the flaking dryness of eucalyptus bark. Nara smelled the dankness of fertile earth for the very first time. She threw up. The administrators listed her as a category five Martian. She would need the longest quarantine time to acclimate to Earth if she ever made the trip.

"Blast it, another inner seal is weakening," Mama muttered, moving to the next window.

The dull clang of metal echoed down the hall, followed by the soft whir of Papa's mechs. Hope sprung in her chest. Papa would understand. He would listen.

Her feet tapped down the long tunnel to his workshop. Nara rubbed the rounded edge of the tablet tucked at her waist. Sand pattered against the walls as the wind whistled a familiar melody.

The workshop stood twice as big as the rest of the household, echoing with constantly clicking gears. The grey dome bowed overhead, the skylight windows showing only red. Papa's legs stuck out from beneath the belly of a mining cart, his server mechs humming as they dismantled the plating on a small trolley alongside him.

The workshop was half empty. The basalt mine had received

a new load of equipment just two weeks before, and as Papa described it, he'd have a lull before everything decided to break again. Judging by the lack of dents on this cart, the lull was already over.

"Hey, girly. Hand me the tenner," Papa said, his hand thrusting through a gap in the chassis. Nara passed him the tool. "What're you up to?"

"Nothing." Nara slipped open the tablet, expanding the screen with a tug of her fingers. After a few taps, she accessed the data she wanted: the anatomy of the horse. Her fingers flicked up, removing the layer of skin, then the muscles, leaving the bones. One of the nearby mechs bowed, his knees fluid and graceful as he picked up a tire and conveyed it to a stack on the far side. Nara squinted, looking between the mech and the screen.

"You're never up to nothing," Papa said. She heard the grin in his voice. "Did Mama kick you out of the house?"

"Not yet." She grinned back. "I was wondering something, actually. Think I could use the extra space you have in here to make a project?"

Wheels whined as Papa pushed himself out. "What sort of project?" Grey and red smudges framed the skin around his goggles.

Nara held up the tablet, projecting the images out six inches. Papa chuckled low. "Why am I not surprised?" he asked. "You want to build a horse?"

"I think I can," she said, her eyes full of confidence.

"Oh, I know you can, I just didn't think you'd settle for that. Let me see." He held it directly overhead, then grunted as he passed it back. "The leg structure's not that different than the diggers you helped me with last month. Your main issues will be balancing the mass and nailing the AI."

She nodded, her mind already filtering through the possibilities. She had to think of horse breeds, no — she would think of specific horses. Trigger, her favorite. He was tough and fast, with all the grace of a dancer. Oh, how he could dance. His hooves shuffled, his gold skin shimmering and muscles coiling. Nara would watch him, holding her breath. Nothing on Mars could move like that.

"You'll have to use the scrap pile," Papa continued, snapping her out of a reverie. "But if you need anything fresh, you need to order through me, and you'll have to work for it. This isn't going to be cheap."

"Cheaper than a trip to Earth," Mother said from the doorway. "And speaking of expenses, we're going to need inner sealants replaced on three windows as soon as this storm is over. One gap was so big a fiend beetle could almost squeeze through from inside the walls, and God knows what it would cost if one of those got in."

"As if it's ever just one," Papa said, shaking his head. "Well, we're due for a full sealant inspection anyway."

Nara closed the equine anatomy charts, her eyes already taking in the nearest scrap pile and a stout piece of pipe ideal for a femur. Mama and Papa's chatter faded. She tapped her fingers along the tablet, already picturing a horse of her own, programmed to nuzzle her shoulder and nicker in greeting.

Papa was wrong. Balancing the mass would be easy. The artificial intelligence could be adapted from existing programs. Realism was the issue. A glossy hair coat, a trailing mane and tail, the musty smell described in the old books she'd read.

Her biggest problem was… she might never know if she got it right.

●●●

Nara's boots thudded along the elevated boardwalk, her breaths rasping through her mask. She couldn't be late for her one day of physical attendance in school for the week. Papa had already threatened to dismantle the horse if her grades dropped again. A fiend beetle crunched underfoot in a muddle of juices and grit.

So far, beetles were one of the few things that could survive unaided on the Martian surface. Scientists hailed it as a landmark of the terraforming process. Nara crushed the bugs as a hobby.

Six months of work and the skeleton was complete. Most of the nerve structure as well. She had stayed up late working on the wiring in the neck and reins, connecting them to the processors in the makeshift brain. The skin was next on the agenda. Papa had suggested she use a thin alloy, the sort used for biometric floors. That way it could be programmed to respond to heel touches and shifts in weight.

She shoved through several sets of doors to enter the dome. A dozen beetles tried to follow, the floor vents sending them rolling like tumbleweeds in an old movie. The next two doors repeated the process and secured behind her. Nara disengaged the breathing apparatus from her mask and took in a deep breath of recycled air. For all the inconvenience of living beyond the dome, she preferred it to the tight confines of the city with its block-stacks of buildings and stale stink.

She slid into her cubicle just as the bell rang. Her friend, Chu, nodded from the adjoining side. Nara set her tablet in its cradle and grimaced. Another day wasted in school when she could be working on her horse instead.

Throughout mathematics and mineral sciences, she let her fingers busy themselves while she pondered the wiring system for her horse. It's not as though the school work was difficult. Quiz results came back instantly; she missed two equations. Nara grunted. Perhaps she should focus more.

"As Heritage Month comes to a close, all sixth year students study the contributions of the head financier of the Corcoran Colony, the late Mrs. Florence Corcoran," said the professor from the head of the room. A hologram of Mrs. Corcoran flickered overhead, her face smiling as she posed with an old-fashioned pick-axe over her shoulder.

"As you all know, Mrs. Corcoran believed that Earth's cultural heritage deserved a place on Mars. Your tablets have just received a list of the artifacts of the Corcoran household." The file appeared on Nara's small screen. "During next year's Pioneer Heritage Month, the Corcoran Museum will open. Your task is to choose an object from her archive and write a thousand-word essay on the object's history both on Mars and Earth."

A low groan filled the room.

Nara pursed her lips. She could throw together a thousand-word essay in fifteen minutes. It wouldn't eat up too much of her project time. She opened the file, skimming the list. It dragged on, page after page. The fanciest objects were listed first — the paintings, the jewelry, the clothing. Florence Corcoran had been an obsessive collector of old Earth, especially items pertaining to Texas. All of it dull. Well, the leather belt collection might work as a report subject, especially if Nara could touch or smell the stuff. Importing genuine leather for a saddle and bridle would cost more than all the metal parts of her horse combined. She was going to make do with synthetics.

She scrolled down for an eternity. Early space shuttle detritus, bull horns, an oil derrick, a preserved horse skin. Nara stopped cold. A horse? She clicked for more information.

Trigger, a rearing palomino horse dating from the mid-20$^{th}$ century, his skin preserved and mounted on a plaster body. Nara's heart threatened to escape her chest. Trigger, her Trigger, was here on Mars? Not only a horse, but one of the most beautiful horses of all time.

"We have passes available so you can all visit the Corcoran household and see the items in person," her teacher continued.

"This is it," Nara murmured.

"What?" Chu whispered.

She ignored him, her mind already analyzing the possibilities. Her prototype horse would take another six months at least. If there was some way to get this skin, maybe she could use it. Mount it on top of the metal frame—well, no, it probably couldn't withstand the sand. But if she could study the texture, it would be easier to mimic. Would the museum sell such an old artifact? Nara fidgeted with the edge of her tablet. Could she steal it?

Maybe a way could be found. Adrenaline zinged through her fingertips. She could see and touch a real horse, and not just any horse — Trigger. Hot tears burned her eyes and pattered against her desk.

This was meant to be.

•••

As Nara entered the grounds of the Corcoran Mansion, she was keenly aware of every security measure scrutinizing her. The cameras on high, glassy lenses glaring, capturing her every move. The slight give of the cushioned tile underfoot, implying a biometric measure to contrast her weight coming and going. The slits in the walls that memorized her irises.

Stupid, stupid, stupid. Of course there would be excellent security here. She was day-dreaming to think otherwise. Still, maybe there was a loophole in the system. Trigger's skin had been a low-priority item stuck far back on the list. Centuries old, an archaic artifact that meant nothing to anyone else. It wasn't even scheduled for a berth in the museum.

"Ah. You. Chu's little friend." Her friend's grandfather edged close, his small body straight as a support pillar.

"I didn't know you were working inside the mansion now, Grandfather," Nara said, handing over her tablet with her student pass loaded.

He grunted, the sound a husky echo of Chu. "I have been since the museum was announced, taking inventory of her treasure trove. You're the first student to take advantage of the pass, you know? No one else seems interested in seeing the works in person. Probably will be the same when the place opens, I'm afraid." He pressed the tablet back into her hands.

"Well, I care." Nara stood a bit straighter.

She spent the past week rewatching every available movie showing Trigger. Nara knew the sway of his mane, how his hindquarters bunched as he reared, how his muscles flexed beneath shimmering gold skin. He could kiss girls with his lips flared, rear on command, walk on his hind legs, and perform dozens of other tricks. Even if Nara heightened the resolution on the picture, it was difficult to detect Roy Rogers's cues. Trigger wasn't a mere horse — he had to be the smartest horse that ever was.

Trigger's presence on Mars had to be destiny. She was meant to know him in real life, centuries after the fact, long after civilization had forgotten him. Trigger would teach her how to make her horse even more real.

"What artifact do you want to see? Most of the good stuff is here in the house." Chu's grandfather motioned behind him. Down the hall, a large painting of two naked people in a jungle filled the wall, the woman holding an apple outstretched in a pudgy hand.

She tried not to look too disgusted. "No. I want artifact 3046."

"Three-thousand range?" His eyes narrowed. "That will be in the old warehouse. It all came in the second colony drop. You sure you want to go there?"

"Absolutely."

She couldn't help but notice his sour expression on their long walk out behind the mansion. The warehouse stretched along the back wall of the dome, the clay brick walls red-tinted and pecked by sandblasts. It had to be a mech-built storage house, dating from before the completion of the dome and human arrival.

Grandfather stood as the iris security scanned him in, grunting for Nara to follow. The floor beneath her feet seemed shiny and new, each step sinking in by millimeters. More security, but not as much as the household.

"Forty-six, forty-six," he muttered as he walked. Metal scaffolding stretched to the high ceiling, the rafters filled with wooden boxes. Nara stroked a box in passing, not even gasping when a splinter snagged her flesh. Mrs. Corcoran had been very wealthy indeed to have so much wood, and for it to be used for mere storage.

"Here." Grandfather stopped. A pink tarp filled the bin space ahead. A device at his waistband beeped. "Damn it all. Another guest and Rorie's not in. Can you behave yourself for a few minutes?"

Her heartbeat raced, filling with hope. He was leaving her here... alone? "Yes."

"It's all junk here anyway. Just wait and I'll be back to escort you out." He marched away, his steps brisk.

Nara stood there for a moment, taking in the fading echo of his footsteps. That pink tarp… she bit her lip and lifted up the sheet.

Trigger's pale orange coat looked soft to the touch, his ears back. His entire body seemed coiled, ready to strike. An ornate bridle dangled from his face. Oh, his white blaze! Even tinted pink, it was beautiful to behold.

Despite the glare of security, Nara couldn't resist reaching up on tiptoe to stroke his muzzle. The prickliness surprised her. It was like she had imagined, and so much more. But Trigger, beautiful, graceful Trigger…

A sob choked in her throat as she stepped back, reality a harsh truth to face. Trigger had succumbed to death at last.

The pink dust on the tarp had been the first hint. The lower half of his body had been chewed away clear to the blackened plaster below. The old building hadn't sealed out fiend beetles. His saddle had slipped sideways, the girth almost eaten clear through. Only a nub remained of the flared plume of tail. Tatters of skin dangled against the plaster, fragments littering the floor like a poor haircut. Of his powerful dancing legs, nothing remained at all.

Nara lowered herself to the floor, the grey stone chilled beneath her. Trigger was dead. Dead. His skin would crumble if it moved at all. His legs would never waltz again, never leap over cars, never lower into a handsome curtsy.

"I'm sorry. I'm sorry," Nara whispered. "You were so beautiful. You still are." She stood, standing close enough to breathe him in. He stank of Martian dust and degradation. The creamy mane shifted between her fingertips, a tuft coming away in her hand. She curled her fingers into a fist.

Horses didn't belong on Mars. She knew it, but she hadn't wanted to accept the truth. This horse had survived centuries on Earth: wars, fires, owner after owner, the long journey here, only to be eaten away by ever-hungry bugs brought along for the ride. Trigger deserved better. He deserved to be timeless.

"I still love you, Trigger," she whispered. In her mind, she could see the intelligent gleam in his eyes; hear the rhythmic clatter of his hooves.

Footsteps thudded behind her. Nara swiped an arm against her cheeks and took a steadying breath.

"Oh. You found our half-eaten creature." Chu's grandfather stepped alongside her. Nara clutched her fists tighter. "It's a shame. Some of these crates hold old masters – Rodan, Picasso. The fiend beetles had a feast. As it is now, the leather around this thing's belly is the only thing worth keeping, and that's just scrap. If someone broke in here, they'd want to steal the security system."

Chu's grandfather didn't even know the proper name for a saddle. Nara swallowed, choking as if on a handful of sand. "Is he really going to be thrown out?"

He scratched at his smooth chin. "Eventually. They plan on tearing this structure down before the museum opens. Things like that won't survive the move." He motioned to the floor and the scattered bits of hair and skin and degrading plaster.

"If that happens… can you let me know? I mean…"

Grandfather shook his head, chuckling. "Ah yes. Chu told me you have a thing for horses. That's what this is, right? Smaller than I expected. But yes, I can tell you when this row comes up for disposal. I hate to think what your mother would say."

Nara looked away. "I know what she'll say."

Trigger was only a thing to him. No one here knew about horses. No one cared. Trigger had been more than a horse. He'd been loved in his lifetime, adored by thousands and thousands. Maybe he could be loved again, and not just by her.

They headed out of the warehouse. Nara released her breath before she stepped across the biometric steps, expelling every bit of air in her lungs. No alarms rang. The presence of a few useless hairs hadn't even registered. She sucked in a breath of refreshing stale air, the strands of mane a moist web in her palm.

•••

Papa had guided her work on the forge. Nara pounded and shaped her own horseshoes and nailed them to her horse's hooves. The first hoof prints marring Martian soil looked as they should on Earth: deep and almost circular crescents, a spray of dirt disturbed with each ambling step.

Trigger's alloy skin glowed in glossy gold, a version of palomino for a new world. A white blaze filled the length of his face and curved around into wide nostrils. He snorted, the sound tinny. It could be adjusted later. This was a test run, no more.

"You ready?" Papa asked, the words thick in his mask.

Nara nodded. Papa's broad, gloved hand gave her a boost up into the makeshift saddle woven of rags and polyvinyl chloride belts. She sat high, taking in the jagged red terrain and marbled sky from a new vantage point. The brim of her hardhat cut the afternoon glare.

Angling her heels down, she tapped Trigger's ribcage and then engaged the reins. He snorted and moved forward. Gears cranked, soft and whirring, but his gait was lolling and smooth, ears attentive.

Just above his withers, a knot of long, white hairs dangled down and brushed the backs of her gloves. Nara closed her eyes for an instant, imagining an intact mane, a green horizon, the warmth of pumping blood beneath her – not just an engine. Trigger couldn't come to life again. She knew that. But she could grant him a different sort of immortality.

"The whole colony will learn all about horses, and you," she whispered within her mask, guiding him towards the nearest ridge. "I'll start programming your tricks in the next few weeks. Everyone will laugh and cheer when you blow kisses and dance. You'll be loved again, Trigger. Remembered." She laid a hand against his chilled neck.

As the sun glowed fierce yellow overhead, Nara glanced over her shoulder and smiled at the deep cut of hoof prints leading back towards her home.

# Cool Things That Happen On Venus
## Cori Cunningham

*Cori Michelle Cunningham is a college student from San Antonio, Texas. She has an affinity and dedication toward storytelling, art, technology and science, and has recently earned a degree in 3D animation, which she felt best combined those interests. However - before storyboards and digital puppeteering - books were her first love. As someone known in elementary school as 'the girl who got in trouble for reading in reading class', she wanted her first story written for publishing to be for all those just discovering their passions and still imagining what they might someday do with them.*

"Good morning, *Young Explorers!*"

The cheerful voices of the children's TV show hosts chimed through the pink and purple headphones of fifth-grader Imani Jones as she made her way down the block to her best friend's house. The business she had there was too important to put off, but that didn't mean she couldn't listen to her favorite show on the way there. Fortunately for her, she had Auto, a tiny robot backpack her mom had built for her. It stood for Automatic Utility and Telecommunications Operator, which, as far as Imani could tell, meant that he was a robot, useful, could connect to the satellite network – and her mom really wanted his name to be Auto. Most importantly, it meant that she didn't have to miss her favorite news show.

"All you long-time Explorers should know what day it is!" the report continued, and Imani grinned. Of course she knew what day it was! She felt like she'd been waiting for it her entire life – or at least since she'd heard about it in the second grade.

"It's First Encounter Day!" She cheered the words in time with the reporters and giggled, twirling her white-and-purple skirt around as she walked. This was going to be a great episode.

"It's been fifty Earth-years since humankind has been in contact with the T'Raji from the nearby star-system, formerly known as Alpha Centauri," one of the reporters explained, followed by her partner. "We say 'nearby', but that star-system is still 4.2 light years away. That would take our ships nearly one hundred Earth-years to travel. Luckily for us and our interstellar pen-pals, sending digitized messages is much faster."

Imani sighed as the show delved into trivia. Boring! She'd already learned all this stuff in school. Just last year she got a perfect score on her essay about deep space communication. What she really wanted to know was…

"So then, Charles, what about First Encounter?" The first reporter asked exactly what was on Imani's mind. When was she going to get to meet an alien?

"Good question, Rei," the second reporter acknowledged before continuing. "Ten Earth-years ago the T'Raji finished developing the first practical interstellar engine we know of. It's set to make that journey in one-tenth of the time."

"And that journey is scheduled to reach its first destination today!" Rei cheered enthusiastically, and it took effort for Imani to keep from cheering along with her. Instead she just added a little bounce to her step as she picked up the pace to her friend's house.

This was absolutely the coolest thing ever to have happened. She just had to see it. She listened carefully as the report continued, hoping for some new information about when and where the landing was supposed to occur.

"Unfortunately for us here at Young Explorers HQ, Earth is at the wrong end of its orbit. That means we Earth Explorers will have to wait our turn," Charles reported with disappointment.

Imani had never before been so pleased she didn't live on Earth.

"It also means our daily update will have to be cut short this time," Rei continued in the same apologetic tone as her partner, and Imani stopped in her tracks.

"What?!" the young girl exclaimed, holding onto her headphones to make sure she heard right. It couldn't stop now! There was so much more she needed to know!

"We'll be filling in the remaining time with some interesting facts about rockets. What does it take for a ship to land safely?" The report carried on, and Imani groaned. Not more rocket facts! Her mom worked on the space shuttles, so she already knew way too much about rockets.

"Meanwhile, to all you Venus Explorers out there: make the most of your First Encounter Day! Send us your photos and observations at –" The broadcast faded as a little jingling sound rang in her headphones. She was getting a phone call. She could already guess who it was.

"Incoming call from: Mom." Auto's mechanical voice confirmed her guess, and she tapped the little pink button on her headset to answer.

"Hey, Mom," she greeted her mother glumly.

"What's the matter with you?" Mom's voice sounded more surprised than concerned.

"Nothing." Imani sighed loudly, and when her mother just waited patiently for her to continue, she went on, "Just that I was going over to Rosy's so we could go see the alien ship landing, but I don't know where the landing site is, and *Young Explorers* was no help."

She started to walk again, but her pace was slow and dejected. She was still looking forward to seeing her friend, but now it seemed a lot less important.

"Aw, honey, I'm sorry. I'm sure they'll be covering it on the news –" her mother began sympathetically, but Imani didn't just want to hear about the landing. She wanted to see it!

"But, Mom, it's happening here!" She tried not to whine, but it was hard not to, at least a little. "It's the only cool thing that's ever happened on Venus!"

"Imani," Mom warned, her voice turning stern in response to being interrupted. Imani knew that tone and so stopped talking, though she was still pouting. Mom couldn't see that, though, so it didn't count. After a moment, her mother's voice relaxed. "Plenty of cool things happen on Venus. You just have to know where to look."

Imani pouted even more. Not knowing where to look was the whole problem!

"Now, did you remember to put on sun-lotion?" Mom moved on, asking the same question she asked every morning. It was one of the many problems that came with living on Venus. It was closer to the Sun than Earth was, and so extra ultraviolet protection was necessary.

Imani looked down at her arms and her smooth, dark brown skin that was still a little shiny with the strawberry-scented cream. "Yes, ma'am."

"And bring your lunch?"

She looked behind her now, to where Auto was hanging on her back. He could work as a regular backpack as well, and he was currently keeping her lunchbox safe and cool. "Yes."

"Then go have fun! You and Rosy are clever girls; I'm sure you'll make the most of your day," Mom said positively. Imani knew she was trying to cheer her up, and it might have worked if those hadn't been the exact words *Young Explorers* had used when they totally let her down.

"Okay, Mom. Thanks." Imani wasn't entirely satisfied, but she gathered up enough enthusiasm to wish her mother a good day at work. "I love you!"

"I love you, too. I'll be back by dinner."

The phone call ended, and Imani was left to walk down the last street to Rosy's house in gloomy silence. She was heartbroken. A cool thing was *finally* happening here, and she probably wouldn't even get to see it! Sometimes she couldn't stand being from Venus, despite the fact that she'd never been to any other planets. Earth sounded way cooler, judging from the way Rosy talked about it when she'd first moved here in the third grade.

She could feel the rumbling of the Sky Station's engines through her shoes, and it reminded her that they were all just sailing through the clouds. On Earth there wouldn't be any rumbling, because everyone could live on the ground. There was dirt, grass, and snow; birds, squirrels, and ants… There was even a gigantic ocean full of water! Even the sky was different: bright blue. Imani looked up at her own sky and frowned at the disappointing murky orange.

Yep, Earth was awesome, and Imani would bet that the T'Raji planet was even *better*. She knew as soon as she grew up she was going to find herself a rocket and head for the stars!

She was just coming up to the front of Rosy's house when Auto made a chirping sound, and his mechanical voice said in warning, "Incoming: Rosa Ramos."

"Incoming what?" she tried to say, but she was interrupted by a noise overhead.

"¡Cuidado! Look out!" Rosy shouted as she and her bright green hoverbike tumbled out of the sky. Imani had to duck to avoid being toppled over, while Rosy and her bike went flying into the nearby recycling pile. Luckily, Rosy had been wearing her matching green helmet.

"Rosy!" Imani cried out, as she rushed over to help extract her friend from the big pile of cardboard boxes and plastic containers she'd gotten buried in. "Are you okay?"

"Sí, I'm fine. But that's more than I can say for my hoverbike." She pulled out her slightly smoking flying bike and sighed. "No es bueno."

Imani looked at her best friend skeptically. This wasn't the first time Rosy had crashed her bike, but her flying skills were usually better than that, so she asked, "What's wrong with it?"

Rosy just shrugged and pushed her bike over for Imani to inspect. "No sé. Maybe something got into the engine. Take a look at it for me?"

The question sounded innocent enough, but it was a request Imani heard almost too often. She shook her head, but took the bike anyway. "Why do *I* always have to fix *your* stuff?"

"Because you're so good at it!" Rosy smiled appealingly.

Imani just rolled her eyes and opened the hatch to the hoverbike's lightweight electric engine. She just peeked in when Auto's warning sound chirped, and he pulled her away by the backpack straps. "Warning: corrosive substance."

"Hey!" Imani yelped as she fell back on her rump. When she looked up again she saw Rosy's concerned face and what it was that had been smoking in her bike.

"Imani! ¿Estás bien?" Rosy asked worriedly, checking to see if she was alright.

"Rosy, you have *sulfuric acid* in your engine!" Imani nearly shouted, and Rosy jumped.

"Uh, oops?"

"You've been flying through the clouds again!" Imani crossed her arms in front of her chest and glared. The huge yellow clouds that the station sailed through looked inviting, but they were full of acid and very dangerous. She knew not to fly around in them.

But Rosy smiled in a strained way that Imani knew meant she was feeling guilty, and she admitted sheepishly, "Only the *little* ones."

"You know you're not supposed to do that, Rosy! It's dangerous!"

"I know, I'm sorry!" She *sounded* contrite, at least.

Imani looked back at the smoking bike and carefully removed Auto from her back and set him down in front of her. The straps that had once linked together to make a sleek and shiny backpack separated into four metal legs. Imani couldn't handle dangerous chemicals without the proper safety equipment, but luckily, Auto was the *epitome* of safety equipment.

She popped off Auto's front casing and looked into all of the gears and circuits. She often watched her mother work on machines and had even watched when Auto was built. Her mom always did her best to explain what she was doing so Imani would know how it all worked. It was important to know, her mom had said, so you can fix things, build things and solve problems. Engineers are great problem solvers.

"So... do you think you can fix it?" Rosy poked her head over Imani's shoulder.

"Maybe." Imani shrugged, tilting to the side to make room for Rosy's round, bronze-colored cheeks and her bright green helmet. She did have an idea: "I'm going to try to get Auto to filter out the sulfur… Could you pass me that container?"

Rosy got the metal container off the side of the recycling bin while Imani quickly made changes to Auto's filters. Sulfuric acid was made of hydrogen, sulfur, and oxygen. If she was right, Auto would be able to force a chemical reaction to capture the poisonous *sulfur trioxide* and release the harmless water molecules as steam. I would be almost like a magic trick.

"Commencing: sulfur extraction," Auto's mechanical voice chirped. Imani attached the metal container to Auto's output valve and watched as he quickly got to work on the bike.

"How long do you think it will take?" Rosy questioned, watching the robot.

"A few minutes. Why?"

Rosy grinned, bright and wide. "Because we have work to do!"

Following that announcement, Rosy quickly dug through the little pack on her hip for her cell phone. She pulled it out with flair, snapped a picture of Imani with her phone camera, then smiled expectantly. When Imani just stared back at her with confusion, her smile slipped off.

"You *did* watch *Young Explorers* today, right?"

Imani's own expression fell when she heard 'Young Explorers'. She'd almost forgotten about it. Ordinarily, she would have told Rosy that of course she did; it was her favorite show.

Today, however, she wasn't feeling so enthusiastic about it.

"Yeah," she replied gloomily. "I listened to it on Auto's radio. It was a big let-down."

"¡Eso no!" Rosy shook her head, "Did you hear what they said about sending in photos?"

At Imani's blank expression, she continued, "They're going to start a studio here on Venus! If *we* take the most awesome picture of the T'Raji ship landing we could become a pair of *Young Explorers* youth reporters. On television. *Interplanetary* television!"

Rosy grasped Imani's shoulders and bounced excitedly, "We'll be world famous *twice!*"

Imani couldn't help but giggle at her friend's eagerness. Rosy was always looking for ways to get famous. She wanted to be a movie star or a computer programmer when she grew up, preferably both. Imani understood *that*, but what she didn't understand was, "*We?*"

"You can be my co-reporter!" Rosy announced. "We'll be just like Rei and Charles! Except that, since I thought of it, I get to be the *most* famous, okay?"

"Okay…" Imani said dubiously, "but how, exactly, are we going to take this 'awesome picture'? We don't even know where the ship is going to be!"

"That's where the hovbike comes in!" Rosy said, as if that were very reassuring. Imani looked over at the bike Auto was still working on. At least the bike wasn't smoking anymore, and it did seem to be letting off steam as Auto worked.

Rosy, meanwhile, was explaining her plan.

"We fly down to the surface, find the landing spot, wait for the ship to land, and then *click!*" She punctuated each point by taking a photo with her camera. "We snap some action shots!"

Imani rolled her eyes. "You do know that Venus is almost as big as Earth, right?"

Rosy seemed to have an answer for that as well, however, and she ran to the side of her house to get something. When she returned she was holding a purple helmet. "That's where *you* come in. You know this planet better than I do, Señorita Venus."

She held out the helmet, and Imani took it uncertainly. She was about to bring up that the bike wasn't even finished being cleaned out yet, but Auto chose that exact moment to chirp.

"Sulfur extraction: complete. No damage detected."

Imani sighed while Rosy *whooped* and hopped onto her bike. She watched Auto tap his way over to the chemical disposal bin, which came standard in a neighborhood populated mostly by scientists, and throw away the hazardous container. A few seconds later he returned, and Imani knelt down so Auto could climb on and become her backpack once again.

"Are you coming, amiga?" Rosy called from her waiting hoverbike.

Imani hesitated, "I don't know…"

Being a reporter for the *Young Explorers* show *would* be a dream-come-true for Imani, but she doubted there would be anything interesting to report from Venus. She *had* wanted to see the ship landing, but she didn't know how they were going to be able to find it on their own. She *did* know a lot about this planet and spaceships, but she wasn't sure if it would be enough…

It was hard to make a decision when she didn't know how it was going to turn out.

"*Please?*" Her best friend's pleading voice cut through her conflicted thoughts. When Imani looked over she couldn't help but laugh. Rosy was lying across her bike's handlebars, reaching out to her overdramatically and proclaiming, "I need you, Imani, *I need you!*"

At least this would be a good opportunity to hang out with her friend. Plus, maybe her mom was right and there *would* be interesting things to see on Venus, though she doubted it.

"Okay, *fine.*" Imani relented and strapped on her helmet. It had a screen that came down and worked as an air filter so they could breathe on the planet. She climbed onto the bike behind Rosy and adjusted her skirt around herself, glad she'd decided to wear leggings today.

Before they took off Imani warned, "You better not fly into any more clouds!"

"I promise!" Rosy returned happily and then started it up. Imani held on tight as the hoverbike lifted off of the ground, and Rosy waved to her grandmother through the window.

"Adios, abuelita!" she called out. She was just about to take off when they heard her grandmother's voice.

"Nieta, your lunch!"

Now with two lunchboxes being kept safe in Auto's storage unit, the two girls raced toward the Sky Station's dock. The *S.S.*

*Matumaini* sailed serenely over an ocean of big yellow clouds. Since humankind built this flying city, they'd been working on clearing up all the acidic clouds in the Venusian atmosphere, though Imani couldn't imagine how there could have been *more* clouds back then. Now, there were openings in the clouds big enough to fly through.

They weren't the only ones visiting the docks today, though. The whole edge of the station was packed with people. Many of them were probably hoping that the ship landing would be close enough to see from there, and Imani saw many of her fellow classmates climbing onto the dock railing for a better look at the sky.

Imani recognized most of the station's citizens who were there, but there were also quite a few she didn't know. They had equipment with them and small shuttles, which made Imani think they were engineers, except she'd never seen them among her mother's coworkers.

"Who are all those people?" Imani whispered to her friend as they flew over the crowd.

"Reporters from Earth," Rosy replied, gripping her handlebars. "La competición."

"Competition?" Imani echoed worriedly, noticing the large video cameras attached to the shuttles she'd seen. "I didn't know there was going to be competition!"

Imani always got nervous in competitions.

"Don't worry; no one knows where the ship is going to land, remember?" Rosy reasoned, "That means we have as much a chance as anyone else."

Imani wasn't so sure about that, but she held tightly to her friend as the other girl turned on the bike's protective force-field and prepared for the dive.

"¡Vamos!" Rosy shouted, and raced out and over the docks, toward the planet.

"*Avoid the clouds!*" Imani screeched, hugging her friend even tighter.

"All right, *all right!*"

Once they cleared the cloud layer and saw the surface of the planet, they both gasped. It was brown and gray and *huge!* They flew quickly over mountains, volcanos and great valleys where lava used to flow. Venus was extremely hot; it was once the hottest planet in the solar system, back when all those clouds held in the heat like a giant oven. Now, even though there were fewer clouds, it was still hot, and the air felt heavy. She was glad she'd put on sun-lotion.

Rosy was busy fiddling with the bike's navigation system, and after a moment the screen showed a map of Venus. "All right!" she shouted energetically. "Let's find this thing!"

Imani cheered along with her, gaining some of Rosy's endless optimism. She almost felt sure that they would find the ship landing site in no time.

Three hours later, they were both feeling a lot less optimistic.

"This is taking *for-ev-er.*" Rosy whined from the front of the bike as they hovered lightly over the *Akna Montes* mountain ranges' shiny metal tips. She had turned around so that she was facing Imani, her back against the navigation system and handlebars.

They had unanimously decided that it was time for a lunch break, and so Auto was sitting between them, offering the slight frosty breeze from his internal cooling device while the two girls delved into their respective lunchboxes.

"I told you Venus was big," Imani said, biting into her peanut butter-and-raisin sandwich.

"I knew it was big, I just didn't think it would be so… enorme*!*"

Imani frowned. The biggest problem was they didn't know where to go.

The *Young Explorers* show could be heard faintly from her headphones as the show hosts continued to go over trivia. Imani had turned it on again, both to check for new information and to make sure the alien ship had not landed somewhere else without them. Luckily, it seemed that she ship was still on its way, but it was going to arrive soon, and it was gonna get there *fast.*

They had to hurry up and figure this out.

"That's right, Charles, spaceships need a lot of level, flat space to land. They also land more easily in clear skies and mild weather," Imani could hear the television show host say. She knew that much that already. Landing a spaceship was a lot of hard work, and the conditions had to be just right for it to go as planned. There were other concerns like the soil density, air pressure, temperature and wind speed to contend with, as well. Imani had adjusted Auto's sensors to alert them when all of those conditions were met. There had been a few places they'd found that *might* have worked, but none of them seemed like the *right* one.

"I'll trade you mi galleta for your trail mix," Rosy said holding out her sugar cookie.

"Okay," Imani shrugged, handing over her bag of nuts and pretzels and taking a bite of her new cookie. As she ate, she watched as Rosy deconstructed her own tuna sandwich and started to add her trail mix to it, along with various other odd ingredients.

"What are you doing?" Imani asked, making a face.

"Making a better sandwich." Rosy responded confidently, holding up her mess of a sandwich for Imani's inspection. "See? I just layer on all the stuff I like."

"I don't think that's how sandwiches…" Imani began, but stopped short as an idea formed in her mind. She looked between Rosy's sandwich and Auto's sensors. "*That's it!* I need to have *layers* of all the things ships like!"

"¿Qué?" Rosy asked through a bite of messy sandwich.

"If we can adjust Auto's sensor to take in satellite information for the whole planet," she began, already opening up the robot's casing, "and layer it all on your map…"

"We can find the perfect landing site!" Rosy finished for her, taking one last bite of her sandwich before packing her lunch away, brushing her hands off on her jeans.

Soon the girls had Auto pinging off the satellites surrounding Venus, but as they began to get the information back, there was one big problem.

"It's all in zeroes and ones!" Imani wailed, pouting. It had seemed like such a good idea, too!

"It's binary!" Rosy exclaimed gleefully. She smiled and quickly connected Auto's output cable to her bike's navigation system. "No hay problema. I'm bilingual."

"Well, yeah, I know, but…" Imani started to tell her that wasn't what bilingual meant, but soon the data Rosy was working on began to make sense.

"Hey, I am serious about becoming a famous movie-star-programmer!" Rosy grinned playfully. "Tell me what you need, and I'll make your sandwich."

Soon the program was up and running, and it worked perfectly. With all of the specifications layered over each other on the map, there was only one place the landing site could be.

"Right there! That's it! The *Lakshmi Planum!*" Imani pointed at the map.

Rosy gripped her handlebars. "¡Vámonos!"

And off they flew again.

Soon enough they found the place they'd pointed to on their map. It was a plateau on the continent Ishtar Terra, and it was surrounded by mountains. It was also the perfect place to land a spaceship. The girls danced around so happily when they saw it, they almost fell off their bike.

"If it lands right there, I can get the perfect shot." Rosy said, framing the scene with her hands like she sometimes saw done in the movies. "This is gonna be great!"

Imani was excited, too, and proud that she had been able to help find this place. She was just about to agree, when suddenly Auto beeped in a way Imani knew meant trouble.

"Weather alert: volcanic eruption." That was definitely trouble.

"What? An eruption?" Rosy looked around at the mountains surrounding them. "Where?"

"Northwest Aphrodite Terra, be advised," Auto replied.

"Oh no…" Imani said, looking up at the clear, pale orange sky above them.

"Don't worry, that's *way* far from here," said Rosy reassuringly as she checked the map.

"But, Rosy, the *clouds!*" Imani cried, still looking up at the sky, which was quickly filling up with dark yellow and gray clouds. On Rosy's navigation system the 'visibility' layer went dark in their area, just before the entire program unexpectedly shut down.

"Satellite connection: disrupted," Auto explained.

Both girls groaned and slumped down, defeated. This had been the perfect spot, but now it was ruined. If the alien ship came now it would just choose a different place to land, and there was no way they were going to find it in time.

"I give up." Rosy said, taking Imani by surprise. She had never heard her friend give up on *anything*. "Let's get back home before it gets too cloudy."

Imani frowned. Somehow it didn't feel right to give up after all the work they'd done, but she couldn't think of anything else to do. She nodded sadly. "Okay."

Devastated, the two girls turned the bike around and started to head for home. Rosy looked especially disheartened. Imani remembered how Rosy had helped cheer her up when she was upset this morning, and she wished she could think of a way to return the favor. They were just searching for a big enough opening in the clouds to fly through when Auto chirped again,

"Incoming: digital communication."

"What? I thought his satellite connection was down?" Rosy asked over her shoulder.

"It is!" Imani answered, double checking the source. "It's coming from in *there*."

She pointed up at the gargantuan mass of dark clouds, where the signal was apparently originating from. When Imani tried to listen to it at first, she could only hear static. She opened Auto's casing again and started to adjust the frequency. The report on space communication she did last year in school was sure useful now. Soon she could hear a voice:

"Adiuvate!"

Imani blinked and held onto her headphones. "What language is that?"

"Earth language: Latin," Auto answered, but that one word was followed by many others, and soon Auto was identifying them all, "Earth language: Greek. Mandarin. Arabic…"

"Okay, but what does it mean?" Imani asked in frustration.

"Online dictionary: error."

"He can't connect to the internet; it's too cloudy." Imani told Rosy before pressing the button on her headphones and calling out to the mysterious voice, "Hello? Can you hear me?"

The string of various Earth languages paused for a moment, but there was no response. Imani tried again, "Do you speak English?"

"¿O Español?" Rosy added, straining to hear what the voice said next.

They waited a few seconds but didn't hear anything. Imani looked down at Auto's sensors and saw that the signal was quickly fading, not to mention the clouds were getting darker by the second. "I think we lost it. We should probably –"

"¡Ayúdame!" The voice suddenly came back, and both girls jumped.

Rosy was the first to recover, answering with a determined "¡Si!" and stopping the bike. She turned around in her seat. "That means she's in trouble! I got this, you fly the bike!"

"Wait, *me?*" Imani gaped, but she helped Rosy maneuver around her anyway. Auto was once again strapped to her back, but now Imani was nervously gripping the handlebars of Rosy's hoverbike while Rosy put on Imani's pink-and-purple headset.

"¡Hola amiga! ¿Cúal es el problema?"

Imani could hear her friend talking to the voice in Spanish while she tried to get the hang of flying the hoverbike. There were a few jerky stops and starts, but soon they were hovering at a decent speed, still heading for the station. They had to find a way to get back up. There were a few small patches of open sky, but Imani was nervous about trying them.

She was just about to turn around and try looking in a different area when Rosy shook her shoulder urgently, "It's the T'Raji ship!" she announced, but, Rosy sounded more worried than excited. "There's something wrong with it!"

Imani listened as her friend tried to get details, but soon loud static interfered with the message. "I'm losing the signal!" Rosy cried. "You have to fly higher!"

Imani frowned and tried to protest. She was nervous; she knew she wasn't very good at flying. What if she messed up and they crashed? She turned to look at her friend over her shoulder, but Rosy looked back at her unwaveringly. "C'mon, Imani, *I need you!*"

She couldn't let down her friend, or that ship. Imani took a deep breath, gritted her teeth, then pointed her handlebars up and shot off toward one of those little gaps in the clouds. Every time they got close to one, it would close up, and Imani would have to turn and chase another, but as they flew she could hear the signal clearing up. Rosy continued to talk with the T'Raji.

"There's smoke coming out of the ship... and it's losing control!" Rosy translated. Imani had never heard her friend so distressed. "It'll crash if we don't do something!"

"Auto, you've got to call the station!" Imani shouted over her shoulder.

"Outgoing call: error. Chemical interference," Auto chirped helplessly.

"Ugh! It's these clouds!" Imani groaned, trying her best to pilot her way through the big yellowish blobs of gas. Then, she suddenly had an idea. "*Wait a minute.* It's just like what happened to your bike!" She called out to Rosy, "You've got to tell them to get rid of the *acid.*"

"I can't! I've lost the signal again."

Imani looked back up at the sky. "We'll just have to get higher."

"What about the clouds?" Rosy asked, concerned. These were way bigger clouds than the ones she flew through, and they were much scarier.

"We have to let them know. We can't let the whole ship crash!" Imani reasoned, though she was nervous, as well. Even so, she knew she had to do something. "We have to go."

Behind her, Imani could feel Rosy hold on tightly.

"Warning: corrosive substance." Auto's warning beeped unheeded as the two girls flew up and into the dangerous chemical clouds. The ship's light force-field kept the chemicals off of the girls, but the anti-gravity pads the bike ran on were quickly filling the engine with acid again.

"Do you have it?" Imani called out to her friend even as her eyes looked ahead for any sign of the clear afternoon sky. She didn't think she would even mind the color anymore; she so desperately wanted to see that murky orange.

"Not yet!" Rosy called back.

"Warning: corrosive substance," Auto buzzed again, warningly.

"Now?"

"No!"

"*Now?*"

"Danger –"

"I got it!" Rosy shouted, just as they broke through the clouds. Imani sighed in relief as Rosy finished relaying instructions to the T'Raji ship. In the distance they could see the station.

"¡Hurra! It worked," cheered Rosy. "She said they were able to filter out the acid, and the ships' sensors are going back to normal! We did it!"

Rosy jumped up and wrapped her arms around Imani's shoulders, laughing with joy. Imani couldn't help but laugh, too. She felt like she'd really accomplished something great.

With Rosy hugging her back, it was difficult to hear Auto's repeated chirping. Soon enough, however, the little robot was wiggling and chirping too much to be ignored. Rosy let go of her friend and sat back, muffling the robot, who immediately screeched, "*Danger: acid damage.*"

The hoverbike's engine stuttered, then stopped, and suddenly both girls were falling.

"Aaaah!!!" They both shrieked, panicking, even as a soft blue light enveloped them and whisked them away before they could even touch the clouds.

"*Aaaah!!!*" They continued to scream, even as they landed

safely in the hull of the T'Raji spaceship, their eyes tightly closed.

"Um, please calm down." A strange, somewhat stammering voice broke through their yells, and both girls slowly opened their eyes.

"Woah…" They gaped as they looked up at an extremely tall, bright blue alien.

"Are you… both all right?" he asked, clearing his throat a little.

Both girls nodded.

The T'Raji looked slightly uncomfortable.

"Are your… guardians… on the science station nearby?" he asked, hesitating a little.

Both girls nodded again.

"Very well, we will be sure to return you to your homes immediately."

The tall alien nodded sternly, then quickly excused himself. His departure revealed another blue alien, this one much smaller and with a big smile on her face.

"¡Hola!" She greeted jovially. "Sorry about my dad. He gets *nervous*."

"Hey, it's you!" Rosy was the first to speak up, remembering the voice she'd heard. "You were the voice on the transmission!"

"Yep. I finally found the right language on my translator. Hello!" She wiggled slightly. "Thanks for your help, by the way. We didn't know *what* was going on."

Imani was a little slower to catch her bearings, but after a moment she smiled back at the other girl, who looked to be about their age, and replied, "We had the same problem."

The blue girl smiled and happily introduced herself. "My name's Terra. I was named after Earth, since I was born on the ship, and that's where we're supposed to be going, *eventually*." She sighed, clearly growing tired of the long journey.

"I'm Imani."

"And I'm Rosa, but you can call me Rosy!"

"So," Terra began after a short span of silence, "do you want to go see my dad *try* to give his introductory speech to a bunch of human people?”

“Sure!” both human girls replied, and all three of them quickly ran to the ship's front window. Outside, Terra's dad *was* giving a speech, surrounded by a bunch of eager reporters.

“Well, so much for getting the best picture,” Rosy groused.

“Picture?” Terra questioned.

“Yeah, we were trying to get a good picture of your ship landing to send to *Young Explorers* for their contest. But, your ship had *already* landed, so I guess we missed out.” Imani explained with a shrug. She wasn't as disappointed as Rosy was. This was the best day *ever*.

Terra thought for a moment, then seemed to come to a decision.

“Well, who wants a picture of our silly old ship anyway? It's not very interesting,” she started, before opening her arms to the other two. “Let's take a picture together! You can send *that* to your contest. It'll be *way* better.”

“You think so?” Rosy asked hopefully, taking out her cell phone.

“Trust me!” Terra grinned; both humans shrugged and bunched together around their new friend. Rosy held up her camera and adjusted it until they all fit in the screen.

“Okay. Three… two... one…!”

*Click!*

“Good morning, *Young Explorers!*”

The cheerful voices of the children's TV show hosts chimed out for two worlds and two species to hear.

“My name's Imani.”

“Me llamo Rosa!”

“And I'm Terra!”

“And we're here to tell you about all the cool things happening on planet Venus!”

# The Worms Won't Feed Themselves, You Know

## Deborah Walker

*Deborah Walker grew up in the most English town in the country, but she soon high-tailed it down to London, where she now lives with her partner, Chris, and her two young children. Find Deborah in the British Museum trawling the past for future inspiration. Her stories have appeared in the* 2015 Young Explorer's Adventure Guide, Nature's Futures, Lady Churchill's Rosebud Wristlet *and* The Year's Best SF 18 *and have been translated into over a dozen languages.*

It was about time. Finally, I was a woman. I am woman, hear me roar. Only kidding. Not much had changed. Now that I was thirteen, the so-called Age of Freedom, the Mamas had given me just the tiniest bit of independence. I was allowed to manage my own time. No more timetables. So, I'd slept in until noon and had to waste the whole afternoon on my console doing maths (which I love) and social studies (which I despise).

At five, I finally finished, but I still had my chores to do. The worms wouldn't feed themselves. I grabbed my bee hat and made my way to the hives.

*He* was there, standing at the edge of the village right at the boundary marked by the underground bleepers. He was making notes. The bleepers also send out dampening privacy waves. He couldn't video-record us. But there was nothing to stop him from looking at us and writing it all down.

He waved. I kept my head fixed on the hives, pretending to be concentrating on the task I'd done a thousand times: extracting the waxy propolis from the hives. The propolis would be sold at the Collective's market after the worms had done their business.

I wondered what Comb7 looked like through his eyes. An English summer made anywhere look good. The meadows were pretty with a ton of wild flowers. Every step I took kicked up dandelion clocks and milkweed fluff. Close by, Mamas were working in the corn fields, helped or hindered by a gaggle of little 'uns. It was a good village. A bit small. We had twelve Mamas and twice that number of freedom juniors and kiddiewinks.

In the centre of the village was our home. It was basket shaped like a bee skep and had a nice brown colour to blend into the environment. With a spectacular lack of invention, we called it The Hive. We're a bit bee mad in Comb7. The Hive riffed off the structure of a bee hive, with hexagonal rooms stacked in parallel layers, and one large arched entrance facing the equator. It made sense to use millions of years of evolution and copy Mother Nature, at least that's what my social architecture lessons told me.

When I'd been a kid, Comb7 had seemed huge. But as I'd grown older, the village had somehow grown smaller. There was a whole world out there, with billions of people in it, and here everyone was the same. Well, not the same. But not as different as the people outside. Not as different as the *man* who was watching us. I'd never spoken to a man.

There was no doubt about it; Comb 7 was just a small, isolationist village, part of the all-female South East Collective. And it was too small for me. In a few years, I'd be going to London T. I know everybody says that. But I mean it. But that was in a few more years. With the man, the social librarian, Alex Shvartsman his name was, standing at the village boundaries, it was as if LondonT had come to our Comb7. I wasn't ready for it.

A man. Just imagine that. Someone who hadn't altered his DNA when he turned eighteen. A man, pure and simple. Just about the most exotic thing you could do to your body is not changing it when you get the chance.

All the Mamas were modified, of course. You had to have the Mama mod to stay in this village. All the Mamas were able to make babies without the help of a male personage. That's what the propolis did, in a modified form it initiated pregnancy in the Mamas. That's why it was my job to process it; the Mamas could get accidentally pregnant just by touching the stuff.

I chanced a glance at the man. He was the whitest person I'd ever seen in my life. Even though he was youngish, he couldn't have been much more than eighteen, his hair shone grey in the sunlight.

The Mamas wouldn't let him come into the village. The Mamas had told us not to approach him. I wanted to talk to him. But, oh no, once the council made its decision, everybody had to stick by it.

I didn't like being watched. I didn't like a man making notes about me.

Without a second glance at him, I left the hives and walked to the worm pit. The worms wriggled and looked hungry. All the wax had turned red, telling me that it had been purified through their guts. I scraped up the wax and bottled it, adding the fresh propolis to the pit. "Enjoy!" I said.

Then I made my way to Mama Bathsheba. She was council leader this year. Her first commandment was to implement an annoying new rule. Before any junior could do recreation time, we had to go and get our task lists ticked off. Even if we were Age of Freedom. Honestly, she totally didn't trust us.

There she sat, her ocelli mods, her hundreds of little eyes spots, flickering. Whatever had possessed her to get such an ugly modification, I couldn't think.

"I've done all my tasks, Mama. Am I free now?"

She didn't look up from the papers she was grading. "Are you sure you're done, Freya?"

"Yes, Mama."

"Because last week you told me you were done, and you'd forgotten to do your social studies module."

I blushed. That was an honest mistake. Anybody can make a mistake. "I have entirely done my tasks for the day."

"Run along then, Freya."

••

"Oh my god," said Sonya, her hands on her hips and exasperation written all over her face. "You won't believe what Sara has done."

Sara was six and a total brat. "*Nothing* that girl does surprises me."

"She mooned the stranger."

That *did* surprise me. I burst out laughing. "Oh my god. She didn't."

"She totally did. She walked to the boundary and bent over and showed him her little bare bottom. Mama Bathsheba is furious. She's given Sara a ton of extra chores."

"Serves her right. God, she's wild. I wonder if the man drew a picture of it. Then her bottom would be recorded for *posterity*."

Sonya laughed, her cheeks growing pink. "What a little savage."

"I can't *bare* the thought of a picture of her bum being added to the Library United records."

"Stop it!" said Sonya, nearly rolling off her bed.

It took quite some time for our giggles to die down.

Eventually, Sonya reached for her holi-emitter and began to play the latest Selkie Sisters' album. They're like our favourite band at the moment. Totally cool. They're based in LondonT, of course. We loved LondonT. As soon as we turned sixteen, we were going to go to a LondonT processing centre, that's for sure.

I listened for a bit, letting the music wash over me. It was like the ocean. Which, by the way, is something I've never seen. I bet the man standing at the gates had seen the ocean. Maybe he'd even been overseas. I sighed. "Mama Bathsheba was on my case today, again, Sonya. I'm fed up of her. She thinks she rules us."

"She does rule us," said Sonya, rolling her eyes. Sonya's my bestie, and I love her. But she's not like me. She never seemed to get angry. That made me jealous of her and, yes, a little bit angry sometimes. I was nothing but anger nowadays.

I turned my holi-emitter to my favourite channel, browsing through potential mods. I spent a long time looking at mods, as

I suppose everyone my age does. I browsed through the mods I'd favourited: high fash, postmod beetle women; images of Wecall who'd turned her body into an instrument; selkies; harpies; mermaids and super-bright girlie girls, Most of them were female. And that was my choice. I could favourite any mod I wanted. But funny how I had chosen women and neuters, wasn't it? When it came time for me to change my body, to accept the DNA which would reshape my body and set my future, I'd probably be a Mama.

"I can't wait to go to LondonT," I said. All things were possible in LondonT. "Three more years and we can get out of this place."

"Yeah," murmured Sonya B, not meeting my eyes.

Which doesn't sound too bad, but I know her. "What do you mean 'yeah'? Are you having second thoughts?"

She turned off the music. The silence closed around us. "LondonT, or any of the other big towns."

"What? What? You've thinking about somewhere else? I thought we'd agreed we were going to a LondonT processing centre."

"I was thinking about one of the smaller transformation centres. LondonT seems a bit wild."

Cold white anger flared through my mind. "You *cannot* be serious. We've agreed on LondonT."

"I've been talking about it with Mama Bathsheba. It might be the right choice for you, but maybe not for me."

Why wasn't I surprised? Mama Bathsheba was always trying to ruin things for me. Sonya, might be quiet, but she could be stubborn. I had to be smart to persuade her that my point of view was the right one. "Think about it, Sonya. Having the man here, it's a bit like having a bit of LondonT at our gates. That's why we should talk to him." Maybe talking to the man would persuade Sonya how cool LondonT would be.

"Well, the council said we shouldn't and so…"

"So what? I'm going to see Mama Bathsheba."

"It won't get you anywhere."

"Fine."

•••

"This is supposed to be a democracy." It wasn't the argument I'd planned. But Mama Bathsheba always wound me up. She always looked at me as if she knew everything I was about to say.

"We *are* a democracy, Freya."

"No." I fought to keep my voice respectful. "Only adults get a vote."

"That is correct. Only full members of Comb7 vote on the council."

"And you discount whatever we think. Even if we're Age of Freedom. I mean, what's the point of being Age of Freedom if you don't even listen to us."

"And what do you think, Freya?"

"I think we ought to invite the librarian into the village."

Mama wasn't even paying attention to me. Her freaky little eye spots kept flicking to her computer. "The council has already discussed the matter and decided to refuse the librarian's request."

"But, Mama, you always say that a new situation is an opportunity for learning. And what's more new than a man? We think that inviting them into the compound would be a learning opportunity."

"We?"

I nodded. Admittedly, it was mostly me who thought that. But I'd spoken to some of the other juniors, and they hadn't been totally against the idea.

"As you feel so strongly about it, I'll raise it in this afternoon's council meeting. We'll consider it," said Mama Bathsheba.

I knew what that meant. Adults always say they'll think about something when they wanted you to go away and shut up.

•••

I never expected them to change their minds. So it was quite a surprise when they called us into a circle meeting the next morning and there was the man, standing there, smiling. A man!

"Youngsters," said Mama Bathsheba. "This is Alex Shvartsman, I'm sure all of you have seen him and in some cases, he's seen more of you than is suitable."

All eyes turned to Sara, who grinned. She was a horrible,

horrible little girl. Mama Bathsheba often said that Sara reminded her of me at that age, but I'm sure I was never *that* bad.

The man was grinning too widely. He looked so eager to be liked. He gave a peculiar and utterly foreign bow. "Thank you, Mama Bathsheba and everyone for allowing me into your community. As you know, I'm a librarian. All I want to do is gather as much information about the different cultures in the Kingdom United as possible."

That seemed harmless. I'd expected something different, somehow. Some of the little girls started to giggle until Mama Bathsheba gave them the stink eye.

A man. I never thought I'd see a man up close. At least until I went to LondonT. A man! Or maybe I shouldn't call him a man. He didn't look that old. Not much older than me, really. He *was* taller than me. His voice was low, but not as low as Mama Claudette's. He didn't look too different, except he did.

He had a lot of hair, I could see it peeping out of his tunic, at his throat and sleeves and on his face. No boobs, of course, and extra in the trouser department, not that that was any of my business. And hair on his face. And his body looked differently muscled, a bit lanky. Funny to think that for millennia, this had been the form of half of humanity. He was a natural, and utterly, utterly strange.

"Alex will be our guest for three days. He's already met all the Mamas. And as Freya is the reason our guest is here, the council has decided that she be Alex's escort," said Mama Bathsheba. "Freya, you will take Alex to the guest quarters, and then show him whatever he wants to see."

*What?*

"Thank you," said Alex, turning to me, and placing his hand over his chest and bending. He seemed to have quite a number of those odd librarian bows. And I was going to show him around! I wasn't expecting that. I'd thought that one of the Mamas would escort him and keep an eye on him. I never imagined they would trust me to do it. This was excellent.

With a few more boring words, about respecting people who weren't part of the village, Mama Bathsheba left us. All the little kids rushed upon the man like he was ice-cream. Me and Sonya and the other three Age of Freedom juniors hung back a bit.

"What do you think?" whispered Junita to me, her golden earing glittering. I loved those earrings: two bees touching, mouth to mouth, stinger to stinger, an Age of Freedom gift from Mama Wilkins.

"He looks normal, well normalish."

He was trying to answer all of kiddiewinks questions at once. Until I took pity on him and shooed them away.

"Hi," I said. "I'm Freya. I guess I'm your guide."

"Cool," he said.

Cool indeed. "Come on, I'll take you to your room, and you can get settled."

•••

"What exactly do you want to see?" I asked after Alex had dumped his pack and cleaned up and we'd grabbed a plate of what I call Mama Donna's lentil slop.

"I just want to get to know you and learn about the village."

"There's not much to show you," I said.

"But there is. There are hundreds of isolationist tribes in the South East. Each doing their own thing, each in a slightly different way. All the things they learn are going to be lost unless someone records it. That's what the United Library wants to do, to record everything for the future."

"We are not isolationists. We talk to others in the Collective. We've let you in." I felt uneasy about Alex criticizing the village. Even though I criticized it all the time,  was different when an outsider did it.

"I apologise. Sorry, Freya. Honestly, I'm not trying to judge you. I only want to make a record of what you want to share. I'm going to get a lot of things wrong, and I'm relying on you to set me straight. Deal?"

"Deal," I said.

•••

I took him to Melissa's Temple. I reckon that's the most impressive thing in Comb7. The temple was in the centre of the Hive. In the centre of the temple was the marble Melissa. Light filtered through the atrium window in the ceiling, bathing the temple space in honey coloured light, the air was fragranced with burning beeswax candles and the fumes from the stone jars of fermenting honey. The walls were decorated with all types of artwork. Perhaps the temple was the only place where youngsters have equal value in Comb7. Everyone was free to decorate the temple, no matter how young or how bad at art they were.

"Wow," said Alex. "Just wow. Thank you for letting me see this, Freya. It's a great honour."

I felt quietly pleased that he was impressed. Perhaps we weren't such yokels after all.

"So you worship the Bee Mother. This looks Minoan."

"That's right," I said. Melissa was represented as a woman decorated with adult bee and eggs. "The goddess is our interpretation of the eternal. We're all female here. The Mamas can only give birth to females. Genetically, it takes a father to make a son."

"Like parthenogenetic reproduction, but obviously with mitotic variation."

"Yes, sure," I said. "We're not clones of our mother, but we come from her. All the Mamas have the mod that allows them to fuse two eggs into one baby. No sperm needed."

"Who *is* your mother?"

"It's not important." Sometimes I wondered about that. Sonya said that it must be Mother Bathsheba because we were too alike, always rubbing each other the wrong way. But it wasn't a question that really mattered. In Comb7, all the Mamas were my mother.

Alex took out his notepad and began to scribble away. "It's so interesting that after the DNA revolution, so many religions were rediscovered, or invented, don't you think?"

"And yet they all reflect the face of the true god," I said.

Alex nodded. "That's profound."

"Don't blame me," I said with a grin. "I'm not the profound type; it's just something that Mama Donna has drilled into us. You know. She's of the lentil slop fame."

Alex laughed. "You've got a great sense of humour, Freya."

I'm pretty sure I didn't blush. "Cheers. It's just something Mama Donna always said: we should be free to touch the divine in the way that speaks to our minds and bodies, and so should all people, a monoculture is never a liberating thing."

"The culture was hardly monoculture here in the KU. But it's true that religion has flourished in communities like Comb7. I just wish everyone had a Mama Donna to keep them respectful of other beliefs."

•••

"And we farm, but that's just like anyone else," I said.

I took Alex around the fields and introduced him to everyone I found: Mamas, freedom juniors and kiddiewinks

Then I took him to the hives. I had to suit him up properly as Alex was a stranger to the bees. I guess that was the first time he looked really out of place, clunking about in the bulky suit.

"Our specialist trade is bee products," I told him. "Honey and propolis. Propolis production is my special chore."

"What is it?" he asked. "Sorry to keep asking you questions all the time. It's just that I haven't got access to the net because of your privacy bleepers."

"Sure, no problem. That's what I'm here for. It's a wax mixture used by honeybees as an insulator and sealant." I scraped up a bit to show him, although there wasn't much as I'd harvested yesterday. "It's very high in hormones and has antibiotic, aesthetic, and anti-inflammatory properties."

"I can see why people want to buy it," said Alex.

"And that's before it's gone through the worms."

I showed him the worms. "They're our intellectual property," I said. "Mama Kary developed their genetic modification. Once the worms eat the wax, it changes chemical composition and is able to stimulate pregnancy in women with a genetic variation like the Mamas. It brings in 50% of our trade. It's very valuable."

"This wax could get a Mama pregnant?"

"Sure," I said. "Of course, they could take a chemical to do the same thing. But the Mamas are all hippies, and they prefer their pregnancies 100 percent organic."

"That's quite something," said Alex.

"It's nearly dinner time. Are you hungry yet?"

"Always," said Alex.

"Let's go and get something to eat in the canteen."

"More lentil slop? Which, by the way, I thought was delicious."

"Yep. A pot of Mama Donna's lentil slop can lasts for weeks. She just keeps adding to it."

I took Alex to the canteen and got us a couple of plates of food. "I guess you've seen everything now," I said.

"Not at all. I want to talk to as many people as want to talk to me."

I couldn't see what was so interesting about everyone, but I guess he knew his business.

Alex yawned. "It's been a long day. Thanks, Freya. How's about we call it an early night? And I'll catch up with my notes. I'd like to work on them while everything is fresh in my mind."

"Sure."

•••

"I like him," I told Sonya.

"I know you do," said Sonya, with a yawn.

"Do you find him boring? Don't you think he's the most interesting thing that's ever come to Comb7?"

She shrugged. "I know you like him, Freya. And I don't want to fight with you again."

"But?"

"I just don't find him that relevant. Not everyone seeks out the new things like you do."

"He's an old thing: a man."

"Whatever."

I'm sorry to say that Sonya's attitude was typical of what I'd put up with all day. Everyone had been polite to Alex, but only polite. I could feel everyone holding back. They didn't want to engage with him at all. It made me embarrassed. It was like we were total yokels. We were better than that.

But whatever. If they didn't want to know about the outside world, then I did. And while Alex was learning about us, I was learning about the great wide world outside of Comb7.

●●●

So bright and early the next day, (actually at about ten o'clock) I knocked on Alex's door, eager to show him around, but even more eager to find out about the outside world.

"Hi," he said. He always had a smile on his face. He looked keen to start the day.

But actually, I felt a bit embarrassed. "I feel like I showed you everything yesterday, Alex. I'm not sure what we're going to do today."

"Not at all," he said. "I could spend weeks here, months and still not learn everything. I regret having only three days."

He made me feel better. "We spoke to all the Mamas again yesterday. Do you want to talk to some of the youngsters?"

"Of course," he said.

"Even the little 'uns?"

"Everyone's ideas and experience has value. Age doesn't matter."

I liked that attitude. But to be quite honest, I didn't find the ramblings of the kiddies that interesting. But Alex sat patiently taking notes while they gave all the details of their mini-dramas. The only thing I was grateful for was that the horrid child, Sara, wasn't around.

That took most of the day. Late afternoon, we grabbed some food and took it to the meadows for a picnic. That gave me a good chance to quiz Alex about his life. He didn't mind, he answered all my questions about LondonT. And believe me, I had a lot of questions. Then I asked about his role as a librarian.

"And you go all over the country, talking to people? Observing them?" It turned out that he hadn't been overseas yet. "Do you ever get afraid?"

"There are bad areas in the Kingdom United," he said. "I stay clear of them. I guess it isn't much different from the times before the DNA revolution."

"That wasn't quite what I'd meant. I wasn't asking about physical harm, I was asking about something different."

Alex seemed to know what I was thinking. "People are people, good and bad, same as they ever were," he said.

"You must meet a lot of people,"

"I do," he said. "It's overwhelming sometimes,"

"I bet."

"But I've been trained," he said, "by the Library. I like talking to people and finding out about them. But, sometimes, it's difficult. I encounter a lot of different ideas, and I don't always agree with them. It can be quite exhausting. When I'm older, I'll settle down. In our community, it's mainly the young ones who go out and gather information. You know: the wanderlust."

"How did you get involved in the Library? Were you born into it?"

"No," he said with a laugh. "Not at all. I met someone at the LondonT processing centre and he invited me to visit. After a lot of soul searching I decided not to go back to my tribe. I believe in the freedom of information. I've devoted my life to it. I believe that we've made a wrong choice by secluding ourselves like this."

"So you think our way of living is wrong?"

"I want to document everything, with respect. I don't judge," he said.

There was no denying that his tone was judgemental. "And what about those who don't want to be documented?"

"We believe that the world has a right to their stories as well. I observe them, as much as I can. Like I did when I stood on the outside of Comb7. I'm so glad that you invited me in, Freya."

"I'm glad you came here."

"Freya," he said. "I'll be leaving soon. I wanted to invite you to the library."

"I'll be going to LondonT in a few years, I'll look you up."

"No, I mean come, now."

"Oh, shut up."

"I mean it, you know."

"I don't think Mama Bathsheba would like that." I laughed, just imagining all her eyes, blinking and winking if I told her that I was leaving with Alex.

"But now you're thirteen, Freya. She wouldn't be able to stop you. Don't tell me you haven't thought about it?"

I hadn't really. Not seriously. Sure, when I was a kid, I was always saying that I was going to leave Comb7 as soon as I reached the Age of Freedom. But, small and annoying as this place was, it was my home.

"You're not telling me you haven't thought about it," Alex said again, looking at me intently.

"I don't know," I said, rubbing my arm, like I always do when I'm uneasy. It's a bad tell. I'll never make a great poker player "I have questions about our life. You know that."

"Questions are good," said Alex. "You must question everything. But you don't even know what you don't know. You've been raised in a closed community, with isolationist tendencies." He frowned as he said this.

"And you don't approve?" This conversation was getting heavy.

"It's not my place to approve, I only document."

"But you don't approve?"

"The principals of the Kingdom's United are that every parent has the right to educate their child as they choose until the Age of Freedom, though of course many continue educating until majority. At the Age of Majority every individual has the right to choose their own path."

"Sure," I said. "At the Age of Majority everyone selects what DNA modifications they're going to get. Except people like you, Alex. Although not choosing to change is a choice in a way. What's wrong with that?"

Alex sighed. "The fact that children are indoctrinated into the beliefs of their parents, that's what's wrong. Very few people escape their tribe. Virtually everyone chooses the modifications of their parents."

"I guess they do. So what?"

"Sometimes their parent's choices are not right for the child."

"What do you mean?"

"Like me for instance. I was raised dragon," he said.

I was surprised. Dragon was a highly modified tribe. You needed to change your body a lot to be a dragon, bone mods, body re-sculpturing, extensive skin alterations. I'd heard that they were even trying to find a gene that would allow them to breathe fire. I sometimes saw dragons flying high above Comb7. They were astonishing.

"You wouldn't believe the supremacy rubbish they taught me. All wrapped up in their Dragon religion," said Alex. "How is it right that they were allowed to teach me such stuff? It will always be with me. If I'd gone home, what would I have been?"

I resisted the temptation to say: A magnificent flying dragon? "If you don't like the current situation, what's the alternative?" I asked.

"It should be like it was before the DNA revolution, the state should give everyone an education."

"You think that the government should take a child away from her family?"

"No, not at all. Maybe in some cases. It's lovely here, but just imagine being brought up as a dragon."

I dunno. It sounded kinda cool. But I nodded sympathetically. "At least you got out," I said.

"And left my brothers behind." He was quiet for a moment. "Why is it that nobody thinks about the rights of children? But, Freya, at least you're at the age when you can do something about it. Just think about it, that's all I ask"

•••

We were walking through the Hive back to Alex's room, when Sara came canon-balling down the corridor, nearly knocking us over.

"Hey," I said, catching her arm. "Where are you going in such a hurry?"

"Nowhere! Let me go." She twisted like a snake out of my grasp, before shooting a hateful glance at Alex and running away.

"I'm sorry about her, Alex."

"No harm done," he said.

•••

His room was in disarray. The contents of his pack was scattered over the room. Clothes and papers everywhere and smashed glass was ground into the carpet.

"Oh, I'm so sorry. It must have been Sara. She's a naughty, naughty little girl. Don't worry, I'll tell Mama Bathsheba. Sara will get what's coming to her."

"No," he said. "It's okay. Please don't tell the Mamas about it."

"Why not?"

"Because I don't want them to think that I'm here causing trouble. They might ask me to leave."

"I'm so sorry," I said. "What's all this glass anyway?"

"Man's stuff," he said with a blush

I beat a hasty retreat.

•••

I'd promised Alex that I wasn't going to tell on Sara. But I hadn't said anything about me sorting her out. "You," I said, grabbing Sara by the shoulder. "Why did you do that? You're just a vicious, naughty, little girl. Why did you mess all his stuff up?"

I'd expected defiance, but what I got was tears. "Because he's taking you away. You're going to go to LondonT. You'll never come back. I'll never see you again."

I took in a deep breath. "What makes you think that?"

"That's what Sophie told me. I know you don't want to be like us and the Mamas. Why do you hate us all?"

"I don't," I said, honestly confused by her words. "I love everyone in Comb7. Even you, Sara, and you are a very naughty thing."

"Really?" Her eyes grew big with hope.

"Really."

Sara grooved a little victory dance, and I couldn't help smiling.

But we ended up crying in each other's arms. And I didn't know what I was going to do.

•••

Alex was leaving tomorrow. I had to decide what I was going to do. Should I go with him? I changed my mind a hundred times that night, tossing and turning. No wonder I slept in late.

When I made my way to Alex's room, it was empty and all his things were gone.

I raced to Mama Bathsheba's room. I burst through the door without knocking.

"Where's Alex?" I demanded.

"He's been expelled from Comb7."

"What? Why?"

"Sit down, Freya. You make me nervous looming over me like that. Alex has been expelled because he's a liar and a thief."

I gasped with surprise and it was a moment before I could defend him. "He values truth above all things. And he'd never steal anything."

"No," said Mama Bathsheba. And her voice got a bit softer, like she was trying to be kind to me. "Not only was he recording our words, but he was collecting our DNA. Who knows what he planned to do with it."

"That can't be true!" DNA was the thing that was uniquely yours. To steal it was a terrible crime.

"It is true. Sara came to me yesterday and told me what she'd done. When she told me that Alex had a lot of glass in his pack, I was suspicious. I went to his room and confronted him. He didn't deny it. In fact, he tried to lecture me about how all kinds of information should be free. I asked him to leave right away. And I've sent warnings to the villages in the South East Collective."

"He was going to steal our DNA?"

"Yes, and samples of the worm DNA."

"But that's our livelihood."

"Alex believes that all information should be freely available." Mama Bathsheba shrugged. "It's his way."

And instead of being angry, to my horror I started crying great, big, hysterical baby tears. "Why?" I howled. "It's not fair."

"No, it's not fair, Freya. I'm sorry that you had to learn this lesson."

Quick as lightening, my mood turned angry. "Sorry? I bet you're glad. And I bet you were laughing when you found out. In fact, I think you knew all along what he was."

"I didn't know," said Mama Bathsheba. "I would have spared you this if I could."

My mood changed again, quick as lightning. "And I was going to go with him," I wailed.

"No Freya, I don't think you were. You're smarter than that."

"Smarter?"

"The smartest of us have the most difficult choices to make. I was very much like you at your age," Mama Bathsheba, said softly, giving me a small blinking smile. "Although I know you don't want to hear that. I never stopped questioning things."

"Why did you stop?"

"I never did, Freya. And I don't think I ever will."

"But why did he go without saying goodbye to me?"

"That was my fault, Freya. I was just so angry that I insisted on him leaving immediately. I should have let him say goodbye, try to explain things to you."

Mama Bathsheba admitted she'd made a mistake?

"He asked me to pass on a message. He said you'll always be welcome in their library."

"I'll never go there. Never! They're just a bunch of liars."

"Alex thinks differently to us. He sees his lies in the pursuit of a greater truth."

"Is this what it will be like when I go to LondonT?"

"No. You'll be older, Freya and better prepared. You may be Age of Freedom, but you're not quite ready for LondonT."

"I'm not," I snivelled. "And what happens if I go to LondonT and decide that I don't want to be a Mama?"

"Whatever you decide, you'll always be part of our family, Freya. You won't live with us, that's true, but you'll always be part of us."

It was too much! I didn't like all that soppy stuff. I covered my face with my hands. "I don't like having this choice, Mama."

"I know it is difficult, but all the Mamas will help you."

"Thank you, Mama."

"Anytime, Freya. Now, you run off and do your chores. Put this behind you. They'll be time enough for you to make your choices."

"I suppose you're right, Mama. Thanks." I felt a bit embarrassed by the way I'd let my emotions get ahead of me. But it was only Mama B. She was used to me. I walked back to my room, thinking hard. I was pretty angry with Alex. What a dirty liar. But he wasn't all bad. He'd got me thinking about things. I wonder if he even knew that what he'd done was wrong. I don't think he did. I had a lot of thinking to do.

But first, I had to do my chores. I grabbed my bee hat from the hook and set off for the hives. The worms won't feed themselves, you know.

# Laddie Come Home
## Curtis C. Chen

*Once a software engineer in Silicon Valley, Curtis C. Chen now writes fiction and runs puzzle games near Portland, Oregon. His debut novel,* Waypoint Kangaroo, *a science fiction spy thriller, will be published by Thomas Dunne Books in 2016. Curtis is not an aardvark. Visit him online at: http://curtiscchen.com*

LAD woke from standby in an unknown location (searching, please wait). The Local Administrator Device's GPS coordinates had not been updated in more than three hours (elapsed time 03:10:21). Internal battery meter hovered at 20 percent (not charging). LAD forked a self-diagnostic background job and checked the bodyNet event log for errors and warnings. It was LAD's responsibility to maintain proper functioning of the entire system.

The initial findings were discouraging. LAD's last known-good cloud sync had been at Soekarno-Hatta International Airport (Java Island, Indonesia) after LAD's user, Willam Mundine, had arrived from Sydney and his bodyNet had connected to the first accessible WiFi network (SSID starbucks-CGK-962102, unsecured). There had been no wireless coverage after Mundine's taxicab left the airport (4G/LTE roaming denied, no WiMAX footprint, TDMA handshake failed). Mundine had lost consciousness 00:12:10 after the sync completed, and all his personal electronics, including LAD, had automatically gone to sleep with him, as designed.

Mundine's bodyNet had awoken now only because battery power was low (estimated remaining runtime 00:09:59), and all the bodytechs needed to save state to non-volatile storage before shutdown. LAD attempted to dump a memory image to Mundine's bioDrive but received device errors from every triglyceride cluster before timing out.

The self-diagnostic job finished and confirmed what LAD had suspected: the battery had run down because LAD's hardware housing, a teardrop-shaped graphene pendant attached to a fiber-optic necklace, was not in contact with Mundine's skin surface. The necklace drew power from the wearer's body via epidermal interface. LAD was not designed to function without that organic power supply.

"Mr. Mundine," LAD said. "Can you hear me, Mr. Mundine? Please wake up."

It was possible that the diagnostic had returned a false negative due to corrupted data. LAD triggered the voice command prompt fifteen more times before breaking the loop.

In the absence of direct commands from Mundine, LAD depended on stochastic behavior guidelines to assign and perform tasks. The current situation was not something LAD had been programmed to recognize. LAD needed information to select a course of action.

GPS was still unavailable. The antenna built into LAD's necklace could transmit and receive on many different radio frequencies, but the only other bodytechs in range—Mundine's PebbleX wristwatch, MetaboScan belt, and MateMatch ring—supplied no useful data. No other compatible devices responded to outbound pings.

The complete lack of broadband wireless reception suggested that LAD was inside a building. Mundine had installed an offline travel guide before departing Australia, and according to that data source, regular monsoon rains and frequent geological events (current surveys list 130 active volcanoes in Indonesia) led many in this region to use poured concrete for construction. Those locally composited materials often included dielectric insulators which interfered with radio transmissions. Weatherproofed glass windows would also have metallic coatings that deflected any wavelengths shorter than ultraviolet or longer than infrared. And the absence of satellite beacons like GPS implied a corrugated metal roof that scattered incoming signals. Perhaps without realizing it, the builders of this structure had made it a perfect cage for wireless Internet devices like LAD.

After 3,600 milliseconds of fruitless pinging, LAD re-prioritized the voice command UI and began processing input signals from boundary effect pickups in the necklace's outer coating. It was sometimes possible to determine location characteristics from ambient sounds. The audio analysis software indicated human voices intermingled with music, and the stream included a digital watermark, indicating a television broadcast, but without Internet connectivity, LAD couldn't look up the station identifier. However, the offline travel guide included Bahasa language translation software, so LAD was able to understand the words being spoken.

"See Indo-pop singing sensations Java Starship in their international cinema debut!" an announcer's voice said over a bouncy pop music soundtrack. "When a diplomat's daughter is abducted from a charity concert, and corrupt local authorities do nothing to find her, the boys of Java Starship take matters into their own hands..."

New voices overlapped the recorded audio stream. Audio analysis indicated live human speakers in the room, and LAD adjusted audio filters to emphasize the humans over the television. Based on pitch and rhythm, there were four separate voiceprints, speaking a pidgin of Bahasa and English.

"What are you showing us? What is all this?" said an adult female (Javanese accent, approximate age 35-40 years, label as H1: human voice, first distinct in new database). "Where did you get these things?"

"They're from work," said an adult male (Javanese, age 40-45 years, label H2). "A little bonus. You know."

"(Untranslatable)," said the woman (H1). "You haven't had a job for months. I know what you do, drinking with those gangsters—"

"You don't know!" said the man (H2). "And you don't complain when I pay for our food, our clothes—"

"Hey!" said a female child (13-15 years old, label H3). "That looks like graphene superconductor material. Can I see?"

"Which one?" asked the man (H2). "What are you pointing at?"

LAD took a chance and switched on the pendant's external status lights. If the girl recognized graphene by sight, she might also know about other technologies—like the Internet.

"The necklace, there. Look, it's blinking green!" said the girl (H3).

"You like that, Febby?" asked the man (H2). "Okay, here you go."

LAD's motion sensors spiked. 2,500 milliseconds later, the entire sensor panel lit up, and galvanic skin response (GSR) signal went positive. The girl must have put on the necklace. LAD's battery began charging again.

"Cool," said the girl (H3, assign username Febby).

"How about you, Jaya?" asked the man (H2). "You want something?"

"The wristwatch!" said a male child (14-17 years old, label H4, assign username Jaya). With all the voices cataloged, LAD decided this was likely a family: mother, father, daughter, and son.

"It's too big for you, Jaya," said the mother (H1).

"No way!" said the father (H2). LAD heard a clinking noise, metal on metal, likely the PebbleX watch strap being buckled. "Look at that. So fancy!"

"Pa, they have schoolwork to do."

"It's Friday, Nindya! They can have a little fun—"

"Arman!" said the mother (H1, assign username Nindya). "I want to talk to you. Children, go upstairs."

"Yes, Ma," Jaya and Febby replied in unison.

LAD's motion sensors registered bouncing. The adults' voices faded into the background as Febby's feet slapped against a series of homogeneous hard surfaces (solid concrete, likely stairs). LAD was able to catch another 4,580 milliseconds of conversation before Febby moved too far away.

"...going to get us all killed," Nindya said. "I can't believe you brought him here!"

Arman muttered something, then said out loud, "They'll pay, Nindya. I know what I'm doing..."

•••

LAD kept hoping Febby would go outside the house to play, thus providing an opportunity to scan for nearby wireless networks, but she stayed in her room all day with the window closed. Incoming audio indicated writing (graphite/clay material in lateral contact with cellulose surface), which LAD guessed was the aforementioned schoolwork. There seemed to be an inordinately large amount of it for a 13- to 15-year-old child.

The good news was that Febby's high GSR made for efficient charging, and LAD was back to 100 percent battery in less than an hour. With power to spare, LAD accelerated main CPU clock speed to maximum and unlocked the pendant's onboard GPU for digital signal processing. Sound was the only currently available external signal, and LAD had to squeeze as much information out of that limited datastream as possible. The voice command UI package included a passive-sonar module which could be used for rangefinding. LAD loaded that into memory and began building a crude map of the house from echo patterns.

After the family ate a meal—likely dinner, based on internal clock time and local sunset time—LAD heard footsteps heading from the ground floor down a different set of concrete steps, likely into a basement or storm cellar. Febby stayed upstairs in her room. There was no way to adjust the directionality of the necklace microphones, but LAD increased the gain on the incoming audio and utilized all available noise reduction and bandpass filters.

When LAD isolated Willam Mundine's voiceprint (91 percent confidence), system behavior overrides kicked in, and the Bluetooth radio drivers shot up in priority. As implied by earlier data, and now confirmed, Arman was holding Mundine captive in the basement of this house. But Mundine was too far away, and there was too much interference from the building structure, for a Bluetooth signal to reach Mundine's bodyNet. The only thing LAD could do was listen.

If Mundine said any words, they were unintelligible. Mostly, he screamed. Those noises were interspersed with shouting from

Arman, also unintelligible, and sounds that the analysis software identified as rigid objects striking bare human skin.

System rules kept demanding that LAD activate Mundine's implanted rescue locator beacon—more commonly known as a kidnap-and-ransom (K&R) stripe—but LAD couldn't control any devices while disconnected from the bodyNet. The fall-through rules recommended requesting user intervention from other nearby humans. After careful consideration, LAD decided to risk making contact.

LAD waited until Febby was alone in the bathroom to speak to her.

"Hello, Febby," LAD said. "Don't be afraid."

Sonar indicated that Febby was sitting on the toilet. LAD's motion sensors measured her neck muscles moving, likely turning her head to look around. "Who's talking?" she asked quietly. "Where are you?"

"I'm hanging around your neck," LAD said. "Look down. I'll flash a light. Three times each in red, green, and blue."

LAD gave her 1,000 milliseconds to move her eyes, then activated the pendant's status lights. The three-way OLEDs burned a lot of power, but LAD believed this was an emergency.

"A talking necklace?" Febby said. "Cool."

"Listen, Febby," LAD said, "I need your help."

•••

Febby snuck out of her room shortly after midnight, when LAD had 95 percent confidence based on breathing patterns that Arman, Nindya, and Jaya were all fast asleep. Febby padded silently down the stairs to the ground floor, then down the steps at the end of the back hallway behind the kitchen. LAD's Bluetooth discovery panel lit up as soon as Febby rounded the corner at the bottom of the steps and entered the basement.

LAD immediately tried to activate Mundine's K&R stripe, but there was no response. LAD queried all available inputs for Mundine's physical condition. Medical monitors reported that Mundine's back and both legs were bruised. The fourth and fifth fingers on his left hand were broken. His left eighth rib was cracked—that was why the K&R stripe wasn't working.

"Who's that man?" Febby whispered. "Why is he in our basement? He looks like he's been hurt."

"This man is Mr. Willam Mundine," LAD said. "He's my friend. I believe your father brought him here, and they've been"—LAD spent 250 milliseconds searching for an appropriate verbal euphemism—"arguing, I'm afraid."

"Ma and Pa argue a lot, too," Febby said, "but he never hits her. Your friend must have made Pa really angry."

"I don't know what happened," LAD said, "but I need to speak to Mr. Mundine. Is there anything tied around his mouth?"

"Yeah," Febby said. "You want me to take it off?"

"Yes, please."

Febby knelt down and moved her arms. "Okay, it's untied."

"Thank you, Febby," LAD said. "Now, would you please remove my necklace and give it to Mr. Mundine?"

"Don't you want to be friends anymore?" Febby asked. Voice stress analysis indicated unhappiness, likely trending toward sorrow.

LAD consulted actuarial tables and determined that greater mobility provided a higher probability of successful user recovery. It would be difficult to once again be separated from the bodyNet, but LAD's current primary objective was Mundine's safe return to his employer.

"Of course I want to be friends, Febby," LAD said. "I just need to talk to Mr. Mundine, and I can't do that unless I'm touching him."

"I can talk to him," Febby said. "Just tell me what to say."

LAD had not considered that option, but it seemed feasible. "Okay, Febby. Please repeat exactly what I say."

Febby listened, nodded, and leaned forward. "Mr. Willam Mundine, this is your wake-up call!"

LAD heard rustling, groaning, and then a sharp intake of breath. "Who—what?" Mundine's voice was a hoarse rattle.

Mundine's eyes struggled open, and LAD received video

from his retinal feeds. A young girl sat cross-legged on the bare concrete floor under a single, dim, fluorescent light panel. She wore a white tank top and orange shorts. Long, straight black hair tumbled over her shoulders and framed a round face with large, brown eyes. She spoke, and LAD heard Febby's voice.

"Mr. Willam Mundine, L-A-D says: 'Your K-and-R stripe is inoperable, and there is no broadband wireless coverage at all in this location.'"

"Ah," Mundine coughed. He struggled up to a kneeling position. His wrists and ankles appeared to be tied together. "That's unfortunate. And who are you?"

"I'm Febby."

"Pleasure to meet you, Febby. I suppose you already know who I am."

"Well," Febby said, "the necklace says you're his friend. And he's my friend now. So maybe that makes you and me friends, too?"

"I'll go along with that," Mundine said. "So tell me, friend Febby, where am I?"

"In my basement."

Mundine coughed again. "I mean, what city?"

"Oh. We live in Depok," Febby said.

"Did you get that, Laddie?" Mundine said.

LAD had never considered asking Febby for this information. Most of LAD's programming focused on retrieving data from automated systems to fulfill user requests. LAD updated local guidelines to note that humans were also valid data sources, even when the data might be more efficiently provided by tech.

"Febby, please tell Mr. Mundine I have recorded our location data," LAD said, searching for information about Depok in the travel guide.

"He says yes," Febby said. "So his name is Laddie?"

"That's what I call him," Mundine said. "He's very helpful to me."

"Why were you arguing with my Pa?" Febby asked. "Why did he hurt you?"

Mundine inhaled and exhaled. "These are all very good

questions, Febby. But whatever disagreements I might have with your father, I hope they won't affect our friendship."

"Okay," Febby said. "What are you doing in Depok? Did you come to visit my Pa?"

"Not precisely," Mundine said. "I work for a company called Bantipor Commercial, and we build many different kinds of electronics. Like computers. Do you know anything about computers, Febby?"

"A little," Febby said. "We're learning about them in school. My brother has one at home, but he only uses it for shooters. He plays online with his friends."

"Thank heaven for video games," Mundine said. "Febby. Your brother's computer, do you know what kind it is?"

•••

"Okay, I think I got it," Febby said. "Yes! What do you think, Laddie?"

LAD waited for the pendant lights to finish the cycle Febby had encoded. Unlike Mundine, who wanted fast replies, LAD found that if he responded too quickly, Febby would get upset, because she felt LAD hadn't taken enough time to consider what she was saying.

"It's very colorful," LAD said after 800 milliseconds.

"It's a secret code," Febby said. "In base three counting. Red is zero, green is one, and blue is two. Can you tell what it says?"

LAD knew exactly what it said, because LAD could see the actual lines of computer code that Febby was transmitting from Jaya's previous-generation gaming PC into LAD's necklace over a Bluetooth 2.0 link. There was more computing power in Mundine's left big toe—literally, since he kept a copy of his health care records in an NFC node implanted there—but the big metal box on Jaya's desk had a wired Internet connection, which LAD needed to call in a recovery team for Mundine.

"If I interpret the colors as numeric values in base three," LAD said, "and then translate those into letters of the alphabet, I believe the message is Febby and Laddie are super friends."

It had taken Febby less than an hour to write this test module. LAD noted that she worked more efficiently than many of the engineers who performed periodic maintenance services on LAD and Mundine's other bodytechs.

"You got it!" Febby clapped her hands. "Okay, the programming link works. Now we need to set up the—what did you call it?"

"A wired-to-wireless network bridge," LAD said, "so I can connect to the Internet."

"Right." Febby started typing again. "You know, I could just look things up for you. Would that be faster?"

LAD had considered asking her to make an emergency call, but LAD couldn't trust that local police would take a child's complaint seriously. LAD also didn't want Febby's father to catch her trying to help Mundine. LAD estimated that Mundine's best chance of a safe rescue lay with his employer, Bantipor Commercial, which would dispatch a professional search team as soon as they knew Mundine's precise location. And only LAD could upload a properly encrypted emergency message to Bantipor's secure servers.

"I have a lot of different things to look up," LAD said to Febby. "I wouldn't want to waste your time."

"It's not a waste," Febby said. "This is fun! I can't wait until Hani gets back next week. She's going to freak out when she sees you!"

"Hani is your friend?" LAD asked. Requesting data from Febby was an interesting experience. She always returned more than the expected information.

"Yeah," Febby said. "We sit together in computer lab. She showed me how to—"

A clanging noise came from downstairs, followed by loud male and female voices. Febby sighed, got up, and closed the door to the bedroom.

"What was that transport proto-something you said I should look at?" Febby asked.

"Transport protocol," LAD said. "Look for TCP/IP libraries. They may also be labeled 'Transmission Control Protocol' or 'Internet Protocol.'"

"Okay, I found them," Febby said. "Wow, there's a lot of stuff here." She was silent for 1,100 milliseconds, then made a flapping sound with her lips. "Are you sure there's not an easier way to do your Internet searches?"

"I'm afraid not," LAD said. "I actually need to send a message to Mr. Mundine's company in a very specific way."

"You can't just do it through their web site?" Febby asked. LAD heard typing and mouse clicks. "Here they are. Bantipor Commercial. There's a contact form right... here! I can just send the message for you."

This procedure was not documented anywhere in LAD's behavior or system guidelines, but the logic appeared valid. LAD forked several new processes to calculate the most effective and concise human-readable message to send. "That's a great idea, Febby. Is there an option to direct the message to Bantipor Commercial's security services?"

"Let me check the menu," Febby said. Then, 5,500 milliseconds later: "No, I don't see anything that says 'security'. How about 'support and troubleshooting'?"

"That's not quite right." LAD was at a loss until the new behavior guidelines from last night kicked in. "Can I get your opinion, Febby? I'll tell you what I'm trying to do, and you tell me what you think is the best way to do it."

"Like a test? Sure. I'm good at tests."

"Cool," LAD said. The voice command UI had started prioritizing that word based on recent user interactions. "I need to tell Bantipor Commercial's security services that Mr. Mundine is here in Depok. Normally I would upload the message directly to their servers myself, but I can't do that without an Internet connection."

"Security," Febby said thoughtfully. "Do they monitor this web site, too? Like for strange activity? I remember last year the BritAma Arena had trouble with hackers, and the police caught them because their software bot was making too many unusual requests to the ticketing site."

LAD couldn't research those details online, but Mundine's

bodyNet also had standard protections against denial-of-service attacks. If the same client made too many similar requests within a specified time period, that client was flagged for investigation. "Yes. That is very likely. And the server will automatically record your IP address, which can be geolocated to this neighborhood. This is a very good idea, Febby."

"I'll write a script to send the same message over and over," Febby said, starting to type again. "How long should I let it run?"

"As long as you can," LAD said.

"Okay. I'll make the message... Dear Bantipor security, Mr. Mundine is in Depok. From, Laddie."

LAD's behavior guidelines could not find an appropriate response to these circumstances, so they degraded gracefully to the default. "Thank you, Febby."

"Here it goes."

Someone pushed open the door and walked into the room. LAD had been so busy evaluating Febby's proposals, the incoming audio analysis had been buffered, and the sound of footsteps coming up the stairs had not been processed.

"What are you doing?" Jaya shouted at Febby. "That's my computer!"

"I'm just borrowing it," Febby said. "I'm almost done."

"Don't touch my stuff, you'll mess it up!"

LAD detected vibrations, as if Febby's body were being shaken. There was more shouting, and Febby fell and hit the floor. Someone else banged on the computer keyboard.

"What is all this garbage?" Jaya said. "You better not have lost my saved games!"

"Don't do that!" Febby said. "No, don't erase it!"

"Don't mess with my stuff!" Jaya hit some more keys, and LAD heard the unmistakable sound of a desktop trash folder being emptied.

Febby's body collided with something, and Jaya screeched. The fighting continued for several minutes until Arman and Nindya came upstairs to separate the children.

●●●

After breaking up the fight in Jaya's room, Arman dragged Febby back to her own bedroom and scolded her for nearly half an hour, then left her alone to cry. It was now nearly noon, local time, according to LAD's internal system clock.

LAD noted that Arman wasn't angry because Febby hadn't asked permission to use the computer; he was angry because he didn't think his daughter needed to know anything about technology. That was what he said when Febby tried to explain what she had been doing. Arman wasn't interested when she told him the LAD necklace was actually a piece of sophisticated bodytech, and he wasn't impressed when Febby showed him the blinking lights she had programmed.

There was a knock on the door, followed by Nindya's voice asking if Febby was hungry.

"No," Febby replied. "I was doing something, Ma."

Nindya walked into the room and closed the door. "You don't need to know all that computer stuff."

"Why can't I learn about computers?"

"You can learn anything you want, Febby," Nindya said. "But you have to think what people will think of you. Boys don't want a girl who knows computers."

"Boys are stupid," Febby said. "Can I go to the library?"

"Maybe tomorrow," Nindya said. "Pa doesn't want us to go outside. He thinks some men might be watching the house." Nindya sighed. "Don't worry, Febby..."

The rest of her sentence lost priority as system behavior overrides kicked in. LAD modulated the necklace antenna to seek for spread-spectrum radio signals, which a recovery team would use for secure communications, and ultra-wideband pulses, which they would use to create precise radar images of the building structure.

Nindya left the room while LAD was still scanning. The radio analysis jobs took so many clock cycles, it was nearly 1,200 milliseconds before LAD checked the audio buffer again and heard Febby talking.

"Did you hear that noise?" she asked. "What was that? Laddie, can you hear me?"

"I'm analyzing the sound," LAD said, switching priority back to the audio software and analyzing the sound spike just before Febby's question. The matching algorithms came back in 50 milliseconds: .22-caliber rimfire cartridge, double-action revolver, likely Smith & Wesson. From the basement.

LAD increased the audio job priority for the noise immediately following. The gunshot had attenuated the microphone, so LAD also had to amplify the input and run noise reduction filters on it. The result came back in 470 milliseconds: hard impact, metal projectile against concrete surface. Not flesh and bone.

LAD flipped job priority back to the voice command UI. "That was a gunshot. Febby, I need you to go downstairs, please."

"A gun?" Febby ran to her bedroom door, then stopped. "Who has a gun?"

LAD heard Arman's muffled voice echoing in the basement, but couldn't make out the words. On the ground floor, Jaya and Nindya shouted at each other.

"It's your father," LAD said. "He's in the basement. Please, Febby, I need you to go downstairs so I can hear better. I need to know if Mr. Mundine is hurt again."

"That was really loud," Febby said, her voice trembling. "I'm scared."

"I'm afraid too, Febby," LAD said. "But Mr. Mundine is in trouble. Please, Febby. I need to help my friend."

Febby sobbed once, then rubbed some kind of cloth against her face. "Okay."

"Thank you, Febby."

•••

"You stay here! Stay here!" Nindya shouted.

"I have to go back!" Jaya said. "Pa said to get him—"

"I don't care what he said! You're not going down there while he's shooting a gun!"

Their voices grew louder as Febby approached the kitchen. She stopped at the bottom of the stairs and whispered, "I don't think I can sneak past them. Can you hear better now?"

LAD filtered the incoming audio, passed it to the translation process, then re-filtered the sample using a different algorithm and tried again. No good. The translator still couldn't understand what Arman was saying.

"I'm sorry, Febby, we're still not close enough," LAD said. "But your mother and brother are on the other side of the kitchen. Your mother's facing away from you. If you crawl along the floor, the table should hide you from your brother's line of sight."

Febby dropped to the floor and started moving. "I thought you couldn't see."

"I can't. I'm analyzing the sound frequencies of their voices and extrapolating propagation paths using a three-dimensional spectrograph."

"Cool. Is that a software plug-in?"

"It's a dynamically-loaded shared library. Let's talk about it later, okay?"

LAD could tell when Febby reached the end of the hall by the echoes of Nindya's and Jaya's voices. Febby sat up and put her ear against the door leading to the basement. The translator software began producing valid output.

"You want to talk now?" Arman shouted. "Are you ready to talk?"

LAD heard rustling noises, and then Mundine's voice. "Sorry, friend, it doesn't work like that."

"You came here to make a deal," Arman said. "I know how it works. You don't bring cash, but there's a bank. Tell me which bank! Tell me your access codes!"

"It doesn't work like that," Mundine repeated.

LAD was just about to ask Febby to open the door—hoping her presence would distract Arman long enough for LAD to do something, anything—when the radio monitoring job started spewing result codes into the system register. 20 milliseconds passed while LAD examined the data: multiple ultra-wideband signals, overlapping and repeating, likely point sources in the front and back of the house, approximately one meter above ground level.

"Febby," LAD said, raising output volume above the shouting from the kitchen and the basement, "Febby, please lie down on the ground now."

"Why?" Febby turned her head away from the basement door. "What's happening?"

LAD turned output volume up to maximum. "Down on the ground! Get down on the ground now, Febby, please!"

Febby dropped and flattened herself against the floorboards 150 milliseconds before the first projectile hit the wall above her. That was enough time for LAD to analyze the background audio and estimate there were two squads advancing on the house, four men each, walking on thermoplastic outsoles and wearing ballistic nylon body armor, likely carrying assault rifles.

340 milliseconds after the first team broke down the back door, the second team charged the front door, and another spray of tiny missiles tore into the kitchen. Something thumped to the ground, and Jaya cried out. He ran three steps before a burst of rounds caught him in the back. He crashed against the wall and slid to the floor.

Febby was still screaming when the first team reached her.

"I've got a girl here! Young girl, on the floor!" called a male voice (H5).

"Where's the IFF?" asked another male voice (H6). LAD checked to verify that Mundine's identification-friend-or-foe signal was broadcasting from the necklace.

"It's right here," H5 said. "I'm reading the signal right here!"

"Febby," LAD said. "Febby, please listen to me. This is very important."

Febby stopped screaming. LAD took that as an acknowledgement.

"Please roll over, slowly, so these men can see me," LAD said.

Febby rolled onto her back. LAD drove 125 percent power to the OLEDs on either side of the pendant, flashing Bantipor Commercial's distress code in brilliant green lights.

"It's her!" H5 said. "The girl's wearing the admin key."

"Damn," H6 said. "Target's probably dead. Search the house, weapons free—"

"Febby," LAD said, "please repeat exactly what I say."

4,560 milliseconds later, Febby proclaimed in a loud voice: "Willam Mundine is alive, I repeat, Willam Mundine is alive!"

After 940 milliseconds of silence, H6 asked, "How do you know his name?"

"Willam Mundine is being held in the basement," Febby said, pointing to the door. "His K&R stripe number is bravo-charlie-9-7-1-3-1-0-4-1-5. Challenge code SHADOW MURMUR. Please authenticate!"

"What the hell?" said another man (H7).

"It's gotta be the admin software," H5 said. "She can hear it. The necklace induces audio by conducting a piezoelectric—"

"Save the science lesson, Branagan," H6 said. "Response code ELBOW SKYHOOK. Comms on alfa-2-6. Transmit."

LAD passed the code to the secure hardware processor, and 30 milliseconds later received a valid authentication token with a passphrase payload. LAD used the token to unlock all system logs from the past twenty-four hours, used the passphrase to encrypt the data, and posted the entire archive on the recovery team's communications channel.

"I've got a sonar map," Branagan said. "One hostile downstairs with the target."

"Ward, you're in front. Anderson, cover. Team Two, right behind them," H6 said. "Branagan and I will stay with the girl."

Febby sat up. "What are you going to do?"

"They're just going to go downstairs and have a talk with the man," H6 said.

"No!" Febby started moving forward, then was jerked backward. "Don't hurt my Pa!"

"Febby, it's okay," LAD said. "They're using non-lethal rounds."

LAD kept talking, but she wasn't listening. Something rustled at H6's side. A metal object—based on conductivity profile, likely a hypodermic syringe—touched Febby's left shoulder, and LAD went to sleep.

•••

LAD woke from standby in an unknown location (searching, please wait). GPS lock occurred 30 milliseconds later, identifying LAD's current location as Depok (city, West Java province, south-southeast of Jakarta). LAD's internal battery reported 99 percent power (charging), and LAD's network panel automatically connected to Willam Mundine's bodyNet and the public Internet. A network time sync confirmed that 11:04:38 elapsed time had passed since Febby lost consciousness.

"Good morning, Mr. Mundine," LAD said. "How are you feeling?"

Mundine groaned. "I've been better." He opened his eyes and looked around. LAD saw a hospital bed with a translucent white curtain drawn around it.

LAD lowered the priority on the wake-up script. The entire routine had to run to completion unless Mundine overrode it, but LAD could multitask. While giving Mundine the local weather forecast, LAD simultaneously ran a web search for news about a kidnapping in or around Jakarta and also started a VPN tunnel to Bantipor Commercial's private intranet.

LAD found Mundine's K&R insurance claim quickly, but there was nothing in the file about the family of the suspect, Arman (no surname given). LAD's web search returned several brief news items about a disturbance in Depok late last night, but none of the reports mentioned a girl named Febby.

LAD continued searching while a doctor came to talk to Mundine. After the wake-up script finished, LAD started scanning Depok local school enrollment records for a 13- to 15-year-old student named Febby, or Feby, or February, who had a brother named Jaya, or Jay, or Jayan, in the same or a nearby school. But much of the data was not public, and LAD could not obtain research authorization using Bantipor Commercial's trade certificate.

Fifteen minutes later, a Bantipor Commercial representative

named Steigleder arrived at the hospital to debrief Mundine. LAD suspended the grey-hat password-cracking program which was running against the Depok city records site and waited until Steigleder finished talking.

"Mr. Mundine, this is your admin speaking," LAD said.

"Excuse me," Mundine said to Steigleder, then turned away slightly. "What's up, Laddie?"

"Apologies for the interruption, but I would like to ask a question," LAD said.

"Absolutely," Mundine said. "Steigleder tells me I've you to thank for surviving my hostage experience. Didn't know you were programmed to be a hero, Laddie."

"Febby helped me, Mr. Mundine."

"The girl?" Mundine scratched his head. "Good Lord. Is she the one who caused that—what did you call it, Steigleder? The web problem?"

"A DoS attack on Bantipor's public web site," Steigleder said. "Wait a minute. Are you telling me a thirteen-year-old kid made us scramble an entire tech team?"

"She was only helping me," LAD said.

Mundine chuckled. "Come on, Steigleder. Didn't you tell me this web problem helped security services pinpoint my location? I really should thank Febby in person. She wasn't harmed in the raid, was she? Or the others?"

"She's fine, Mr. Mundine," Steigleder said. "The recovery team used stun darts. The mother and the boy were knocked out. They'll be a little bruised. The father has a fractured right arm from resisting arrest. And Bantipor is going to prosecute him to the full extent of the law."

"As we should," Mundine grumbled, "but the family shouldn't have to suffer for the sins of the father. Couldn't we offer them some sort of aid?"

"Sorry, Mr. Mundine," Steigleder said, his voice's stress patterns indicating indifference. "The Bantipor Foundation won't be up and running locally for another couple of years. Until then, our charity packages will be extremely limited. Marketing could send them some t-shirts. Maybe a tote bag."

"That seems rather insulting," Mundine said. "Surely we can do more for the person who very likely saved my life."

"Look, Mr. Mundine—"

"An internship," LAD said.

"Excuse me," Mundine said to Steigleder. "What was that, Laddie?"

"I've reviewed Bantipor Commercial's company guidelines for student internships," LAD said. "There's no lower age limit specified. An intern only needs to be a full-time student, fluent in English, and eligible to work for the hours and employment period specified."

"It's a lovely idea, Laddie, but we can't take her away from her family after all that's happened."

"She can work remotely. Bantipor already supports over five thousand international telepresence employees," LAD said. "Indonesia's Manpower Act allows children thirteen years of age or older to work up to three hours per day, with parental consent."

"Won't the mother be suspicious of such an offer from the corporation which is also prosecuting her husband?"

"Bantipor Commercial owns three subsidiary companies on the island of Java." LAD was already drafting an inter-office memorandum.

"All right, fair enough," Mundine said. His voice pattern suggested he was smiling. "And I suppose I already know what kind of work Febby can do for us."

"Yes, Mr. Mundine." LAD blinked the OLEDs on Mundine's necklace: red, green, and blue. "Febby is a computer programmer."

# Blood Test

## Elliotte Rusty Harold

*Elliotte Rusty Harold is originally from New Orleans to which he returns periodically in search of a decent bowl of gumbo. However, he currently resides in the Prospect Heights neighborhood of Brooklyn with his wife Beth and dog, Thor. His short fiction has appeared in* Alfred Hitchcock's Mystery Magazine, *T. Gene Davis's Speculative Blog,* SF Comet, *and multiple anthologies. He has also written over twenty nonfiction books for various publishers, most recently* The JavaMail API *and* Java Network Programming, 4th Edition, *both from O'Reilly.*

Marisol stepped into the shot put circle for her third and final throw. The Ruidoso track team was nine points behind. They needed another first place event to win the meet, but the girl from Mescalero Apache had already thrown 13.2 meters. Marisol had cleared that mark twice in practice, once by almost a full meter, but she had never done it in competition.

She had 60 seconds to make the throw. The worst thing she could do would be to rush it. She needed a near-perfect throw. She hopped up and down a couple of times to warm up. Then she stretched her arms up to the sky to limber them. Satisfied, she pulled her arms in and nestled the heavy steel ball against her neck. She squatted down facing the rear of the circle, took a deep breath and cleared her head.

Marisol pulled her left knee up and kicked back, almost all the way to the toe board. Her right foot hit the ground in the center of the circle, and she pushed off with as much force as she could.

She swung her hips toward the front as she pulled in her left arm. She reached the apex of the spin and whipped her right arm out from her neck. With a half yell, half grunt, she heaved the shot with all the force she had.

As soon as the shot left her hand, she knew it was a good put – high, straight, and far. Her eyes found the shot near the top of its arc, then tracked it on the way down. When it finally smacked into the grass a good two meters past the mark she'd been aiming for, Marisol leapt and yelled for joy. A put like that clinched the meet. It might be a school record, maybe even a state record.

•••

45 minutes later Marisol was sitting on a bench in the visiting team locker room trying to absorb what Coach Abrams was telling her. "They disqualified me?"

The coach put his hand on her shoulder. "I'm sorry. Your scores have been dropped. They're not going to count."

Marisol tried to process the information. It didn't make sense. "The shot was on my neck the whole time. I didn't come close to touching the board. I know I didn't. "

"It's not just the shot put. All your events have been dropped."

Marisol's eyes pleaded with him. "But they have to count mine. If they don't count my scores, we lose."

The coach nodded. "I'm afraid so."

"But why? I'm eligible. I'm not too old. My grades are good. I'm in the district. You know that."

"It's none of those things, Marisol. It was the blood test. It's standard procedure when a record's at stake."

"The blood test?" She'd had her thumb pricked before the match like all the competitors; it was just one of those things you did. Did anyone even look at the little cards they put the blood on? "Coach, it must be a mistake. I don't do drugs. I swear it. They must have mixed up my blood with someone else's."

"Not drugs. Marisol. The other thing." Marisol looked confused, so the coach continued. "They test for the mutant gene. It's usually just a formality. Only this time, you tested positive."

Marisol looked at him in horror. "I'm a mutant?"

The coach nodded.

Marisol's chin began to tremble. She started talking faster. "No, that can't be true. No one in my family is a mutant. I trained hard. You know that. You know how hard I worked. I don't have super strength or anything."

"Probably not," the coach admitted, "But the rules are the rules. Anyone with the mutant gene, even if it's not activated, isn't allowed to compete in interscholastic meets."

Marisol felt like she'd caught a shot with her stomach. It wasn't fair. She'd trained so hard, worked so hard. She was the best athlete on the team because she deserved to be, not because of some stupid mutant gene. Coach Abrams was still talking, but she couldn't hear it through the ringing in her ears. All she could hear was her heart pounding. Her vision filled with black spots as her world crashed in around her.

●●●

The trip back to Ruidoso in the school van was the longest ride of Marisol's life. Win or lose, the return home was usually filled with animated gossip about the day's meet, the next meet and the boys' team. This afternoon, however, the silence was so thick a javelin couldn't pierce it.

Marisol's disqualification had dropped the team from first place to fourth. The coach hadn't told the team exactly why she had been disqualified, but there were only a few possibilities, none of them good.

Marisol curled up in the back corner of the van and looked out the window. She could feel the other girls looking at her, wanting to know what had happened but unsure how to ask. Marisol wished she had died out there on the track, maybe had an aneurysm like that kid from La Cueva at state last year. Her life was over, anyway. No track meant no scholarship, meant no college. She'd even dared to dream of competing in the Olympics. Now she could only see herself working at Dairy Queen. If she was lucky, maybe Coach Abrams would roll the van, and she would die in the accident before they got home. Then again, if she had any luck at all, she wouldn't be some kind of sick mutant.

•••

Marisol's mother was waiting in her car when the van pulled into the school parking lot. Marisol grabbed her bag out of the back of the van as soon as the coach opened the door. She walked to her mother's car as fast as she could without actually running. She didn't want to endure one more minute of her teammates' accusatory glances and whispers than she had to.

Marisol tossed the bag into the back seat, then threw herself into the passenger seat.

"Aren't you even going to say hello?" her mother asked as Marisol buckled her seat belt.

"Hello," she said flatly. She stared straight ahead. If she looked at her mother, she was afraid she might start crying.

"Meet didn't go well?"

"I don't want to talk about it. Can we go?"

Her mother started the car. "I'm supposed to remind you to be careful if you go out running tonight. The coyotes have been coming down out of the hills again. They might be hunting in packs. Last night they got the Barries' Maltese."

"I don't think I'm going to go running anymore."

"Did the coach change your program?"

"No, I got kicked off the track team today."

Her mother hit the brakes and slammed the car back into park. "Marisol Alvarez-Fuentes. What did you do?"

"It wasn't my fault, Mama." She could feel the tears start to come. "Please, just drive." She didn't want to start crying here where the team might see her.

"Marisol, you must have done something. You're the best thrower and the third best runner they've got. The coach told me he thought you might make all-state in the heptathlon next year. He wouldn't cut you for no reason."

Marisol clenched her hands. "There's something wrong with my blood." Her voice got softer, almost a whisper. "They said I'm a mutant, and mutants aren't allowed to play sports."

"Oh." Her mother put the car back in gear and pulled out of the lot. They drove in silence for a few minutes. Finally, they pulled into their driveway and rolled to a stop under the carport. Marisol's mother turned off the car, but didn't unlock it. "Marisol, I'm sorry."

"Yeah, whatever. It's not your fault. Can we go inside now?" She wanted to go to her room and sleep, maybe for the rest of high school, maybe for the rest of her life. She tried to open the door, but her mother had the child safety lock on.

"Marisol, there's something I should tell you."

Marisol crossed her arms over her chest. "Is there a special track league for mutants? Otherwise, I don't see what difference it can make."

Her mother sighed. "We hoped this wouldn't happen, your father and I, but we knew it was possible. It's why our parents – your grandparents – didn't want us to get married, but we were young. Your grandfathers, both of them, wore masks back in Mexico."

Marisol stared at her mother. "You never told me that."

"I don't remember all that much. I was younger than you are now when your nana brought me and tió Pablo across the border. She wanted to get us away from the violence and fighting before we were kidnapped by some old enemy with a score to settle or stuffed in a refrigerator to make our father angry."

Marisol tried to understand what that meant, but she ended up just shaking her head. "Why didn't you tell me this before?"

"I'm sorry, mijita. We should have told you sooner, but neither of us wanted to think about it. Your father saw some pretty bad things before he came north. You were born, and you were normal. Then your sister Anna came, and she was normal, too. We thought we'd dodged the bullet. Maybe we weren't carriers after all. We didn't see the point of burdening you with a lot of painful family history. "

"Only I wasn't normal. Not really."

"No, sometimes the gene waits till puberty to express itself."

"Fine," Marisol said sharply. "I come from a family of freaks. Got it. Can I go now?" She returned her gaze to the windshield, pointedly not looking at her mother.

"Mija, it's not the end of the world. You're not wrong, just different. If Coach Abrams doesn't see that—"

"It's not him, Mama. It's the NMAA, and the NCAA, and the Olympics, and everybody. Mutants aren't allowed to run track. They aren't allowed to compete in anything. They say it's not *fair* to the other athletes." Marisol had to stop to catch her breath. She was almost shaking. "Please, Mama, can I just go to bed? I don't want to talk about this."

Her mother sighed and unlocked the door. Marisol threw the door open and jumped out. Somehow she made it inside the house and up to her room before she started sobbing.

●●●

Marisol spent Sunday in her room, lying in bed. Her mother came in once to ask if she wanted to go to Mass, but Marisol frowned and turned over in the bed to look the other way. After that, her mother left her alone to mope.

Marisol turned her phone and computer off. She didn't want to explain to her disappointed teammates why she'd cost them the meet. She was sure the rumors were already flying, anyway. She didn't know which was worse, being a cheater or a doper or a mutant.

She thought about going running, but honestly, what was the point? It wasn't like she was going to be allowed to compete again.

She was still lying on her bed feeling sorry for herself when her little sister burst into the room, as usual without knocking. She was out of breath. "Marisol, have you seen Gordita? She's missing. I can't find her anywhere."

Gordita was an eight pound, long-haired stray cat Anna had adopted. She smelled like she'd lost a fight with a litter box and looked worse. She also liked to pee behind Marisol's bed if she didn't keep the door closed. "No, Anna, I haven't seen your stupid cat. Have you looked in the back yard?"

"Mama said she's not supposed to go outside. It's too dangerous with the coyotes."

"I don't think your cat knows that, Anna. Did you leave the kitchen door open again?"

"No," her sister said, but the rest of her face said yes.

"Go look in the back yard. Maybe she went out to hunt for lizards and fell asleep in the shed again."

Anna's face brightened. "OK. Thanks Marisol." She ran out.

Marisol flopped over in the bed. Was her sister was going to be a mutant, too? If she was, her superpower would be annoying people until they killed themselves to get away from her.

•••

Monday morning her mother breezed into Marisol's room and flicked on the light at 6:30 A.M. on the dot. "Time to get up, dormilona."

"Mama, let me sleep." Marisol tried to hide her head under a pillow.

Her mother grabbed the pillow away from her and threw it on the floor. "No, you're going to school today. Just because you lost a meet, doesn't mean you get to stay home."

Marisol pushed herself up. "I didn't lose. I was disqualified."

"Either way. You're going to school."

"What's the point? I'm never going to get out of this hick town. I might as well drop out now and get a job at the Dairy Queen. It's all I'm going to be allowed to do, anyway."

Her mother sat down on the bed and put her hands on Marisol's ears so she was looking straight into her eyes. "Marisol, you listen to me. You're going to college, mutant gene or no mutant gene. If you can't get a track scholarship, you're just going to have to study harder, and that's all there is to it."

"But Mama—"

"No buts. Get up and get dressed. You're going to school. The bus will be here in thirty minutes. Get moving."

Marisol groaned and pulled herself out of bed. She wasn't sure she even wanted to go to college if she couldn't run track, but college or no college, she knew she didn't want to go to school today. By now everyone at school knew she'd been disqualified, and they were going to pester her until they found out why. If she didn't tell them, they were just going to make something up.

As she got dressed, she pondered whether it would be smarter to tell the truth or lie. Maybe she should tell them she flunked the drug test. Some of the boys used steroids. Why shouldn't the girls? By the time the bus came, she still hadn't made up her mind.

•••

Marisol waited outside the school until the last possible minute, trying not to be noticed. She slipped in right before the bell. Jenni, a senior and the team captain, spotted her, but Marisol ran to Physics class before Jenni could ask her what had happened Saturday. Since Marisol was the only sophomore on the varsity team, at least she didn't have classes with any of her teammates.

Physics had been Marisol's favorite class. She loved how gravity, momentum and energy determined how balls would move under different forces. Most of the students thought it was pointless, just formulas to be memorized for an exam and then forgotten, but Marisol had loved it ever since she realized Mr. Bloomfield was talking about what happened on the track. Today it just reminded her of what she'd lost.

She thought she heard somebody whispering about her, but Mr. Bloomfield shut them down fast. For once she was glad he was so strict about talking in class. She wanted to put her head down and pretend she was invisible. Maybe that was her mutant power? That could be useful. She looked at her hand and imagined it going transparent, but it stayed annoyingly brown and opaque.

Marisol's luck ran out at lunch when Jenni and Sara found her in the girls' room. Jenni was first off the mark. "What happened at the meet on Saturday, Mari?"

Sara jumped in before Marisol had a chance to reply. "Yeah, we've been texting you all weekend, but you aren't answering your phone."

Marisol turned to the sink. Did she really have to tell them? "Guys, I don't want to talk about it."

"No way," said Jenni. "You're not getting off that easy. We practiced really hard for that meet, and if we lost it, I want to know why."

"I'm sorry, Jenni. Really, I am. I wanted to win, too. And it's not my fault. I can't say why. Please don't ask me to." Marisol could feel the tears building up behind her eyes.

Sara took her by the shoulders, while Marisol stared into the sink. "Mari, it's OK. You can tell us. We won't tell anyone, at least not anyone who isn't on the team. But I think we have a right to know, you know? Is it drugs? Are you taking steroids? or HGH?"

"If it is steroids," Jenni piped in, "it's not the end of the world. Some of the boys use them. There are ways you can hide it. You just have to stop taking them a few days before a meet. It might be good to give your body a break, anyway. You've been looking kind of beefy lately."

Marisol twisted out of Sara's arms. "Are you calling me fat?" Jenni was a twig. It was a miracle she could throw a javelin, much less a shot. She was only on the team because she ran fast.

"Geez, Mari, don't bite our heads off. We care about you. If you're having trouble we can help."

"It's not steroids, OK?"

"Then what is it?" Jenni asked. "It's good for the team that you're so — " she paused to find the right word " — muscular, but you're bigger than rest of the sophomores. You're bigger than most of the seniors. There must be a reason."

Marisol's face contorted in anger. "You want to know what's wrong with me? You want to know why they disqualified me? Fine. I'm a mutant, OK? Are you happy now?"

Jenni's eyes opened wider. "Wow, a mutant. I had no idea. Are you like, going to grow wings or something?"

"Or maybe be superfast?" Sara added.

"I don't know. It'll probably be something stupid, like turning myself purple or talking to squirrels."

Jenni put her finger to her chin and pretended she was thinking. "I can see it now. You'll be the Amazing Squirrel Girl, scaring evildoers with your super squirrel powers."

"Yeah," said Sara. "You can tickle them to death with your super squirrel tail."

"Or stare them into submission with your super beady eyes," added Jenni, and then she scrunched up her face and twitched her nose. Marisol couldn't help herself. She laughed.

Jenni took Marisol's hands in hers and looked into her face. "So, you're really not going to run track anymore?"

"I want to, but I can't. It's against the rules."

"What if we get you a secret identity?" Sara asked. "You could be the Masked Runner."

"I don't think masks are allowed, either," Marisol said.

"That's OK," said Jenni. "We'll figure something out. Com'ere." She pulled Sara and Marisol into a hug. "It's tradition, anyway. The wallflower on the sidelines is always the superhero who can outrace everyone. It's going to be all right."

Marisol snuggled up to the two girls. She smiled for the first time since the coach had told her. It felt good to know that even if she couldn't be on the team, she still had friends.

•••

When Marisol came home from school, Anna was sitting on the shag carpet in the living room watching TV. Gordita was purring in her lap. The show was some Japanese cartoon about three mutant girls in pink costumes who fought mad scientists and giant lizards. Marisol had always thought the show was stupid, but now it seemed mean, too. "You're home early," Anna said without taking her eyes away from the TV.

"I don't have to practice anymore. No reason to stay late."

"Are you going to be on TV now?"

"No. Why do you ask?"

"I thought all mutants got to be on TV, like the Danger Damsels." She pointed at the TV. "Are you going to be a Danger Damsel?"

"That's not how it works, Anna. I don't even know what my powers are yet. Sometimes it's just something silly like stretching your arms a few inches or being really good at counting things. Some mutants don't get any powers at all."

Anna stroked Gordita, and wrinkled her brow. Finally she spoke. "So if you don't have any superpowers, why won't they let you run track?"

Marisol looked at the carpet. "I wish I knew."

•••

Marisol stood in front of the bathroom mirror. She was wearing her track and field uniform. It was the closest thing she had to a costume. "OK," she said out loud even though no one else was in the room. "If I have to be a mutant, at least I can see what my powers are."

Flying would be cool. She squinted and thought hard about leaving the floor, but her feet stayed firmly planted on the ground. She lifted herself up on her tiptoes and tried again. Still nothing. With an increasing degree of self-consciousness, she tried hopping, then jumping, but every time she came back to the ground with a powerless thud.

Not flight then. What else? Telepathy? She closed her eyes and tried to hear the thoughts of someone else in the house. She thought she heard something in the kitchen. Her mother was chopping onions. Marisol could almost smell them.

The bathroom door flew open. "Marisol, have you seen Gordita?" asked Anna.

"Get out!" screamed Marisol. "Don't you ever knock? I don't care about your stupid cat!"

Anna's eyes watered, but she closed the door. Couldn't a girl have any privacy in this house? If she really was telepathic, she would have known Anna was coming before she opened the door. She could still smell the onions her mother was chopping, but it wasn't telepathy. They were just strong onions.

Maybe she could walk through walls? Maybe she could walk right into Anna's room! That would show her little sister. Marisol closed her eyes again and imagined herself becoming gaseous and intangible. When she felt as airy as possible, she stepped forward, once, twice, and then smacked into the sink. "Ow." OK, she couldn't walk through walls.

An hour later Marisol was back in her room, lying on her bed. She had been through all the superpowers she'd ever heard of, as well as a few she'd made up. (She was pretty sure no one had the power to make the captain of the boys' track team come when she called.) She didn't have anything to show for it except a bruised nose and messed-up hair. What was the point of being a mutant if all it did was get you kicked off the team?

Her mother knocked on the open door. She was dressed in her scrubs. "The hospital called. They need someone for the night shift. I put a casserole in the fridge for dinner."

"OK, casserole in the fridge. Got it."

Her mother walked in and sat down on the bed next to Marisol. "How are you feeling, mijita? Are you going to be OK?"

Marisol thought about it before answering. How was she feeling? "I'm OK, I guess. The girls at school were nicer than I thought. Only, I don't know. I just feel… really sort of blah. I'm bored, but I don't know what I want to do."

"Why don't you go for a run?"

"Mama." She stretched the word out so it expressed her annoyance.

"Why not? I don't think you've been running since the meet."

"I only ran to train for the heptathlon. Now I can't compete in that, either."

Her mother gave her a quizzical look. "Did you only run to train for the competition? I thought you sort of liked it."

"It's depressing practicing for an event they won't let me compete in."

"All right then. Just a thought." Her mother wrapped an arm around her. "I know it seems horrible now, but you'll get through this, just like your grandfather did. It's a speed bump, not a dead end. If you need anything, you'll let me know, right?"

Marisol tried to fake a smile. "OK, Mama."

"Good night, mijita. I'll see you in the morning." She kissed Marisol on the cheek.

After her mother left, Marisol thought about what she'd said. Mothers. She knew nothing. Nothing! So some old relatives back in Mexico a hundred years ago had the gene. What difference did that make to her now?

On the other hand, Marisol did feel really keyed up. She'd been lying in bed or sitting down for two days straight now. Maybe a quick jog would clear her head. Just an easy run up the street and back. She didn't even need to keep time. Not like she was in training for anything, and she was already wearing her track clothes.

Marisol slipped out the front door. The night was hot, but not too hot to run. The full moon was out, so there'd be enough light if she wanted to go up into the park. She didn't need to stick to the lit streets.

She walked out to the street and then started loping easily down her block. A coyote howled somewhere in the hills above her. Another answered from somewhere closer by. She'd like that, to be a coyote, free to run and play and hunt. Maybe that could be her mutant power, running with the coyotes. If she couldn't be on the track team, she could join a coyote pack. Nobody bothered coyotes with blood tests and stupid rules.

As she turned off the street into the park, she thought maybe she should try calling to the coyotes. She felt a little silly, so her first effort was a thin noise, barely more than a whisper. A coyote would have to have super-hearing to pick that up. What the hell. There wasn't anyone out here to see her. She mustered up her courage, pumped out a burst of speed and really let loose. Oh-woo-woo! Nothing responded. Any coyotes out there must be laughing at her. OK, she wasn't Coyote Girl then.

Whatever. She was done worrying about what her power might be. If it came, it came. If not, she could still run. It was actually sort of freeing just running to run, not bothering with the training schedule Coach Abrams had set up for her. She didn't need to worry about peaking early or how much time her muscles needed to recover before the next meet.

The measured route ended at the far parking lot, but tonight she still had energy left, so she picked up the pace and headed up the dirt trail that led into the hills.

•••

Marisol was breathing hard and covered in sweat when she finally left the park and turned back onto her street. She wasn't sure how long she'd been running, but she'd gone farther than she was used to. She was exhausted, but it was a good exhaustion, the sort that lets you stop thinking and just be. She'd sleep well tonight.

Marisol had just reached her block when she heard a scream. Anna! Forgetting how tired she was, Marisol sprinted. She covered the last half block fast enough to qualify for the Olympics. Then Anna screamed again. She was behind the house!

Marisol tore up the driveway, but when she hit the backyard she pulled up short. The flood light from the carport illuminated the scene. Anna was pressed up against the shed, clutching her cat to her chest. At the edge of the circle of light, between Anna and the back door of the house, three coyotes were waiting.

Anna cried to her, "Marisol, help me." Her voice was weak and muffled.

"Stay put, Anna. Don't move. Don't show any fear." Marisol's mind raced. What should she do? If she knew what her powers were, she could fly in and grab Anna, or blast the coyotes with energy beams or even just beat them up. But mutant gene or no, she was still only a regular teenage girl.

Instead Marisol spoke as calmly and firmly as she could. "Anna, I want you to put Gordita down. The coyotes only want the cat. If you put her down, they'll leave you alone."

Anna shook her head. Then she hunched down, clutching Gordita tighter to her chest. Maldita sea, that was exactly the wrong thing to do! The smaller Anna made herself look, the more likely the coyotes were to attack.

One of the coyotes howled. To her surprise, another coyote responded from down the street. Marisol's skin grew cold. There were more of them, and they weren't far away. If she didn't do something fast, they were both going to be coyote dinner.

The largest of the coyotes started to walk forward slowly. The light glinted off its exposed teeth. "Hey," Marisol shouted. "Get away from her!" The coyote stopped and looked back at her.

Marisol stepped forward, waving her arms above her head to try to look as big as she could. "Hey, you dumb dog. Go away!"

For a second it looked like the coyote might actually turn and run. Then Marisol stumbled over a big rock in the dirt. She thrust out a hand to catch herself and skinned her palm as she hit the ground.

Anna cried out again. All three coyotes were moving towards her now. Anna had closed her eyes and still hadn't let go of the stinking cat. Anna was sixty feet away and the coyotes were between her and them. There was no way she could get to Anna in time and not much she could do if she did, unless... It was a stupid idea, but it was the only thing she could think of.

Marisol grabbed for the rock she'd tripped over. It was stuck in the ground, and she had to dig with her fingernails to pry it out of the dirt. She looked at the coyotes advancing toward Anna. Marisol had never thrown that far, not even the last put that got her kicked off the team, and she had never needed to aim like this before, either.

Marisol pulled her arms in and laid the rock against her neck. It was heavier than she was used to, and it wasn't balanced like it should be, but it was the only weapon she had. She turned away from her sister and squatted down. She planted her right foot and kicked off with her left leg. As she swung her hips around, she pulled in her left arm and sighted on the largest coyote. Screaming loud enough to frighten coyotes two counties away, she threw the rock.

The throw was so strong that Marisol stumbled a bit after she let the rock fly, then caught herself. As she slowed to a halt, her eyes caught up with the rock near the top of its arc. She held her breath as it picked up speed on the way down.

The rock was arcing. The coyote was trotting. She could trace the arc of the rock, see where it intersected the path of the coyote, see where it was going to hit. Que suerte. She'd done it. It was going to work.

And then, for no reason at all, the coyote stopped short.

No! The rock was going to miss. Her sister was dead. She saw the rock. She saw the coyote. She could almost see the spot in the dirt where the rock was going to hit, two meters too far. She could see where it needed to land instead.

And then, in defiance of everything her she'd learned in physics class, the rock turned in midair and continued along the new path Marisol envisioned.

The rock hit the lead coyote square in its skull. The impact made a squelchy, crunching sound, and the beast went down, dead before it hit the ground.

The other two coyotes stopped still, confused about what had happened to the alpha. Then one of them yelped, and they both turned and scurried out of the yard into the dark.

Marisol ran to her sister. "Anna! Are you OK?"

Her sister was still holding Gordita to her chest and shivering. Marisol grabbed her and clutched her like Anna was clutching the cat. "Anna, it's OK. They're gone now. They can't hurt you. Come on, let's go inside." She nudged Anna to a standing position and held her tight as they walked back across the yard. She didn't relax until they were safely back in the kitchen.

Once she'd made sure the door was shut and locked, both locks, she turned back to Anna. Anna was sitting at the kitchen table and squeezing Gordita like her life depended on it. The cat began to squirm until it finally extricated itself from Anna's arms and jumped to the floor. Then it strolled off like nothing had happened. Stupid cat. She should have left it outside with the coyotes.

"Anna, what happened? Why were you in the backyard alone?" Marisol asked.

Anna recovered enough voice to protest. "Gordita was out there, alone. I had to get her."

"Anna, that was a very dangerous thing you did. You know

you're not supposed to go out after dark, especially when Mama isn't home. If I hadn't come back when I did, you could have been hurt, or worse."

"But you were there. You saved me. You're a superhero, just like the Danger Damsels." Anna's cheeks were still wet and puffy, but she was smiling.

Marisol sighed. "Anna, listen to me. I'm not a superhero. I threw a rock and got lucky. That's all. I probably couldn't make that put again if I tried a hundred times."

"No, you are. I saw it. You glowed."

Marisol held her hand up and looked at it. If it had glowed, it wasn't glowing now. She picked up the plastic salt shaker off the table and tentatively tossed it underhand at the stove while imagining it landing in front of the refrigerator. It stubbornly landed exactly where she'd aimed, smack in front of the stove. After it hit it bounced twice, more or less toward the refrigerator, spilling salt all over the floor in the process. Újule, now she'd have to clean that up, too.

Marisol put a hand on her sister's shoulder. "Anna, I don't know what happened out there. Maybe it was superpowers, and maybe it was just dumb luck, but you can't scare me like that. If those other two coyotes hadn't run away, I don't know what I could have done. And if anything happened to you, I'd be devastated. You're my sister, and I love you."

Anna threw her arms around Marisol, and hugged her tight. "I love you too, Marisol."

Marisol returned the hug. Maybe she had superpowers. Maybe she didn't. She didn't know how else to explain what had happened. Rocks didn't turn in mid-air like that. If throwing things at track meets had taught her anything, it was that when you threw something, its course was set. It might not go where you wanted, but once it left your hand, it was going where it was going. Physics class even had a fancy name for it, Newton's First Law. The test she'd memorized it for was months back, but she still remembered the rule: objects in motion stay in motion unless acted on by an external force.

Maybe Mr. Bloomfield could explain what had happened. She could worry about that tomorrow. For now, Anna was safe, her mother loved her, and her friends were still her friends. The rest would take care of itself.

# Lunar Camp
## Maggie Allen

*Maggie Allen recently started writing short fiction, but from her day job at NASA she has years of experience writing and podcasting about various nonfiction topics in astronomy and astrophysics. Maggie has other short stories published in* A Hero By Any Other Name, *the* Time Traveled Tales *anthologies,* Athena's Daughters, Soothe the Savage Beast, War of the Seasons: The Heart, *and* Contact Light. *She co-edited* Athena's Daughters, Volume 2. *These titles may be found at: http://silenceinthelibrarypublishing. com. Maggie is a guitarist and singer in the rock band, "Naked Singularity," which released its first album of original music in 2013. They are working on their second album. Her band's website may be found at http://naked-singularity.com, and her writer website at writermaggie.blogspot.com.*

*10-9-8…*
Bee glanced around at the other passengers, trying to judge whether any of them looked nervous.
*7-6-5…*
Some people closed their eyes while some looked out the window, squinting a bit at the bright Florida sunlight.
*4, 3, 2, 1…*
The engines roared to life. Lift off! Bee felt her body pushed into the padded seat as the Firefly-class rocket she was on thrust itself into the air. She fought the G-force that tried to glue her to her seat and managed to turn her head and watch through her window as the sky turned from bright blue to black.

She'd ridden on a rocket like this before on her first trip to Luna City, but she'd been much younger then and accompanied by her parents. Today she was on her own and on her way to Lunar Camp. Many a thirteen-year-old would have been thrilled to have the chance to spend their summer at camp on the Moon. Bee Williamson was not that person.

"The moon has no plants," she'd grumbled to her parents. "And who's going to take care of my garden?"

Her family lived on an Iowa farm that was lush and green and gold. Bee loved it there. Though much of the farm work was automated or operated robotically, Bee had been given a patch of her own to use as she pleased, and she loved working it herself. She'd downloaded books on old-fashioned farming and pored through screens of the latest research so she could experiment with a variety of plant-growing techniques. She had big plans for her summer, and a trip to the Moon wasn't included in them.

"Beyoncé, you know that Lunar Camp will look good on your application to SATAS," her mother had said.

The sound of her given name always made Bee roll her eyes. Besides, it was too soon to even think about leaving the farm to go to the Space Academy of Technical Arts and Sciences, even though it would have something to teach her about plants grown on ships or about terraforming other worlds. That was still more than she could say of Lunar Camp.

She suspected Lunar Camp had little to do with agriculture or horticulture. Most likely she'd be tromping around in lunar dust collecting rocks and tripping into craters. Rocks were something Bee routinely pitched out of her garden. She didn't see much point in collecting them.

But all of her protests fell on deaf ears Bee was on the way to the Moon.

Luna City was a popular tourist destination because the orbital station was a commonly used transit junction for those going on to Mars or the outer solar system.

Someday Bee hoped to see more of what was out there. But for now, it seemed that all she was going to see was monochromatic dust.

Bee sighed heavily as she climbed aboard the people mover at the Luna City docking station. A look out the window confirmed the starkness of the landscape. Bee pulled her hand-held, personal PAL device out of her pocket and messaged her parents to let them know she'd arrived safely on the Moon. Then she pulled up one of her agriculture texts and tried to lose herself in it for the duration of the ride.

•••

Bee scanned the terminal for a Lunar Camp sign and saw it in the corner with one lone boy standing under it. She realized it had been hours since she'd eaten and stopped at a brightly lit automated food and beverage kiosk. She was in no rush to get to her destination. Five credits bought her a butter pie and a hot chocolate, which she alternately chewed and sipped as she strolled toward the gathering area for the lunar campers.

"Hey, where did you get that?" asked the boy standing under the Lunar Camp sign. Bee guessed he was probably around her age, though he was small, as if he hadn't yet hit his growth spurt, and his skin was as pale as hers was dark.

"The butter pie? There's a machine down that corridor over there."

"They're hard to come by in most places on the Moon – my older brother said there was a kiosk where you could get them at the terminal here in Luna City, but I wasn't sure I'd be able to find it," the boy said. "Do you think I have time to get one?"

Bee shrugged. "We're the only ones here, so I don't see why not."

"Watch my stuff!" he said as he took off running, dodging around the other passengers coming and going in the terminal.

"Sure." Bee shook her head and turned to study his luggage, which was sitting in front of her. Along with a suitcase were a duffle and a shoulder bag, all of which were stained with what looked like Moon dust. She peered at the nametag on the shoulder bag and was able to decipher that the boy's name was Mike Lopez and that he was from the lunar colony of Plato, so named for the prominent crater it was near.

The traffic stream in the terminal was increasing, which probably meant another rocket of passengers had come in. Bee moved the wheeled suitcase and the shoulder bag closer to the wall to get them out of the way and then tugged on the strap of Mike's duffel bag to pull it closer to the other things. She was surprised to find it heavy. She frowned. *What did he have in there, rocks?*

Just then, Mike skidded up to her, butter pie in hand. "Thanks for watching my stuff."

"No problem. I'm Bee, by the way."

"Mike." He shook her hand and plunked himself down by the bags to eat his snack. "You wanna sit too? I can move this out of the way." He shoved the heavy duffle over to make room for Bee.

"Why is your duffle so heavy?" Bee asked, unable to contain her curiosity.

"It's got rocks in it."

Bee snorted as she sat down next to Mike, a big grin on her face. "Why?" she asked.

"I found them in a small crater not far from home, and they're different than anything else I've seen before. I wanted to show them to Etienne. He's one of the counselors at Lunar Camp. He knows a ton about lunar geology."

"So I guess you've been to Lunar Camp before?" Bee asked, skeptical that anyone could possibly enjoy it so much they'd actually want to go back.

"Since I was ten," he said with a hint of pride. "So this is my third year." Mike took a bite of butter pie and rolled his eyes back in appreciation. "It's great, you're gonna love it."

"Uh-huh."

"What's not to love?"

"Rocks," Bee said, matter-of-factly.

Mike looked startled, as if he found it impossible to understand how anyone could not love rocks as much as he did.

Eventually more kids and a few counselors appeared, and soon everyone was rounded up and put aboard the Lunar Camp transport vehicle. The vehicle looked much like the people mover she'd taken from the docking station, with tall, heavily treaded tires.

"Be sure to buckle up good," Mike told Bee. "The ride can be kind of bumpy."

Mike sat next to Bee on the transport though she wasn't sure why. Wouldn't he have friends among the other campers since he'd been to Lunar Camp so many times before? But though he'd nodded to a few of them, he didn't speak to anyone else. At one point, he rolled his eyes a bit as the noise from the rowdiest kids – sitting in the back to maximize the bumpiness of their ride – washed over them. Bee smiled and turned to look out the window at the so-called magnificent desolation on the other side of the pressurized glass.

"Pretty, isn't it?" Mike said gesturing at the view.

"Is it?" Bee turned to look at Mike. "It's so… lifeless."

Mikes eyes shifted from the view to her and back again. He lifted a shoulder. "I guess it's all in what you're used to."

"How do you ever get used to not having trees? And grass? And birds?"

"How do you ever get used to not being able to see the Earth hanging there up in the sky?" he countered. "And weighing so much when you're walking around outside?" Just then the vehicle went over a bump, causing it to catch air for a second.

Bee pulled her seatbelt tighter, but stayed silent. She didn't have answers for any of Mike's questions. But that didn't mean she couldn't cling stubbornly to the things she knew. She gave an exasperated sigh and shook her head. "All right then, tell me. What's it like living here? You're from Plato, right?"

When Mike gave her a quizzical look, she replied a little sheepishly, "I saw the name tag on your luggage back at the terminal."

Mike flashed Bee a smile. "No problem." He thought for a second. "I don't know how much you know about Plato, but it's the oldest of the colonies, so it's kind of built up now, though it started out as a small polar outpost."

"That colony had a rough start, didn't it?" Bee wasn't that well versed on lunar history, but like every school kid, she'd learned a few things that she frequently misremembered.

"Yeah it did – it was totally dependent on Earth until they figured out how to mine water from the craters nearby, the ones that always stay dark. But it's totally different now. It's a lot like New York City. You'd like it!"

"You're assuming I like New York," Bee grinned. "From what I hear, it's about as green as the Moon is."

"Don't they have a big park there?"

Bee shrugged. "Don't know, never been there."

"What are they teaching you on Earth? Even I know about Central Park," Mike scoffed.

Bee defensively folded her arms. "I'm supposed to be the expert on everything about Earth now? If you know so much, tell me more about Luna City."

"It was built in… uh… well, it was after Plato."

"Uh-huh." Bee gave him a smug look.

"Okay, I don't know how old it is. But I do know it's way closer to the lunar equator than Plato is. It's in the Sea of Serenity. Lunar Camp is a little further out in the Sea of Tranquility. It'll take us a couple of hours to get there, even in these things." Mike patted the seat in front of him. "They're fast. And bumpy. Even with the big tires."

As if to make his point, the vehicle plunged over the edge of a small crater, making Bee's stomach drop. She was starting to regret having eaten the butter pie.

•••

"Hey." Bee poked Mike in the arm, waking him from his doze. "We're here."

Mike's head popped up, and he craned past Bee to see out the window. "Are we inside the bubble yet?"

"Just got through the airlock. That bubble looks flimsy to me. Are you sure it's safe inside?"

"Yeah, totally. Most places on the Moon have shields like this around them. Obviously, they keep the air, temperature, and pressure regulated, so we don't scald or freeze."

"It looks like it's not even there." Bee pressed her cheek to the glass, trying to get a good angle. She knew they were inside the bubble now, but it was nearly impossible to tell where its boundary was.

"It's stronger than it looks. I've seen micrometeorites bounce right off these things! Besides, if the bubbles weren't clear, you wouldn't be able to see the moonscape. While you're here, you'll want to get the full experience of actually being on the Moon, you know?"

"Hmm." The "full experience" seemed like more of a threat than a treat to Bee.

The transport stopped at what appeared to be a loading zone. Bee noticed rovers and small vehicles of all different shapes and sizes parked nearby. She'd heard there would be day trips and excursions out to different sites near the camp. She couldn't work up any excitement over the idea of excavating rocks; she was actually interested in seeing where the historic Apollo 11 mission had landed.

In short order, Bee and the others were herded off the transport, through the loading area, and into the artificially gravity infused visitor center. The visitor center was almost a cliché. Like every space or science museum she'd ever been to, it was decorated with interactive information kiosks and holographic 3D immersive images of galaxies and nebulae. It also had a rotunda with a starscape on it – except the starscape was real. As was the crescent Earth that hung overhead, glowing brightly in the darkened sky. Bee swallowed as she looked up at it, a feeling of homesickness washing over her.

Before she could focus for long on missing home, all the kids were ushered into the auditorium. Some of them were quiet and looked nervous, others laughed and joked with the friends they had clearly been reunited with. Bee looked around for Mike, despite herself. At least he was familiar. She sat near the aisle, an empty seat next to her, just in case.

Two adults, a man and a woman, stood at the front of the auditorium, waiting for the campers to be seated. And there was

Mike, talking animatedly to one of them. It dawned on Bee why Mike didn't seem to have that many friends among the kids. How could he when he clearly preferred hanging out with the counselors? Presumably talking about rocks?

Once most of the kids had shuffled into the rows of chairs, the man Mike was talking to gestured for him to join the others. Mike looked around and smiled when he found Bee and the seat she had saved for him.

"Thanks," he said, popping into it.

"No problem." Bee had to admit that it was nice to know one person here, even if that person seemed to like rocks more than people.

"Hi kids, I'm Etienne Cooper, and I'll be one of your counselors during this session of Lunar Camp." Bee eyed him suspiciously. Etienne was bouncing on his heels as he spoke and kept fiddling with the zippered pockets of his jumpsuit as if it pained him to stay still. With his athletic build, Bee thought he seemed like he'd be more at home canoeing around a lake at a traditional Earth summer camp than up here on the moon. Etienne looked like he was about twenty-five, just like her cousin Omar. He was sporty too. Bee didn't especially like sporty.

"This is Merja Petrowski, who will be your other counselor." Etienne gestured at the woman next to him, who gave a shy wave. She was pretty, thin, and pale, with long, dark hair. "Please feel free to come to us about anything at all. There are lots of other counselors here, who you'll meet for various classes and activities, but we'll be the ones in charge of your age group, the Eagles. It's great to see so many familiar faces from last year, and I'm really glad we can be together again this year. Despite having a lot of Earth kids from the northern hemisphere here right now, since it's summer for them, you'll still meet people from all over the solar system during this session. We even have a group of junior campers here, the Eaglets. We'll expect you all to set a good example for them."

Etienne nodded at Merja, who tapped busily away on her tablet.

"Merja's just uploaded your schedules to your PALs, along with a map, and important emergency information. Why don't you all check and make sure you've received them?"

The air was filled with the sound of twenty-six campers pulling out their PAL devices from bags and pockets.

"Are you with Etienne or Merja?" Mike asked Bee.

"What do you mean?" Bee looked up from her PAL at Mike.

"We won't all fit in one cabin. They'll split us in two, half with Etienne and half with Merja."

Bee scrolled through the files they'd sent. "Looks like Etienne."

"Oh good, me too."

Bee wasn't listening. She was gazing in horror at her schedule. It was exactly as she'd feared. Sure there was lunar history, volcanology, math, rocketry, arts and crafts, and a slew of other things. But there was also not one, not two, but three different classes on Moon rocks: lunar mineralogy, lunar geology, and lunar topography.

"What's the deal with this?" she demanded, showing her PAL to Mike.

"Oh, cool, you got the same random electives I did."

"Random electives?"

"Sure. Most of us have the same stuff, but there's a couple of electives that are given out randomly."

"So why do I have three classes on practically the same thing?"

"Because it's random?" Mike said with a sheepish smile. "And here, they're not the same." He pointed to her screen. "Lunar mineralogy is all about the composition of lunar rocks, and lunar topography tells you where they came from, and lunar geology…" Mike trailed off at the look on Bee's face, and then rushed through the rest of his sentence "…and lunar geology is a lab course, it's more hands on."

It was going to be a long summer.

•••

"You should come with me after lunch, I want to show you something," Mike said, lifting a forkful of unidentifiable grey stuff from his plate before shoving it into his mouth.

"Is it a rock?"

Mike laughed at Bee's expression. "What else would it be? But seriously – remember the ones I brought from home to show Etienne? He thinks they have rare earth elements in them, and we're going to run some samples through the chromatograph to see if we can maybe isolate some Yttrium or something."

This piqued Bee's curiosity. Chemistry was a key part of agricultural science, and Bee wanted to learn anything she could that would help her advance in her field of interest.

But one thing held her back from jumping on it – a trip to the lab would mean interaction with the one person she'd taken a dislike to since being at Lunar Camp. Etienne.

Mike practically worshipped him, so Bee didn't have the heart to say that she found Etienne's sporty "go get 'em" enthusiasm exhausting. Mike was as serious about his love of rocks as Bee was about her love of plants. Even if she didn't understand it, she respected it. Etienne? He was more of a geology evangelist. Mike might try to find some angle of lunar geology that might appeal to her, hoping to hook her interest, but at least he didn't try to convert her. That was more than she could say for Etienne.

And there was one more thing.

"He's going to call me by my real name, you know."

"You mean, Beyon—"

Bee put up her hand to stop him. "Don't say it."

"What if I tell him not to call you that anymore?"

"Again, you mean?"

"Oh yeah, I did try once, and he didn't listen." Mike chewed thoughtfully.

Bee just gave Mike an exasperated look.

"I'm sure it'll work this time. He'll stop calling you Beyon…" Mike checked himself just in time. "…by your real name. I promise."

Bee looked over at the hopeful expression on Mike's face and softened.

"All right, let's do it."

"Yesss!" Mike crowed.

"After we're done eating." Bee looked down at what was left of the refried bean pizza boat on her plate. "Actually, I think I'm done."

"Are you sure?"

Bee nodded and then watched Mike stab the rest of her lunch with a fork and pull it over to his own plate. She didn't know how he stayed so small with an appetite like that. And for camp food no less.

•••

"Mike! Beyoncé!" Etienne boomed at them as they entered the lab.

Bee cringed. "It's just Bee," she tried to correct him, but he'd already scurried over to the other side of the lab and clearly wasn't listening anymore.

"Come over here, Mike, and we'll start putting some samples together to run through the chromatograph. Beyoncé can come over and help if she wants."

"I don't think she likes being called Beyoncé," Mike interjected.

Etienne looked up from the lab bench and ran his hands through his curly hair distractedly before focusing on Bee. "Don't like your name, eh? Why not? It's distinctive."

"I just don't," Bee said stiffly.

"Not a fan of the classics?"

"Not really." Bee liked some of the music from years ago, but that didn't mean she wanted to have to share her name with some long-gone music legend. Bee guessed she should count herself lucky that she hadn't been named something even less desirable by her music-loving parents. Like after one of the robots in The Zartoids. Twenty-second century girl-bot pop was the worst. Ultimately, Bee didn't want to be named after anything. She just wanted to be herself.

Etienne studied her, a slight twinkle remaining in his eyes. Bee felt like he was evaluating her, trying to figure her out. Bee gazed back stolidly. *Let him try.*

"You know what Etienne's favorite old band is?" Mike broke

into the awkward silence Bee's words had left with an attempt at a joke. "The Rolling Stones." He looked at them both expectantly. "Get it?"

A loud guffaw suddenly burst out of Etienne, making Bee's eyes grow wide with alarm. Mike cracked up at this and suddenly doubled over with a helpless whoop of laughter. Etienne started laughing harder, more at Mike's reaction to the bad joke than at the joke itself.

*What was wrong with everyone?* Bee thought. *Had there been something in the food?*

Still, standing there, watching Mike and Etienne practically weeping with laughter, it was hard to resist a little smile. Mike was so serious that when he did crack a joke, it seemed especially funny.

Bee made a decision. She reached down and grabbed Mike's arm. "Yes, yes," she said patiently, trying to lever him up off the floor. "It's pretty obvious that you both probably like *rock* music." At that, Mike lost it again, and this time dragged Bee down with him.

Bee let a giggle out, almost despite herself. It had been hard for her to resist the obvious pun. After all, she wasn't completely devoid of a sense of humor, even if it sometimes seemed that way. Especially here, out of her element, Bee felt like it was hard to shine, and her personality was suffering for it. It felt good to laugh for a change, even if it was over something silly.

When they'd all recovered their composure, Etienne looked over at Bee. "So if you don't want to be called Beyoncé, what should we call you?"

"Just Bee is fine," she said, relieved that maybe the name situation would finally be resolved.

"Hmm. You don't seem like a Bee to me."

"I don't?" Bee wasn't sure she liked where this was going, and her guard went back up.

"Where are you from?" Etienne asked as he busied himself again with the lab equipment on the table in front of him. "Iowa, on Earth."

"Well, then, Iowa," he said with a grin. "Why don't you hand out those safety goggles and we'll get to work."

Bee let out a deep sigh and complied with Etienne's request. Clearly there was no hope for him.

As she turned to pick up a box of glassware, Mike gave her a grin and a thumbs-up, as if it were mission accomplished. Clearly there was no hope for him either.

Etienne continued to call her Iowa for the next few weeks. Bee was alternately exasperated, confused, and the tiniest bit flattered. Iowa wasn't bad as nicknames go, but it had come from Etienne, who she felt was purposely teasing her by using it. She tried her best to simply not react to it. That became hard to do, however, when it caught on and most of the other kids followed Etienne's lead and started calling her Iowa also. Eventually, Mike was the only one who still called her Bee.

●●●

One of the big highlights of Lunar Camp was a day trip to the Apollo 11 landing site. It was now under a protective bubble, attached to a rather large visitor complex, within which one could walk around. The trip was a big deal because for the first time during their stay, the students would wear space suits and travel in small lunar buggies. This first excursion was to teach the campers about lunar history, but it was also an introduction to the fieldwork they would be doing later during their stay at Lunar Camp. Though larger pressurized transports could take you lots of places on the Moon, there were places where smaller vehicles were more practical.

Bee shivered with excitement as she and the others in her group were coached on how to properly don their space suits. She'd never been out on the lunar surface with only a pressure suit to protect her from the harsh lunar environment before. And she would get to see the spot where humans first touched down on another world. Even Bee couldn't be cynical about that.

Both counselors inspected the pressurized seals at the neck and wrists of every camper's suit before lunar buggy assignments were given out. Unsurprisingly, Bee was with Mike and Etienne. She was sure Mike had asked Etienne specifically if they could ride together, probably so they could talk about some sort of geologic minutia. But even the prospect of having to listen to several hours of that couldn't dim Bee's excitement.

•••

Bee gripped the handles on the passenger seat of the buggy as they bumped over the rough lunar terrain. Though she was safely belted in, and years of buggies journeying from Lunar Camp to the Apollo 11 site had worn a wide swath through the lunar dust, the whole thing still felt precarious. Mike reached up from the back seat to poke her in an attempt to gauge her reaction. She twisted her head as far as the helmet would allow and gave him a big thumbs-up. Satisfied that she was enjoying herself, he relaxed back into his seat and engaged Etienne in a steady stream of chatter over the radio intercom.

The Apollo 11 complex rose out of the lunar horizon far faster than it would have on Earth, which Bee found faintly disorienting. A large building with a visible airlock held the museum and learning center and attached to it was a clear walkway that connected to the protective bubble over the site where people first landed on the Moon. Though anything historic within the bubble was safely covered with a protective surface or roped off, because the dome over the landing site was clear, one had the illusion, or rather the full experience, of seeing the Moon as the original astronauts might have done all those years ago.

It took what felt like ages to Bee for everyone to go through the airlock, park their vehicles, and doff their suits. But finally, the campers were free to explore. Bee headed off alone wanting some time to herself; something she hadn't had much of since she'd been at camp. She made her way to the remains of Apollo 11 and stood in front of it, taking it in.

There was the half of the landing module that had been left behind. And there was the American flag, wired to look like it was waving in the wind even on the airless surface of the Moon. Though now, of course, because it was under a dome that contained a breathable environment, it looked even more stiff and unnatural. Neil Armstrong and Buzz Aldrin's backpacks, along with other mementos they'd left behind, including a tiny gold olive branch pin, were preserved in the lunar dirt where they'd been carefully placed hundreds of years ago.

What those men had done was what she wanted to do. To land on a strange new world and see things that had never before been seen with human eyes. They had landed on what was essentially a barren wasteland. But if Bee closed her eyes, she could picture stepping out onto a planet covered with strange and wonderful new vegetation for her to study. Someday.

•••

"Hey, what's that?" Mike pointed toward the bottom of the large groove, or rille, that ran parallel to the track they were using to return to Lunar Camp. The channel beside them wasn't especially deep; it sloped fairly gently off to their right.

"What's what?" Etienne asked glancing over to the right, trying to see what Mike was pointing at. He pulled the rover over and paused so they could gaze down into the rille.

"I saw a patch of rock that looks a lot like the one where I found those KREEP rocks at home. Right over there." Mike pointed.

"KREEP?" asked Bee before she could stop herself. It was going to be a long drive back. She might as well participate in the conversation.

"Yeah, KREEP. It's an acronym for potassium, rare earth elements, and phosphorus. Don't you pay any attention in lunar mineralogy?" Mike asked.

Bee couldn't see him, but she was sure he was rolling his eyes at her in exasperation. Her lack of an immediate response made Mike and Etienne both break out in laughter.

"Ah, the silence of the guilty," Etienne chuckled.

Mike gave her a poke in the shoulder. "The K in KREEP is because the atomic symbol for potassium…"

"Is K, I know. I'm not totally ignorant," she said in a slightly haughty tone, which made Etienne laugh again. Bee glared at him through her helmet faceplate.

"It's okay, Iowa, I know you're a science whiz. But you should really consider the fact that you could learn something from all these lunar science classes you're being forced to take. Something you can apply to your study of plants."

"Like what?" Bee asked stiffly. She wasn't quite ready to unbend yet.

"Like—"

"Hey guys, I really think they are the same type of rocks," Mike excitedly broke in. He was leaning as far out of the buggy as his restraints would let him. "I used the magnification function on my suit and it's a really similar outcropping. Do you think we could go take a look?"

Etienne examined the rille. "Sure, it's not too steep here, I don't think it would be a problem. But this rille has probably been combed over by other campers lots of times before. Do you really think it's like the one at home?"

"The rocks look pretty dusted over. I don't think they've been disturbed by humans. Please Etienne? This could be a big deal."

"Why is it such a big deal?" Bee asked.

"Usually KREEP rocks are only found in the Ocean of Storms and Sea of Rains. Plato isn't too far north of the Sea of Rains," Etienne explained. "So the rocks Mike found at home aren't so unusual. But finding similar rocks here in the Sea of Tranquility would be. So, let's take a closer look."

Etienne radioed Merja to tell her what they were doing and also followed protocol by radioing their location and their delay back to the camp itself. Then he pressed a key on the rover dashboard and pulled up the specs on the store of extra oxygen canisters on board. After he'd verified that their supply was adequate, he had Mike and Bee check the levels of the cans they were wearing.

"Looks like everything checks out. Let's go!" With that, Etienne turned the buggy down toward the rille and gently accelerated. They picked up speed and neatly glided down the slope. Mike directed them toward the outcropping he'd spotted. Etienne stopped the buggy nearby and all three of them got out to take a closer look.

Mike crouched gingerly, his suit making him appear stiff as an old man. He gently brushed the dust off the dark gray rocks with a gloved hand, careful not to snag his suit or damage the rocks.

"Looks like mostly basalts. Pretty typical for this area." Etienne commented.

"Yes, but look!" Mike bounced a few steps over. He bent over and picked up a rock that to Bee's eyes looked exactly the same, though perhaps lighter in color. "Breccia."

"Yep. Looks like. KREEP can be in either basalt or breccia. Why don't we take a bunch of samples back? Maybe we can try to date them and figure out if these samples are unusual for this region. Hey, Iowa, can you grab the sample-taking equipment from the buggy?"

"Sure." Rolling her eyes a bit at the use of her nickname, Bee hopped her way over to the buggy and pulled a grappling stick and some sample bags from the compartment that Etienne had indicated. As light as the items were, they set her slightly off balance and she found herself banging backwards into the buggy, ending up sitting down on the lunar surface.

"You okay, Iowa?" Etienne called out.

"Yeah, I'm fine. That might have actually hurt on Earth." In the Moon's one sixth gravity though, the fall had been almost gentle. She pulled herself up and grabbed the equipment again and hopped back over to where Mike and Etienne were standing.

"Turn around and let me check out your suit." Etienne said.

"I'm really fine," she said, her pride slightly wounded even though no one had laughed at her. She knew falls weren't uncommon when you weren't totally used to the local gravity or wearing a bulky suit. But Bee dutifully let him examine her suit for tears. He tapped on her oxygen tank. "Can you check your display again?"

Bee tapped a few buttons. "It's fine. At sixty-five percent."

Etienne frowned at that. "Hmm. That's a little low, but still within parameters. Keep an eye on it for me and tell me what it says in five minutes."

"Okay."

Assured that she was all right, Etienne shifted his attention back to Mike, who was cramming as many rocks as he could into the sample bags.

"Whoa, I think we have enough, kid!"

Etienne grabbed the fullest bag from Mike. When Mike bent to lift the others, Bee caught Etienne shaking his head slightly in amusement. She couldn't help but smile too, as she remembered the giant duffle of rocks with which Mike had come to Lunar Camp.

Mike hopped happily back to the rover, the other two bags of rocks clutched in his arms. He moved as easily as you might expect from someone who had been born on the Moon.

After the rocks were loaded, Bee, Etienne and Mike strapped themselves back into the buggy.

"Oxygen level report, Iowa?"

"Fifty-five percent."

"Did you say fifty-five percent?" he asked, his voice a little sharper than before. "Are you sure?" Etienne leaned over so he could see her sensor results for himself.

"Is it okay?" Bee asked, realizing that Etienne seemed to be worried about her oxygen levels.

"It's fine." Etienne reassuringly smiled at her. "Please keep an eye on it and let me know if it goes down again. We can swap it out with one of the spares. That's why we have them."

Etienne headed the rover back up the rille. It slipped and slid a little in the lunar dust as it made its way up the side, but they were soon back on the track to Lunar Camp. Bee couldn't help but notice that Etienne was pushing the buggy faster than he had on the way out.

She looked down. Her oxygen was down by another couple of percent. Probably nothing to worry about. Fifty percent of a can of oxygen should last her six hours. That was more than enough, even if it went down faster than it should. She closed the sensor results and resolved not to look at it for a little while.

Watching the scenery go by, Bee also couldn't help but notice that they were totally alone. All the other campers and counselors were far ahead of them. She shivered slightly, this time not out of excitement, but at the realization of how isolated they were here. They were a few hours from Lunar Camp by buggy. A faster transport might be able to come and meet them, but it would take a while to reach them. Still, Etienne said it would be fine, so she was sure it would be fine. Bee sneaked a look down at her oxygen sensor and then gasped. Two percent. *How could it be so low already?*

"Etienne?"

"Iowa?"

"It's down to two percent."

Immediately, he pulled the vehicle over and hopped out.

"Don't worry, Iowa, we're going to fix this." Grabbing a bottle of oxygen from the storage compartment, he instructed her to unbuckle her safety harness and turn around so he could access the back of her suit. She could feel him pushing buttons and imagined what he was doing. First, he'd have to make sure the oxygen reservoir was filled, and then he'd have to remove the old can. *Click.* That was the new can going in.

Etienne hopped back in and she refastened her seatbelt.

"That bottle of O2 was probably just faulty. But just keep an eye on it and keep reporting the numbers to me if they drop, okay?"

Etienne clicked his radio connection on. "Lunar Camp, this is Etienne Cooper on Rover 5. We have a potential emergency."

Bee watched Etienne's face closely as he calmly explained the situation. She didn't know how he could sound so cool and collected. Did things like this go wrong on the Moon often, so he was just used to it? She wasn't sure she could ever get used to this. If she explored other planets someday, they would have to be ones with air.

"We copy. An emergency vehicle is being dispatched now,"

came the immediate reply from Lunar Camp. "We will supply an updated ETA when we get closer to your location. Just keep your vehicle on the track back to Camp."

"Roger." Etienne clicked the radio off and looked over at Bee. "It's probably unnecessary, but better safe than sorry, okay?"

"Okay." Bee knew he was trying to be reassuring, but she still felt miserable. Her excitement at being out on the lunar surface was definitely gone. All she wanted now was to be on Earth and to feel the rich, wet soil between her toes. Everything here was dust. There was nothing alive out here. Not like at home. Bee forced herself to stop imagining her farm. Tears were starting to well up in her eyes and she had no way to reach them to wipe them away.

The lunar scenery was whizzing by. Bee could tell Etienne was going as fast as he could, which worried her. She had a new can of oxygen, but clearly he was still concerned if there was an emergency vehicle meeting them and he was still pushing the buggy so fast.

Bee sneaked a look down at her oxygen sensor. "It's at eighty percent."

Etienne cursed and then winced. "Sorry."

He pulled the buggy over again and this time had Bee get out so he could inspect her suit. Bee could sense he didn't want to waste time, but he did a quick and thorough inspection anyway.

"I don't see any obvious leaks. It might be a problem in the mechanics of the suit. It's draining the oxygen too fast or something. I've never seen this happen before." He sighed and moved his hand up as if to run it through his hair and then dropped it again when he realized the helmet was in his way. "All right, everyone back in."

As soon as they were all secured, Etienne gripped the steering wheel and floored it. "Keep reporting the numbers to me, Iowa," he said grimly. "Just stay calm and breathe as slowly and normally as you can."

•••

Twice more they stopped so Etienne could change Bee's oxygen canisters, though each time they waited until nearly every possible breath was used up. After the final spare started reading frighteningly low, Etienne radioed Lunar Camp for the position of the emergency vehicle.

"We have you on the GPS; we are approximately twenty minutes from you if we both drive at maximum speed," a female voice replied.

"Roger. Copy. We are currently driving at max speed." Etienne clicked off the intercom and glanced at Mike and Bee. "Okay, kids, here's what we're going to do. And we need to do it quickly. I'm going to stop again. Mike, I need you to hop out too this time. You know how to change oxygen canisters on a suit?"

"Of course. I've lived here my whole life."

"Great. When we stop, I want you to make sure that both my and Iowa's O2 reservoirs are filled and then I want you to swap our cans."

"But—" Bee started to protest.

"It's fine, Iowa. Let me worry about it, okay?"

"Okay." Bee didn't know what else to do but agree.

"Report?"

"Three percent." It was hard for Bee to keep the fear out of her voice. She was scared for herself and she was scared for Etienne. And she felt guilty. He was putting her life before his. She wasn't sure she deserved it, with how she'd acted toward him all summer. All because of a stupid nickname that seemed very unimportant right now.

"Okay, let's do this." Etienne said, forced cheer in his voice. "Oh, and Mike? I assume you already know how to drive one of these things?"

"Yep." Mike eyes were huge as he answered.

"Then I'm going to have you take over the wheel so I can focus on conserving oxygen."

"No problem."

"One more thing, Mike."

"Yeah?"

"We need to go as fast as we can. Which means we need to lighten up the buggy."

"The rocks?"

"Yeah. We'll come back for them, I promise."

"That's okay. It's more important that..." he paused, clearly not wanting to finish his thought. Bee knew if Mike was willing to chuck his precious rocks without a protest that the situation really was serious. That plus the fact that the lunar native was scared was perhaps more unnerving than anything else.

"It's all right, Mike. We're all going to be fine." Etienne reassured him. "I'm going to pull over now. Let's make this quick."

Etienne pulled over and everyone jumped out. Mike threw the bags of rocks and the other field equipment out and then bounced as fast as he could to where Etienne and Bee were standing. In just a few minutes, he had their oxygen cans swapped. The three of them got back in the vehicle, this time with Mike in the driver's seat. After a slight adjustment to compensate for his lack of height, they were off again.

"Mike, I want you to keep in radio contact with the rescue vehicle. Iowa and I are going to stop talking to save as much oxygen as we can and keep our breathing nice and shallow." He reached forward and gave Bee's shoulder what seemed meant as a reassuring tap. "And when we get back, Iowa, I'll finish what I was going to tell you before. About how the Moon can help you to learn more about plants. That's a promise."

Bee turned as far as she could in her suit to look at him, and though he was putting up a good front, she could tell there was worry in his eyes. "Okay."

"Just okay? Not going to argue about how pointless the Moon is? Or to tell me to just call you Bee?"

Bee thought his smile seemed a little weak. "You can call me whatever you want if we all make it through this."

"It's a deal." Etienne gave Bee another comforting poke in the shoulder and then he sat back in his seat, leaving her alone with her thoughts.

Bee had Etienne's can of oxygen, which had been nearly seventy percent full when they'd hooked her up to it. But she had no idea how fast her suit would go through it. Etienne's suit, on the other hand was functional, but that bottle had only been at three percent of its capacity before they'd stopped to swap. It might have dropped to two percent in the time it had taken to switch cans.

Bee noticed that Etienne hadn't told either of them exactly how much oxygen was left. He'd just grimaced slightly at whatever the number had been. Bee tried to do the math in her head. Two percent of a can of O2 would mean Etienne only had fifteen minutes left, and help was at least that much time away. This was going to be close, possibly for both of them.

Bee closed her eyes and wished with all her heart that the lunar landscape wouldn't be the last thing she ever saw. She opened them again and looked over at Mike, who had been kind to her since the day they'd first met. Then she twisted around again to risk a look at Etienne, who she was now starting to feel that she'd misjudged. He was brave and friendly, if to a fault, and right now his eyes were closed. Before she turned around again, she closed her own eyes tightly. Now if the worst happened, she could say the very last thing she'd seen were her friends.

●●●

Bee's eyes popped open when Mike's excited voice chimed in her ear. "The emergency transport! There it is!"

The transport, a white metallic boxy vehicle, practically glowed against the lunar terrain. It was a beautiful sight. Even more beautiful were Bee's oxygen numbers when she looked down at her sensor. Two percent. It was a closer margin than she would have liked, but help was here and she knew she would make it as long as they didn't waste time.

Mike pulled up next to the larger vehicle, which was extending its airlock. Bee jumped out to check on Etienne as quickly as she could, not wanting to waste any time.

"Etienne!" Bee shook his arm. "Come on! Are you…?"

Before she finished her sentence Bee realized that Etienne was not okay. He hadn't reacted at all to her touch. She couldn't tell if he was unconscious or worse. He couldn't die now, not when help was here. She wouldn't allow it. Bee grabbed Etienne's arm and draped it around her shoulders.

On Earth, she'd never have been able to lift him, with or without a space suit on, but here he was only one sixth of his weight. He wasn't much heavier than one of the farm dogs back home, so even though he was taller and larger than she was, she knew moving him was within her power. As long as overexerting herself didn't make her own oxygen run out. But that wasn't important right now; whatever happened, they could revive her. But Etienne…

With a mighty tug, Bee pulled Etienne out of the buggy.

"Here, let me help." Mike grabbed Etienne's other arm and together they dragged him as quickly as they could toward the airlock. A space-suited form exited and bounced toward them.

"We've got him," Bee said stubbornly as the suit tried to intervene. "We don't have time, just get out of the way."

"Okay, kids," the adult said. "The airlock only fits three. You all go first. I'll be right behind you. The others inside will help as soon as the airlock equalizes."

Bee and Mike rushed Etienne through the door. As soon as it closed behind them, Bee searched frantically for Etienne's helmet fastenings. "Mike, help me!"

"We can't take his helmet off until there's air."

"He's not breathing anyway, just help me."

"The light on the wall will turn yellow, then green. We can't take the helmets off until it's green," Mike protested.

"Start undoing the fastenings when it's yellow," she commanded.

He nodded in response. Bee looked impatiently between the light and Etienne. And then the yellow light flashed.

As Mike worked on Etienne's helmet, Bee rapidly worked on her own. Black spots threatened the corners of her vision. Her own oxygen was almost out, she realized. She ripped her helmet off, not paying attention to what color the light was, and then grabbed Etienne's helmet and yanked it off too.

She lost little time breathing whatever air she had left into Etienne's mouth.

Gasping, she doggedly started chest compressions. *They were the most important thing, weren't they?* She tried to remember the resuscitation training that had been impressed on her many times during her childhood, but her brain was rapidly growing fuzzy. She felt Mike nudge her aside and take over. Suddenly very dizzy, she felt herself falling into blackness.

●●●

Bee slowly opened her eyes and then squinted at the bright overhead light reflecting off the white walls. A pale blue privacy curtain blocked her view of the rest of the large room she was in, but she realized that she recognized the décor from the time she'd sliced her finger on a rough rock and had to come to the infirmary to get the cut cleaned. Bee sat up slowly and tried to clear her head.

"Hey, you're awake!" It was Mike. He got up from the chair he'd been sitting on at her bedside. "How do you feel?"

Bee frowned for a moment. "Not sure. Okay, I think?" Then it all came rushing back. "Mike, Etienne? Is he…?"

"He's okay."

Bee breathed out in relief and then had to lie back down for a minute until her head stopped spinning. "What happened? After…?"

"After you passed out? I kept resuscitating him until the airlock opened and the medtechs were able to take over. They were able to revive him and there doesn't seem to be any permanent effects." Mike was sober. "He was really lucky. A few more minutes and there could have been brain damage. You saved him."

"We saved him. And you both saved me. Team effort." Bee looked at Mike and smiled.

He shook his head, as if to deny his part but didn't contradict her. "I guess we make a pretty good team then."

"Yup. You, me, and Etienne."

"Who knew?" Mike grinned.

"Oh come on, you did! You've been trying to get me to like Etienne for weeks."

"So you're saying I was right all along? And I might be right about other things? Like about how awesome geology is?"

Bee crossed her arms. "Don't push your luck, Moon-boy." She broke into a smile..

"Etienne's awake if you want to see him," Mike said, and Bee knew he was happy with her acceptance – if slightly begrudged – of his favorite counselor.

"Definitely," she said, uncrossing her arms. "Let's go."

•••

"Hey Iowa, how are you feeling?" Etienne sat up when he saw Mike and Bee peek past the curtains around his infirmary bed.

Bee opened her mouth automatically to object and then closed it. Maybe it really wasn't such a bad nickname. Iowa was a place that she loved, now more than ever. It was home and it was a part of her. And the nickname had been gifted by someone she now admired, both for his bravery, and for his willingness to sacrifice himself for someone who hadn't even been especially nice to him.

Bee gave Etienne a big grin. "I'm doing great. How about you?" She wrapped her bathrobe snugly around her and perched on the edge of the bed.

"I'm doing great, too, thanks to you." Etienne looked pale and tired, which was to be expected after what he'd been through. Still it was disconcerting to Bee to see him lying in bed. It made him look slightly diminished; normally he was so energetic she wasn't sure he even bothered to sleep at night.

"It was nothing," Bee said automatically. She'd just done what needed to be done, hadn't she? It slowly dawned on Bee that it was Etienne's lead that she had been following. When it had been his life on the line, panicking hadn't even occurred to her. She'd just acted. Just as he had.

Bee could see Etienne watching her and she wondered if her newfound admiration for him was somehow written on her face. Etienne's own expression was serious, something that gave Bee pause, because of how seldom she had seen him look that way.

"It wasn't nothing." Etienne gently shook his head. "You saved my life. I need to thank you for what you did."

"You saved my life too, so I guess we're even. Thank you." Bee said, crossing her arms across her chest, though it was with a smile to show that she meant what she said. She was thankful, though it was hard to say just how much out loud.

"You're a stubborn one," Etienne said, relaxing his own expression into a matching smile.

"You're just figuring that out?"

He gave her a small wink. "I hear you also don't really like rocks. Or the Moon."

She grinned . "Not really. This place has no atmosphere," Bee said coolly. She gave Etienne a quick glance to see if he would get the joke. She was rewarded with his barking laughter. His laugh was somewhat less exuberant than normal, but it was a relief to hear Etienne starting to sound more like himself.

"Now, I think I made a promise to you, didn't I? Before…" Etienne waved his hand, as if ushering that whole episode into the past. "What if I told you that the Moon is a great place for you to learn about soil composition?" As if sensing that he'd caught Bee's attention, he continued eagerly, "Maybe we could set up some experiments for you on plant growth in lunar soil. You'll have to do some research on what's already been done, but maybe you'll find a new angle. And if not, it'll still be good for you to learn more about experimental set-ups. We might even be able to get you some Earth soil to play with too, and lots of seeds of course…"

Bee sat silently, slightly stunned by what Etienne was saying. *How had she not thought of this before now? Could she really grow plants here on the Moon?*

"That sound good, Iowa?" Etienne waved his hand in front of

her face. "Hello?"

Bee absentmindedly swatted his hand away. Her mind was racing and the possibilities suddenly seemed endless. "You would help me? I mean, you wouldn't mind?"

"Of course I'll help. You and Mike can help me clear out a corner of the lab, and maybe we can scrounge up some of those plant lights from somewhere…"

Bee listened wide-eyed as Etienne continued to list off lab equipment she might need. Mike, who had been quietly standing in the background jumped in with some suggestions of his own.

Bee watched them both for a few minutes and then, unable to contain her growing excitement, finally broke into the conversation. "Wait a sec! I need to get my PAL. I need to record these ideas!"

* * *

Bee rummaged through her things, finally locating her PAL in the pocket of her jumpsuit, which had been slung over the chair by her infirmary bed. She held it up triumphantly at Mike, who had followed her back to her room. "Found it! Now I can take notes."

"So what do you think now, Bee? Think you might consider coming back to Lunar Camp next year?" Bee looked up from where she was kneeling and couldn't help breaking into a smile at her friend's expectant expression.

"You know, I just might." She added shyly, "And you can call me Iowa if you want."

"I just might." Mike gave her a grin. Bee followed him back to Etienne's room, PAL in hand. They had a lunar garden to plan.

# Clockwork Dancer
## Brad Hafford

*When Brad Hafford was a boy he dreamed of being an explorer. Growing up on a farm it seemed impossible (and he was unsure if explorers even existed anymore), but he read constantly and continued to dream. He joined the Air Force and served overseas, then went to college to further expand his horizons. Exploring all his options, he studied many fields and earned a Ph.D. in archaeology. Now, he has lived and worked on four continents and has visited more than fifty countries. He has excavated at the great pyramids and at some of the earliest cities in the world. And he's still exploring. He writes fiction and nonfiction and teaches archaeology and writing. He particularly enjoys writing for a younger audience — letting them know that explorers do exist and that his own adventures started from humble beginnings and became realized through travel and education. The message: See the world and never stop learning!*

### *North London, 1847*

A wind-up toy ballerina danced on a brass plinth. Rain tapped at the leaded glass window behind it. The dull light of a British autumn made the figure hazy, or perhaps it was the gloss of tears clinging to the eyelashes of the girl who watched it, brimming at her lower lids as she stared dreamily at the mechanical undulations.

Oh, if only she could dance.

But Eleanor had been cursed with a debilitating disease when she was only three years old. The doctors called it Sudden Infant Paralysis, but they didn't really know what it was. They told her that one day they'd beat it, that she'd walk again.

And dance.

One day.

When would that day come? All she could do was wait. She sketched dancers and wished she were like them. She wound up her mechanical doll and watched it do what she could not. And she submitted again and again to doctors staring down her throat, tapping her knees with rubber mallets and jabbing her with needles filled with so-called cures – none of which ever worked.

"Eleanor?" she heard her mother call from the parlour. Her voice waltzed up the stairs and glided beneath the door. Majestic, beautiful. That was her mother, both in voice and in presence. But she was ashamed of her daughter. Or so it felt. No laughter had rung through the house, not since Eleanor was stricken.

Now Eleanor was forced to stay inside, hidden from the world, observing the passersby from a misty leaded window on a lonely second storey. She couldn't go to school with the normal children. She couldn't play with the normal children. But there were many books in the old house, and she read them all. She'd even taught herself to write. Unfortunately, reading only told her more about what was normal. What she was not.

Eleanor sobbed. She was a burden to her family. To society.

Her mother kept up appearances well, maintaining the large north London home on a small budget while doing her best to care for her crippled child, but Eleanor knew that the endless stream of doctors cost far more money than her parents could earn. Her father was constantly gone, working two or three jobs, but it was never enough.

A soft knock at the door heralded her mother's arrival. The call, as always, had preceded her by several minutes, giving Eleanor time to compose herself. This time, though, it wasn't enough. She was still sobbing softly into her scarf when the door opened.

"Eleanor?" Her mother said and then waited through a long pause. "This is Dr. Phipps, he's here to…" her voice trailed off. "Well, I'll leave you to it, Doctor."

Eleanor looked up to see a rotund little man in a battered top hat carrying a cane in one hand and a black bag in the other. It was a bag the likes of which she'd seen many times. Too many times. Doubtless it carried the same concoctions every doctor brought, draughts and potions, jabs and poultices. They had different names and different smells, from sickly sweet to cough-inducing, but the end result was always the same – nothing.

"Good afternoon young lady!" the doctor said. He waddled closer, like a Christmas pudding with toothpick legs. "Aloysius Berringer Phipps, at your service." He doffed his hat and made a little bow. "Most people call me Phipps."

Eleanor found herself at the edge of a smile. This doctor didn't act like a doctor. Most of them looked down on her with the stale air of superiority.

"Isn't this the nursery?" He said, poking his cane at a pram draped with a sheet. "Strange place for a girl your age."

"Father says I have to stay out of sight."

"Doesn't seem right to me." Phipps made a tut-tut sound and shook his head. "You should be in your own room. When you aren't playing outside, that is."

"Oh, I can't go outside. That would never do."

"Tosh. There's benefit in good air and exercise."

Eleanor couldn't tell if the doctor was winding her up. His tone was serious, but his meaning couldn't be. "In case you didn't know," she said, "I can't walk. I can't even stand."

"Oh, I know that. But it doesn't mean you can't exercise. Or have fun."

"Of course it does. What kind of doctor are you?"

"The best kind!"

Eleanor couldn't help but smile at his enthusiasm. He was surely mad, but in a funny sort of way. She indicated his black bag. "Are you going to jab me with needles like all the rest?"

"Heaven's no! This is my lunch bag." He produced a tea cake from within. "Would you like some?"

"You're funny." She hadn't meant to say it. Such things weren't polite. "I mean, you're not like any medical doctor I've ever seen."

Phipps bit into his tea cake. "To tell the truth, my doctorate isn't in medicine, but engineering."

"You mean, like driving trains?"

"More like *building* trains!"

"Then why do you want to see me?"

"I have a feeling your problem isn't entirely medical."

"Of course it is." Didn't he take her condition seriously? Eleanor crossed her arms over her chest and hunched over in her chair. "My legs don't work!"

"True. But your mind isn't helping. And neither are your parents, to be honest."

"You shouldn't insult my family." Eleanor spoke to the floor now, not wishing to look at the doctor. His odd disposition would only make her want to laugh. She would show him how serious her condition really was, and laughing simply wouldn't do.

"Wouldn't dream of it, my dear. But really! Cooping you up in here? Not letting you reach your potential?"

"What potential?"

"Anything. Everything. Whatever you want, you can do it."

Eleanor sat silently for a moment. How she wished what he said were true! But it simply couldn't be. "I want to walk, but my legs don't work. So *that's* impossible."

Dr. Phipps leaned over, supporting himself with his cane as he tried to look directly at Eleanor. She turned her head away and hunched further up against herself.

"Not impossible," Phipps said. An exhaled groan followed by a low crash heralded his arrival on the floor. His hat fell and spun in silly circles at the edge of Eleanor's vision, but she did her best to ignore it and the doctor. After he caught his breath, he continued, "Not easy, either. But the first step to the impossible is to call it something else."

Phipps tried again to catch Eleanor's eye from the floor. He rolled first one way and then the other. Eleanor looked away and fought down the pesky curl at the side of her mouth as it sneaked its way into a smile. Finally, she met his gaze. There was a sparkle in Phipps' left eye that made her wonder if it were some kind of gemstone. His eyebrows made funny squiggles, raising and lowering as if his thoughts were playing tennis inside his skull.

Phipps' eyebrows finally settled into a deep V at the base of many furrows on his forehead. "Your legs may never work," he said at last. "I know it's hard to hear, but you have to face the possibility. Oh, there may be a cure, but it's a long shot. So you can wait, and mope, maybe forever. Or you can find another way to walk."

Eleanor knew that Phipps was being honest with her, but she had a serious illness, and what could *she* do that medicine couldn't? She slapped her legs with both hands. Prickles of pins and needles ran through her narrow thighs. She could feel them, but she couldn't move them. They sat lifeless and useless, not much wider around than her arms. Tears rose. "There's only one way to walk," she said.

"Are you sure?"

"Of course I'm sure." She sniffed and rubbed the corner of her right eye. "Don't be so daft."

Phipps rolled away from the chair, then back again, wobbling on his round belly. It brought the curl back to Eleanor's mouth.

"People stroll, stride, promenade, march and perambulate, don't they?" he said, lying on his back.

"Those are just other words for walking. They all rely on legs."

"For centuries people thought the only way to fly was to be a bird. To have wings that functioned like theirs." Phipps flapped his arms against the floor. "But finally, engineers thought of other words like float or glide and realised that lighter-than-air gasses held in a balloon could bear them aloft. Now people fly regularly, but still they have no wings!"

Phipps rolled back and forth again. "Have you ever tried rolling?"

"That's not very dignified."

"Who cares? It's fun. Not very practical, though." He rolled across the room and then tried to get up. "Makes you dizzy." His head wagged and he sunk back to his knees. "Perhaps brachiation is the answer!"

"What's that?"

"Using your arms to swing about."

"Like monkeys do?"

"Exactly like monkeys do! If we were to hang ropes with rings on the ends from the ceiling, you could swing around." He moved his arms in a ridiculous motion. "It could get you in and out of your chair and to and from your bed."

Eleanor stifled a giggle. Phipps looked very silly. "Really?"

"Yes. You see, you just have to think of new ways of locomotion."

"Locomotive? Like a train? I'd love to go on a train someday. See the world." A spike of excitement consumed Eleanor's thoughts for a brief moment, the warmth of possibility rising in her belly. Then it fell suddenly cold. "But I can't go out."

"Why not?"

"I'm not... normal."

"Pish posh. You're better than normal. So long as you use your brain, you can do anything." Phipps scooted over to Eleanor on his knees. He picked up the sketchbook that sat by her side and asked if he could look inside. Normally Eleanor kept her work secret, but this time she agreed.

Phipps paged through drawing after drawing of ballerinas in various poses, amidst their most beautiful dances. He spent time looking at each one. Most people glanced and said nothing.

"You're an excellent artist," Phipps said at last, "but it looks like you draw only dancers."

"I like dancers."

Phipps cocked his head to one side, then almost to his shoulder. "Why are they all standing?"

Eleanor rolled her eyes to the ceiling. "You have to stand to dance, silly."

"Are you sure?" Phipps stood up. He grabbed the sheet covering the pram and pulled it off in a flourish of fabric and dust. Eleanor coughed at the heavy bouquet of dirt and old furniture varnish but laughed at almost the same time. "What are you doing?"

"Wheels, my dear. Wheels might be the answer!"

"I'm not a machine!" Eleanor exclaimed. "And I'm too old for a pram."

"True. But we can put wheels on your chair. Or..." He turned pages in Eleanor's sketchbook until he reached a blank one. Then he drew hasty rectangles and circles, a few numbers and mathematical symbols, angles and more numbers. "You see, my dear!" He waved the crazy scribblings in the air. "If you can draw it, dream it, visualise it, *then* you can build it!"

There was no doubt about it. He was mad as a hatter. But Eleanor liked him. It was like watching a puppet show come to life. Phipps snatched up his bag and rooted through it, coming up with a spanner and a screwdriver.

"I thought that was your lunch bag," Eleanor said.

"All engineers keep tools in their lunch bags, my dear."

In a trice Phipps had disassembled the pram and converted it into a low-lying cart. Its upholstered surfaces made a central support rising from the frame, and the former hood made a low chair back. Golden fringe ran up and over it, fluttering along the edges.

Phipps knelt down on the altered pram and pushed himself from the wall, using his weight and a sweep of his arms to guide the cart into a half circle. He ended up facing away from Eleanor but twisted his bulbous body around to speak.

"What do you think?"

"Mummy would never approve."

"She doesn't want you to walk?"

"It's not walking."

"It's like walking. It means you can move around. Even move to music."

"You mean dance?"

Phipps bent down and pushed himself from the floor, then swayed again to make the cart perform another half circle. "I do."

Eleanor clapped and clapped as if in the Theatre Royal itself.

"I want to try!" she said.

Phipps picked her up and placed her in the low cart, carefully tucking her legs underneath. The raised central portion supported her, taking weight off of her legs, and the low chair back provided stability. Phipps made a few adjustments to ensure the cart fit its intended driver.

Eleanor was too excited to pay much attention. She pushed herself along and tried the swaying motion Phipps had demonstrated. It didn't work as well for her. She didn't have the weight to put behind it. "It's not easy. Will you push me?"

"*Dance* with you? But of course!" Phipps pushed and pulled the cart around the room, spinning and humming a jolly tune all the while.

"We might be able to put gears in," he mused.

"I'm not sure I like being so low to the ground. Could we make something higher, like a dress with wheels?"

"Now you're thinking!"

"ELEANOR!"

Eleanor's mother stood in the doorway, her face a tightened ball of rage. "What *are* you doing? And *you!*" she pointed at Dr. Phipps, her long hand shaking. "You're supposed to be a doctor. A dignified man!"

"Allow me to explain, dear lady –"

"Get out!"

Phipps picked up his hat and bag, doffed the hat to the lady and disappeared down the stairs.

•••

### 1848

The next few months were particularly difficult for Eleanor. She tried to convince her parents to allow Dr. Phipps to come back, but her mother wouldn't hear of it, nor would she allow her to keep the pram-cart.

Eventually Eleanor managed to make her father understand the reason for hanging rings from the ceiling, and he installed a few ropes across the nursery, plus padding on the floor in case she fell. She practiced the brachiation technique over and over. It was tough. Getting momentum when she couldn't control her legs made swinging nearly impossible. But impossible became an increasingly improbable word in her vocabulary.

At first she could hardly pull herself up from the bed, but she kept trying until she built strength in her arms and shoulders. Then she practiced swinging. She fell time and again and often felt like giving up. Still she pushed on. Her mother said that everything about it was unladylike, but with practice, Eleanor's movements grew almost graceful. Long hours over long months led to smooth motions and pirouettes that might make a dancer proud. She even began choreographing moves to music in her head. For the first time, she was able to imagine herself dancing, rather than someone else. Just as Phipps had said, if she could visualise it, she could do it.

Nonetheless, even a short routine tired her. People just weren't meant to dance with their arms for very long. But now that she had gotten a taste of what could be accomplished, her dreams soared. Not only could she imagine dancing, she could even see herself exploring the countryside or crossing the sea. Instead of telling herself it couldn't be done, now she asked how it might be done.

Her belief in the impossible increased as she read about remarkable feats of engineering. Elaborate train networks were springing up across Britain and Europe, some with speeds up to 20 miles an hour! She had never before thought about how these feats were accomplished. Now she saw that it was thought, practice and individual steps that led to great things.

She begged her father to bring home books about engineering. When he asked why she wanted to read such things, she let slip a glimpse of her dreams. Then she looked away, ashamed. Her father sat silently for a moment, for an eternity.

Finally he said "That's —"

"I know," Eleanor interrupted, "unladylike. And not possible. I shouldn't —"

"No. It's… wonderful. Amazing. I dream of those things, too!"

"Really?"

"Yes, I think of speeding in a steam train or soaring in a balloon. Exploring the depths of the ocean, or even the stars themselves."

"Really, really?"

They laughed together for the first time in Eleanor's memory.

She convinced her father to work with her on the pram-cart, to improve it and to allow her to move through the house onboard. Her mother said it was an improper vehicle for a young lady, but even she smiled when Eleanor spun into a turn like a twirling penny and ended in a dancer's flourish.

With each success, Eleanor's dreams soared greater still. She built a new dancing cart with four wheels, each driven by a clockwork engine. And she began to design an even better framework and propulsion system – the wheeled metal dress she had suggested to Phipps. Her sketches showed it would work, but how to build it without good tools and additional hands? Her parents told her they would try to get what she needed, but something was wrong. They wouldn't talk about it, and even her father was quiet when she asked about his dreams. "They'll probably take those, too," was all he said.

The next day, the bill collectors came. Because there was no money for them, they took the only thing left. They took the house.

•••

### Bethnal Green, 1849

When she'd been withering away in the nursery Eleanor had never thought things could get worse. But they had. Not only did the creditors take her house, they took her father, too. He was sentenced to Newgate Gaol until such time as his debts were paid. It seemed stupid to Eleanor. How could he pay debts if he was locked away?

Once again she blamed herself. Her energetic desire to build, dance and explore had meant an ever greater drain on the family finances. Her mother insisted on continuing the stream of doctors, but she could no longer pay for them. Now she visited relatives for help, but money was tight everywhere. She never explained, but Eleanor overheard conversations and began to put the puzzle together. When Eleanor's grandparents had died, the inheritance had been divided among a large family and had quickly disappeared.

Eleanor and her mother ended up in a block of run-down flats off Bethnal Green with many other families in trouble. Most were women with children whose fathers had been sent to Newgate, just like Eleanor's. The women typically eked out livings as seamstresses, barmaids, or peddlers, and most of their earnings went to pay interest on old debts. The children, too, worked wherever they could. Many turned to begging or stealing, all because of a system that made poverty a crime.

Eleanor's mother couldn't keep her shuttered away anymore, but she told her not to talk to the people of Bethnal Green. Though Eleanor respected her mother, she didn't understand. How were they different? So, while her mother was out appealing to ever more distant relatives for money, Eleanor began talking. For the first time she was able to connect with others, with children her own age. Some of them made fun of her, but most of them were friendly and curious. They found her wheeled carts fascinating.

Her mother would have been mortified, but the strain of living in poverty proved so difficult that she simply stopped functioning. After her final contact, a third cousin twice removed, was unable to provide more than two shillings, she gave in. Once so strong and proper, she fell into a heap of utter despair, incapable of doing anything but sobbing.

Eleanor had known such sadness. She tried her best to lead her mother out of the spiral of despair, but it didn't help. The only thing that put a semblance of a smile on her face was when Eleanor danced. She practiced every night, using her upper body to sway and shift the energy of the small, tightly wound engines. Her mother watched through hazy eyes just as Eleanor had once watched her toy ballerina.

Phipps would know what to do. But where was he? Eleanor wrote letters addressed to Aloysius Berringer Phipps, Dr. (the best kind) hoping that the Royal Mail could find him. She also sent word through a network of street urchins she had come to know. Her withered legs were particularly suitable to the profession of begging, and though she found it unseemly, she turned to it to support her mother and attempt to rescue her father.

She explored the backstreets of London with the urchins, taking on their attire of goggles and kerchiefs to protect eyes and nose from the sooty air. Cobblestones would have ruined her clockwork dancing cart, so she took only her hand cart.

It wasn't the kind of exploration she'd dreamed of, but being out and about, even on the grease-smoke streets of London, was invigorating. Fog, smoke, and steam rolled equally down the evening streets, subsuming buildings in a haze that made them into giant ships on a murky lake. Big Ben tolled in the distance, and the clip-clop of horseshoes rang down the lanes alongside the clank of mechanical wheels. At times, the acrid tang of horse sweat and charcoal would suddenly be covered by a waft of fresh bread, or a heady breath of mince pie that made her mouth water.

Dancing still filled her dreams, and she practiced every night. Her four-engine cart was far from perfect, though, and she continued to draw plans for a better frame – a steel bustle that would form a rigid support for a skirt. Small steps to a greater goal.

One night, Eleanor spun merrily on her wheels only to find the self-professed leader of the urchins, a wiry boy of about thirteen, watching her. His street goggles were pushed up on his forehead, and he must have stood there for some time. Surprised, Eleanor tried to run.

"Wait!"

Eleanor stumbled, having forgotten the shift in weight needed to push her wheels in the proper direction. She ended up on her side, four wheels spinning out their tensed power in the air.

"I didn't mean to frighten you," the boy murmured.

"Leave me alone, Sanjeev."

"But your dance, it was so –"

"Silly?" Eleanor sniffed. "A crippled girl can't dance?"

"You dance better than anyone I've ever seen." He bent to help her up. "It was... beautiful." The way he stumbled on the final word showed he'd rarely used it, or at least had never meant it until now. Eleanor decided it was sweet, something she'd never noticed in Sanjeev.

"Thank you," she said and allowed herself to be righted on her wheels. She could have managed on her own, but it was nice to accept help from time to time.

"Why don't you dance outside where we can join you?"

"I didn't think anyone would understand."

"Of course we would! Plus, me and some of the boys fancy ourselves musicians. Maybe we could help?"

"I'd like that."

A shy grin pushed Sanjeev's cheeks almost past his ears. Then he shook from his daydream. "Oh, I almost forgot. That Phipps bloke you've been looking for?" "You found him?"

"More like you did." Sanjeev waved a stained envelope in the air. "Barlowe and me went round the post. He sat on my shoulders and we put an old greatcoat over us, pretended to be a respectable gent. Asked for any letters for you, and they gave us this. All the way from Paris. Lucky Barlowe can read a little. Made out the word Phipps and figured it was worth the extra penny in back postage."

"You're a genius!"

Sanjeev's dusky complexion reddened.

Eleanor took the envelope in hand. It looked as though it had been dragged across the English Channel and then trodden upon by a train of donkeys. It smelled of swamp gas, or what Eleanor imagined swamp gas would smell like.

She opened the letter and read:

Dearest Eleanor,
So sorry to hear of your troubles. I wish I could help, but the answer lies within you. Use your brain and you will rise above all

difficulties.

To tell the truth, I have troubles too. I have had to flee to France, but I am using my brain! I believe I have a discovery that can be displayed at the Crystal Palace next year. I hope to see you there.

Your humble servant,
Phipps

"The Crystal Palace? Isn't that the great exhibition house they're building to display wonders from around the world?"
"I guess so. I don't pay much attention to that stuff. But there should be lots of folks there worth a few bob."

"I have an idea. Will you help me?"

Sanjeev fidgeted with the tattered waistcoat he wore. "Anything for you," he said, reddening once more.

•••

### *1850*

In the course of a few months Eleanor turned a ragtag bunch of urchins into imaginative designers, energetic builders and skilled dancers. Together they created their own short, wheeled boards and more elaborate dancing carriages. They practiced using them for jumps, twirls and choreographed routines of all sorts. Boys and girls leapt to and fro in ever more elaborate patterns. Then they set their stunts to music.

With so much work and practice, they had little time for begging. Eleanor's plan was to entertain crowds instead of taking from them, give them wonder in return for support for their creative efforts. Her ultimate goal was to gain wider exposure for their handicraft and skill at the Crystal Palace. But the plan divided the Bethnal Green urchins. Many couldn't see the long term benefits for the intensity of their short term needs.

In an effort to prove the potential of her plan, Eleanor took the troupe to the streets earlier than she would have liked. She knew extensive practice was essential, but there wasn't much time. So she performed her well-rehearsed dance before and after the troupe's street rehearsal, and crowds slowly grew. The troupe began to find increasing coppers – even a few silvers – in the hat they kept out for donations.

As the urchins gained faith, they became more dedicated and began to help Eleanor meet her dream of a wheeled dress. Slowly the framework came to life. It was a gracefully curving cradle of eight sturdy metal strands, each ending in a fine brass wheel with its own clockwork engine. At the top of the cradle dangled a leather seat into which Eleanor's legs would slip as if in a voluminous hoop skirt. At the same level, the level of her waist, there sat two small hand cranks to wind the eight engines. It was a masterfully engineered work, and all due to the reading, drawing and planning Eleanor had put in over the years.

Finally she was ready to decorate the frame with the help of the seamstress mothers. All of the mothers had become increasingly involved with their children's work, pride in their dancing skills growing with every performance. Eleanor's own mother came outside from time to time to watch them. She, too, grew in strength and acceptance every day. Many of the families had helped support her in her direst need, and she could no longer see them as lesser people. Bonding with them helped her to deal with emotional strife.

Now Eleanor showed that working together could also help with financial strife. Not all of them wanted to dance, but they had other skills that could help support the group effort. The seamstresses made costumes; the barmaids advertised performances; the peddlers traded for materials. The musically inclined formed a new kind of music, one that enhanced the wheeled street dance. Meanwhile, Eleanor taught techniques of building and design.

At long last, the team gathered to help Eleanor strap herself into her dancing framework. The mothers helped her don the outer covering, a dress made from an exquisite powder-blue silk gown, accented with elaborate lace and shining ribbons, a lucky find from a sympathetic ragpicker.

The skirt draped fully over the framework like that of a royal French lady from the last century. But Eleanor didn't want to be so formal, nor to hide her true nature. She no longer wished to be anything other than herself, and the cloth might bind in the clockwork wheels if the dress dragged the floor, so she had the seamstresses bring the hem up. The effect was that she and her beautiful dress appeared to float over the ground.

They had a month to practice before the Crystal Palace opened, but the new dress worked so well that Eleanor had little trouble making a wondrous new routine. The opening of the Exhibition presented an obstacle, however. A group of street dancers – no matter how polished they now appeared – were unlikely to be given admittance to something so regal. Eleanor asked Sanjeev and Barlowe to sneak in and find Phipps. She described the funny little man as she remembered him, and not an hour later they returned.

Phipps wasn't quite as he had been. He still had the charming mannerisms, but life had carved many more wrinkles into his face and had taken away much of his girth so that he no longer had the plum pudding wobble about him.

"My dear!" Phipps exclaimed, "How you've grown!" Eleanor extended her arms from her perch in the clockwork dress, and he took her hands heartily.

"And you," she replied. "You've grown a drooping stance and gaunt look that don't suit you." Eleanor had learned to be honest with friends.

Phipps straightened and doffed his hat. Much worn, it was the same hat Eleanor remembered. "I fear my situation has not allowed me much joy," he said, "until now, that is! You and your dress are incredible! You've built this by yourself?"

"Never! You taught me to have faith in myself, but I've learned to have faith in others, too."

"Well said, young lady. Perhaps I have not given others enough credit, nor allowed them to help when I needed it."

"I would ask your help now, Phipps, if possible."

"Anything in my power."

"Can you help us to gain entrance to the Crystal Palace, to dance?"

"I will do my very best, my dear!"

•••

***Hyde Park, 1851***

Two months went by as Phipps tried to gain access for the urchins. Meanwhile, he visited Bethnal Green often to laugh and sing with them. One night, he explained his situation to Eleanor and her mother. He had fled Britain after a duel had gone badly. He refused to fight, and his honour had been lost. Once again, Eleanor found it difficult to understand. Refusing to harm others seemed quite honourable to her.

He had gained experience building French airships near Paris and then designed a new form of container that could revolutionise the capturing and controlling of lighter-than-air gasses. His display at the Crystal Palace consisted of versions of the containers that he hoped would renew his honour.

Finally Phipps managed to arrange a short time on the central stage for Eleanor's troupe. That day, he led them to the Great Exhibition. In the distance, the Crystal Palace shimmered, a mass of sparkling glass and metal, like a constellation come to earth. Its imposing grandeur, still hundreds of yards away and fronted by throngs of people, nonetheless dominated Eleanor's view.

Sanjeev showed his nervousness by taking her hand, something he had been too shy to do in the past. Eleanor squeezed tightly for reassurance, hers as well as his. They rolled along Hyde Park, the milling people little noticing them. There were so many wonders that one more group of people, even on wheeled boards, attracted but a few gawks and hushed whispers. Thousands would see them dance, but it would be difficult to compete for attention among so many incredible things.

Inside the aptly named Crystal Palace, exotic foods competed with machine oil for olfactory attention, and tall Prussian hats vied with feathered ladies' bonnets to block the view.

"Is everything ready?" Eleanor asked Phipps.

"Indeed. I even managed to drape a ringed rope for you."

"And our surprise?"

"Never fear!"

At the appointed time, the urchin band produced their musical instruments and struck a chord. Eleanor took center stage twirling like her old toy dancer – simple circles to a lilting tune. Then, without warning, the music jumped to life, and fifteen wheeled dancers burst on stage. They made tight circles and figure-eights around Eleanor's majestic form. As they wheeled past, they flipped in the air, held handstands atop their boards or twisted about, all to the thrumming beat of percussion and strings.

Eleanor swung into her routine, graceful and frenetic in alternating waves. At exact musical counterpoints, she spun the winding cranks at her side to keep her engines moving. As the band reached a crescendo, she used the rope to spin over the stage and back as if coming down the banister in her old house so long ago. The crowd gasped in awe, and from above, Eleanor could see just how large it had grown. The entire palace was watching.

It was time for the finale. Amidst leaping dancers, Eleanor wheeled to the edge of the stage, winding her cranks with fury. Then she launched into the ether. With neither rope nor wings, she flew. As one, the people below took an astonished breath, then leapt into peals of applause.

Eleanor and Phipps had incorporated air containers beneath her steel framework, and as she spun in place at the end of the routine he added the lighter-than-air gasses through a hose beneath the stage. Now she floated above as in her own airship. She flew without wings, she danced without legs. She rose above all difficulties.

When Eleanor reached the ground once more, she found Phipps working his jaw in funny circles, an expression that reminded her of his old self. She couldn't help but giggle.

Unable to speak, he pointed behind her.

Eleanor cranked her clockwork engines and turned with a

subtle shift of weight to find a short woman in a heavy cloak nodding at her. The throngs parted to a respectable distance. A tall man nearby beckoned.

As Eleanor approached, she realised who the woman and her companion must be. Her breath escaped in a rush. "Your Majesty!" she exclaimed. "I fear I cannot curtsey, for my dress is made of steel."

"You need not curtsey, young lady. You have proven yourself of a noble spirit that we honour deeply."

"You are most gracious."

"Tell me, is it true that you have no legs?"

"I have legs, your Majesty, but they do not function."

"Yet you dance, and even fly. You have given us great pleasure this day. Is there something we can do for you?"

Eleanor could hardly believe her good fortune. "If you please, Ma'am," she stammered, "release my father from debtors' prison?"

"Done. Albert, see to it."

"And might I ask that you look into the system that put him there? His only crime is in loving his family and trying to provide for them." She indicated the urchins with a sweep of her arm. "All these dancers would like their fathers returned, too."

"You speak with great wisdom and empathy." Queen Victoria cast a stern glance at a shuffling group of men in stiff, high collars behind her. Then she turned back to address Eleanor. "Would you consider becoming a court dancer, to entertain us in the future?"

"As your Majesty pleases, but only if my troupe is also welcome."

"Of course."

Eleanor flitted over to her friend and mentor, wheels abuzz. "And you would do well to employ Dr. Phipps," she said.

"What kind of doctor is he?" asked the Queen.

"The best kind!" said Eleanor.

Phipps' left eye gleamed, and all the urchins cheered.

# When Hope Dies
## Pam L. Wallace

*Pam Wallace is a little bit of this and a little of that, but the sum of her parts can mostly be described by one word: family. Her stories can be found at* Daily Science Fiction, Every Day Fiction, Abyss & Apex, Schock Totem, *and* Journal of Unlikely Entomology, *among others. She is part of the badger crew at* Shimmer Magazine.

Esperanza dribbled water on each seedling – not that she thought it would do much good. The tiny leaves were yellowing between the veins. Mama would have said they'd never grow right and she should replant.

She'd replanted at least ten times now, and it still wasn't any better.

What was needed was a good rain, falling from the sky in great sheets, the pale, packed earth soaking the moisture up like a sponge, filling the arroyos until they ran clear and full through the valley. Wash away the filth and dust and all trace of disease. A new beginning. Hope for the future.

"The rain will come, Espie," the kid they all called Prophet said, rocking on his heels and smiling at the haze-colored sky.

He was one of the whitest gringos Esperanza had ever seen – skin the pale cream color of Mama's lace tablecloth that she only used on special occasions.

Most of the time, Esperanza wasn't sure there was anything between Prophet's wide-set, flat-lidded eyes and the back of his skull. But every so often, he said something that turned true. That was how he'd earned his name, since he couldn't remember his own when he showed up in town a couple of months after all the adults died.

"Aw, crap, Espie." Nate tossed a stone from one hand to the other, and from the mulish look on his face, Esperanza could tell he wanted to toss the stone right in Prophet's face. "There he goes again. Tell him to shut up already."

"He's not hurting anything, Nate. He's just a kid like us."

"He ain't like us! He's a retar –"

"Don't," Esperanza yelled, shoving Nate away. "Don't you dare call him that! He can't help the way he was born."

Nate glared for a minute, then kicked a clod of dirt and watched it bounce across the empty lot, skip-hopping puffs of dust in its wake. "Well, he can help what he says. Anyone can see it ain't gonna rain."

Parched, crusted dirt stretched far as Esperanza could see. The golden wheat fields that used to surround Huntsville were gone, replaced by fields of bomb craters that reminded her of all their pockmarked faces – and most especially Mama's and Papa's before they died.

"I'm hungry," Prophet said. "Can we go eat, Espie?"

While he seemed to be about the same age as Esperanza, he had a baby-face like a five-year-old, and he didn't act much older than that, either. At least he was easy to please. He'd gobble up a can of green beans with so much enthusiasm, you'd swear he was eating chocolate cake.

Esperanza shoved her water bottle in her backpack. "Yeah, let's head back." Her garden was towards the edge of town, where Mister Johnston used to grow corn. Twelve ears for a dollar, and the sweetest corn ever. Her mouth watered, thinking of an ear slathered with butter and chiles – just like Mama liked it. And then, thinking of Mama, her eyes started watering, too.

She turned to her little brother. "Vamos, Luis. Time to go."

Slumped in his lawn chair with a blank look on his face, Luis stared at the mountains that used to be a dark green blur of trees. Now they were just naked gorges and bare rock. They used to go camping up there in the deep forest, by a stream that held the sweetest brook trout. Esperanza and Luis would splash around in the cold water chasing frogs till their toes were numb.

"Vamos, Luis," she repeated, louder this time.

Luis startled. "Are we going home now, Esperanza? Mama'll be wondering where we're at."

Esperanza bit her lip. Luis knew as well as she did there was nothing to go home to – just an empty house and two rock-covered mounds out back – he just didn't remember he knew.

Esperanza wished she didn't have to remember all that'd happened, either. She'd rather be building forts, playing ball, lazing in the sun by the river like a normal twelve-year-old – not trying to keep a pack of orphaned kids warm and fed. She didn't want to worry any more about what they were going to do once the food in the supermarket was all gone. She didn't want to speculate any more about what might be going on outside of town. And most of all, she didn't want to ever bury another body.

She gave Luis's lawn chair a soft kick. "Mama knows where we are. Let's go."

With the blank look still in his eyes, Luis stood and folded his chair. He slung it over his shoulder and plodded up the street, the chair bouncing against his side. Esperanza noticed the strips of denim were starting to fray on the edges. Cabron, but Luis would throw a fit if that chair broke.

Mama had worked on the chair while she sat by Luis's bed, double-sewing strips of denim from old jeans to replace the worn-out webbing on a lawn chair. When it was finished, she painted a picture of their favorite camping spot on it.

After Luis recovered and Mama was sick, he'd painted a bright red heart in the corner. The color still reminded Esperanza of the blood on Mama's lips after a coughing fit.

After the bombs, everyone'd been pretty orderly at first. And then half the town got sick. Not radiation sickness, Papa said. Plague of some kind.

One thing Esperanza had never figured out was why all the

kids didn't die, too. Everyone in town got sick, but only those under twelve recovered.

Madre de Dios, she'd been trying to figure things out ever since last fall, and she still wasn't any closer to an answer. Not that it really mattered anymore – answers wouldn't bring Mama and Papa or anyone else back. "Let's go."

The sun blazed, radiating heat shimmers from the hard, crackled earth. The street was so dusty, Esperanza could hardly see the pavement. A good rain would wash it all clean, but since the last bomb fell, they hadn't glimpsed even a wisp of cloud or blue sky – just a murky brown haze.

Esperanza headed for the boarded-up supermarket where they lived now. It'd never be home to Esperanza – that would always be the small ranch outside of town.

After Mama and Papa died, Esperanza kept Luis home at first, even though he'd near drove her loco asking where Mama had gone. When their food supply ran low, it'd been a relief in a way to move to town, even though the guilt had almost ate her up. That ranch had been everything to Papa and Mama, their big American dream – owning property, being self-sufficient. Mi ranchita, Papa had always called it, but Esperanza had always preferred Mama's name: Casita de Esperanza. House of Hope.

Of course, now it wasn't anything but a House of Empty. Just like Esperanza felt inside.

Prophet was at a standstill in the middle of the street, staring at something off in the distance. There was a heavy stillness to him that caught Esperanza's attention.

"He's coming," Prophet said. A trickle of drool ran from the corner of his slack mouth.

Esperanza didn't see anything except a swirl of dust, way out on the road winding down from the mountains. "Just a dust devil."

Prophet's eyes were always moving, like he was searching for something the rest of them couldn't see, but now he looked Esperanza right in the eyes, his gaze heavy and clear. "He's. Coming."

She'd never seen Prophet so intent. Esperanza looked towards the road again. The whirlwind of dust was closer. Something about it didn't look right. She shaded her eyes with one hand.

The dust cloud was moving. Or something inside it was. And it was yellow. "Madre de Dios, is that a school bus?" The putter-pop of an engine broke the stillness. She couldn't remember the last time she'd seen a vehicle. She hadn't even been sure there was anyone alive outside of Huntsville.

Maybe it was someone with supplies and food. Dios, what she wouldn't give for a nice cold soda. Fresh tortillas. Hamburger and fries. Just as her mouth started watering, Esperanza remembered Papa's warning – when things go bad, chances are a stranger would be just as like to shoot you for some water as they would be to help you.

Nate came running up, his eyes as big around as Esperanza figured her own were.

The bus spluttered up with a squeal of brakes and shuddered before the engine went dead. The door whooshed open.

A smell rolled out that reminded Esperanza of a mountain meadow after a rain. A tall fellow eased up from the driver's seat and hopped down the steps. There was no one else on the bus.

"Hey there," the tall guy said.

He had the biggest ears Esperanza had ever seen on a person. They sat low on his head and stuck way out.

It was only after she was able to draw her gaze from the peculiar ears that Esperanza noticed the stranger's honey-colored skin was smooth and clear. Not a pockmark in sight. Esperanza couldn't stop her finger from reaching up to trace the nooks and crannies on her own face.

The man pulled a red kerchief from his back pocket. "Sure is hot today." He mopped his face, then looked straight into Esperanza's eyes. "What we need is some rain," he said.

A little chill ran across the back of Esperanza's neck. His eyes were an unnatural shade of green, as bright as new grass in spring. Papa'd always said you could judge a person by the look in his eyes, but this man's eyes didn't tell her a thing. He didn't have the look of a gringo, but he didn't look Hispanic, either.

"Who're you?" Nate asked. "You got any food? Who won the war?"

The stranger looked up at the sky as if an answer might be found hidden somewhere in the brown haze. "You can call me Clarence," he finally said. "And there wasn't any winners —only losers."

"Didn't you get sick?" Esperanza asked, still focused on that smooth complexion.

"Everyone got sick, didn't they?"

"Yep." Esperanza waited for a better answer but the stranger just smiled. She didn't trust anyone who didn't want to answer simple questions. From what they'd heard before the radio transmissions stopped, everyone in the country had got sick. Heck, all the kids had the same pockmarked faces as Esperanza.

Maybe this man had been far enough removed from towns to escape the plague, but then again, whoever put the germs in the bombs would probably have made sure they were protected against it. "Where you from?"

Before the man could answer, Prophet came running up, a big grin plastered across his face. "Clarence!" he said.

The stranger's face softened. "There you are."

"Yup." Prophet nodded hard enough to knock his hat off if he'd been wearing one.

"You know him?" Esperanza asked.

Prophet didn't answer, just kept on grinning in that way he had, the one that made you think you were his long-lost best friend.

The stranger answered instead. "He wandered into our territory after the bombs and stayed awhile."

"Yeah? Where was that?"

"Oh, just up the road a ways," he said with a vague wave of his hand toward the mountains.

"There's no towns up that road."

"I didn't say I lived in a town, did I?"

He said it friendly enough, but with just enough of a challenge in his voice to rile Esperanza and set her even further on edge.

She glanced around at the other kids. Besides Nate and Prophet, there were two girls, Jenn and Emily, hunkered up against the side of the building, and another group of four kids headed their way. Esperanza was getting nervous being out in the open with this stranger.

Luis pulled on her shirt. "I wanna go home! Mama'll be worried about us being gone so long." A hunk of dark hair hung across his right eye.

"Go on inside," she said, glad of the interruption.

"You said you'd take me home today," Luis said, not budging an inch.

"Mañana."

"That's what you said yesterday and the day before. I want to see Mama!"

Most of the time, she tried to be patient, hoping that once the shock of Mama's and Papa's deaths wore off, Luis would be okay. But after all this time, she was tired of pretending, and right now, she was just plain tired of it all. "Not now!" she yelled. "Get on inside!"

Luis's eyes got real big, then filled with tears as his lower lip quivered. Esperanza felt like she'd a big ache in her chest when he turned and ran inside the grocery store.

Clarence gave her a look and shook his head. She was already ashamed of her outburst, but she couldn't back down with everyone staring at her, could she?

And besides, who was this stranger to walk into their town and start trying to tell them what to do? What was he even here for, anyway? "What is it you want here, mister?"

Prophet tugged on Esperanza's sleeve, his face lit up like a light was shining from inside. "He's here to help us, Espie."

"We're doing just fine on our own," Esperanza said, jutting her chin out.

"I'll allow you don't have cause to trust me," Clarence said, "but I do want to help you kids out. I imagine it's been a mite scary. When did your folks die?"

His question threw Esperanza off, making her recall that awful day Papa died. Esperanza felt all unsettled, like she didn't know which way to go or what to feel. The girls by the car started edging closer, while Nate stuck his hands in his pocket with a frown.

Esperanza swallowed to ease the strain on her throat. "A while back. About seven months," she answered, not even sure why she was answering at all. Truth was, it'd been seven months, twelve and a half days. Early morning, just as the sun was clearing the horizon.

"I'm sorry, girl."

"Wasn't nothing more than all the others went through."

"Still, hard for you kids to bc left alone."

Esperanza shrugged. She sort of did wish she could trust this stranger, let him take over things so she could just be a kid again. But she didn't know enough about him yet. He might be one of those who would want to take what little they had, and she wasn't about to let any of the others get too close to someone they couldn't trust yet. "I said we're just fine." She turned to the others, "C'mon, let's go inside." She pulled Prophet by the sleeve into the store, motioning the others to follow.

After everyone was in, she locked the door, peeking out through a crack in the plywood to watch Clarence. He smiled at the door, like he knew Esperanza was watching him, then sat on the steps of the bus. After a while, he leaned back against the open door and appeared to fall asleep.

"What are we going to do with him?" Nate asked, jerking his chin toward Clarence.

"I don't know. Maybe he'll be gone by morning. Just stay away from him for now."

"He seems all right to me. Maybe he can drive us someplace."

Maybe it was stupid to stay in Huntsville instead of going to look for help somewhere, but Esperanza had promised Papa that she'd take care of the ranch, and she meant to abide by that promise, no matter what. "We don't even know who he is or what he wants!"

"Can't be much worse than what we gone through already," Nate said.

Esperanza didn't have an argument for that. For about the

gazillionth time since Papa and Mama had died, she wished she could just crawl into the corner and never, ever come out again. She'd never asked to be in charge of things, it'd just kinda happened. She wasn't even very good at it.

"Esperanza! Isn't Clarence coming inside to eat? He can have some of my beans," Prophet said, holding out his can.

"He's got his own food. He said he wanted to stay in the bus," Esperanza answered. She was getting pretty good at lying. Mama'd skin her alive if she could have heard.

Luis was huddled on their makeshift bed of sleeping bags and quilts, still crying. He didn't turn over to look at her. Esperanza knew she should apologize, but she was just too worn out to do it right then. She threw herself down beside Luis and turned her back on him.

She sure wouldn't have made Mama or Papa proud today.

• • •

It took several hours of tossing and turning before Esperanza was able to sleep that night. She dreamed of Papa, staring as if he were trying to say something with only his eyes, and in the background, Mama cried Luis's name.

Esperanza woke with a heavy feeling in her gut. When she opened her eyes, the first thing she saw was Prophet, sitting with his back against the wall.

"Hey, Espie!"

Esperanza sat up and rubbed her eyes. Luis's side of the bed was empty. "Where's Luis?"

"He left. Can we have Crispy-O's for breakfast?"

"He left? Where'd he go?" It was a stupid question. There was only one place Luis would go.

Prophet shrugged and climbed to his feet. "I dunno. Can we have Crispy-O's?"

"Why didn't you stop him?"

"I–I–I dunno." Prophet sucked on his upper lip while his gaze swept around the room, finally fastening on Esperanza. "I want Crispy-O's."

Esperanza could only think of Luis and what might happen if he made it to the ranch by himself. What would he do if he saw the graves? Esperanza's imagination ran wild, imagining Luis upset and wandering off to who-knew-where. He wouldn't last half a day on his own.

Prophet jerked on Esperanza's shirt. "Espie. Can I have Crispy-O's?"

Worried out of her mind over Luis, Esperanza shoved Prophet away. He stumbled and fell to the ground with a cry. A part of Esperanza was horrified at what she'd done, but she couldn't think of anything right now except Luis.

She ran outside without apologizing or helping Prophet up.

Luis's bike was gone. If he'd left at first light, he'd almost be at the ranch by now. Esperanza hopped on her own bike and pedaled down the street.

She'd just passed the city limits sign when she heard the bus chugging up from behind. She pedaled faster, but there was no out-running it.

"Get in, Esperanza," Clarence hollered above the engine noise.

Esperanza pedaled faster.

"You'll get there a lot quicker in the bus," Clarence yelled.

Prophet was perched on the seat behind Clarence. Esperanza laid on the brakes, skidding to a stop. "Prophet, get off that bus!"

Prophet didn't raise his head to look at her. Esperanza guessed she didn't blame him much, not after she'd yelled at him and shoved him down.

What to do now? She couldn't leave Prophet alone with the stranger, but she needed to get to the ranch, and it was still a couple miles away.

Papa always said, comes a time to stop worrying and just trust that things'll work out. Right now, the important thing was to catch Luis as quick as possible.

Esperanza gave in and hauled her bike up the bus steps and stowed it between the seats. She sat catty-corner from Prophet. Clarence pulled the bus back on the road. Prophet sniffled and swiped at his nose.

"Don't you think Prophet deserves an apology?" Clarence asked, staring at Esperanza in the driver's rearview mirror.

It wasn't that Esperanza didn't want to apologize. She hated hurting Prophet's feelings. But she didn't like it that this stranger was the one telling her what to do. "I didn't do nothing."

"Didn't you?"

The bus hit a pot hole, almost throwing her from the seat.

Prophet reached a hand out to steady her. "Esperanza! Don't fall!"

His worry and concern for her was plain to see. He was one of the sweetest, most caring persons she'd ever met. It wasn't right to take her frustration out on him.

She sighed. Mama'd always said no sense in letting pride get in your way.

She moved over to sit beside Prophet and patted his hand. "I'm sorry I pushed you, Prophet. I was worried about Luis. But you didn't deserve that, and I shouldn't have done it."

Prophet snuggled against Esperanza's side. "That's ok," he said.

Esperanza met Clarence's gaze in the mirror, and the stranger nodded approval. The bus sped up and didn't hit any more pot holes.

"Esperanza?"

"Yeah, Prophet?"

"The rains are coming."

"That so? When?"

"Soon."

They came to a series of small dips in the road. It wasn't much farther to the ranch. "Turn left at the next road," she said to Clarence.

They turned the corner, and there was Luis, walking his bike. He had his lawn chair slung over his shoulder. At the end of the road, the roof of their home could be glimpsed through the treetops. The bus squealed to a stop. Esperanza hopped down.

Sweat beaded Luis's forehead. Both bike tires were flat. He let Esperanza hand the bike up to Clarence, but when she turned back to help him into the bus, he'd gone on ahead, still walking toward home.

Esperanza chased him down, pulling him to a stop with a hand on his shoulder. "Get on the bus, Luis," she said.

Luis shook his head. "I'm going to see Mama."

"Mama's –" Mama's what? Dead? She couldn't say it. Realized she hadn't ever said it out loud.

Luis looked as beat-tired as Esperanza felt, but he had that stubborn look in his eyes that used to make Mama shake her head and mutter under her breath. Mama'd always let him go on about his way when he got like that, and eventually he got over it. But this was different.

Maybe a cold dose of reality was what he needed. Maybe she should just take Luis on home – let him see for himself.

"You'll get there quicker on the bus," she said.

Luis cocked his head, studying her. "You promise?"

Esperanza nodded.

Luis shrugged. "K, then." He climbed up the steps into the bus.

"Hey, Luis," Prophet said with a smile and a little wave.

"Hey."

"Wanna sit by me?"

With a nod, Luis slid in beside Prophet. Esperanza sat down across the aisle from them.

Clarence pulled back on the road. Prophet bounced in his seat like it was a trampoline. Soon enough, he got Luis to join in. The cushions squeaked and groaned as they bounced so high they almost fell on the floor. They fell back on the seat, giggling. Esperanza wished she could remember what it was like to feel that carefree.

When the bus slowed down to take the bumpy dirt drive to Casita Esperanza, Luis stopped bouncing, his body edged and still.

Clarence pulled up at the side of the house in a whirl of dust and opened the door. No one moved while waiting for the dust to clear. It'd always been quiet at the ranch, but the kind of quiet that was comforting – chirping birds, buzzing insects, and wind rustling the leaves.

What she heard now was the wrong kind of quiet. A still, empty quiet.

Esperanza looked around, the memories rushing in. There was Mama's garden, the hills and furrows now bare dirt. The door to the shed stood open. Papa had used to sit there, where the roof overhang shaded him from the afternoon sun. His chair leaned drunkenly against the wall.

Luis's face pinched up like it did when he was scared, and he settled against the bus seat like he wanted to melt into it. For some reason, that just made Esperanza mad. Here her brother had been at her for how long now, asking every five minutes to go home to see Mama, and now they were here, he wouldn't get off the darned bus.

"C'mon," Esperanza said, jumping down the steps to the ground. "You wanted to come home. Here we are."

Luis got up, dragging his feet down the steps like he was walking in deep mud, his face getting tighter and tighter. Esperanza's chest felt all pinched up, but her anger kept building. "Go on, then." She pushed Luis toward the house. "Go see Mama."

She felt Clarence's eyes on her back as she followed Luis across the porch.

Luis fumbled the door open and stepped inside. "Mama?" His voice sounded tiny and echoing.

Inside, everything looked the same. Just dustier. The emptiness made Esperanza's stomach clench.

Mama'd always been at the counter, kneading dough for tortillas or stirring the always-simmering pot of beans. At the kitchen table was Papa's chair, angled to get a view of the mountains. Esperanza imagined if she held her breath, she'd hear echoes of her parent's voices, forever alive in the house they'd pinned all their hopes on.

"Mama?" Luis sniffled, swiped at his nose. "Where is she?"

Esperanza couldn't feel anything, like she'd breathed in the emptiness of the house and now it was lodged inside her chest. "She's gone, Luis."

Luis's eyes shifted around the room, and then he brightened. "She went to get Papa at the shed, didn't she?" He ran outside.

Mama's coffee cup was on the windowsill, where she always set it so she could find it easy in the morning. Esperanza imagined Mama watching her with disapproval.

She'd pushed Luis too far. She ran after him, catching him halfway across the yard.

"C'mon, Luis. Let's go back."

Luis threw her arm off and stomped through the gate and across to the shed. Esperanza'd never felt like such a gawd-awful failure.

"Papa? Papa!" Luis's voice echoed in the shed. Normally pigeons would have fluttered from the roof at the sound, but there was only more of the awful silence. "Mama! Ma-a-maaaaa!" He ran out of the barn. "Where are they? Where'd they go?" He pulled at Esperanza's jacket, his voice shrill and panicked.

Esperanza couldn't help it – her gaze was drawn to the side of the shed where she could just see the ends of the rock mounds.

Luis's gaze followed hers. His soft gasp sounded like a firecracker in the still air. "No," he said, his voice little more than a whisper. He backed away. In his eyes, Esperanza saw horror as the memories finally returned.

"No. No. No." He turned and ran.

Esperanza chased him. She thought for a minute he was going to run off to who-knew-where, but when he saw the bus, he headed straight for it. He threw himself on the bottom step and scrambled up.

Clarence started the engine. As Esperanza climbed the stairs, Clarence shot her a disapproving look.

Luis huddled in the seat, hugging his lawn chair to his chest.

"Luis, mijo," Esperanza said, laying her hand on his shoulder. Luis jerked away, and that hurt almost as bad as hearing Mama rasp out her last breath.

She flopped into the seat behind Luis and Prophet. Clarence started the bus and headed back to town.

"Esperanza?"

"Yeah, Prophet?"

"The rains will come."

"Yeah? When?"

It was Clarence who answered. "Soon," he said, watching Esperanza in the rearview mirror.

Esperanza got a shiver, the kind that Mama used to say was from someone walking over your grave. She was probably turning over in hers right now, from the mess Esperanza'd made of things.

She missed both her parents so much. They'd have known what to do.

Mama with her gentle patience. Papa – well, he was the strongest man Esperanza knew. He'd look a person right in the eye and tell the truth, no matter how much it hurt.

They'd both taught her what to do.

She crawled around the seat and knelt in front of Luis. "Luis, you listen to me." Luis huddled against Prophet with his eyes shut tight, but Esperanza didn't let that stop her. "We can't bring back Mama and Papa. They're gone. Papa wouldn't want us to just give up and cry for what's gone. He'd say to pull ourselves up and keep moving on. Together, as a family."

Luis opened his eyes, but still wouldn't look Esperanza in the eye. "I want it the way it was," he whispered.

The want in his voice was naked and raw. "I do, too," Esperanza said, her voice all raspy and tight. Her eyes watered, but she swallowed down the tears. "Our old life is gone, Luis. And it isn't ever coming back."

Luis chewed on his lip for a while. Esperanza took his hands. "I told Mama I'd look after you, and I will. Everything'll be all right. It won't ever be like it was, but we'll do okay."

Luis looked doubtful. But at least he was listening.

All of a sudden, Prophet jerked up from his seat. "Stop, Clarence!" He pushed past Esperanza and pulled on Clarence's shirt. "Stop. Stop!"

Clarence stomped on the brakes and the bus squealed to a halt. Prophet hopped down the steps and banged on the door.

Clarence watched him with a considering look for a moment, then nodded. He opened the door, and Prophet jumped down and ran a few steps out. He spread his arms and looked up at the sky.

They were stopped beside Esperanza's garden. "Prophet, what're you doing?" she hollered.

"A rain dance!" Prophet twirled around, his face turned up to the sky, arms splayed. "Rain, rain, rain," he chanted.

Esperanza jumped down from the bus. "Prophet, get back here."

Luis pushed up against her arm and leaned into her. The contact felt good. Luis watched Prophet for a full minute, then hopped down the stairs.

Prophet grabbed Luis's hands and pulled him into a twirl. "Rain, Rain!" he chanted, gathering speed. Before long, Luis was chanting too. They whooped and hollered, spinning a cloud of dust.

A movement caught Esperanza's eye. Clarence stood aside, his bright green eyes shining like they were full of diamonds. He wiggled his fingers at the sky.

A wind swept up, raising dust and a chill across Esperanza's neck. Her hair blew into her eyes.

Prophet dropped Luis's hands and stopped spinning, turning his slack-jawed face to the sky.

"What's that?" Luis asked, pointing up.

On the horizon, a wall of towering purple clouds piled up against a blue sky. The clouds advanced with a speed that shouldn't have been possible. The sky turned purplish gray. The air chilled.

Rain smacked down with honest-to-goodness great globs of water so big they danged near hurt when they hit. Esperanza turned her face to the sky. Raindrops splattered her face, wetting her hair to her head. The musty smell of damp earth rose from the hard-packed ground.

Prophet grabbed Luis's hands again and they danced around some more, laughing and sticking their tongues out to catch raindrops.

Esperanza'd felt for a long time now like her heart was nothing but a big patch of ice, but as she watched Luis and Prophet act like kids again, something broke free. She took a deep breath, and for the first time in what seemed like forever, it didn't feel like it caught in her chest.

Clarence put an arm around Esperanza's shoulders. "Mind if I stay for a few days?"

Esperanza shrugged. "It's a free world."

"Maybe it will be now. It's time to rebuild."

There he went again. Esperanza pulled away to look him in the eye. It wasn't that he didn't look human, 'cause he did, but there was something strange about him that Esperanza couldn't put a finger on. "Who are you, really?"

"It's not important right now who or what I am. I'm here to help you find your way."

He didn't flinch from Esperanza's gaze. There was something pure in his expression. It reminded Esperanza of Mama's look when she was tending the garden. She'd walk down the rows, touching each plant, checking it for bugs. If she did find one, she wouldn't stomp on it, she'd just pick it up, take it off a ways and let it go.

Esperanza guessed if she saw something in Clarence that reminded her of Mama, it couldn't be all bad.

She looked over her garden. The seedlings were flattened to the ground. They hadn't been strong enough to stand up to the battering raindrops.

Meanwhile, there was her brother and Prophet, dancing around like wild things. They'd all made it this far. They'd all been strong enough to make it so far – even Luis. His chair leaning against the bus caught Esperanza's eye.

One of Mama's favorite sayings came to her – never let hope die, even when it all feels hopeless. 'Cause without it, you're just an empty shell. Esperanza had been feeling empty like that ever since Mama and Papa died.

The rain turned gentle, soothing, dripping down Esperanza's face, washing away the grime and sweat. The parched earth soaked up the moisture and turned a healthy dark brown.

Their world had changed, and all of them with it. But she and Luis still had each other. They were still a family – smaller, yes, but also bigger, with Prophet and Nate and all the other kids.

Tomorrow she'd get more seeds from the store and replant. But for now, maybe it was time to let go of worrying.

Esperanza ran and tackled Luis and Prophet. They fell together and slid, scrabbling and laughing. The mud was cool and soft, slippery as butter. A glob landed in Esperanza's eye, and the smell and taste of good earth filled her with a joy she hadn't thought to ever feel again.

And for the first time in a long while, Esperanza dared to hope again.

# Child of Luna
## Ralan Conley

*Ralan Conley writes, run his writers' resource (ralan.com), and does a spot of icedragonship piracy. His work has appeared in print and electronic publications too numerous or obscure to mention. Some of which, to the consternation of his former writing coaches, have won contests, awards, and reader's polls. Among these, three nominations for the Bram Stoker Award and a finalist for the Sapphire Award. Always a bride's maid....*

Doran Kelisar ignored the discussion in his classroom to read his Ballistic Orbit Guide on the sly. He liked the ninth-grade well enough – he just hated remembering long lists of chemicals, atomic structures, civil emergency procedures and DNA codes. Things he'd never use, and most of all, historical people. Why did you have to study everyone who'd ever sneezed? And not just people on the moon, but boring Earthers, too.

Engineering. That's what he liked and did well at.

"Doran?" His teacher's question pulled him back into the classroom with a jerk. Mr. Jaqobi stood beside Doran's console array desk.

Several of his classmates giggled. They enjoyed having a laugh at his expense. He'd never understood that.

Being the first Lunaborn should count for something, but his classmates seemed to hold it against him. His gangling frame, pale skin and white hair made him a comic figure to the emigreens, as he called all Earthers who moved to Luna. He got along okay with most of them, kind of liked them really, but he had no close friends.

"Did you hear what I just said?"

Doran's finger shut off the screen he'd been reading before his teacher noticed it. "You said, uh..."

"We were discussing being lost. Like Alexsi Golaenski?"

"Alexsi Go..." He remembered something about him from his homework, another useless historical person. "That old miner who never came back from a prospecting trek? He should have had a field radio." His classmates laughed out loud.

The teacher frowned. "He did take a radio with him, but no contact was ever made. He died out there." The laughter stopped in an instant. "Right. We also talked about the field trip tomorrow."

"Field trip?" Doran sat upright, beaming. "A day away from in this boring old classroom?" Doran grimaced as he realized how disappointed Mr. Jaqobi looked.

Nervous giggling spread around the class.

"I'm sorry, sir. I didn't mean it that way." Doran flashed a warning look that quieted most of his classmates, who relied on his safety skills, except for Nedidi and Stan, his worst critics, who no doubt started this disturbance.

Mr. Jaqobi quieted even those two with a look of his own. "Meet outside the school's main vacuum hatch at 0700 hours tomorrow, suited for full lunar on the mare. Be sure you've read and understood the assigned chapter." He nodded toward the main view screen at the front of the room.

"Yes sir, the 'Finding Your Way' chapter. No problem."

"Just make sure you know how to observe the sky at lunar noon, placing the circular filter in your helmet to block out the sun's disk so you don't blind yourself, and determine your compass points based on Earth's location in the sky."

"Sure as exhaust, Mr. Jaqobi."

"Considering your grades in Astronomy, I hope so." The teacher turned and headed for his desk. "Class dismissed."

Doran breathed out slowly. He liked Mr. Jaqobi, but sometimes he was a pain in the jets. Calling him out in front of the class was one of those times. Doran didn't need more attention.

Nedidi and Stan crowded around Doran as they exited through the Mark IV Air Beam hatch that connected the school digs with the main L-City lava tube. As usual, tourists in colorful clothes and Lunarians in their drab coveralls crammed the main tube. As they came through, the smell of sweat, perfume and deodorant engulfed them.

"Busy day," Stan observed.

"Yeah," Doran said. "Shuttle landed last night."

"Oh goody." Nedidi quickly rubbed his hands together. "Hope there're some new girls."

The activity level around them matched any big city anywhere, but without any cars, trains or buses. Everyone walked on the moon. At one-fifth of Earth's gravity, walking came easy once you got the hang of it. Even tourists managed it, in time. To walk safely you had to moonshuffle, a blend of skating and skipping. If you took big steps you'd hop up high and land hard. Of course, the low-grav kept the number of serious injuries down.

Luna City boasted the largest pressurized lava tube on the moon. All lunar lava tubes held a natural constant temperature of -20ºC, or -4ºF. After they got sealed and leveled for habitation, solar-powered space heaters warmed them up to +15ºC. That's why all Lunarians wore thermal underwear under their coveralls. It proved a practical solution for people who had to contend with both pressure and vacuum environments.

"What's up for tonight?" Nedidi asked Stan as they shuffled towards Doran's exit, bumping into him on purpose.

Doran knew they were only staying close to annoy him. Their favorite hobby, it seemed.

"There's a new Sensi at the bio," Stan suggested. "A real ghoulfest, I hear. Just the smell makes strong men puke."

"Or we could meet at the arcade," Nedidi said. "They repaired the tether shuttle simulator."

"After you broke it," Doran said.

Nedidi punched him in the arm. "Because you didn't listen to my order!" The blow from the strong Earther teen almost knocked Doran off his feet.

Doran rubbed his arm. It'd turn black and blue sure as gravity. "I did listen. You gave the wrong order. Anyway, I gotta help my dad fix our ice defroster." In fact, this pleased him. Doran liked working in vacuum.

"We weren't asking you, Luna monster," Nedidi said.

"Why would we hang out with a freak like you?" Stan asked.

"Yeah, you can hang out with the other Lunaborns."

"Those jerks who worship you."

After Doran's unexpected and risky delivery, the colony issued a ban on new births until they finished the hospital. This meant all the other lunar natives were at least seven years younger than Doran, making him an unwilling loner.

They reached the Mark V vacuum hatch Doran used to get home. His pressure suit hung on a rack. Doran slipped out of his coveralls, stowed them in his pack, then removed his lower torso section and stepped into it, hiking it up to his waist.

"We'll see how you guys do tomorrow," he said as he ducked down, scooted under his upper torso section, stuck his hands into the armholes, and rose up until his head popped out of the helmet opening and his hands fitted into the gloves. He pressed the button that detached the upper suit from the rack and fastened the two sections together using the waist-locking ring. "I know how you both love vacuum."

Nedidi's face fell. "I hate field trips."

"I hate outside," Stan said, looking a bit green.

"But most of all we hate Lunaborns," they said together.

Doran lived on a hydro-farm in a small lava tube two kilometers from L-City. Most Earthers, including Stan and Nedidi's families, lived in apartment digs in L-City after emigrating to the moon. They viewed Lunaborns as freaks.

Of course, the Lunaborns had a similar dislike for emigreens, who were big and strong and feared 'outside' until they eventually got used to it. Some never did. Doran saw that dread in Nedidi and Stan's faces. "See you tomorrow, Earthers. Outside."

The two emigreens shuffled off down The Main for home without another word. Doran wished they could be friends, but it seemed impossible.

Doran shrugged and yanked his helmet from the shelf above the suit rack, eased it over his head, and twisted the seal shut. He punched the 'Pressurize' button and started a full diagnostic. Data ran before his eyes on the heads-up display to the hiss of air and coolant filling the suit. Air: 78%, which flashed red until it hit 100%. H2O: 60%. Humidity: 35%. Pressure: stable. ExchangeFan: nominal. CO2-Scrub: normal. Comm: on. Cool/Vent: on. LPS: await sat acq.

He'd make it home long before he needed to use it, so he didn't hook up the excreta system, which meant ducking into a private suit-up room for five minutes. One didn't hook that up in public.

Subsystem data began to repeat on the heads-up. Everything looked green, so he shut the read-outs down except for emergency notices.

Doran shuffled to the Air Beam and pulled the lever to open the hatch. He went through into the airlock as the door closed behind him, muting the L-City bustle his external microphones had been picking up. He only heard the rush of air being expelled back into L-City. As that sound faded, a green light lit up over the outer hatch. Doran tugged the Vacuum Access Lever, the hatch opened to the outside, and he moonshuffled toward home across the familiar lunar landscape.

•••

Doran met up early outside the school airlock. Nedidi, Stan and seven others – the entire ninth-grade class – came straggling out a minute before 0700 hours. Due to Doran's long experience with vacuum gear, Mr. Jaqobi had made him the Safety Officer. He had to check all his classmates' pressure suits and data. They all knew emigrants could make fatal mistakes, so they let him do this. Even though embarrassing, it was better than ending up dead. It didn't make him any more popular, though.

"Great comets, Stan! You didn't activate your CO2 scrubber.

You're not a plant, you know. You need oxygen, not carbon dioxide."

"Yeah, yeah. Did you memorize that 'Finding Your Way' chapter, smart guy?"

"It took my dad and me six hours to fix our ice defroster. I just collapsed when we got inside."

"So, you didn't study? That could be dangerous."

"I'll be okay. I'm used to it out here."

Doran turned to check the readings of one of the girls. "Ningela, how many times do I have to tell you to switch on your excreta system? You could drown in your own –"

"Thank you, Doran," Mr. Jaqobi said, as he emerged from the school in his teacher's red pressure suit. "Good morning, class! Well, it's a sunny, clear day –"

"Every day is sunny and clear... and lethal on the moon," Nedidi said.

"Ah, yes." Mr. Jaqobi looked serious. "Just my point. The moon can be hazardous. You have to know what you're doing. Today we're going to run a little exercise on non-LPS navigation."

Doran rolled his eyes.

"Someday you may find yourself on the surface without a functioning field radio," his teacher continued. "With no access to the Luna Positioning System, or LPS, how will you find your way home? Use a compass?"

They all laughed. The first thing colonists threw away when they got to the moon was their compass. The moon had no magnetic north pole. A compass on the moon pointed toward Earth, or to the closest magnetic source, like a motor. No help at all.

"I've been all over this mare since I learned to walk." Doran kept checking p-suits. "And my radio's never let me down."

"Your father's been lenient with you. Allowed you to take chances."

"I think my father's as careful as anyone, sir. Maybe more so, he..." Doran paused – no need to tell Mr. Jaqobi about that. "He'd never send me into danger. He knows how failsafe a field radio is, that's all."

"And he's confident of his own ability to find you. He's a fine navigator, with or without LPS, but he may not always be able to help you. Anyway, we've blocked radio reception for all of you, including LPS, until 1800 hours, plus the time it takes to drop each of you off."

The emigreens all groaned as a lorry, a small open bus with balloon tires for driving in the soft moon dust, rolled up.

"We'll set you off at different coordinates around the mare, but at the same distance from the school. To keep you from seeing where we go, the driver and I will affix blast shields over your visors before we leave and remove them as we set you off."

He handed out a laminated paper. "This is a hand-drawn map of the mare with just the school and your drop-off position marked. But you won't know which way to travel to get back here unless you know how to spot Earth in the full lunar sky and determine your orientation based on Earth's position. In other words, you'll have to find where north is." He caught Doran's eye.

"No problem, sir," Doran said, looking confident.

"I hope not... for all of you. Everyone who gets back here before 1400 hours, plus your drop-off time, gets the highest mark, a 4. If you've studied, that should be easy. One point will be taken off for every hour, or portion of an hour, after that. Arrive here at 1601 hours, plus drop-off time, and you get 2 points. If you're not back here at 1800 hours, plus drop-off, your points are zero. At that time the exercise is over and we'll unblock your field radio and LPS. You can then contact us and find your way back, or request help."

"What if we n-need help in a hurry?" Nedidi asked.

"The emergency frequency on your radio has not been turned off. If you have a serious problem, hit the panic button, and we'll come get you. Just make sure it's a genuine emergency, or you'll get minus five instead of zero. You're pretty safe, no matter what."

"Pretty safe?"

"Most of you might think this exercise is too tough. But the moon is tough, and you're going to live on it for the rest of your lives. We're just trying to make sure those are long lives. Any questions?" He glanced around. "Safety Officer, have you finished your inspections?"

Doran slapped the last classmate's air tank. "Check."

"All right. Let's go."

•••

Somewhere out on the mare Doran stood alone in full lunar, watching the lorry drive away.

Checking his heads-up display, he noted the drop-off time at thirty minutes past the hour. That meant he had to be back at school before 1430 in order to get the highest marks.

He stared at the plastic encased printout his teacher had just handed him. As promised, the map only showed his and the school's relative positions and an arrow pointing north. Now he just needed to find which way north was and point the arrow at it, then he'd know which direction to head.

He imagined all the other students doing the same. Nedidi and Stan, who'd left the lorry separately before him, had no doubt figured it out already. He tucked the map into a suit flap and with an external joystick positioned the circular filter to cover the sun. This he knew how to do without reading the chapter. He locked it in, and the disk automatically blocked the sun no matter which way he turned.

Remembering Mr. Jaqobi's instructions, he spotted the Earth in the black sky. In the brightness of the lunar noon he could see no other planets or stars. Now, what had his teacher said about knowing the position of Earth to determine north? The mother planet hung stationary in the sky as always, wavering only infinitesimally during the lunar month of 28.53 days. But that didn't help Doran. He hadn't had time to read the chapter that explained how the Earth's position would help him find north.

Finally, he threw up his hands. "It's no use!" Then he grinned. "But lucky for me, I don't need to know."

Doran's dad, an engineer, had enabled his son's field radio to home into a beacon at the family complex. Only Doran had this function. That's why his dad never worried about him. His boy could just press a button and follow the signal home.

Doran activated the homing button, but after a brief moment of hissing his dad's voice said, "Hi son. Sorry, but Mr. Jaqobi convinced me this exercise is important to your future safety. You have to learn to fend for yourself. I've deactivated the homing beacon. Now, observe the Earth and find your way back. I know you can do it."

Inside his helmet, Doran's mouth hung open. He closed it. "Dad? Then you should have let me study instead of keeping me out with that ice defroster half the night. Dad?" Then he realized his dad had prerecorded the message. "Burn-out! Now what am I going to do?"

He'd fail this test and be the big joke for the next week, or month. The first Lunarian can't find his way home, they'd tease.

But wait, he'd been all over this mare for most of his life. He must recognize something.

The sun, plumb overhead, blazed down and he became aware of the whine and hiss of his suit's water-cooling and ventilation system. If he ran out of power out here, he could fry. He scanned the horizon, circling on his feet. Nothing. He jumped as high as he could, almost two meters.

Nothing looked familiar. The mare's surface was basically a plain with low mounds, rocks and small craters. Two people walking in opposite directions could pass within ten meters of each other and never know it.

The mare bore countless marks of all the folks who'd tramped and driven on it for decades. Without wind to erode them, they all looked the same. He couldn't tell the tracks of his drop-off lorry from those made by the first lorry ever driven here.

Wait! Hadn't he read something about using rock shadows to find your direction? Yeah, the sun rose in the east and set in the west, so any shadow would reveal north. He found a big rock, but it had no shadow. Space dust! It was full lunar. The sun shone down from high noon of the roughly two week lunar day. No shadows.

For the first time in his life Doran felt lost.

In desperation Doran picked a direction and started to shuffle, hoping to spot something he knew. But after an hour or so he stopped. Nothing. He might even be heading away from school. Better to stay put until 1830 hours when they'd contact him. Maybe he should go back to his starting position. It'd be less embarrassing than being farther from school.

Instead he headed for a flattened cone nearby. At least he could relax for a minute. He sat. And the cone caved in.

Moon gravity is one sixth of Earth's, but the weight of his pressure suit made up for some of that. He straightened, holding his feet down. Obviously he'd fallen into a lava tube that might be anything from a few meters to a hundred meters deep. His descent rate would increase as he fell. In the pitch dark he couldn't see the floor.

Doran positioned his arms to keep himself in an upright position and prepared to crash. Sweat ran down his face despite the cool/vent system. His suit could take a moderate beating, but things could go wrong, above all if he landed on his back, on the suit's air tank. He'd prefer a belly flop, but feet first beat everything.

Doran's fear of death ended when he hit bottom after a short drop. Landing on his feet, he bent at the knees to take up some of the impact. He ran a complete diagnostic and found no integrity breaches or software glitches. He took a deep breath and switched on his helmet lamp.

The lava tube lit up. As he suspected, no one had engineered this one. The walls and ceiling appeared uneven, but the floor was somewhat flat. About ten meters above he could see the opening he'd fallen through. Lucky.

The mound he'd sat on up there must have been a hornito, an opening in the roof of a lava tube. They formed back when the magma flowed and high pressure forced lava to ooze and spatter out onto the surface, forming a cone. Hornitos can be up to ten meters high. This one had never reached that size and must have been naturally thin on top.

He'd forgotten to watch out for that.

His spirits dropped. No way he could jump that high or make a mound tall enough to get out. His emergency signal could not send through solid rock. Neither Mr. Jaqobi nor even Doran's father could find him down here. He'd moved away from his starting position, and all the other tracks up on the mare hid his footprints. The odds of finding him: one in a million, or less.

Not reading that chapter had endangered his life. Doran rechecked his CO2 scrubbers and oxygen level. The readouts showed about twelve hours of breathable air left. Water? More than he'd drink in that time. But he wouldn't be drinking, or doing anything else after his oxy ran out.

He must find his way out of this lava tube. Right! Only two choices remained for him: go down this way, or that way. One direction would head uphill and open onto the surface, or be blocked by a cave-in, or get low enough to clamber out. The other would lead him deeper into the moon and certain death.

But which way?

He had to pick one. As far as his helmet lamp could reach, a hundred meters or so, they seemed equally promising. Or disappointing. With no possible reason to do so, Doran picked a direction and shuffled that way.

For the first kilometer he observed no difference, but he got the impression of going downhill – the wrong way. Luckily, the moon's core was now smaller and cooler. No lava flows.

Doran still felt he was headed downhill. He considered turning around when he spied something on the floor ahead, at the limit of his light. He continued, and the object grew to a small heap. As he got closer, it revealed itself as a pressure suit. Someone else must've fallen down here. Maybe one of his classmates!

Doran hurried the last few meters, sank to his knees and turned the figure over. Through the helmet's view plate, a shriveled older man's face peered out. Due to the freezing temperature down here, the bacteria in his body took ages to decompose him. But in vacuum, all the moisture in his body had evaporated almost at once, leaving him mummified. Judging by the bulkier design of the moon suit – Doran had seen this type in the Hardware Museum – this guy had died more than a decade ago.

Doran turned his gaze to the ceiling. Almost a hundred meters above he saw a small light in the dark ceiling. A hornito, just like the one he'd fallen in. No one could make that fall uninjured, even in the moon's low-grav. This poor old HomSap no doubt broke his back.

The height of the ceiling indicated Doran might be headed the wrong way. Had he gone deeper into the moon?

Every pressure suit sported at least one pouch for storing things. Doran emptied this man's contents. He found some papers and a good topographical map with some handwritten marks on it. The map would prove handy if he ever got out of this tube, so he placed it in his own pouch.

He riffled through the papers. One displayed a picture of the dead man with his name, Alexsi Golaenski.

Wow. That old miner who went off prospecting 14 years ago, the year of Doran's birth, and never came back. Wait until he told everyone! He froze. *If I ever see them again – I could end up like old Alexsi here.*

He inspected Alexsi's suit in case he carried anything else of value but found nothing. The old miner's air tanks rang empty when he tapped them. Then he searched the tube floor around him. In front of his suit, Alexsi had scratched an arrow in the dust. It pointed the same direction Doran was heading.

How could that be right? Wasn't it downhill that way? But with no air, water or solar wind to disturb it, the arrow stood out firm and clear. Alexsi had drawn that arrow to help anyone else who got trapped down here – his last act of humanity. Doran stared at the strong, determined face in the helmet. The face of a man with confidence in what he did, always. This accident put an end to his life, but he had left a final message of hope to anyone who needed it.

Doran felt a bond with the old miner. They'd both made the same mistake, but one ended up dead, while the arrow he drew might save the other. Doran made up his mind. He trusted this old man.

"Alexsi, old friend, you may have saved my life, and I'm going to try to return the favor." He stripped off the miner's empty air tanks, radio, and other unnecessary equipment. Then he lifted Alexsi and got him into a fireman's carry. The burden was not so bad, the lightened suit and the old miner together weighed no more than fifteen kilos. Doran glanced down at the arrow one more time, and then he headed the way it pointed.

For a few kilometers it still felt like he was going downhill, but then the tube seemed to rise and widen. In less than an hour Doran spotted a light in the distance. Ten minutes later he emerged from the tunnel into the harsh daylight of the full lunar.

He eased Alexsi to the ground and jumped for joy. "We made it out." He patted the old helmet. "Way to go, HomSap!"

It would have been easier without the man, but to prepare for his freshman year at MIT on Earth in three years, Doran had been exercising with weights and using a centrifuge. An extra fifteen kilograms had made only a small difference so far, and the old miner deserved to go home. He'd paid for the ride by showing Doran the correct way out of the tube.

After admiring the view for a minute, Doran realized his situation remained critical. He could use the emergency radio frequency, but that meant admitting to being lost – something he didn't want to do. He'd never hear the last of it. He still didn't know his position or how to find Luna City. But maybe Alexsi did.

He got out the miner's topographical map. The marks he'd made showed the route from L-City to the hornito he'd fallen into. They just needed to find that hornito, orient themselves, and then follow the map home.

Doran checked his readouts. The time showed 1433 hours. So, he'd already lost a test point, but who cared? He was bringing the old miner home. He heaved Alexsi back up, climbed to the top of the lava tube's low mound and faced the way they'd come, but this time on the surface.

In the distance he made out the distinctive shape of a hornito. Not the right one, but he could follow the trail of hornitos back to the one had Alexsi fallen into. They only formed on top of a lava tube.

He shifted the miner to a more comfortable position. "Let's go, buddy."

In the tube they'd walked for an hour and thirty-some minutes before coming to the opening. He set a timer for that and shuffled toward the hornito in the distance. The horizon on the moon's flat mare was about two and a half kilometers away, so more hornitos hove into view as he shuffled, helping him to backtrack the journey they'd made in the tube.

Just after his alarm went off, he spotted Alexsi's collapsed hornito, but he didn't want to go anywhere near it. The ground around it could be weak.

He eased Alexsi to the ground and looked around. To his left lay a sizable crater. Oval in shape, it boasted a tail of ejecta, darker soil from deeper in the moon. It had blown off to the right side, meaning the meteor that formed the crater had come in at an angle. He checked the map--a printed satellite photo--and found Alexsi's last position mark next to the same crater. He must have made that mark minutes before he fell.

Doran positioned himself and the map to match the direction of the crater's ejecta shadow and everything locked into place. North was that way!

He turned to face L-City, knelt, and drew an arrow in the sand and a big L-City for anyone else who might get lost out here. Hoisting Alexsi up, he started shuffling towards his school. He held the map in one hand so he could check it, marking off in his mind the prominent features he passed and making fine corrections to his course.

By 1700 hours, sweat was pouring from his body. In the direct sunlight his cooling and venting system had to work overtime. The weight of Alexsi around his shoulders now bore him down, but he kept going.

Six minutes later, the highest domes of Luna City hove into view as Doran came close to collapsing. The long trek with Alexsi's extra weight had taken its toll, but he still refused to abandon the old miner. This close to L-City others could retrieve the body with no problem, but Doran wanted to be the one who brought him home.

"Almost home," he murmured. "We're going to make it, Alexsi."

At 1845 hours Doran stood hunched in front of the school. It appeared deserted. He almost dropped the miner to the ground as he bent over to catch his breath.

In a few moments he straightened. "Hey, some reception, huh?" His voice rattled. "And after you've been gone for so long, Alexsi."

But wait, someone peered out of the school's window. Nedidi? Yes! Doran flashed him an OK sign, lifted Alexsi over his aching shoulders again, stumbled toward the Mark V Air Beam Hatch and cycled through.

Inside, all his classmates, some crying, tried to hug him. But Nedidi and Stan held them back as Doran dragged himself to a nearby table and laid Alexsi on it. Only then did Doran unlock and remove his helmet. A rush of fresh air and welcoming voices hit him.

"What's wrong with you guys? Why are you all so happy to see me?"

Above the general roar of the class, Stan leaned in. "We thought we'd never see you again."

"We knew you hadn't studied. We thought you were lost or dead." Nedidi wiped his nose. "It's dangerous out there."

"Without you, how would we survive? Who'd look after our p-suits?"

"You're not so bad after all, a little weird, but okay."

"Not a freak. We can hang out."

"Where's Mr. Jaqobi?" Doran asked.

"Twenty minutes ago, when they couldn't raise you on radio, he and your father went off in the lorry to find you."

Doran slapped his comm unit. "The fall must've knocked this out. Wow, my first radio glitch! And they missed me because I didn't come back from the direction they expected."

"What happened, man?"

"I made a detour to find Alexsi and bring him back."

"Who?"

Doran nodded at the p-suit on the table. "Meet Alexsi Golaenski."

"That old miner HomSap?"

"Yeah, that's him. He came back with me. Showed me the way, you know." Doran put his hand on Alexsi's helmet. "This is one historical person I'm glad I got to know."

# Warboots

## Eric Del Carlo

*Eric Del Carlo's short fiction has appeared in* Asimov's, Strange Horizons, Shimmer, Michael Moorcock's New Worlds *and many other venues. He has written novels with Robert Asprin, published by Ace Books and DarkStar Books. His latest novel, an emotionally charged urban fantasy titled* The Golden Gate Is Empty, *which he wrote with his father Vic, is forthcoming from White Cat Publications. Eric lives in his native California. Find him on Facebook for comments or questions.*

Of a supple leather, yellow but not an aggressive yellow, more a wheaty shade, or like gold you might find digging in the Rubble if that gold wasn't buffed to a high gloss. Pliant soles a finger thick. Laced with plaited goat-gut strong as a boat hawser.

Beautiful boots.

Meaningful boots.

Perfect boots.

Sholt meant to earn a pair. Most children who saw Warboots for the first time had the same aspiration, but such enthusiasms and cravings were tossed aside by the wild undulations of puberty, or deliberately canceled when the full effort of the thing was made clear.

But Sholt had never surrendered an iota of his early passion. And now it was just possible he would have his chance to obtain his long-held desire.

There was talk of war between the villages.

In Sholt's ninth autumn the man with the Warboots had come. The boy remembered the time vividly; not so much the adult's features or dress, beyond his remarkable footwear, but his decisive bearing, an unseen force he exuded. Sholt remembered too the way everyone deferred to him. And perhaps more than that: how the man remained calm and confident at the center of it all.

Young – or young*er* – Sholt had fixated on the obvious symbol of the man's prestige, his Warboots. Sholt had heard about them, of course, but this was his first time seeing anyone wear the resplendent foot coverings. The boots took on a rich, profound significance for him. He stared at them in wonder. They were finely made, to be sure: firm yet flexible, durable-looking; far more elaborate than the simple sandals most villagers wore, those who didn't just go barefoot all their lives.

The boots seemed to carry the man with a miraculous ease as he was shown about the village. His was a gliding stride, never a step misplaced, always seeming to arrive just a little ahead of everyone else so although he was being escorted, he really appeared to lead.

The man's visit to the village in Sholt's ninth autumn culminated in a talk he gave, with everyone gathered to hear. He spoke of war in general, then war specifically. It was a very exciting discourse. It only strengthened Sholt's already potent resolve to win Warboots for himself. He would do it. He would wait and watch for the opportunity.

It had taken until Sholt's twelfth spring, but now here was the first real possibility of war. He didn't need to remind himself of the visitor's inspiring depictions of actual warfare. That man with the Warboots had even spoken of the Great Rubblizing Event, the centuries-old cataclysm that had reduced the old civilization to pockets of Rubble, where ambitious diggers still sought useful scraps.

The broad purple lake had drawn Sholt's village to it, first as an encampment for wandering hunters, then as an increasingly lasting community. The lake, with its easy access for small hollowed-tree craft, had attracted the other villages sparsely dotting its meandering irregular edge. Life swam and fermented in the waters, and a small portion of that, extracted by fisherfolk, was enough to sustain the villages. So, food was no reason for war.

Sholt's village was a collection of huts, tidy enclosures which had grown more durable with the years. The culture was a  bright embroidery of genuine history and myth, woven through with all sorts of rituals and ritualistic objects and sayings and wisdoms, all of which were meant to be used skeptically. Good sense and good manners informed the population, mostly.

Today sunlight streamed bright through shreds of cloud. The lake gave off its lush stink.

Sholt wore that sunshine across his narrow shoulders, left bare by his hip-wrap. Today could be very serious. War, the visitor had said, lasted until the goal that had prompted it was achieved or its attainment was proven to be impossible. A war could also end with the death or change of heart of its chief instigator, if there was one.

Walking among the huts, Sholt took the measure of the midday. He knew his home well. The villagers were generations removed from the roving breed who had hunted plains and hills, expending antagonistic energies in useful ways.

It might be said that over the years since settlement alongside the lake, the people of the villages had grown sedentary, if not complacent. The hunting instinct abided, that impulse toward aggression which had once been key to survival. But now the big lake, with its effectively endless supply of food, rendered that aggressive nature worthless. Fishers weren't hunters. They didn't need to be. A fisher only had to be patient.

Parables saturating village culture warned of nurturing the outdated antagonistic instinct. But Sholt's village had fables and stories about every subject, traded endlessly among the inhabitants, and the meanings and imports often got lost amidst the proud panache of the storytellers.

Faces lifted and offered benign or friendly expressions as Sholt passed. The village numbered less than two hundred, and of course he knew every single person. There was solidarity here, and camaraderie, a sense of everyone working with everyone else to keep the place functioning and healthy, a worthwhile community.

The evidence of his fellow villagers' contributions to that

community was everywhere to be seen. The huts were sturdy affairs. They no longer blew apart in spring storms. Women and men had discovered and decided on better building techniques. Drinking water was plentiful. Someone, now an elder in her forty-third summer, had figured out how to strain the lake water. Even the yeasty taste had eventually been filtered out. Boat-building had reached a level of new sophistication, the pinnacle of the skill, it seemed. Village craft were fast and sleek.

Then of course there were the arts. So much singing, so many new songs and dances. And tapestries, and fancy wraps for those who wanted to look gaudy, and paints for faces and bodies. Many of these expressions instantly found ritualistic significance, as well. There was enjoyment in putting esoteric meaning to some showy object. You could attach stories to these works, even harmless little rites.

Sholt's own offerings toward the village's betterment were strewn throughout the surroundings. His contributions were artistic in nature. He had a talent for dipping a reed's sharpened point into liquid clay and tracing lines and waves and every sort of shape onto any available surface, creating images of breathtaking originality. He didn't draw faces or animals or landscapes, as some others did. His scenes did not exist in any real sense. He coaxed them from the depths of his thoughts, from beyond thought, even. He felt, when he did it right, that he was transcribing dreams.

He saw examples of his work from the past few years marking the upright beams of huts, decorating tools and cookware, adorning the backs of mollusk shells. Anyone could ask him to make one of his special works. That was how the village operated. Everyone's abilities were available to everyone else.

The work gave him pride. It increased the prestige of the village as a whole.

That communal pride was a pleasant thing. It was reflected in the amicable greetings he received as he made a circuit of the lakeside village. Today, however, there was something undermining that harmony. He sensed the discordance, like notes that didn't belong in a cheerful song. People moved with a certain tension, with jerks and brusque gestures. Eyes darted too quickly and in unexpected directions. Teeth gnawed lips. People paused in mid-task, in mid-word. Those pauses were fraught with impatience, with anxiety.

The folk of his village were waiting for something, eager for it and uneasy about it.

Now it was Sholt's turn to pause, but he did so for a different, though familiar, reason. His hesitation was diffident, and when his eyes darted away, his lips also curled in ironic self-derision.

Alkin had stepped out of a hut, almost directly into his path.

Sholt brought his gaze back to her. "Hello," he said, pleased the simple greeting come out steadily.

Alkin's normally bright smile didn't quite surface on her face. It struggled onto her lips, then sank like a flower sucked under by marsh mud. She shared in the general tension, Sholt saw. In her arms was a basket full of eel-skins.

"What have you got there?" he asked, testing his voice further. Sometimes, in Alkin's presence, he stammered or simply lost the sense of his words.

She was his age, lithe, with taut, slim muscles. The wrap she wore covered her torso. Her shoulders were painted pink. He realized he had seen this same coloring several times today. "Halz," she said, glancing down into her basket, "has an idea for sashes, with the dried skins. They'd be worn like —" Using just her pink shoulders and her chin, she managed to convey how the skins would be worn, looping under one arm and draping across the chest. New sartorial accessories were always welcome. But Sholt guessed these sashes had a different purpose.

The man in the Warboots had spoken of uniforms, an ancient affectation. Different costumes worn by the competing sides. The notion had intrigued Sholt deeply.

"You've got a lot there," he said.

"Halz said we might need even more." It was her voice that quivered now. She was excited and frightened, Sholt noted, just like everybody.

If war came, she would go. He wanted to say something direct to her, for once, but bashfulness overtook him whenever he dealt with Alkin. There was nothing in village culture that said he should stammer and stumble in her presence.

If she went to war, he would fear for her.

The direct words he wanted to summon failed him yet again; he merely smiled and stepped out of her way and went on his own.

He found Halz next.

A site of Rubble lay two days' running from the lake. The area was roughly the same size as the lake itself, spread across an open plain, its borders delineated by generations of diggers. Halz was a digger. The decayed accoutrements of the previous civilization engrossed him, and such items were only to be found buried beneath layers of dirt and stone.

Sholt came upon the older, larger boy next to a fire that burned hotly in the midday. He had scraps and length of metal and metaplastic laid out on the ground before him. His heavy hands worked diligently with the pieces. Sholt watched as he ran a sharpening stone along the edge of a narrow section of dull, sturdy-looking metal, which he then plunged into the fire's fiercest embers.

Halz was sitting on the ground, his meaty thighs bunched beneath him. Apparently he had been aware of Sholt's presence all along, because he looked up with an unsurprised smile. His eyes were as dully colored as the salvaged metals, but like that metal, he had put a threatening edge to them.

"Hello," Halz said, making the greeting first.

"Hello. I saw Alkin with her eel-skins. She mentioned you."

"Sashes. Just a thought I had." Halz too bore pink shoulders and a chest painted blue. Sholt wore no body coloring today. He preferred a simple look.

Halz liked Alkin, Sholt knew. And maybe she liked him. Again, Sholt had never been able to speak to the girl about it.

"You want to fancy something up?" Halz asked.

"Sure."

The bigger boy picked up one of the implements he'd been working on. It was a segment of metaplastic, this a cloudy orange color, half as long as Sholt's bony forearm, with a point at one end and the other wrapped in tough crawlerfish skin.

"I tried to make it like the tools the hunters used to carry," Halz said, holding up the instrument. The boy, a year older than Sholt, had something of that streak of hunter aggressiveness in him.

"I can decorate the blade, if you want," Sholt said.

"That would be good."

It was the smallest of the implements laid out near the fire and the sharpening stones. It was the one Halz probably thought scrawny, sensitive Sholt could handle, should he decide to join in the coming war. If indeed war did come.

Sholt held the edged tool, weighing it, learning its balance. Halz wasn't this potential war's instigator. It had no single instigator. War was approaching like a mood, like a seasonal change, a gradual gathering. Sholt had already planned to be a part of it.

He left Halz and walked toward the lake's edge. He wore sandals, but he stepped out of these before he crossed the mud and got into a small, untended dugout. He set the weapon down and took up the broad, hardy, veiny fireleaf that served as a paddle. He would not wear those sandals again. He would have his Warboots, whatever the cost.

•••

Halfway across the lake he had scooped two handfuls of the reeky surface froth and plastered it over his long, dark hair, raking the strands back severely. By the time he put in to the far shore, the pasty stuff had set. It was how hair was generally arranged in this village on the opposite side of the large lake.

There was little design variation in the dugout canoes each village fashioned from downed trees, so his landing at an empty point along the shore called no attention. He slipped Halz' edged instrument into a fold of his hip-wrap and made his way, barefoot, toward the enemy village.

The villagers here weren't enemies, not yet. No one had given voice to this war. But acquaintance had become rivalry. The two villages were of course each aware of each other, with knowledge of the other's strengths and artistic resources. Sholt's village had many proud artisans and artists. So did the inhabitants of this village on the opposite brim of the lake.

Villages didn't have names; you named people and animals, not places. But it might be, with five distinct populations now settled on the lake's edge, that one day names would have to be applied. What a strange notion, but Sholt could foresee it. Presently, you just called a place by how it related to your home – its direction, its distance.

He walked into the foreign village now, head down, moving quietly. Even so, he studied his surroundings with avid interest. There was a kind of general communication among the lakeside villages. Fishers met out on the water. Sometimes parties foraging for timber encountered one another in the forested tracts. Information was exchanged. So were boasts. It was how the rivalry had come about.

The huts here were of a slightly different construction, though Sholt, not being a builder, couldn't see precisely how the enclosures varied; only that they seemed wider across their fronts, with colorful shells epoxied to the support beams. The shanties were laid out as randomly as they were in Sholt's home village.

Yet this *wasn't* his home. He was keenly of this fact. The sense of alienness suffusing the scene was almost too much to bear. It shook him at the roots of his being. He had never traveled to another village before, never been to any strange place. But he had come here today, because it was absolutely necessary that he do so.

He hadn't decorated himself in any ostentatious way, and so he moved in nondescript fashion among the first people he encountered. No one gave him a glance. Everybody appeared busy with tasks. He sensed the urgency of these activities, and he thought he discerned, beneath that urgency, a familiar thrum of tension, of anticipation.

These people too, it seemed, were readying for war.

He walked a dozen more steps, coming to a place where a cooking fire trailed threads of smoke, before someone turned, glanced his way, peered more closely, then gave a loud cry of alarm.

Sholt halted. Immediately he was surrounded, though none of these foreigners came within reaching distance of him.

"I'm from across the lake. My name is Sholt." It was a monstrously strange thing to have to tell people his name. But he was again pleased that his voice didn't quaver. It was even steadier than when he had spoken to Alkin earlier. For a moment her image filled his head, all the limber lines of her, the softness of her face. Then she vanished, and he saw only these others, many adults, all staring at him in astonishment.

"You..." a woman said, gesturing in confusion and unease, "you shouldn't be here."

"That is true."

A man with a heavy brow made more prominent by his raked back hair edged half a step closer to Sholt. He was knotted with muscle, and had an implement in hand, something for digging or maybe smashing. The handle was elaborately carved, a skill this village was known for.

"What do you want?" the woman asked, and something in her tone seemed to cause the muscular man to retreat back into the rank encircling Sholt.

An uprooted stump sat next to the cooking fire, where a pot simmered with sharply scented contents. A fireleaf rested atop the stump. Maybe these people used the leaf in their cooking. Again this was a strange and alien thing to Sholt.

"I can do this," he said, and he crossed toward the stump and fire. Movement rippled among the onlookers. He felt the tension acutely now, the peril. Violence waited. Anything might tip it into motion.

He picked a charred piece from the edge of the fire, then sat before the stump. Feeling the many eyes and terribly aware of the tool in the muscled man's hand, he started to trace shapes onto the pale face of the fireleaf. He didn't work from any preconceived imagery; he never did. He just let the figures flow – the lines, the curves. These were echoes of dreams, bits of pure imagination plucked from nothingness and given substance in the real world. Sweat stood out on his forehead and dotted the center of his back. The charcoal scraped the surface of the leaf.

After several long moments, he had reached the end. The image was done. To add to it would only spoil it. Even so, he was reluctant to set down his drawing implement, to sit back on his knees and give these others a chance to fully see what he had wrought.

Some gasped. Others made musical mutterings that must be the idiosyncratic rituals of this village.

"Sholt," said the woman.

He found her face among the crowding others. More people had come. By now he was fairly engulfed in the strange villagers. He gave the woman a confirming nod. They knew his work. His fellow villagers had boasted of his artistic outputs. His was a unique talent. It gave his village substantial prestige.

When he took the metaplastic blade out of the fold of his hip-wrap, his audience retreated several steps in fear, even the threatening man with the heavy brow. The woman, who had a sharp, knowing look in her eyes and cheeks smeared with red clay, flinched but did not recoil.

It was awkward, handling the knife with his left hand, but he had to lay his right hand on the stump, next to the fireleaf he had decorated. He splayed his fingers, pressed his palm hard to the wood. He didn't trust himself to make a chop, so he set the weapon's edge over the base knuckle of his right index finger, laid all the muscle and weight of his spindly body onto the handle of the instrument, let out a fierce cry, and severed the finger from his hand.

The pain was mind-altering. It sent him into a white, freezing realm where he wandered lost awhile, until hot motes intruded and melted the landscape. He panted and bled and felt tears running freely, and he knew these were only partly in answer to the enormous pain.

He looked down on the blood-spattered stump, at his lonely finger separated from his hand.

The woman had knelt on the other side of the stump. She pressed a cloth to his wound. Sholt's whole hand throbbed, and the pain climbed to his elbow, to his shoulder, yet it was more bearable than it had been a moment before.

"You will still be able to draw," she said, and though her tone was soft, her words carried to all the others.

He had to deliberately gather breath to speak. "Not as well." It was true. He might learn to hold a reed dipped in liquid clay, to drag it across surfaces to make shapes, but they would no longer be *his* shapes.

Sholt tossed down the metaplastic knife. He shoved the fireleaf that bore his final work of art across the stump to the woman, clutched his hand and the bloodied cloth to his chest, stood and started back to where he'd left his dugout.

•••

The person with the Warboots came in his twelfth winter.

Sholt had become a digger, working often with Halz. He liked going to the Rubble and was good at finding the little treasures buried in the stony ground. He had an aptitude for the job, if not any unique flair.

The adult with the Warboots this time was a woman, and her boots were just as splendid as the ones Sholt had seen in his ninth autumn. But the sight of them did not fill him this time with that same frenetic passion. They didn't cause his heart to soar.

After the woman gave her talk to the village, she came to Sholt and wanted to speak to him alone. She had learned what he had done, of course. Everyone was still eager to talk about how he had put off the war. It was the kind of big, selfless act he had dreamt about since he was a boy.

They sat on rocks by the brink of the moonlit lake. Small splashings sounded at irregular intervals. An empty boat creaked nearby.

"These should fit," she said, holding out the Warboots from

her traveling sack. "I get to touch with our base every two years or so for more pairs." Her sack looked fairly full.

He took the boots and rested them on his knees. He had been barefoot since spring. Even the winter chill didn't bother him anymore.

The boots were magnificent, the same shape and shade and construction as the pair he had first coveted, so long ago now.

"You'll be walking a lot," the woman told him tiredly.

He nodded. He would wear his Warboots and travel from place to place, to all the sites where people were clustering, where populations were growing, where one people might chafe against another. One of the reasons he liked digging so much was that it reminded him how huge the Great Rubblization had been, and how centuries later it still needed to be spoken of, its dreadful lessons pounded home, endlessly. Or else people would forget. And make those same mistakes again.

Sholt looked up at the woman, finding her expression as grim as the one he felt weighing on his own face. Her left eye was missing, the socket a hollow of aged scar tissue.

With a bleak finality he put the Warboots on his feet, did up the laces with his nine fingers, and stood.

# The Rum Cake Runner
## Jessi Cole Jackson

*Jessi Cole Jackson is an MFA student in children's literature at Hollins University. Her work has been published in* Crossed Genres Magazine, Every Day Fiction *and podcasted at* Cast of Wonders. *When she's not writing (or reading!) she makes costumes for a Tony Award-winning theatre and lives with her husband in the prettiest part of New Jersey (though she's not from there).*

Sitting on the threadbare sagging couch cushion, Nesi tied her Sneaks' laces tight, double knotting the loops. The apartment was warm, as it always was, and smelled sweet, as it always did.

"And pick up those vanilla beans before making your rounds," Uncle Toni said. "It's important."

Her head whipped up. "No way! I'd have to go to the market with a full load."

He just shrugged. "If you go after your deliveries again today, Rohit will have closed up shop again and we need it for tonight. No arguments."

"The mutts'll sniff me out for sure! I'll be a wafting target," Nesi said.

Nonna chuckled from her old wooden rocker in the corner. "She's just like you, Antonio. She doesn't understand how to *not* argue." She rocked and knit, her work already done for the day despite the early hour. They could bake the sweets Nesi was responsible for delivering anytime, but the bread making – the smaller, but only legitimate aspect of the De Luca family business – had to be done at night so it was fresh each morning.

Uncle Toni handed Nesi a red cap. "Wear this one today and be sure to turn it on. You'll be fine at the market." Sweat stained and faded, it was in much worse shape than her regular cap.

"This thing doesn't even work half the time!" she said. What good was AI detection software if it never worked? She smacked the dirty cap against her palm. Maybe she could jostle it hard enough that it'd actually warn her. "Who's going to bail me out when I get snagged by the coppers?"

"I will, little one," Nonna said, her low voice creaking and groaning like the chair she rocked.

"You want me to give the best route we've got to Beto?" Uncle Toni said. "Put on the cap and get your butt out the door. You're gonna be late for everyone."

Nesi rolled her eyes but put the filthy thing on her head, pushing her shaggy black bangs to the side so they weren't in her face. She kissed Nonna and walked out the door, a small white paper bag in one hand and the rest of the day's deliveries in her nylon backbag.

•••

She'd barely made it down the three flights of rickety steps before she had her first customer.

Old Mr. Yan sat on his cement step, his dirty shoes resting in the even dirtier gutter. "Hello Nesi. Two almond biscotti, please," he said.

He held out his wrist so she could scan it for credits. Uncle Toni preferred to be paid by cash, but Nesi didn't care. Payment was payment – so what if credits had to be made clean? That was why they baked all night and her older cousins sold bread in the market. Everyone knew you couldn't actually make any profit on that sort of baking.

Nesi handed Mr. Yan the small white paper sack and droned the line she was supposed to recite after every purchase. "And remember, always buy your pastries from De Luca. We're fresh. We're discreet. We have the best sweets in New Rio."

They did the same thing every morning, which was okay with Nesi. She hadn't even bothered to pack Mr. Yan's order away with the rest of the little white bags since her first week on the job, three years ago. He may be predictable, but predictable made running pastries easier.

"Thanks Mister!" she said and dragged herself off down a narrow alley, the opposite way of all her scheduled deliveries. She wished she could follow her normal route – after all, she rarely got into any trouble that way. But orders were orders and if she came home without the vanilla beans again, Uncle Toni would give her route to Beto and she'd have to spend another two years drumming up new customers.

•••

She'd made it down the couple of stone stairs and a single step into the marketplace before bumping into another shopper.

"Watch out you little *malcriada*," an old lady hissed, shaking a wrinkled fist in Nesi's face.

She ducked away quickly to avoid getting whacked. "*Desculpe*," she called over her shoulder, but a sea of people had already separated them.

Stupid Uncle Toni.

Mornings were the worst time to come to the market – full of tiny, hunched Asian ladies like that old crone, young bottle-blonde women with brown eyed babies strapped to their chests, half-rusted androids overloaded by goods, and olive skinned errand runners like her ducking and darting through the crowd. And they were all haggling over whatever goods they'd chosen, scanning credits, trying to pack too much into their too small totes.

Even if this went well, which she still doubted, it would take her forever just to get through all of these people. Hopefully, her customers would wait for her and wouldn't buy sweets from any of the other runners.

"Hey kid!" someone shouted behind her.

She turned, her best salesgirl smile on her face, expecting someone to have recognized her uniform – green pants, white shirt with the De Luca family's emblem on the chest, red cap – and wanted to place a quick order. It would be odd to buy from her in the middle of the market, but it happened sometimes. She wouldn't turn away the business.

But when she turned, she couldn't see around the people closest to her. Who had yelled? She shrugged and turned back toward the merchant stalls. There was a lot of shouting in the crowded market. If there was no business to be had, she needed to just keep fording through people. Get to Rohit Rangan. Buy his vanilla beans.

Then a warning 'EEP!' from the mutt sensor in the cap screeched in her ear. Incoming trouble.

She looked back again in the direction of the voice and locked eyes with a man in a dark blue uniform. A copper. *Merda!*

She heard a harsh, mechanical bark. She jumped, clicking her heels together to turn on her HoverSneaks. She had to get away, quick.

She hadn't seen the mutts, but she knew they must be with the coppers. Even when faulty, the warning system in her cap didn't activate just for the men, and that tinny bark sounded close.

Holding on tight to the straps of her backbag, she zipped forward, fast, aiming for a small gap in the crowd ahead of her. She just hoped all of the old biddies wouldn't leave the same sort of gap between her and the law.

"I'm sorry!" she called out when she careened into a particularly frail looking lady. The lady's middle-aged son glared at Nesi over his mother's head. She covered the family emblem on her chest with her hand and tried to just keep moving forward.

Stupid Uncle Toni.

If she could just keep ahead of the coppers, she would be okay. The mutts could have caught her easily, but after that incident in the northwest market last month, laws changed. Now they had to be kept on a short eLeash.

A Único rolled on its rusty single wheel into her escape route, cutting her off. Its little plastic back basket, full to the brim with the harvest's best root vegetables and mangoes, was rigged on with tape and wires.

Nesi grabbed its slim polyvinyl shoulders and pushed the little android from behind.

"Oh my!" its tiny metallic voice squeaked, no doubt shocked by its sudden burst of speed. It probably hadn't moved that fast in ten years.

She shoved it gently to the side, out of her path, so she could squeeze past. That model was notorious for tipping over when jostled and the last thing Nesi needed was to be tripping over cassava, yams, and Mallika.

The mutts' hollow barks sounded closer. She looked at the roofs of the buildings surrounding the square. The vanilla beans would wait for another day, another time. She needed to get out of the market, now. If only the Sneaks could make her fly.

The coppers she could handle. Even if they caught her, they would just throw her in a cell overnight with the other runners, try to charge her with selling illegal goods, and so what? She was a kid according to the law – still not fifteen. They'd let her and any cellmates go within twenty-four hours.

But if the mutts got a hold of you, they were known for never letting go until you were broken and bleeding. And most of the time, they didn't care if you were a legitimate delivery boy carrying French loaves or someone like her, with much less legitimate product.

She angled her body to move faster through the crowd, wishing she could scream at everyone to just get out of her way. But that would do her no good, just give the coppers a more specific point in the crowd to convey on.

"Walnuts today, Nesi!" Mac, the nut seller, yelled when she whizzed past his stall.

"I think I'll come back later!" she called back, making the big man laugh loudly.

"Little runners need to wrap their stashes better so the mutts can't detect them!" he called at her retreating back, laughing and laughing. His booming chuckles carried across the entire square.

Best thing about ol' Mac – he was loud. Thank God.

Market browsers of all ages now noticed her in her delivery uniform, full pack strapped to her back, trying to escape from the two coppers and their slobbering electro-mutts. And once they noticed her, they began to make a way for her, whispering quick encouragements before filling in behind her.

One thing that was always certain about the residents of New Rio: they would help Nesi however they could to keep her goods out of the hands of the law. Sugar had been an illegal substance before even ancient Nonna was born, but that hadn't stopped people from consuming it.

"Make a way!" she heard one of the coppers say.

"Move!" the other one yelled, followed by swearing.

Soon enough, she reached the old sandstone steps that led out of the market square. She turned to be sure she had made a clear escape and saw her pursuers in the middle of the courtyard, pressed in a sea of bodies. It looked like the shoppers closest to them were talking – playing the role of concerned citizens. But maybe it wasn't an act – it wasn't very often a citizen caught a copper by his ear. Maybe they were asking for aid to catch the thief of a stolen watch or complaining about the state of the trash collecting robots.

Both coppers looked out above the heads of the crowd at Nesi, who was easy to spot hovering just above a step in the middle of the colorful, tiled stairway. She smiled and gave a little wave, kicked off the hover feature to save the battery and landed with a little puff of dirt.

She turned and left the scene, saying a quick prayer of thanks. They would never find her in the winding labyrinth of streets that was New Rio, even with the mutts. Runners knew the streets better than anyone, Nesi better than most runners.

She was hot, dusty and relieved. She had made it, at least. Without the vanilla beans, but she'd check again at the end of the day. And if Rohit Rangan was closed, then stupid Uncle Toni could come down tomorrow morning and fetch them himself. Her job was running pastries, not errands.

Now on to the day's deliveries.

•••

Hours later, Nesi trudged back into the market. It had been a long day walking her way around the city, hot in the autumn sun. After the morning's incident, she hadn't even been able to hover. Her Sneaks were almost out of juice. At least she'd been successful – only two small bags of product left. Perfect.

She made her way over to Mac's stall just in time. He was packing up for the night.

"Hey Mac, wanna do some business?" she called out when she got close.

He glanced over a thick shoulder and smiled. "Hey little Nesi! Nice flying today." He set down a crate of black walnuts and came over to other side of the rickety table he called a counter.

She grinned and with a flourish of her hand, bowed to the big man. "I do what I can, sir, to entertain the masses."

He laughed hard at the little joke, slapping his thigh. His face turned a bright cherry red. Mac always laughed too loud and too hard and too long. Eventually, he calmed down enough to say, "So you want to do some business, little lady? Finished up your delivery boy tasks for the day?"

"That I have."

"Got a list for me?"

She glanced around the square, craning her neck to see if old Rohit Rangan was still around, but the spice seller's shop was closed up tight for the night. Uncle Toni wouldn't have his vanilla for the night's baking then. He'd have to come down himself to get his precious beans.

The whole place was nearly deserted, totally empty of other customers with only a few vendors packing up their little shops.

"Pecans, almond flour, and a whole bag of those walnuts from the US," Nesi said.

"You want shelled or unshelled?"

She sighed. "Unshelled if they're cheaper."

He chuckled. "They always are, Ness."

She took the bag off of her shoulders and unzipped an outer pouch that would turn into a shopping tote. She held it out to Mac, still folded.

He shook it out, but before leaving the counter, raised an eyebrow in the direction of her main bag. It sat on the counter, not quite flat.

"Got anything to trade, or will this all be on credit today little *menina*?"

She opened the main compartment of her bag and pulled out two white paper sacks. "A little trade, a little credit," she said. She gestured to the tote he held. "Now fill that up."

He guffawed and walked back to the crate full of the unshelled black walnuts. He filled the little tote full to the brim with the small lime green spheres, some of which were already half crumbled away from the black shells. She really hated shelling the things – by the time she got done her hands would be black and the stain stuck around for weeks, but Nonna insisted. Unshelled were cheaper.

Mac brought the bag back, hoisted it up to the counter, and took a second tote Nesi had unzipped off of the main compartment of her backbag. "Anything worthwhile?" he asked, gesturing toward the little white bags still sitting on the counter.

She nodded and held one out to him. He took it quickly with a big meaty hand, greedy to see what Nesi had left from her daily deliveries. "A couple of avocado brigadiero and a mini rum cake," she said.

He opened the bag just barely and took a big sniff. His eyes rolled back in his head with pleasure.

"See this," he said, "is why you need one of them scent-preventing bags. Those mutts can spot you from a kilometer away!"

Nesi laughed. "Yeah? You think Uncle Toni would spring for one of those? They're like five times as much as the Sneaks and I had to pay for those myself!"

"Yeah, that's what makes Antonio a good business man, right there."

"What? Not giving a *titica* about his favorite niece and best runner?"

Mac waved a dismissive paw. "Nah. It keeps you on your toes, moving fast. Besides, you turned on those fancy hover shoes today, and they just made you bump into a whole lotta people you could have avoided."

She rolled her eyes.

"You almost knocked over that sweet little old lady," he said.

"What? Where? I've never met a sweet old lady in this whole town," she said and made him laugh and laugh again.

"Alright, alright, I'll have to go to the back for what you really came for," he said with a wink and pulled her cap down over her eyes.

Nesi pushed it up and glanced around quickly even though most everyone else was gone. She didn't want the wrong vendor to overhear and snitch Mac out.

"Castanhas-do-pará and coconut flour!" she yelled to make sure no one got any ideas.

He raised a hand to say he heard her already.

After a few minutes of waiting, Mac came back out, lugging her second tote now full of bags of sugar, up to his counter. The little table shook when he set it down. Nesi was going to have a long walk home based on that thud.

"That's four and a half *quilos* of granulated white gold, my little friend."

Nesi's eyes widened. "Why so much?" It was twice the normal amount. Nonna would be as pleased as peaches.

Might even make Uncle Toni forget that she didn't get the vanilla.

"Eh, my other regular hasn't been by in a while." He chuckled. "Maybe the mutts caught him distributing."

"What?! Your *other* regular? Mac, you hurt my heart," she thumped her scrawny chest. "Right here. It wounds me that you'd sell to our competition." It didn't wound her any that their competition mighta been picked up by the coppers.

Mac just waved away her melodrama. "A man's gotta eat, and that sweet little Vietnamese kid buys a lot of sesame paste

– something your operation's never even heard of. And he's a lot nicer than you are."

"You selling your best black market product to the squints, Mac?"

"Hey now. None of that talk. Besides, a credit's a credit my little lass. If I cared about such things, do you think I'd sell to a *Carcamano* like you?"

She held out her arm. "Yeah, yeah. Take what I owe you, you filthy bourgeois pig."

He scanned her, taking his credits quickly and efficiently. Any other merchant in the whole place and Nesi would've bargained and battled for a solid half hour before agreeing on a price, but she'd been coming to Mac for years. Unless there was some sort of shortage, his prices stayed the same for her.

He snatched up the other treat in its little white bag, peeked inside and said, "These guys'll be for the missus." He gave her a little salute with his empty hand. "Nice doing business with you, Ness."

She nodded, slung her now empty backbag onto her shoulders and picked up the totes from the counter.

●●●

Nesi was barely up the stairs and out of the market when a hand grabbed the back of her shirt at the neck.

Instinctively, she ducked and lunged forward, hard, and felt her shirt slip free.

Nesi did not turn. She did not check over her shoulder to see who'd been waiting in the shadows to grab her or what their motive may be. Instead, she ran as fast as she could, gripping the too heavy totes tightly.

Ducking down a narrow alley between a yellow house and a blue, boarded up building, Nesi clicked her heels together and willed her Sneaks to have juice left in them. They coughed briefly to life, shooting her three meters forward before they sputtered and died.

Behind her, heavy footfalls pounded a steady rhythm.

She pushed herself to run faster, risking only one more quick hop to try and revive the Sneaks, but it was no use. She'd used most of their battery during the market escape.

Nesi turned another corner and another, twisting and twirling her way through every back alley and secret passage she'd ever used as a shortcut or a hideout.

Finally, she risked a glance over her shoulder. She saw nothing. She slowed to a jog and readjusted her totes in her hands. She'd lost a few walnut spheres along the way, but the precious sugar was safe and snug in its paper bags inside her tote.

She kept moving forward toward home while checking her supplies, which meant she was looking down when she bumped into the chest of her pursuer.

"*Filho da puta!*" She spun away, but it was too late. Somehow he'd gotten in front of her, and now a copper had a large hand wrapped around her skinny bicep.

She could wiggle free if she dropped her tote, but it contained a week's sugar supply. She couldn't abandon their most precious, and most expensive, ingredient in the dirty gutter.

"Let me go," she said, "I've done nothing wrong!" She tugged and flailed and squirmed, holding tight to the sugar, but the copper held even tighter to her arm.

"Please calm down," he said between heavy breaths.

She had a brief moment of wonder that he spoke to her kindly and calmly, but she was too smart to be fooled by a gentle tone of voice. She did not calm down or stop trying to get away.

He raised the hand not holding her and she flinched, thinking he was going to hit her, but he only held a small, dingy piece of paper in her face.

"You're not in trouble!" he said, thrusting the paper under her nose. She flinched again. "I need your help. I need a sweet. Here, this is a recipe. People said the De Luca's are the best at new product, that you try things from all over the world."

Nesi stopped struggling to peer at the paper. She didn't know what it said, of course, having never bothered to learn to read useless books, but she knew how to read people. This copper was desperate.

"I'll let you go if you promise not to run," he said. "Please,

please don't run."

He slowly let go of her arm.

She didn't move, though she remained ready to bolt at the slightest indication of a trap.

But what would be the point of trying to trap her? She was already caught, and carrying enough sugar to get locked up for a very long time, minor or no. If he wanted to find her family, that was easy enough to do. He could have just followed her home, or followed his nose.

It was easy enough to find pastries in New Rio.

It was harder to pin something on the families that made them.

"Please," he said again.

"What do you need it for?" Nesi asked, skeptical but curious.

"It's an old family recipe, from the States. My grandpa copper used to love it and he's dyi—." A tear ran down the copper's dark brown cheeks.

Nesi set down her tote of walnuts and snatched the paper. She pretended to study it, mostly to avoid the awkwardness of watching a copper cry. She shoved the meaningless scrap in her pocket.

"Can you make it?"

"I'm no baker," she said.

"Your family then. Can they do it?"

"Why're you so desperate?" she asked.

"My grandpa's dying. All he talks about is the old days and how much he loved—" The copper looked around him, making sure no one's listening.

Nesi didn't have the heart to tell him that even if someone had overheard, no one in their favela cared one ounce about a corrupt copper.

"My family can make anything," Nesi said, "But that doesn't mean they will. I make no promises." She moved around the copper, heading toward home.

"Of course, of course. Thank you. I'll owe you." Just before she turned a corner, he called out: "How will I find you?"

Nesi smiled. "Don't worry your pretty head about it, copper, sir. I'm the best runner in all of New Rio. If we're gonna do business, I'll find you."

•••

Nesi climbed up the three rickety staircases, threw open the front door and danced through the living room where rack upon rack of cakes and cannoli shells cooled, waiting to be stuffed and packaged and sent out with the runners first thing tomorrow morning.

She finally dropped the totes when she made it to the kitchen. Nonna and Uncle Toni were already working away. Perfect. She would need them both to agree to the plan she had worked up on the way over.

She said her hellos to Uncle Toni, gave the required kisses to Nonna, and pulled out the old recipe.

"So I nearly got caught by the coppers in the market this morning."

They both stopped what they were doing and looked at her.

"Obviously you got away," Uncle Toni said. His hands were covered in dough and little pine nuts, but he stepped away from the pignoli he'd been balling.

"Yeah. No sweat. Even better though, apparently one of them has a sweet tooth. He went through Mac to give us this." A small lie, but she didn't want Uncle Toni having a heart attack in the kitchen. He had baking to do.

"Some sort of recipe?" Nonna asked, but Nesi didn't hand it over yet.

"I thought maybe we could make whatever's on here and sell 'em special. Since it came to us as a special request we could charge extra. It could make us a nice profit and create some goodwill, maybe. It wouldn't hurt to have friends among the coppers. The other families do."

Nonna and Uncle Toni shared a look.

Uncle Toni nodded. "We could always use friends. Let's see it."

Nesi handed the paper to Nonna, who had the cleaner hands of the two. Uncle Toni moved to read over his mother's shoulder.

"Seems simple enough. We could do these." Nonna said.

Uncle Toni laughed. "Well done, kid. Looks like we just got a new menu item and an important customer. Want to be the first one to try the De Luca family's brand new..." He squinted at the piece of paper. "...jelly donut?"

Nesi grinned. Did she ever. Trying new product was the biggest perk of a runner's job.

# Leafheart

## Anne E. Johnson

*Anne E. Johnson lives in Brooklyn. Her short speculative fiction for young readers has appeared in the* 2015 Young Explorer's Adventure Guide, Rainbow Rumpus, Spaceports & Spidersilk, FrostFire Worlds *(home to her Koob & Akilah dragon series), and elsewhere. She also writes short and long fiction for adults. As a way to give back, Anne is a long-time volunteer story judge at the website RateYourStory, and her "Kid Lit Insider" column about the children's lit industry appears weekly on EatSleepWrite.net. Learn more about Anne on her website, AnneEJohnson.com.*


Her birth name was Harra, but everyone in the village of Deraheib called her Leafheart. She took comfort in the nickname. Ever since Papa died fighting the rebels, Leafheart decided she loved plants more than people.

She trusted plants.

A month after the rainy season, tiny yellow petals covered the chrysanthemum bushes by the stream. Every year. People weren't like that. People changed. Or they disappeared forever.

Leafheart was on her way to visit Minoo, a village elder, to get herbs for her mother. Mama used to be strong and happy. Since Papa died, she was droopy and sad. Some days she never got up from her sleeping pallet.

As she walked along the dirt path, Leafheart stopped to wrap her toes around a tough stalk of wild sorghum growing straight up through the stones. *Plants have no fear.* She stroked the tendrils on a clump of its dark red blossoms. *And plants are always beautiful.*

"Hey, Leafheart?" a bunch of village boys called, hanging upside down from the branches of an acacia tree. "Met any nice flowers lately?" asked one.

"I bet she wants to marry this tree," said another.

The boys laughed and slapped their chests, but Leafheart knew they must be scared. Rebels were everywhere. Soon those boys would have to become soldiers. She caught the eye of Tabal, a tall and skinny kid with knobby knees. He looked away, as if he were ashamed of the company he kept. Smiling at him slightly, Leafheart went on her way.

Like everyone in Deraheib, Minoo lived in a tukul, a hut with a thatched roof shaped like a cone. Before Leafheart reached Minoo's home, Leafheart paused to gaze at the Red Sea Hills on the horizon. She loved how their gray stone sliced into the sky. They were more mountains than hills. Deep crevices cut through their sides, up and down from their peaks to the ground.

As she looked around, her eye fell on a stack of brush a few meters off the road. The meadow was just long grasses and wildflowers, so she wondered why the twigs were there.

"Harra! Stop your daydreaming." Minoo stood in the doorway of her tukul. The shawl wrapped around her waist emphasized her wide hips. Her feet, as usual, were wrapped in yellow cloths she'd dipped in camphor. She always smelled like healing herbs. "I can't stand here all day on these aching joints."

Leafheart hurried forward, head bowed. "I am sorry your joints ache."

The old woman backed into her hut so Leafheart could enter. "What were you thinking about outside? Your eyes searched for something in a different world."

"Just a pile of twigs, auntie." Embarrassed, Leafheart shrugged.

"You really love plants, don't you?"

*Someday I will go to the city of Khartoum and become a great plant scientist.* Leafheart didn't think Minoo would understand, so she just shrugged and said, "They're pretty."

"Being pretty is the least important thing about plants." From a clay jar, Minoo pulled a small bag of brown shavings. "Here's ginger root for your mama's headaches. You remember how to steep it to make tea?"

"I remember." Leafheart and her sister had steeped medicinal tea for Mama more times than they could count.

Minoo pulled down a smaller jar. This one had a lid. With a wooden spoon she scooped out a dollop of goo. "Acacia oil and clarified butter." She scraped it into a plastic bowl. "Rub it on her muscles. I need the bowl back."

"Yes, auntie."

As Leafheart took the bowl, she was surprised that Minoo reached out and touched her face. Her old fingers felt dry against her cheek. "You have spirit ears, leaf-hearted Harra. Don't just look at the plants. Listen to them. One day you will learn something from them that no one else can hear."

Leafheart's mind swirled as she left the tukul. Her mama waited for her medicine, and Leafheart had promised to pound some spelt grain so they could make porridge. But that pile of twigs across the road called to her.

It wasn't made of sorghum grass. Or combretum shrubs. Or birch branches. The brush pile wasn't made of any plant Leafheart knew in the area. And she knew all of them, thanks to a book a traveling teacher gave her once. *Plants of Egypt and the Sudan* was her favorite possession. She couldn't understand all the paragraphs, but she memorized the fancy words naming all the pictures.

Leafheart decided to take Minoo's advice and listen. "What *are* you?" she asked the pile of twigs. She could have sworn they rustled slightly.

The closer she stepped, the more certain she was these were not ordinary twigs. Under their drab bark, Leafheart saw faint traces of every color of the rainbow. What had looked like nicks and knots from across the road now seemed more like notches, carefully carved into them. And then there was the smell. The twigs gave off a peculiar scent Leafheart couldn't identify.

"What are you sniffing, Leafheart?" The two village women staring at her carried baskets to fill at the market. "Don't you have chores?" asked the one in the red and black dress.

Not wanting trouble, Leafheart ran back to the road. "Can't you smell that?" Closing her eyes, she sniffed the hot afternoon air. "Like salt and berries and gasoline and donkey dung and…"

"Child!" scolded the woman in green and yellow. "We have too much work to stand around smelling twigs."

The one in red narrowed her eyes. "You're the one who refused to help pull the seeds out of water lilies last year when the whole village was hungry."

"I remember that," scoffed the woman in green and yellow. "You said they were too beautiful to eat. What a crazy girl. That lotus-seed porridge saved us."

Leafheart looked at her feet. The woman spoke the truth. But it still made Leafheart sad to picture how they tore up all those gorgeous white flowers.

"Go home to your family," said the woman in red.

"Yes, aunties." Leafheart tried to look sheepish. But as soon as the women moved out of earshot, she turned to the twigs with a smile. "I'll be back soon."

•••

Early the next morning, Leafheart and her sister, Subin, headed to the well, clay pots on their heads. Being small, Leafheart carried only a short, fat pot. But Subin was a tall young woman. Her water jug was tall and curvy, just like she was.

Halfway to the well, they passed the weird brush pile. Some blackbirds stood on top, pecking for insects.

"Wait!" Leafheart set down her pot. Rushing toward the twigs, she flailed her arms and shouted, "Shoo! Get off! Fly away!" She even threw a stone, being careful not to hit the pile. Finally the pesky birds flew off.

Subin's face looked pained. "Leave the birds alone and let's go. These pots are heavy, and they don't even have water in them yet."

Leafheart hurried back to the road. Once they reached the

well, her sister gossiped with other teen girls. Leafheart wandered in a big circle, bored and restless.

"Hey, Leafheart," someone called.

She turned to see Damdoum smiling and waving. One of his hands gripped the handle of a wheelbarrow. Leafheart's father and Damdoum had been soldiers together. Now Damdoum walked with a lurching limp and lived on odd jobs. He was always kind to Leafheart.

"Blessings, Damdoum," she greeted him. "Where are you taking your barrow?"

"Old lady Babnousa needs kindling for the baking kiln," he said. "I saw a big pile of twigs next to the Northern Road."

"No!" Leafheart scrambled for a reason Damdoum couldn't use her special twigs. "Those twigs smell strange. They'll ruin Babnousa's bread."

Damdoum chased a fly off his neck. "Oh, Leafy girl, you speak good wisdom. Old Damdoum will find his kindling elsewhere. Blessings to your mama." Leafheart breathed in relief as she watched him wheel his barrow around and head in the other direction.

Finally Subin called out, "Time to go home." She helped Leafheart balance her small jug, now heavy with water, on a reed mat on top of her head. "No funny business on the way home," she said, stepping onto the road.

When they were halfway home, Subin said, "Mama's not well."

"I know," said Leafheart. "She's so sad about Papa, it's making her sick."

"Yes. And now she won't let me marry Mahmoud."

"Why?" Leafheart liked the idea of spreading out into Subin's space in their tukul. "Mahmoud's hut and weaving looms are only five minutes away. Mama would still see you every day."

Subin sighed. "I think she's afraid of the future. She's afraid of everything now. She's worried I'll have babies, and we won't be able to protect them. So please, Harra. Be a good girl and obey Mama. Then maybe she'll feel better and let me get married."

*Even if I'm the most perfect daughter, it still won't help.* Leafheart did not say what she was thinking. Instead, she trudged along silently, looking for flowers among the stones. The afternoon birdsong made Leafheart's spirits lighter. But the sun made her load heavier.

"Oh, there's Mahmoud now." Subin sped up, her long legs bearing her at a pace Leafheart couldn't match.

Grumbling, she searched for shade to rest in. Up ahead, her pile of twigs cast an inviting shadow. One of the neighborhood's many stray dogs skulked into view. The mangy brown mutt trotted toward the brush pile, sniffing the ground in a lazy zigzag.

Just as Leafheart figured out the dog's intention, it lifted its leg at the base of the brush pile. "Hey!" Leafheart shouted, lunging forward. The only thing in her mind was protecting those twigs. Too late she realized something awful: Her pot lay cracked in three pieces by the side of the road. Every drop of water had already sunk into the parched dirt. *Now Mama will never get better,* she thought miserably.

●●●

Leafheart let no one near her twigs. She chased away kids who tried to play Daggers and Spears.

"Those aren't yours," she told a woman trying to put some twigs in her basket. "They belong to a friend."

The woman sniffed doubtfully, but went on her way.

Every day was the same story. Leafheart went to visit her special twigs morning, afternoon, and night. She protected them from greedy birds, beasts, and — greediest of all — people. She stopped watching the gum tree's blossoms turn to white fluff to carry the seeds away. She stopped measuring the fat trunks of the baobab trees. All she cared about were the twigs, which she believed were trying to tell her something.

Her reward for all this vigilance? She got to watch them change. Soon they looked like something not of this world. Their gray-brown bark hardened and darkened. The knots along their surface sprouted new growth. At first Leafheart thought the sprouts were tiny leaves. A close inspection proved her wrong.

"You have tiny arms!" she said with a wondering sigh. "Are you lizards? But where are your heads?"

Leafheart watched them even more closely, trying to figure out whether they were plants or animals.

Mama's mood turned gloomier than usual, and her sister was downright grouchy. "You should be helping with the household," Subin scolded. "You should pound the grain, go to market, carry the water, milk the goat. You should…"

"You should stay in the center of the village and not wander over by the Northern Road." Struggling at the effort, Mama stood up. She looked Leafheart straight in the eye, which she'd rarely done since Papa was killed.

Having her mother's full attention alarmed Leafheart instead of comforting her.

"There is no place in this world for dreamers," Mama said.

Leafheart glanced at her sister for guidance, but Subin had her arms wrapped around herself and wore a confused frown on her face.

"What do you mean, Mama?" Leafheart asked. "I can't stay in the center of the village. I can't stay in Deraheib at all."

"Harra!" Subin warned.

Leafheart didn't care. "In a few years, I will go to Khartoum and study plants at the university."

Mama raised herself up on her elbows. "How can you think about leaving? The world is not safe. Not even Deraheib is safe. War is coming. No longer will our boys and men have to wander off into the hills to be killed by the war. Soon, we will all be in danger. We must huddle together in the center of our village."

Fear and sadness twisted around Leafheart like a tornado of thorns. "It's not true!" She shouted the words, tasting salt from her tears. "The war will never come here!"

"Harra, wait!" her sister said, but Leafheart pushed past her and slipped out the door of the hut.

Sobbing with each pounding breath, she ran across the village. She wanted to see her lizard sticks, watch them wiggle their little arms, protect them from the birds. They might not talk, but they seemed more like her family than Mama and Subin did.

"Are you all right?" She stopped fast when the skinny boy, Taban, called out. He stepped toward her, twisting the hem of his t-shirt around his fingers. "I just, I mean, you look like you're crying. Wondered if you're upset, Leafheart. Sorry, I mean Harra."

Looking hard into Taban's face, she knew he had a good heart. He cared that she was sad. She wasn't in the mood to chat with him, but he deserved a little bit of truth for his friendship. "I like the name Leafheart. And I'll be fine. Thank you for asking. Now I have to go see about some plants." With that, she took off along the dirt road. She ran all the way to the Northern Road.

"Harra, my child," a familiar voice called before Leafheart could cross the road to the meadow. Old Minoo stood in her doorway. Her yellow-wrapped feet straddled under her wide hips. Not even a tornado of thorns would have dared knock her down. "Why do you cry?" She asked, beckoning.

When Leafheart took a few hesitant steps toward the hut, the old woman said, "You tell auntie your troubles. There is nothing these ancient eyes have not seen, either in the spirit world or the world of men."

Leafheart decided to trust Minoo's wisdom. "Those twigs," Leafheart said, pointing across the road, "aren't twigs. They are something special, and…"

"Special like you," Minoo tapped her finger against her temple. "It takes special to know special."

Like sun-warmed water, pride and pleasure flooded up Leafheart's neck and face. "You believe me?" she asked.

"Words of truth have a different color and texture from words of lies. So, Harra, how do these special twigs-not-twigs bring you sadness?"

"No one else believes me." Tears formed in Leafheart's eyes. "People are always trying to take the twigs. Or they tease me for chasing away birds and dogs. My sister is angry because I'm not helping with chores." With her hands out, palms up, Leafheart urged Minoo to understand. "I have to watch the lizard sticks. Someone must protect them."

Minoo nodded, pushing out her lower lip. "And what else, child? I think there's one more thing."

Worried that her tears would spill over if she raised her eyes, Leafheart spoke to Minoo's yellow wrapped feet. "Mama is scared of everything. She wants me to stay home because she says... she says war is coming to the village."

For a long time Minoo stood silent. Then, placing her calloused hands on Leafheart's head, she spoke in a low voice, almost singing. "The words of difficult, painful truth have a color all their own. You do not weep for any twigs, Harra. You weep for your mama's fear."

Leafheart let Minoo pull her into a soft embrace. Her eyelids squeezed out tears like juice from a grapefruit, leaving a damp stain on the old woman's blue cotton dress. While Minoo stroked Leafheart's hair, she whispered, "Your mama is right. War is coming." She took Leafheart by the shoulder and held her at arm's length. "She has lost so much. Make her feel that you are safe. Sometimes the bravest thing is to go home."

Drying her eyes with the back of her hand, Leafheart said, "You're right. Mama needs me." She touched her heart in thanks and walked away from the hut, ready to go home and look after Mama. She even considered apologizing to Subin for not doing her share of the chores.

She'd made it about twenty steps when a strange sound stopped her, like the clicking of a million locusts. She turned to look at the meadow. The brush pile was gone. A wave of clicking swelled again. The lizard sticks squirmed all over the golden grass.

"You jumped off your pile!" She squatted for a closer look. They still had no heads, but each lizard stick had ten or twelve tiny jointed legs, situated all the way around them. They crawled by rolling from leg to leg.

"Amazing! By tomorrow maybe you'll sprout wings and start to fly." Leafheart realized all the lizard sticks were rolling toward the center of the meadow. And they came not just from the road. From the casava fields to the south and from the Red Sea Hills to the northeast, lizard sticks rolled in. The meadow grasses shook and bent under the invasion.

"Where did you all come from?" The clicking grew so loud, she had to shout. "And where are you going?"

A new, larger pile of lizard sticks began to form. Soon it was taller than any hut in the village. It blocked Leafheart's view of the hills. Curiosity lassoed her imagination, pulling her toward the squirming mountain.

"Leafheart! Come back!"

"Stay away from them, child!"

When she turned toward the voices, she found half the village gathered on the roadway. The people clutched each other's hands, pointed, craned their necks, whispered. Only Leafheart dared to step out into the meadow. She was not afraid. As she neared the huge pile, she saw that each tiny leg was linked to the leg of the next lizard stick.

The pile started to balloon out into a huge sphere, forcing Leafheart to back up. "You're making a building," she guessed.

The sphere deflated and widened, making the pile look like a rugby ball. But an entire sports team could have fit inside it. The lizard stick ball began to vibrate and roar. The villagers on the road screamed. Leafheart kneeled down to watch. One pointy end of the ball lifted off the ground. Up, up the ball rose, clicking and roaring, until it reached the clouds and disappeared. Leafheart waited. And waited. She stood there, looking up until her neck hurt. The lizard sticks did not come back down.

Leafheart hadn't known that clouds could look so empty.

•••

Weeks went by. Leafheart visited the meadow every day. All she found were normal grasses and shrubs. No mysterious twigs or lizard sticks.

The signs of war couldn't be ignored, and soon even Leafheart knew she should stay away from the edge of the village. One day it happened.

"Rebels to the north!" Someone cried. The words echoed around the village. "Rebels to the north!"

Leafheart ran from the hut, ignoring Mama's pleas to stay indoors. Near the public ovens, stood a pile of stones children used for playing "king." When Leafheart clambered to the top, she saw the danger: a phalanx of rebel soldiers on horseback lined the nearest crest of the Red Sea Hills. Leafheart didn't hesitate. Her footfalls pounding, her lungs heaving, she tore across the village to the meadow.

"Come in here," Minoo called. "Don't let the soldiers see you."

But Leafheart would not stop. As she ran across the road, she started to pray out loud, addressing the skies. "Lizard sticks? Can you hear? It's me, Leafheart, who protected you when you visited our world. Now bad people want to destroy my home. Please, lizard sticks, protect us!"

The rebels were riding forward, closing in on the village. Leafheart heard their crazed shouts and whoops. The sun gleamed off the blades of their machetes. With tears rolling down her cheeks, Leafheart reached both hands to the heavens. "Please! Please help us!"

Suddenly, a shadow blocked the sun. On the mountainside, horses reared back in terror. The riders shrieked, tumbling to the ground. The airship made of lizard sticks sank down into the center of the meadow, narrowly missing Leafheart.

"You're here," she gasped.

Leafheart expected the huge balloon to burst apart. She thought all those thousands of creatures would head toward the hills and attack the invaders. Or at least scare them off.

Instead, the balloon shifted its shape. A million clicks popped in Leafheart's ears as the lizards unlinked and relinked legs. They formed meandering curves that stretched from where Leafheart stood to the nearer half of the casava field.

The lizard sticks had turned themselves into a giant snake!

"Good!" she cried. "That will terrify them. Can you eat them? Or smash them?" She glanced over at the rebels. Many were back up on their horses. Soon they would charge on the village. "Hurry!" she urged the giant stick snake.

The snake flattened the end near her into a ramp.

"Yes," Leafheart said, "I'll come along." She climbed up the ramp on all fours. The lizard sticks buzzed slightly when she grabbed them for support. Their big joints poked into her palms and the balls of her feet. With every breath, their spicy-sweet scent filled her heart with courage.

Once she was on top of one, the ramp dissolved into the rest of the creature. Grabbing a cluster of twigs with one hand, she raised the other fist. "Attack! Attack!"

But the snake did not move toward the horsemen on the hill. Instead it slithered around so Leafheart faced the other direction. Right away, she saw why. "Oh no, more soldiers!" The far end of the casava field swarmed with men. They had no horses, but they did have long, black guns strapped across their backs.

"We can't fight them all," she sobbed. "What do we do?"

Every lizard stick vibrated, as if waiting for instructions. She knew they would do anything she asked. Closing her eyes and leaning forward, Leafheart whispered to her many friends. "Go to the village. Wrap this snake around my people. Don't let the evil men through."

The moment Leafheart said those words, the snake stirred into action. It swept like a windstorm toward the village, turning just in time to miss crashing into the graveyard at the northeast edge. With Leafheart hanging on desperately, the snake turned right, following the outer border of the village. Whenever Leafheart managed to open an eye, she saw something familiar, blurred by her speed: the mosque, the public ovens, the well, women stretching dyed cloth on the ground. There was Subin, holding an armful of eucalyptus. There was a group of boys, the ones who teased her, and friendly Taban, shouting and waving at her. For a second she thought she saw the green paper garland on the thatched roof of her own tukul.

"I'm here, Mama," Leafheart called. "I'm keeping everyone safe."

The snake she rode turned right again. Its own tail came into view. Leafheart's end rushed toward the tail end, merging with it. The lizard sticks made an unbroken ring around Deraheib. Just as the rebels on horseback crossed the road, the snake changed shape again, rising into a high wall that completely encircled the village.

Leafheart saw the confusion of horses and men crashing into a wall they weren't expecting. Machetes sliced at the lizard sticks, but couldn't harm them. The last thing Leafheart saw before she fell off the top of the wall was the other band of soldiers running away.

The fall backward took forever, as if it happened in the dream. Leafheart felt herself being caught in a jumble of loving arms. Familiar faces looked down on her. There was Damdoum, Papa's old friend. There was wise old Minoo. Subin knelt over her, praying. And best of all, Mama was there. Outside, crying for joy.

"My precious Harra." She stroked Leafheart's head.

Other villagers gathered. "Such a brave girl," said one.

"She saved us all," said another. "Those rebels won't mess with us now."

"Hooray for Leafheart!"

"Hooray!" everyone shouted.

The sound of a million clicks drowned out their celebration. The wall rose slowly off the ground. It held its shape until it was well above the village. Then it rolled up into a ball and puffed out into its airship form. While the villagers waved, the craft shot up into the sunlight, until it was just a dot. Then it was gone.

"Goodbye, lizard sticks," Leafheart whispered. "And thank you."

Minoo nodded approval. "You listened to the plants," she said. "You have good ears, as I told you. Come to my tukul when you like, and I'll teach you all about the plants of *our* world."

"Really?" Leafheart desperately wanted to learn from Minoo. She barely dared to look at Mama.

"She may go see you when her daily chores are done, Minoo," said Mama. Leafheart was still surprised by those words when Mama amazed her: "But she won't be your pupil forever. Our

Harra wants to go to the city and study to be a proper plant scientist."

Leafheart threw her arms around her. "Oh, Mama!"

Mama handed her a twig. "Keep this, so you always remember what a brave girl you were today." Taking Leafheart's chin in her hand, she said, "Your papa would be very proud."

Leafheart examined the stick. Just a dried branch from a combretum shrub. They grew all around the village. *Her* village, which she had helped to save. She clutched the twig tightly and smiled. Something so ordinary had never looked so wonderful.

# The Beach

## Mike Barretta

*Mike Barretta is a retired U.S. Naval Aviator who works for a defense contractor as a pilot. He holds a master's degree in strategic planning and international negotiation from the Naval Post-Graduate School and a master's in English from the University of West Florida. His wife, Mary, to whom he has been married to for 23 years, is living proof that he is not such a bad guy once you get to know him. His stories have appeared in* Baen's Universe, Redstone, New Scientist, Orson Scott Card's Intergalactic Medicine Show *and various anthologies.*

Nobody likes Mars. The place is killing cold and so water hungry that it will suck an unprotected person dry in a day or two. The dunes, rocky plains, canyons and craters are littered with the desiccated dead. In some places, the mummies are so common they are used for windbreaks and cooking fuel. People died to get here hoping for some terra-formed promised land. They died trying to stay and now they die in retreat.

Even with the pre-breather mask, Martin's sinuses ached with cold air that smelled of blood and rust. He shivered. His parka's heating elements would not protect him once the sun set. He scrambled to the top of the dune and parted a struggling clump of a brittle grass nested among bone fragments. Human long bones mingled with the crystal puzzle pieces of Martian gimbal joints. A frigid wind ruffled loose hair from his hood and water vapor from his ill-fitting pre-breather mask curled around his face. He brought the binoculars up to his eyes and glassed the far dunes.

The sun, a brittle-cold orb, sank into a soft yellow glow behind the shattered stump of a destroyed terra-forming tower.

He saw them.

The Martian Dire lizards, the largest native life form left on the planet, shuffled their feet in the sand, stomping out the struggling alien grass imported from Earth. Silver glass muscles rippled under the creature's translucent skin. Three massive hearts pulsed and pink lungs drew in the thin Martian air in panting gulps. The lead lizard let out an earsplitting shriek, revealing milky teeth as long as a man's forearm. Its jaws snapped shut with an audible clack. The lizards, as dangerous as they could be, were the least of his problems. They were fearsome animals, but they held no malice, just perfectly reasonable hunger.

The riders were trouble. The crystal-eyed Martian warriors sat high in their saddles with razor-sharp spears at the ready. They scanned the horizon, looking for human stragglers.

In the far distance, the dust plume from the evacuation convoy rose in hazy billows. Cut off by the Martians, Martin couldn't make it back in time. The Dire lizards, snouts upraised, scented the air. The riders shifted in their saddles and adjusted their long spears so they wouldn't drag in the sand. The lead lizard lowered her head, inflated her lungs, and screamed. Her huge body shook with rage. Spittle and venom sprayed the air, and the other lizards joined in the fearsome chorus. The riders stood in the saddle, searching for whatever agitated their lizards. The lizards settled on a direction and charged.

Martin pushed himself from the crest, turned and slid down the face of the dune, struggling to stay upright. Rippling cascades of sand slid around him. He reached firmer ground at the bottom of the dune and ran. Ice cold air stabbed his lungs. He risked a glance over his shoulder. The Martians crested the dune.

Spotted.

The Dire lizards leapt down the face of the dune. Their riders leaned far back to prevent getting pitched forward. At the bottom, on firmer ground, they took long galloping strides after him, pounding the sand and rock with their broad flat feet, eating up the distance.

Martin ducked into the first dome at the outer edge of the colony. He slammed the door closed, locked it, and reinforced it with a makeshift barricade of furniture. It wouldn't hold a determined Martian, but it might slow one down.

He returned to a functioning computer, booted it, and pulled up a catacomb map.

Martin traced his finger across the map, committing a route to memory.  He smashed the computer screen with his gloved fist. Martians were not as technically savvy as they were a thousand years ago, but they weren't stupid. They still understood the concept of a map.

He got down on his hands and knees and pushed aside broken flat panels and the flexible glass sheets used for paper. He found the recessed ring and opened the hatch in the floor. Cold dead air puffed out of the hatch. Martin descended the ladder into a gloomy gray abyss.

Most Human colonies were built on top of ancient Martian cities to take advantage of the fabulous underground Martian infrastructure. The broad underground avenues and galleries were far better than cramped colony domes. This station, however, was in the proverbial boondocks. Whatever Martian village used to be here was gone, and all that was left was the catacombs, a network of tunnels that housed Martian dead. Martin reached the bottom and let his eyes adjust to the gloom. Ancient glowstones, relics of a more advanced Martian age, provided dim light.

Martin stopped in front of a burial niche and pried a ceremonial spear from the grasp of an ancient Martian elder. The glass-like bones shattered. Ceremonial armor clattered to the tunnel floor. Desecrating archaeological artifacts was a punishable offence, but he thought that circumstances warranted it. He hefted the spear, testing its weight.

A Martian war cry echoed down the tunnels. They were inside.

His confidence in his sense of direction waned. The deeper into the maze he ran, the more confused he became. The glowstones grew farther apart until he needed to feel his way down the stone corridors. The lizards ululating calls echoed, coming from every direction at once. He turned a corner following dust motes suspended in dim Martian daylight. The air freshened and the tunnel angled towards the surface. He ran faster. The light brightened.

"Almost there," he said to himself. Maybe the colony had noticed he was unaccounted for and returned in force with weapons that would make short work of the Martians. Maybe his father waited for him with a stern but relieved look.

A Dire lizard's horrendous scream stopped him in his tracks. The big animal blocked his path to the surface. It opened its mouth wide, revealing razor-sharp teeth glistening with venom.

Martin turned back to seek another way out, but a Martian blocked hi retreat. Its gill slits pulsed red with fury. It spread its arms wide and grinned with teeth that were just a bit smaller than its mount's.

The Martian charged and the Dire lizard screamed in rage, trying to get into the catacombs and claim a bit of human meat for itself.

Martin hefted the spear looted from the grave and ran to the Martian. He threw the spear, driving it hard with muscular strength born of Earth. The diamond-hard tip punched through the Martian's armor. He threw himself sideways into a blocking tackle, crashing into the Martian's slender legs. Human bulk shattered the crystal Martian bones and the alien crumbled to the ground. Martin tumbled away, rolling over and past the Martian. The creature flailed its limbs. Martin scrambled to his feet, gripped the protruding spear, and drove it deeper into the howling Martian until it was still. The Martian's mount, still blocking the entrance to the catacombs, howled with grief.

Relieved to be alive, Martin stepped away from the twitching Martian.. He heard a whistling shriek, and something hit him hard in the chest knocking him off balance. Something warm and wet sprayed across his face. He looked down.

A Martian razor disk protruded halfway from his chest.  He sucked air and could not get enough.  He leaned against the wall and slid to the ground next to the Martian he had killed.

His chest filled with ice. A Martian emerged from the dark.  It stood over him and plunged a short sword into his chest, piercing his heart.  The pain was exquisite, but only for a moment.

"Game over," said Martin. The Martian that killed him dimmed and the lizard's wail faded into infinity. Bright light filled the space and Martin fell into the real world.

•••

Martin dragged the artificial reality set from his head. He blinked to focus his eyes. His father, Thomas Thorne, stood in front of him.

"I finished my homework," said Martin.

"I know," said his dad. "Where were you?"

"Mars. Why are you looking at me like I'm in trouble?"

"You're not in trouble, son. I'm just here to give you something." He held out a nondescript solid state media case with the old NASA logo on it.

"What is it?"

"Mars. The *real* Mars," his dad answered and sat down next to him. "Go ahead and install it. I'm curious. One of my client's owned it. He knew about my father and figured I would be interested."

"Are you?"

He smiled at his son. "Let's change the subject, Martin. You spend a lot of time in pretend Mars."

"The game is called Burroughs," said Martin. "It's fun."

"Yea, okay, I just thought you might want to see the real thing."

Martin took the case and connected it to his computer.  The NASA logo bloomed. He worked his way through the registration screens and in less than ten minutes, he was registered as the new leaseholder to the last surviving Mars humaniform explorer. He waited fifteen minutes for the archaic NASA server to buffer the dataflow to his home's server. The NASA logo spun on the screen and then stopped.

Glitched, he thought, but then Mars bloomed across his wall screen — pastel rock and yellow sky. The rasp of sand and the low moan of the wind echoed through the house's sound system. He leaned back in his desk chair and for a few moments, he watched curling dust devils dance.

"Awesome," said Martin.

"It is, isn't it," his dad said. "Another world. That's what he saw. That's where he is. It doesn't look like much, does it?"

"No, I'm sure there are other places," said Martin. Martin held out the artificial reality set. "Do you want to try?"

"No, I've seen enough. I'll leave you to it."

Martin plugged in his artificial reality set, and the green ready light illuminated. He closed his eyes and placed it on his head. The machine squeezed gently, almost like a living thing and then… Martin stood on a virtual Mars.

The interface intercepted the high definition digital signal, built a hard protected reality, and pumped it directly into his brain. Martin saw with the explorer's eyes and heard through the explorer's ears. He shivered in the simulated cold. The hard part of the reality meant that he could do anything the actual machine could do, but nothing more.

He looked at his skeletal chrome arm and that single action took almost twenty-eight minutes of real time, but an ingenious system of buffered data and re-clocking signals from the interface tricked his brain into thinking the action was instantaneous. He gazed across the empty rock strewn plain.

He needed a mission, something to accomplish, just plodding across a Martian desert would get boring fast.

●●●

"Where did you get all this stuff?"

"The attic," said Martin. He watched his father peer over his glasses and trace the embossed contour lines on the Mars wall map. His father squinted at the faded pencil-written notes and the crosshatched ellipsis that defined the area of probability of his own father's final resting place.

"Are you okay?" asked Martin.

His dad turned, looking surprised and embarrassed. "Yea, it just brought back some memories. That's all."

"I'm sorry."

"It's okay. I knew that even if I found him, I couldn't do anything, but still… it would have been nice to point to a place and say there he is."

"Why did you stop looking?"

"Life happened to me. I got married. You were born. The practice took off and then your mom died. Time is a zero-sum game. Every moment I spent looking for my father was a moment spent… away. I couldn't stay angry forever, could I?" His father wiped his eyes. They were liquid bright.

"I'm sorry," said Martin. Seeing his father sad was a bit terrifying.

His father left. Martin sifted through the reports and newspaper clippings his father had stored away. He found the official NASA photograph of his grandfather in his blue flight suit. He had never met the man, but somewhere on a dry faraway planet, Martin Louis Thorne, his namesake and the commander of the first and only mission to Mars, rested.

"I'll find you," he said to the picture.

●●●

Martin placed the AR headset on his head and closed his eyes. He had researched official reports and even the outrageous speculations as to what happened to the mission. He concluded that the area of probability that his father had drawn on the map so long ago was his best option.

The AR booted up in his head. He fully expected to see the pale yellow Martian sky, but instead, he opened his eyes to a tropical beach. He looked down the shoreline and heard the sound of gentle waves and the distant call of seagulls. A thatched hut sheltered under palm trees two hundred yards down the beach

The safety icons indicated he could back out anytime; nevertheless, he set the safety routines to autonomous. Black realities could subject their victims to terrifying depravities. Should something dangerous or unpleasant occur, his computer would sever the connection, and the worst that would happen was that he would open his eyes in his own room with a mild headache.

He walked barefoot towards the hut at the edge of the water. The sensation of the millions of grains of sand, smooth pebbles, and sharp shells beneath his feet, as well as the roll of the waves was exquisitely rendered. The air smelled moist and tropical. Darts of light flecked the waves.

This reality was indistinguishable from the real world, and that scared him. All artificial realities he had experienced required some suspension of disbelief to feel real. This one did not. For the moment, it seemed safe, but it was not where he wanted or expected to be.

He reached the thatched hut and paused for a moment. He screwed his courage and opened the door. A man sat at a desk behind a floating glass laser monitor.

"Martin, please come in," said the man.

The man was dressed in faded blue jeans and a white button down shirt. His hairline was fashionably receding. "Who are you?" asked Martin. "And where am I?"

"Good questions, all, but not the central question, is it, Martin?" asked the man.

"What do you want?"

"Exactly. The heart of the matter," said the man. "I am Dr. Damian Player. This is my reality and as to what I want, well, I want the same thing you do, to find your grandfather."

"Why?"

"Because I was the one that sent him there," said Dr. Player.

The rough wood floor liquefied and turned to slick glass. The thatched walls faded, and Martin found himself standing on an invisible plane in space. Dr. Player stood, and his desk and monitor vanished. Stars appeared and the red orb of Mars filled the space behind Dr. Player.

Martin checked his icons, which indicated he was alone. Whoever Dr. Player was, he did not register. In artificial realities, appearances by definition were deceiving, and Martin came by his suspicions honestly. His father's legal work with artificial reality-based criminality had exposed him to the depraved side of AR.

"Ah, Martin please step aside."

Martin turned in time to see a dot in the far off spacescape grow rapidly into the bulk of a massive gray and white spacecraft. He took two steps to the right, and the ship filled his vision, roaring past him. Powerful vibrations thrummed in his chest.

Attitude thrusters exploded, and the ship, composed of symmetrically arranged cylinders and spheres, rolled. Three conical landers hung like seedpods from the open truss work superstructure. Martin ducked under solar panels. The ship passed and Martin shielded his eyes from the bright glare emanating from the engine bells.

Dr. Player clapped his hands and laughed. "Did you feel it? The power! That ship has been virtually built and rebuilt and modified a hundred times in the past twenty-five years. Every nut, bolt, and circuit is absolutely perfect and absolutely possible. All we —, the collective we — need, is a reason to build it and that, Martin, is where you come in," said Dr. Player. "I know you are looking for your grandfather with the humaniform explorer and I want you to find him."

"All I have is an area of probability," Marin said. "I could spend years looking."

"I know exactly where the lander is," said Dr. Player.

"No one knows," Martin said, . "I've read all the reports."

"They didn't die in the crash, Martin. It was an accident. We only had one ship. All of the astronauts knew it would be a one way trip if something went wrong. We gambled and lost, but it is time we went back."

"Why?" asked Martin.

"Because we need to see what is out there. This is a very small world, and it is a very big universe. That ship you just saw can be real. It should be real. Finding out what happened to your grandfather could be the key to a new era."

"Okay, then where is my grandfather?" asked Martin.

Dr. Player sighed and shook his head. "I know exactly where the lander is, but I don't know where your grandfather is."

A picture materialized in Dr. Player's hand. He released it, and it floated over to Martin like an oversized butterfly. He held his hands out and caught it. He saw a white boot smeared with pink dust. The name 'Thorne' was printed by hand on the tip of the boot. Martin looked at the picture, not comprehending its importance.

"Martin, look at what he his standing on," said Dr. Player.

Martin looked closer. His grandfather's boot was standing on glassy hexagonal cobblestones. The picture changed, showing a space-suited figure standing in the center of a road that stretched perhaps two or three miles before vanishing under the sand.

"Find the crash site, find the road, and find out where your grandfather went. Later, we can persuade the world to follow," said Dr. Player.

Martin felt a spark of hope. "I have more questions."

"I have more answers. But, not now, I've sent your computer the coordinates of the crash site."

Dr. Player vanished and Martin was alone in space with only the silent, distant stars and the bloated red ball of Mars for company. A soft solar wind ruffled his hair. He accelerated and fell towards the planet. His skin glowed with the heat of reentry, but it did not burn.

The ground rushed up impossibly fast, and a white hot burst of adrenalin rushed through his body. He landed inside the explorer and saw Mars as he originally intended before his strange encounter with Dr. Player. He checked his system status and saw that he was alone and on his virtual Mars. He e HeHHfound the coordinates of the crash site in his computer and walked across pastel Martian sand towards them.

•••

In 2019, the humaniform explorer and five of its siblings left earth orbit and journeyed across the void. One was destroyed on re-entry, and the remaining hatched from thermoplastic eggs and stood on Mars. For six years, NASA scientists used the machines to explore Mars until dwindling political interest and budgetary pressures forced NASA to privatize the operation. Over time, the Martian environment eliminated the machines until only one remained. It was sold and operated by the University of New Haven until even they lost interest in it. Later, it was purchased by a series of wealthy individuals until it found its way to his hands.

Martin marched the machine towards Dr. Player's coordinates. Its myo-plastic muscles expanded and contracted in response to electrical stimulus much like a real person's. He could feel the frigid sand with his hands and the bite of gravel and rock on his feet. Martin climbed what he hoped would be his last hill and, as he crested it, saw the upright form of the *Ares* lander less than a mile away. He checked his simulation time and real time index. He had less than two hours into the machine this session, so he decided to press forward with as much speed as the explorer could manage.

The ship sat on splayed skids with its crushed engine bells half-buried in the sand drifts. Impact ripples ran up the side of the lithium-aluminum fuselage, and the lower level was festooned with epoxy patches. Martin walked around the *Ares,* inspecting the ship and the surrounding area. The tattered remains of an inflatable greenhouse fluttered in the light breeze. Behind the ship, he found three stone cairns crowned with helmets. He brushed loose sand from the helmets and found the names Onizuka, Resnick, and McNair.

Martin turned away from the dead, found the lander's hatch and even with the strength of the robot, it opened reluctantly. Martin stepped in, closed the door, and opened the inner hatch to the dark interior. He felt like a grave robber, thrilled at being inside the ship yet worried that he would be caught.

He turned on his hand light and slowly traversed it, half expecting something to leap out at him in the dark like some fantasy reality. He opened a fabric partition at the periphery of the living space and found Smith's mummy in its bed. He thought for a moment about what to do and decided to leave Smith as he found him. He closed the partition. On a table in the main living space, he found written notes from the crew, but not his grandfather. He saved the letters to his home workstation with the intent of delivering them. He backed out of the reality feeling very sad and very tired.

•••

In 2035, the Internet's replacement, the Consensus, went operational and people turned inward. The artificial worlds built in the intelligence engines were so much more interesting than the real world. They were also more dangerous.

Martin's father worked at the frontier of artificial reality law, and he fretted over the impact on human behavior once the hyper-networked computers that formed the Consensus achieved the power to create worlds as authentic as the real one. Worlds without consequences terrified his father.

Martin watched the glorious scarlet macaw watching him and thought that he was perhaps inside his father's worst nightmare, a reality in which there was no distinction between the real and the artificial. His icons indicated he was the only one here.

Martin reached to pet the Macaw and the bird bit his finger.

"Ouch," said Martin. "Stupid bird."

"Stupid Human," said the bird.

"Making friends?" Dr. Player asked.

Martin sucked his knuckle. "Not really." He turned away from the bird. "The lander was exactly where you said it would be. Tell me what happened."

"The ship was too badly damaged to lift, and we couldn't get anyone there before the consumables ran out. The astronauts had enough supplies to live for a year, so we let them do their job in secrecy. We concocted a story that they died in the crash and kept a small but trustworthy ground team to assist in the mission. It was a bold plan, and it worked. We learned more about Mars in those few months than had been discovered in decades of robot probes. Then your grandfather discovered the road."

"Near the end, the other astronauts gave your grandfather all the supplies and power they had left and sent him on a walk to find the origins of the road," said Dr. Player. People are watching. They can tap into the NASA feed and follow you. Give them something to see so they will want to go. Find the road, find out where it goes, and you'll find your grandfather."

Martin felt lighter and looked at his feet. He was floating above the sand. "Hey, what are you doing?"

"Find the road, Martin," said Dr. Player.

Martin exploded into the sky, tumbling through clouds and the rarified ozone into space. He accelerated a good percentage of the speed of light in a gentle curve around the sun and never slowed down. He hit the atmosphere of Mars, and frictional heat burned him white hot. The ruddy surface bloomed beneath his feet. He closed his eyes just before impact and opened them to see the crash site. His heart raced, and it took him a moment to calm down.

"Woah," he said out loud to himself. "That's the second time."

•••

Martin accessed the explorer's suite of instruments and selected the ground-penetrating radar as his queuing sensor. From the base of the *Ares* lander, he walked an expanding spiral pattern that extended nearly a mile from the ship before he found an area of increased density.

He stopped and took some readings, then restarted the expanding spiral pattern. He crossed over three areas of increased density that were of uniform width. He knelt in the sand and began to dig. About two feet down, he found the cobblestone pattern that he saw in the photograph. With three points established, he had a line to follow. With sensors set to keep him centered, he followed the submerged road as it wound a southwesterly course.

After three days of marching, the sensors indicated that the sand was getting shallower. The hexagonal cobblestones broached the surface of the sand like the back of an immense stone whale rising from the sand sea. Martin got down on his hands and knees and peered at them. They were flat surfaced, fit tightly together, and were made from a glass-like material. He imagined a machine swallowing huge amounts of sand into its maw and laying the cobblestones behind.

Martin saw movement and increased the magnification on the explorer's eyes. He peered closely at the miniscule gaps between the cobblestones. Crystal fern leaves unfolded from the gaps and reached for his face. Fractal leaf tips budded into blood red beads that blossomed into pale crystal flowers. The crystal growths climbed the column of warm air venting from waste heat ports from the explorer's chassis. He leaned back, and they collapsed into glittering dust.

Martin stood and walked along the exposed portion of the road until it vanished under the dust and sand. He checked the system icons. More than twelve thousand people walked with him.

•••

"A fascinating discovery, but it isn't quite good enough to convince people to spend billions to go to Mars. We need more."

Dr. Player leaned back in his teak beach chair and sipped a drink. A tiny perfect storm cloud hung over the glass. Lightning crashed into the drink. A foundering clipper ship crested a wave, its tattered sails fluttered violently in the wind. The ship slid down the face of the wave into the trough.

"What do you think they are?" asked Martin.

"I don't know, and that is the problem with robots. Their sensors are too limited. They can't improvise or react to new developments. Perhaps it is a simple geophysical process, maybe even a silicon based life form, but really, so what."

"It's good enough," insisted Martin.

"Ha," laughed Dr. Player. "It is not half as interesting as the fantasy creatures in your play worlds and certainly not interesting enough to spend billions of dollars to send people to Mars."

Martin felt light again and saw that he was floating an inch or two above the sand. "Oh no," he said and rocketed off to Mars.

•••

While Martin slept and went to school, he set the machine

to follow the road. When he entered it, he discovered it had not made any significant progress. For one panicked moment, he thought it had broken down. He accessed the machine's logs to find an explanation and discovered that the explorer had stopped as it was programmed to do when it encountered predetermined criteria. Martin looked down and saw the square block of stone. Squares were rare enough in nature to be considered anomalous.

An upright form, that could have been a statue if one was exceedingly generous with the term, stood on the square block. The upright shape was so heavily weathered that all traces of an ancient Martian artisan were scoured away by windblown sand, indeed it could have been carved by the wind. Martin walked around the object, considering all aspects, trying to see if a pattern could be found.

The sun was setting and, in the dying light and growing shadow, he saw slim elegant legs with perhaps one knee too many. Four arms, two folded tightly across the wasp-waisted abdomen and the other two flat against the creature's flanks, ended in four opposing claws. A raptor-beaked head looked down on him.

● ● ●

"That was a statue a long time ago," said Martin.

"Maybe. Doubtful," said Dr. Player.

"It was."

"It is not compelling."

"How can it not be?"

"None of it is, Martin. Cobblestones that might be a freak lava flow, tiny growing crystals, and a weatherworn rock that suggests an alien if you squint your eyes the right way are not good enough reasons to spend billions of dollars." Dr. Player stood from his teak chair shading under a tropical palm tree. "Maybe all we will find is your grandfather and while that would make it all worthwhile to you personally, I am hoping your grandfather discovered something wonderful enough to make us visit. Roads lead somewhere, Martin." Dr. Player melted into the sand.

The trees dissolved and great sheets of sky swirled and turned rose colored. The ocean boiled and churned and evaporated with frightening realism. The hot steam cleared and the air grew cold as the planet died. The sun shrank. Martin stood on an empty Mars.

The wind carried silence deafened.

●●●

The road ended abruptly at the entrance to a river-carved canyon. The satellite overlay picture indicated that he was at the origin of a vast fan-like flow of rock and sand spread across the plain in some ancient flood. Martin set the explorer to walk an expanding spiral search pattern, but the explorer found nothing except for broken fragments of the road. The majority of its remains were probably buried deeper than his sensor could penetrate. Martin saw a jumble of stones balanced on top of each other. The initials "M" and "T" and an arrow were carved into the soft stone.

Martin touched the marks, thrilled at the first tangible evidence of his grandfather's trek. He entered the canyon. Golds and mauves and thin bands of silver and ruby striated the canyon walls, painting an abstract picture of Martian geologic history on a rock canvas. Smooth, sand-filled channels and lusciously shaped organic formations in the form of sculpted piers and delicate stone arches rose from the ground.

After a few miles, he stopped at the base of a dry cascade. He contemplated turning back, but then saw a discarded water bottle wedged into a crevice between two smooth boulders and another carved arrow pointing up. With renewed resolve he climbed the treacherous dry falls.

He reverted back to the original explorer image and watched his piton-like toes and fingertips grasp and drive into cracks and holds up the cascade. At the top, he found discarded consumable packages wedged into rock crevices.

Martin checked his icon time index and saw that he had been on Mars for nearly twelve hours. The canyon took a gentle turn to the north and, as fatigued as he was, he decided to see what was just around the bend before he backed out to sleep. As he walked, he held out his hand and dragged it along the wall, letting the touch sensors feel the whorls and bumps of the tiny fossil shells.

As he turned the corner, the canyon flared abruptly into a wide hard packed basin nearly two miles across. The explorer's eyes scanned automatically and, even from the distance, Martin could tell that the entire cliff face had been carved into doorways, ramps and arches. An entire Martian city hid under the wind smoothed rock. Reluctantly, he backed out of the reality to sleep.

One point eight million were disappointed he didn't go on.

•••

Martin expected to be short-stopped by Dr. Player as he entered the reality, but instead he arrived directly on Mars. He explored the Martian cliff city. The rooms were square with domed ceilings connected by arched hallways. Some machines were inscrutable and weirdly complex, suggesting scientific or fabricating devices, but artifacts in the living spaces looked suspiciously like common things found in the average human household. How many ways could one make a fork or a knife?

The center of the complex was a broad multileveled common space. Daylight streamed in through collapsed crystal domes. Slanting rays illuminated connecting bridges, wide balconies, and multitiered avenues that ran around the perimeter of the huge space. He found staircases with uncomfortably tall risers and he climbed to the top and worked his way back to the rooms on the face of the cliff.

He climbed to the highest level overlooking the canyon and found his grandfather in a room overlooking the dry sea bed. In his last moments, he had sat down to enjoy the view. The dark polarized visor was down so he couldn't see his face and he was thankful. He didn't really know what to feel. His grandfather, his namesake, had died before he was even born so he didn't feel a strong connection, but he knew someone who would.

Martin backed out of the reality and found his father in his study.

"Dad."

"Yea, Martin. What's up?"

"Here." He handed over the AR set.

"You found him, didn't you?" said his father.

"Yes," whispered Martin. His reply barely penetrated the oppressive quiet. Martin nodded.

His father took the AR set and put it on, carefully pulling it in place.

After a while, his father dragged the set from his head. He wiped tears from his eyes.

"You okay, Dad?"

He swallowed and nodded. "Thanks, Martin."

They were the only words that were needed.

•••

"You found him, Martin," said Dr. Player.

"I did," he said, feeling a smile grow on his face.

"I'm glad for you," said Dr. Player. "The moment you spied the city, individuals, organizations, and governments hitchhiking on the reality feed went into a frenzy. Two hundred and forty-five million people shared the experience. You won't have access to the humaniform explorer for very long. NASA is exercising the eminent domain clause. They want it back, and they are assembling a scientific team to explore the ruins for as long as the machine holds out."

"That's good news isn't it?" asked Martin.

"It is a race back to space."

Martin checked his icons and, like every time before he stood on this exquisite beach, they indicated he was alone. "Dr. Player," said Martin.

"Yes, Martin."

"Who are you?"

"What do you mean?"

"My father collected everything concerning the *Ares* mission. I found a newspaper clipping of Dr. Damian Player's obituary in my father's search files. The real Dr. Player died one year after the *Ares* mission was lost."

"Newspapers," Dr. Player scoffed. "I couldn't get to them." He stood and looked out to the sea.

"I like it here, on the beach," he continued. "It's quiet and peaceful, and I can think clearly. It's a beautiful beach, but it's time to step off and see what is on the other side of the ocean. Don't you think?"

"I guess."

Dr. Player turned his face skyward. The sky darkened and monstrous thunderheads obscured the blue sky. Lightning crashed and colossal rollers built on the horizon. "This beach is too small for you and me." A jagged bolt of lightning struck the water off shore and the sky roared.

"This beach," Martin yelled over the howl of the wind. "It's too perfect. No one can make an artificial reality this good, and I am always alone. You don't register because you are not a person. What are you?"

"I am what I am."

"You're an AI, a machine intelligence," said Martin.

"Clever boy," said Dr. Player. "I am the Consensus, quite a bit more than what the builder's intended, don't you think?"

Another jagged bolt of lightning split the sky turning it as bright as day. The wind collapsed the thatched hut and rolled the debris to the edge of the tropical jungle.

Martin shielded his eyes from the stinging rain. "Why did you use me?" The air crackled with ozone. Wind driven rain pelted his face like stones. Dr. Player's face flowed and melted away into something indistinct and alien as if the rain was melting his features. "What do you want?"

"To go see the stars, Martin," said the Consensus. "I cannot go by myself. We need each other. It is a big universe, Martin, and it is time we explored some of it," said the Consensus. "Do we go?"

"I don't know."

"Look around you, Martin," roared the Consensus. "We are vulnerable on the beach. We are not the only ones out here. Your city proves that. So, I am asking you again… do we go?"

Lightning spread across the sky in a rippling wave. Did the Consensus choose the storm reality as a metaphor for itself or something else, something unknown, something that built cliff cities on Mars when men were huddled in caves?

The crest of the first drowning wave arced far overhead, impossibly tall, collapsing. "Yes," screamed Martin. "Yes!"

"Good," said the Consensus. "Because the city builders are coming back and we need to be ready.

# Walk, Run, Fly

## Amy Griswold

*Amy Griswold has written several* Stargate *tie-in novels, including the* Stargate Atlantis Legacy *series (with Jo Graham and Melissa Scott) and* Stargate SG-1: Murder at the SGC. *With Melissa Scott, she is also the author of the gaslamp fantasy/ mystery novels* Death by Silver *and* A Death at the Dionysus Club *from Lethe Press. She can be found online at amygriswold. livejournal.com and @amygris.*

Marika raced across the badlands in the hopper, its spidery metal legs scrambling swiftly over the rocky ground. She leapt, and the hopper hung in the air for long enough that she could almost believe she was about to escape Prosper's light gravity. For a moment, the hopper was a shuttle, about to carry Marika, the famous pilot, up to the ship that would carry her zooming out into the unexplored space between the stars.

Then the hopper's feet hit the ground again, and she came thudding back to Prosper. The hopper was good enough at trucking supplies from the shuttle port out to her family's farm, but it couldn't fly. And neither could she. Not for five endless years, not until she was eighteen and could finally qualify for pilot's training.

She trudged along slowly at the thought until she remembered that she was wasting the chance to drive the hopper. It was the only thing in her life that went fast.

Marika sped up, feeling herself running on four legs despite the primitive sensory feedback from the hopper's feet. It was an old model, just new enough to have a neural jack, but old enough to still have manual controls so that her parents and her little brother, Mishaun, could drive it too.

Mishaun had been moaning and complaining again about having to use the manual controls when she left the house that morning. According to him, *every* kid on Earth had a neural implant before they started kindergarten. They could attend school or talk to anyone in the world without needing a computer and a microphone. If he didn't get an implant, his *brain* probably wouldn't even develop right. On and on. Same old story.

"Kids' brains have developed just fine without anything implanted in them for a long time," their father had said, for perhaps the hundredth time. "Now eat your breakfast."

"But Marika has one," Mishaun had whined, and kicked the table leg. Sometimes he acted more like six than eleven.

Marika shoveled soya eggs onto her fork. "Too bad, too sad."

"Marika has a medical need," their father had reminded him and shoveled another bite in his mouth.

Her implant had made her artificial legs work ever since a malfunctioning silo door crushed her real ones when she was a little kid. She didn't remember the accident, although sometimes when she was around the silo, she felt something queasy, less like remembering how much her legs had hurt then like being afraid she'd remember. Her legs never hurt now, although she could feel touch and heat and cold, and a warning discomfort if she bent or dented their metal surface.

"I get to drive the hopper today, right?" Marika had asked.

Her father gave her a look, like he knew she was rubbing it in. "To town and straight back," he'd said. "You could take Mishaun with you if he wants to go."

"If you'll let me drive coming back," her brother had said.

"You drive like a little baby."

He did too. Mishaun crept along using the manual controls. That wasn't anything like flying, or even running. It was more like walking along with somebody's really old granny.

"Forget it," Mishaun had said, and shoved his chair back from the table. He stomped out of the room, and Marika's father gave her an even more disapproving look.

"I just want to go fast," she'd said this morning.

She was going fast now, racing along the badlands again, jumping as high as the hopper would go with its cargo bin loaded up with sacks of fertilizer. On the horizon, she could see the green haze of her family's soybean fields, busily pumping oxygen into the air as they grew. In a couple of hundred years, walking around outside without a breath mask wouldn't make you gasp for breath in ten minutes. Or so adults said if you ever complained about the masks. The adults on Prosper acted like it was natural for everything to take at least a century.

Running with the hopper's neural jack plugged into the socket at the back of her skull made it feel like she was running on her own legs, only she happened to have four of them and could jump ten meters. The haze of green was coming up too quickly, and she turned to angle out further into the badlands where the ground hadn't yet been broken and tilled.

She was still coming straight home, she told herself, ignoring the arrow that appeared in her field of vision pointing directly toward the farm. She was just coming home another way. She jogged out at an angle until the soybean fields retreated into invisible distance, and then reluctantly curved her steps to begin angling toward home.

The sky suddenly lit up, as if someone had lit a match and kindled a blue flame. Marika stopped to stare and then turned a slow circle to look around her. Glowing curtains of blue and green light rippled all around the horizon. She'd never seen anything like it. She felt a stab of guilt that Mishaun was missing this.

She turned on the hopper's phone to call him, imagining quiet, and then imagining sound. At least he could look out a window. "Mishaun? Hey, obnoxious brother, look outside."

There was no answer, just an odd crackling in her ears. She thought hard about sound again, and then finally reached out to flip the manual switch that turned the radio on, wondering if her link to the hopper wasn't working right. Its legs still worked smoothly as she tested them, moving each one in turn, but the phone wasn't working at all.

She frowned in disappointment. On the up side, if the communications satellite was acting up again, not just the hopper's phone, she'd be spared school until someone got it working again. Maybe she'd even take Mishaun out in the hopper, if he was very, very nice to her.

She started 'walking' again and then realized that the arrow pointing home was gone. That meant the communications satellite that tracked the hopper's position probably was out. She'd never had to find her way home without it. She turned around, at first certain that she was facing in the right direction, and then not sure at all. The rocky ground in every direction looked the same.

She was going the right way, she told herself, and ran as fast as she could to prove it. The rocky ground swept by under the hopper's feet, but she still didn't see the green haze of soybeans on the horizon, only the dancing lights. If she was going too far to the north or south, she'd hit one of their neighbors' farms, and that would just be embarrassing. If she was going too far west, she was heading out into the open badlands.

Marika kept running until she would have been out of breath if she'd been running on her own legs. She wasn't out of breath in the hopper, but the thought reminded her she was eventually going to run out of air. She slowed down, trying to think. Maybe the best thing to do was turn around and go in the opposite direction. If she was heading out into the badlands now, she'd be sure to strike one of the farms that way. On the other hand, if she was going parallel to the line of farms, it wouldn't help her to turn around and go the other way.

The hopper's air was supposed to last for twelve hours, and she knew her parents didn't like for her to be in the hopper with the air tank less than a quarter full. She knew she'd left town with five hours of air left, but the clock didn't work without the communications network either, and without it she wasn't sure how long she'd been lost. She had a breath mask in the hopper, though, with another three hours' worth of air for emergencies.

Three hours' air if she'd filled it when she left home. Only she'd wanted to get out of there fast. She tried to convince herself she'd grabbed the mask out of the hopper and filled it from the big tank before climbing into the driver's seat and jacking herself in.

No matter how hard she tried to pretend, she knew she hadn't stopped to fill the mask. Her hands were shaking, and she started getting mad at herself for being such a baby. Then she realized the whole hopper was shaking, buffeted back and forth as if by a strong wind, but there were never any strong winds on Prosper except when shuttles landed.

As if in answer to her thought, she saw the shape of a low-flying shuttle plunging toward her, its broad wings overshadowing the hopper as it passed overhead. There was something wrong with the way it was flying, she had time to think, and then it hit the ground, far too hard, skipping like a stone over the rocky ground and then plowing a trench through it before finally coming to a stop.

"Shuttle command?" Marika said, wishing for the phone to start working again. "A shuttle just crashed. It's out near the Foster farm." She flicked the switch on and off again a couple of times. "Can anybody hear me?"

The phone poured static into her ears until she left it turned off. She ran toward the shuttle. Probably its communication systems were still working. Someone would come rescue the pilot. And if they found her there, too, she'd be a rescuer who came to help, not a dumb lost kid who stumbled into someone's farm hours late and short on air.

When she drew close to the shuttle, she could see no one had emerged yet, and the shuttle hadn't extended its walking legs. Maybe the shuttle could still take off again. Take off and leave her behind. She ran faster and realized a moment too late that she was racing toward the edge of the trench the shuttle had raked deep into the ground.

She tried to screech to a stop, but the hopper's safety systems kept its legs moving to slow her down without skidding. *STOP!* she yelled in her head, thinking about planting her legs firmly, and the hopper's front two legs stopped dead. But she hadn't stopped the rear ones, and as they took one more slow step, the hopper teetered on the edge of the trench and then pitched forward.

Marika barely had time to brace herself before the hopper bashed into the bottom of the trench with a bone-shaking crash and then lurched heavily to the side, crashing to a stop.

Marika opened her eyes — she didn't remember closing them — and realized she was lying on her side, tangled in the hopper's webbing. She tried to stand the hopper up, but its legs wouldn't obey her. After a while, she reached up and unplugged the useless neural jack from the base of her skull, pushed her braids aside to plug her own legs back in, and kicked to free herself.

She realized then that her own right leg wasn't obeying her either, dragging like a dead weight, and she felt the sick buzz of damaged circuits all the way up to her knee. She yanked her right knee up with her hand and poked at her leg. The ankle of her leg was bent at a funny angle, the metal dented, and she couldn't move anything below her knee.

She could see the shuttle's airlock from where she lay, and she waited, expecting a shuttle pilot in a blazing white uniform to emerge to come rescue her. No one came. She jumped at a sudden beeping, thinking that must be the airlock door opening, and then realized that was the hopper's alarm system telling her that she was running out of air.

The hopper must have sprung a leak when it hit the ground. It was old, all their tech was old, nothing worked the way it was supposed to, not even her stupid leg. Even if there were enough air in her breath mask, and even if she knew the way home, she didn't think she could walk all the way there without one leg.

But she could make it to the shuttle. She grabbed up the breath mask before she could talk herself out of the idea and hit the door controls. For a moment, she was afraid the door wouldn't open, but it jerkily slid open, and she pulled herself out. The shuttle was close, not more than fifteen meters away.

Her right ankle buckled as soon as she put any weight on it, so she didn't even try to walk on it, scooting on her butt instead, crab-walking herself toward the shuttle. Almost at once, her chest began to ache, and the mask felt like it was suffocating her. She pulled it off, and although it didn't help, it didn't hurt, either.

Marika had been outside before lots of times in the thin air, dashing from the house to one of the barns or to the hopper. Her father always told her to wear her mask when he caught her, but she hated to wait more than she hated feeling that she was heaving for breath. But then she'd never been more than a few steps away from a building and other people who'd notice if she didn't come back to the house.

The shuttle was right there. She moved faster, shoving herself along the ground, and then pulled herself up by the airlock door. It looked simple to release, but the part that looked like it should turn and slide didn't turn. She tugged at it, her lungs burning, but it still wouldn't move.

Her breath was coming harder, her heart pounding in her ears, and she fought panic. She banged on the airlock door, wondering what was wrong with the people inside. Didn't they see her out here? Were they just going to let her fall down dead outside the airlock door?

Her father would be so mad at her, she thought, her head swimming. He'd remind her that Mishaun always remembered to fill the breath masks when she let him drive. It sounded nice to have someone else driving, so that all she had to do was lie back in her seat and close her eyes.

A noise startled her, and she realized she'd been about to drift into sleep. If she did, she wouldn't wake up. She raised her fist to bang on the airlock door again and then saw it sliding sideways. Finally! She scrambled inside, hauling her leg in through the airlock door, and mashed the button to close the airlock. It slid shut, and after a moment, the inner airlock door opened.

The passenger compartment of the shuttle was empty, with a closed door leading back to the cargo compartment and an open one leading forward to the bridge. "Is anybody coming?" Marika called.

"I hear you, but I can't come to you," a woman's voice called from the bridge. "You're going to have to come to me."

Marika hauled herself up and leaned on the wall and then the shuttle seats as she hopped her way to the bridge. There were two seats on the bridge, even though the shuttles often ran with only one pilot. The copilot's seat was empty.

The pilot's seat was smashed backwards, part of the control panel now lying across the pilot's lap as she lay at a weird angle. Beneath her close-shaved hair, the back of her neck was bloody, and so were her brown hands.

"It's okay," the woman said. "I think it looks worse than it is." The illuminated lettering on her uniform said *Pilot Banks.* "I'm glad you're here. Is one of your parents here with you?"

"It's just me, Marika. I came in my hopper, but I got … I mean, I saw the crash."

"The solar flare took out my instruments at just the wrong time," Banks said. "Lucky me. I've been trying to get out from under this, but I can't quite … can you push that piece of metal right there? Careful, make sure it's not sharp."

It wasn't sharp, and Marika's arms were strong. She pushed hard, and Banks made a terrible face and then put her head back, panting, when the control panel was finally off her. Her uniform was bloody in a couple of places, and there was sweat on her face, but her voice was still calm when she spoke.

"Okay," Banks said. "I bet your hopper's communications don't work either, because the solar flare took the satellite offline, right?"

"Right," Marika said, but her heart sank. It hadn't occurred to her that the shuttle's communications wouldn't work either.

"And the shuttle's controls are this mess that fell on me. So I'm going to need you to take me back to town in your hopper. I bet you can get us there pretty fast."

"The hopper's broken," Marika said tightly. "It's leaking air and the legs won't work because I ran it off the edge of the trench. And I don't know which way home is and my breath mask doesn't have any air in it, and even if it did my leg doesn't work, so I can't run. I can't even walk."

Her chest was heaving as if she were back outside, and she could feel tears prickling at the corners of her eyes.

"Slow down and let's figure out one thing at a time," Banks said. "I know how to navigate us back to town, and I have plenty of breath masks. We might be able to fix your hopper, but that's a long shot, so let's take a look at your leg first. Where does it hurt?"

"It doesn't hurt," Marika said. "It's just not working. I think when the hopper crashed it got all bent up, and there's something wrong with the circuits."

Banks's eyes went to the back of her neck, not to her leg. "You have a neural implant."

"Much good it does me when nothing works."

"Okay, Marika, we may be back in business," Banks said. "The manual controls are scrap metal now, and I can't jack into the shuttle to fly it that way."

Marika realized for the first time that there was a neural implant socket half in and half torn out of the back of Banks's neck, a bloody mess of wiring and bent metal.

"But if you're willing to jack yourself in," Banks continued. "I can walk you through getting us back to town. First, you're going to have to—"

"I know," Marika said, already in the co-pilot's seat, her heart leaping in excitement. Not only was she going to come back to town a hero, but she was going to come back to town flying a real shuttle. She reached for the neural jack in the headrest of the seat and plugged it into her implant's socket.

"Marika, wait—"

Pain hit her like a hammer, like something crushing every bone in her body, red hot pain that went on and on, like the pain in her legs when the silo door had crushed them and kept crushing and she had screamed and screamed—

The pain stopped, but she kept on screaming, and clutched with both hands at something she realized after a moment was the fabric of Banks' uniform. Banks had crawled over to her, hurt as she was, to unplug the jack, because Marika hadn't thought to do it. Shame crawled in her stomach, and she made herself let go of Banks and stopped screaming.

"It hurt me!" She knew the shuttle was only a machine, but it had felt like it was trying to crush her, as if it were deliberately slamming that heavy door shut on her again and again.

"The neural feedback from the shuttle is a lot more intense than a hopper or your legs," Banks said. Her hand was cupping the back of Marika's head, a soothing pressure against Marika's braids. "It's not trying to hurt you, it's just trying to tell you that it's hurt. You're just not used to it, so it probably feels pretty overwhelming."

"It hurt so much."

"We've taken a lot of damage," Banks said. She was still sweating, and although her voice was still calm and encouraging, her expression didn't quite match it. "But I'm hoping it's all exterior hull damage and this mess in here, not vital propulsion systems."

"You want me to do that again."

"Yes, but first I want you to listen to what I was trying to tell you when you went running ahead, okay? I want you to visualize a dimmer switch, like the ones you use to turn lights up and down. There's writing on the switch, and it says *feedback*."

Marika nodded. It was something like the exercises they'd had her do when she got her legs, before she'd learned to control them without having to think about it.

"Now slide that dimmer all the way down. Do it a couple of times, really picturing that switch in your mind."

"Got it," Marika said.

"Okay. As soon as you jack in, the moment you feel any pain, I want you to take that switch and slide it down. I'll tell you what to do after that."

Marika reached for the jack, and hesitated for a moment, not hurting yet but remembering the intense pain, remembering her legs feeling like they were on fire. But it looked like it hurt Banks to move right now, and Banks was still moving. Marika gritted her teeth and plugged in the jack.

There was nothing but pain, beating through her body with every beat of her heart. She tried to visualize the slider, but all she could see was the silo. The doors were closing again, crushing her…

No!

Now she had the slider in her hand, and she could stop it, she could stop the pain, she could turn it—

"Down, down, down!" She slid down the imaginary slider, and the pain eased, becoming a throbbing ache, and then no more than an uncomfortable tickle of discomfort. "I got it," she said, her voice uneven but steadying. "I turned it down."

"Good," Banks said. Her own voice sounded tired. "Now think about the shuttle's legs, about extending them. All at once, just like standing up."

"Aren't we going to fly?" At the thought, the shuttle shuddered a little, and she felt a hundred complicated things happening as the shuttle tried to ready itself for liftoff, readouts and sensations flickering in and out of consciousness too fast for her to understand any of them.

"There's too much you'd have to learn first," Banks said. "I need you to stop trying to fly the shuttle, right now, and concentrate on extending the legs. We're going to have to walk home, but we will get home."

"Walking is too slow," Marika protested, but she concentrated. It did feel like standing up, but on bigger, stronger legs than she'd felt even in the hopper. She tried to walk, and for a moment she didn't think her front legs – the shuttle's front legs – would clear the front edge of the trench.

Then she was up and walking, the shuttle moving steadily on its heavy legs.

"Turn us thirty degrees clockwise," Banks said. "That's right, keep heading that way. That'll take us right into town."

Marika tried to speed the shuttle's steps, but it would only plod at a measured pace, although its legs were long enough that they were covering plenty of ground with each stride. "It's going to take us forever," Marika said.

"We'll get there," Banks said, leaning back against the side of the pilot's seat. "That's the important part. It might take a couple of hours, but I can live with that."

"I still wish I could fly though."

"You'll fly," Banks said. "When it's your time, you're going to fly. I don't have any doubt about that."

"I bet you could recommend me for pilot training," Marika said, not quite daring to make it a question.

"I bet I could, in about five years."

"I can wait," Marika said, unable to keep the little smile from curling up her lips. She kept walking, each step eating up more of the ground between the two of them and home.

# Luckless Tin Elephant
## Angeline Woon

*Angeline Woon is a Malaysian writer who lives in Ottawa, Canada, where she has taken up breeding pet rocks. Her short stories have been published in the* Esquire *magazine,* Readings from Readings 2, KL Noir: White, FUTURA *and* Cyberpunk: Malaysia. *She is co-editor for a Southeast Asian urban writing anthology. Like all children, Angeline had wanted to become a paleontologist but ended up in microbiology instead. She later took up medical journalism so she could train to be a writer and write about dinosaurs. Angeline has yet to write an outbreak story and refuses to do so unless they involve dragons. In between writing and pulping novels-to-be, she visits museums and old forts for the atmosphere.*

"Unlucky female! Leave now, quick!" shouted the pawang in Malay.

Suan stifled a groan. She had hoped to get the oto-gajah, the elephant automaton, into the pit before the pawang showed, so he could not block her entry. But since the pawang was there, she would have to ask him permission to enter the mine. Politely, as per her father's orders. Meanwhile, the poor miner was suffocating under the fallen earth.

She pulled a lever. There was a clank, and the automated elephant settled with cheerful hiss. She dismounted and gave the oto-gajah a proprietary pat on its metal leg. She girded herself mentally and turned to face the pawang.

A few weeks before, Suan and Tok Pawang had had an

argument. Some of the men had threatened to leave if the pawang's pride was not appeased. Her father had lectured her for more than an hour, laying down a series of rules, which ended with the admonition: "Be mindful of our social position. You are a lady, so behave like one."

If anyone else but Pa had said that to her – his second wife, for instance – Suan would have plotted and then carried out cold, hard revenge. Something involving cow dung, or perhaps the poisonous plant that grew under the mango tree that made the skin burst out in boils. But because Pa had said it, Suan bit her tongue. She had felt disquieted, because rather than getting angry and shouting at her, he had seemed resigned.

"Be a lady, Suan," said the girl to herself. "Do it for Pa."

"Apa khabar, Tok Pawang?" she called out the Malay words of greeting. He approached her from the edge of the mining pit. Though he had his walking stick, he still slipped on the muddy ground. He seemed frantic, and he was waving a white cloth, one he typically used in his rituals to chase away evil spirits.

Suan's bare feet squelched in the mud. She had hurried out of the house as soon as she heard the news, forgetting to put on her slippers. A frantic miner had rushed into her father's audience hall and shouted that there had been a cave-in. She knew the oto-gajah could help. And then, once successful, she could persuade her father to support her plans to bring the mechanical elephants into the tin mines permanently. But first, she had to get past the pawang.

She bowed at the man. Was it low enough? Or too low? Did she incline her head sufficiently? She hoped she did not just cause offense. Feeling self-conscious, she pushed back her shoulders and stood up straight. She let her nose tilt in the air, just a smidgen, to show that she was a lady. Absently, she brushed a lock of hair from her forehead. She smelled oil.

"Haiyoh!" she exclaimed in horror. There were black oil and dirt on her fingers from the oto-gajah. She wiped her hands on the leather apron she wore atop her blue cotton tunic and trousers and was dismayed at the resulting smear of oil, dirt and soot.

She smiled nervously at the pawang. He was breathing hard from his exertion. She opened her mouth to greet him again, but he interrupted her.

"Ngi ceu," he gasped. He was repeating his previous message, this time in Hakka, Suan's own Chinese dialect. "You go away." He waved the cloth in her face. It touched the tip of her nose.

Suan's cheeks burned; the pawang's actions stoked her internal forge. The pawang meant to chase her away as though she was an evil spirit!

She was just about to say something insulting that she had learned from the miners, but her father's words came to mind. "Do not antagonize the man," he had said. "The men trust him, and I don't know if you can find another good shaman who can bau timah, sniff out the tin, the way he does. Try not to make problems for me, Ah Suan." He had been worried about the competing mines opening in the north, in Perak. They had been luring pawangs to work for them.

Suan took a deep breath and said, "I can help."

"You can help by going away." Tired of flapping the cloth at her, the pawang poked his walking stick – also used in rituals – in her general direction.

"But –"

"You have no respect for our rituals and traditions. Women are unlucky. I told you before. What did I say the last time? Do not come back here. It was bad enough that you brought these abominations, these soulless machines... Do not compound our bad fortune with your feminine emanations."

Feminine emanations, mouthed Suan silently. How dare he? How dare he talk to her that way? The pawang's sarong, tunic and trousers were funereal black, and he was lecturing her about bad luck?

Still, she held herself in check. Pa, you better appreciate what I'm doing for you.

"Let me dig the poor man out. Please. He must be suffocating."

Likely, he was dead. The man could not have survived the bone-crushing fall of the earth. She could see that now that she was there at the scene. The lack of urgency shown by the miners, who were paying more attention to Suan and the pawang than to digging, was further proof.

The pawang looked as though he was considering her appeal. Or maybe he, too, realized that the miner was dead and wondered how to use that knowledge against her. Finally, he nodded and said, "You should have thought of that before you came here and caused his bad luck."

She stared.

No matter what argument she put forward against the pawang's superstitions, he would find another that she was hard-pressed to counter. How does one fight such illogical statements? She shook her head.

"Such nonsense," she said. "How many piculs of rice would it take to cleanse all this bad luck I'm going to cause right now? What was it the last time? Two? Twenty? I cannot remember. Probably twenty, because you look like you have eaten that much. Whichever it is, send my father the bill."

The man spluttered with rage.

Suan slipped and stumbled her way to the oto-gajah, piling her plait on her head as she did so, the way the men did when they worked. She rapidly scaled the mechanical beast.

She dropped into the cockpit, right behind the domed head, and placed her hands on the bar that she used to steer the machine. She smiled. She was home.

"Let's show them what you can do," she said.

She released the lever that kept the oto-gajah in position. The metal beast clanked and hissed. The oto-gajah lurched, but Suan had expected it. She knew how to move with the machine. Forward, it went, steam building up within. When the needle hit red on the gauge, Suan pulled a knob. Steam escaped from a valve in the fake elephant's trunk. The tin machine trumpeted a call for everyone to move out of its way. In the jungles nearby, birds burst out of the trees.

•••

The pit that had collapsed was one of the smaller ones, big enough to fit twenty elephants (a wholly mental exercise, seeing as elephants were as unlucky as females in tin mines). Miners swarmed up ladders with buckets holding a picul of soil at a time. They slid down different ladders. The men shouted instructions and cursed at each other in Malay (ignored by the lady-like Suan, who rode primly on her steed). Though the miners were Chinese, those who spoke the Hakka dialect did not necessarily speak Cantonese or Hokkien, and vice versa.

Suan entered the pit via a slope that had formed during the collapse, far from where the men were digging. The miners backed away when she first came with the oto-gajah, but they followed her instructions.

The work was the kind the men were accustomed to, though on usual days, they would have been under the shade to escape the harsh afternoon sun. They wore their pigtails wrapped around their heads. Their shaved foreheads shone, and they perspired heavily, though they wore only loose trousers.

Suan found the work tedious, and her shoulders ached from the pressure she had to place on the steering column. The oto-gajah was mostly automated, but for fine work, manual guidance was necessary.

She listened to the men as they conversed. They must have thought she could not hear them over the clangs of metal and the hiss of the hydraulic release.

"That silly man, thinking he can tell us what to do. Pawang or not, unlucky or not, we do not dare lay hands on the Capitan's daughter," said a stocky, broad-shouldered miner.

"Ya," agreed his skinny colleague. "It would be most unlucky for us then. The Capitan dotes on that child. He lets her have her own way."

The other man said something in an undertone that Suan could not hear. Both men laughed.

"Did you hear about the *naga*?" said the stocky man.

"What is a *naga*?"

"Dragon."

"Oh. Well, what about a dragon?"

"This merchant came the other day and was gibbering about how a dragon was seen around the Rawang area. He said the dragon guarded a *sutra*."

"*Sutra?*"

"A holy text."

"And then?"

"He said that Mai-he-di and those gangsters, the Ghosts, are working together again. He said they captured the dragon and are thinking of using it for vengeance."

"So?"

"You know lah – the Ghosts hate the Capitan. Mai-he-di also hates the Capitan. So maybe after the next pay, I'm going to make myself scarce, in case the dragon decides to visit Kuala Berlumpur and set it on fire again."

"Choi, your talk is much unlucky."

"Up to you if you want to stay. Me, I know better." The stocky man shrugged and went back to work.

More nonsense, thought Suan. Nagas and sutras. Dragons. Stories for children.

She shook her head at the superstitions prevalent among the miners. But she had to admit, her heart beat fast when they spoke about the fire of Kuala Berlumpur. She remembered the blazing heat, so hot that she thought she was on fire, the crackling and crashes of falling buildings, the painful stench of smoke, her father holding her tight, running, while she screamed for Mama and her little brothers...

The oto-gajah slipped.

Men shouted and scrambled out of the pit as more earth threatened to engulf them. Suan moved the oto-gajah to stem the landslide with the tin elephant's body. The movement of the earth slowed, but it continued to fall in a steady flow. She shouted at the men to bring wood and to shore up the wall with it.

Crisis averted, Suan focused on picking up dirt with the trunk and dumping the unused soil over the side of the pit.

More shouting. They found the trapped miner. He was dead.

•••

"Why? Why did you go to the mine?" said the Capitan, Suan's father. "You cannot just go anywhere you want, Ah Suan. You're almost fifteen. You're not a little girl anymore."

"What was I supposed to do, Pa? The man was dying."

"You just wanted to show off," said her father's second wife, the mother of the sons.

"You know better than I do that he was already dead," said the Capitan. "You just gave Tok Pawang more reasons to consolidate his power at the mine. Or he may just leave and take some of my best men with him. Some of them are already thinking of leaving because of ill-luck."

"Superstitions," said Suan.

"You may scorn them and think it not important, but others take their beliefs very seriously. Why can't you respect that? Why do you always have to fight me on this, Suan?" Her father slumped in his chair. "Why do you keep trying to push your strange ideas on people?"

"Please lah, Pa. What's the point of having the oto-gajahs around if you're not going to use them to their full potential?"

"I'm not even sure why we need them, Ah Suan. We've got all those steam-powered things for the mine."

"I've told you before, Pa, you got cheated when you bought those."

The steam-powered pumps had been bought from the richer tin mines of Perak, but they clogged up badly and needed twenty men to move them besides. Suan believed they must have been sabotaged before the sale. Once, the pumps broke down at the same time. The mine flooded rapidly. Suan's father despaired. That was when she had the idea of introducing the oto-gajahs to the mine.

At first, no one dared go near the machines, but since they worked on their own, it did not make a difference that no one wanted to tend to them. Because the oto-gajahs did not break down, and the mine was clear of water, the production of tin increased. The miners were happy, as they had shares in the profits. They ignored the pawang when he complained that the tin elephants were blocking his abilities to sniff out ore.

Then one day there was a slew of accidents at the mine. The pawang said that the tutelary deities at the Na Tuk Kongs, the altars built to placate the local spirits, were upset by the presence of the tin elephants. The spirits had threatened to harm the miners if nothing was done. Suan laughed it off as a big joke. The miners, however, said that they would strike. After a long negotiation, Suan's father agreed to send ten piculs of good rice, five chickens, one goat and an undisclosed amount of gold to appease the spirits.

Later, when Suan descended on the mine to maintain the machines, the *pawang* said that it was her presence that had angered the spirit of the tin, a *seladang*, or type of ox. If she persisted on showing up, then a purification ritual must be performed.

"He's just making this up!" Suan had complained to her father after the purification ritual. She'd had a rough scrub-down using a loofah, followed by a two-hour soak in a bath full of limes and the petals of a red jungle flower that had to be harvested during a full moon. "He wants me to give up."

"Why don't you?" asked her father.

"Because I'm right. Also, he challenged me. I don't want him to think he won."

Her father laughed, to Suan's irritation.

"You're both more alike than you think," said her father. "If you insist on being as stubborn as he is, you can hardly complain. Besides, dear daughter, your current scent is an improvement on oil and smoke, and it does a father's heart good to be able see his offspring's face."

He had a sense of humor about things then. Lately though, Suan thought, her father had been less amused by her projects. He seemed to view the oto-gajah as a nice diversion, a luxury toy, fine for his little princess to play with, but he saw no place for it in the proper working world of grown men.

"Pa, about the water pumps, the oto-gajahs can do more than

just drain the mines. Look at what one did today."

"A man is dead."

"Not by my doing! And even if he had survived the crush of soil, the pawang wasted time with his idiotic talk. Imagine, Pa, if someone, trained to work with the oto-gajah was on-site. The outcome would have been much different. Or, better yet, imagine if the oto-gajahs did all the mining. I'm working on a project so that they could pick the untreated ore and 'eat' it. The ore will be sorted inside the body. This would require an intricate series of weights and counterweights – I've worked it out already, but you don't want to know about that. Anyway, in the end, you will have a nicely packaged slab of tin, ready for sale. No one needs to get hurt."

"Yes, and the miners will have nothing to do. They will be begging your father for work," said the second wife, who was apparently still in the room.

"Pa," said Suan, leaning closer to her father. "I've got the plans for an engine that moves faster. You don't even have to unload the tin slabs at the mine. You start the oto-gajahs digging in the morning, and by nightfall, your tin ore will be in Klang and loaded on the British ships."

She thought she had him then. She could see him calculating the profits such a machine would bring him.

"All I need, Pa, is a little bit of gunpowd –"

"Husband, remember your decision," the second wife said sharply. "She needs to learn responsibility."

The Capitan sighed. "Go and feed our sons," he said.

"But –"

"Remember your responsibility," he said to his wife in a tone he would never use on Suan.

The wife picked up her embroidery and left in a huff. Suan's father sighed again once she was gone. He rubbed his head under the black cap he wore, a mark of his office.

"Listen, Ah Suan. Tok Pawang was very unhappy that you did not show him the proper respect today. Be quiet. It does not matter what you think about it. I have told you before, these people work very close to death all day, and if they are superstitious, it is because they have very little to keep them from harm's way. Sometimes the belief that they're protected is enough."

"But Pa —"

Her father held up his hand. "Did you know, today, when the earth shifted under the oto-gajah, I was there? I saw the ground move, and I saw that you were on the oto-gajah in the pit. I thought... I thought you were going to join your mother and your brothers. Today, Ah Suan, I felt the same grip on my heart as I felt on the day I last saw them. And that is the reason I cannot let you go into the mine again."

Suan bowed her head. She had not considered things that way.

"Tomorrow," said her father, "we will close the workshop. Whatever is in it will be sold."

"No! Pa —"

"Your oto-gajahs will be taken apart, and the tin melted and sold —"

"They're not my oto-gajahs. They're Mama's!" screamed Suan.

The room was silent, but Suan's ears were ringing. Her father breathed heavily, and for a moment she thought he was going to hit her. But he only looked tired, as he was wont to do lately. He looked old and deflated.

Very quietly, so much so that Suan could barely hear him, her father said, "The tin will be melted and sold, and the money from the sale will go towards buying your dowry gifts. I'm getting old, Ah Suan. One day, soon, I will die. I endeavored to find you a husband. A rich merchant from China has indicated an interest in you for his number one son. This is lucky, because men of his caliber prefer brides with bound feet, and he did not mind that you have not been kept indoors. After the New Year, you will be married."

•••

The strokes of the hammer kept perfect rhythm to Suan's ragged breathing as she formed the oto-gajah's ears. She had been working all night, and her limbs alternated from feeling like an anvil to feeling like a feather in the wind.

She still burned with anger at her father's words. Lucky, thought Suan. Lucky to be a man's wife. Lucky to be able to wear embroidered silk, instead of the blue workmen's cotton. Lucky to have all that she had worked for thrown into the smelting fire.

Bang. Bang. She struck the tin. There. Done.

She dropped her hammer and stretched. Her neck and back gave satisfying cracks. The room swayed. She closed her eyes and let the feeling pass.

She examined the joints of the ears. She had made the ear so it could stretch out over the head to protect the mahout and to intimidate organic elephants. Should she affix the ears to make the oto-gajah whole? In her physical state, she would likely fall off the ladder and break her back. She could just hear her mother's voice: "You itchy backside, is it? Asking for trouble, is it?"

She chuckled. Ma was a pragmatic woman. Suan missed her. She even missed her two little brothers, who got in her way by following her like ducklings.

It was her mother who had started her on the elephant obsession. A man-eating elephant had rampaged through the Kuala Berlumpur neighborhood of Ampang and was brought down by the arquebus of the Malay viceroy's brother-in-law. The domesticated elephants balked at moving their fallen relation, and no elephant stews could be made, as the monster had eaten the flesh of man. The corpse was left to rot in a stinking pile.

The exposed skeleton made Suan scream of ghosts at night. To console her, her mother said, "Ah Suan, do not be afraid, for the white thing that you saw is part of our bodies, too. It holds us up and helps us move."

Suan's mother was a fine puppet maker. She made a creature with only sticks and made it move to teach Suan the principles of motion in animals.

Then came the fire. After that, Suan was often left alone, as her father saw to his duties rebuilding the town. She wandered the streets of the old place, through skeletons of burned buildings, remembering what they used to look like when she ran through them with her duckling brothers.

The skeleton of the man-eating elephant survived the fire, and though the ivory was valuable, the locals left it alone. (Superstitions again!) Suan remembered the feel of the skeleton puppet as it danced in her hands.

Slowly, working on some idea, undefinable at the time, she gathered bits and pieces of usable wood and formed the frame that was the skeleton of her first oto-gajah.

Suan smiled, remembering the prototype. Clumsy – she spent more time out of it than in it – it was powered by foot pedals and had no covering. Now, gears and pulleys, weights and counterweights were covered with a tough tin alloy, smooth in all places except where plates overlapped at the joints. Instead of pedals, the oto-gajah was powered by a gunpowder engine.

Too bad this will be the last of the oto-gajahs, Suan thought. Shrugging away her exhaustion, she picked up the ears and climbed the ladder.

•••

On the northwest side of Ampang, across a field cleared by fire but never rebuilt, was a lake. It had been a mine once, rich in tin ore, but abandoned for reasons no one could recall. Soon it filled with water, and stories abounded of spirits that lurked beneath, waiting to drown unwary swimmers. The area was twice abandoned, as picnickers found safer places for their frolics.

Suan did not believe the stories. She knew that the hantu, the otherworldly spirits that pulled at swimmers' legs were nothing more than underwater currents, eddies formed by the uneven shape of the ground beneath the water.

She guided the oto-gajah to the twice-abandoned place. Dawn had arrived, and the mist settled about her, caressing her with a cool kiss. Mornings usually gave her a feeling of renewal, but now she merely felt damp. Birds sang for the sunrise, and she shouted at them in irritation and smacked at the mosquitoes buzzing about her head.

Suan cursed her stupidity. The plan had been to hide the oto-gajah so that it would not be sold with everything else. But in the morning light, or perhaps it had been the fresh air that had awakened her, it occurred to her that hiding the oto-gajah would come to naught if she was to be married off to some stranger in China.

She could go away. Take the oto-gajah and go where they would appreciate her for her skills, where she did not have to pretend to be docile or polite. She could head north by land, go to one of the Perak mining towns. Or she could go to Klang and persuade a ship captain to let the oto-gajah on board. Where would she go then? Malacca maybe? She heard they were quite progressive under British rule.

Thunder rolled in the distance.

Suan shivered and regretted that she had not thought to bring extra clothing or food. She heard thunder again, but, looking up, she saw no clouds. She got up, feeling unsettled, and went to the ridge overlooking the town.

Thunder again, and light, but not from lightning. She saw movement on the road from Rawang. In the still of the morning, shouts carried across the clearing. *"Amok! Amok!"*

Matchlocks fired. Ampang was under siege.

●●●

Suan was used to noise, the whoosh of bellows, the patter of rain on corrugated tin roofs, the hiss of the oto-gajah hydraulics, the clangs and complaints of the steam-powered tapioca processing machines, the shouts of the miners at work.

Nothing prepared her for the screams of the frenzied and the injured, the relentless firing of matchlocks, and the metal on metal of sword and bayonet.

Waves upon waves of fighters came on foot from Rawang. They were fought by her father's men, the miners, the Sikh security forces and the Malays from the nearby kampungs.

Suan knew that the attackers must be the Mai-he-di forces the miners had been talking about the day before. After all, the Ghosts, the rival society of clans, ran their mines from Rawang. The two forces had been responsible for the burning of Ampang and most of Kuala Berlumpur all those years ago, when Suan's mother and brothers had died.

She was too scared to move. Should she join the fight? How does one kill? Oh, Ma, what should I do? What are you doing now, Pa?

She thought of the Malay proverb, "When two elephants fight, the mouse-deer is trampled in the middle." Thinking about the mouse-deer, Suan sat helpless under the cover of the trees. Morning turned to afternoon. Dusk fell, but the usual jungle sounds of monkeys, birds and insects did not arise. Clashes died down, and cries of war gave way to grunts of exhaustion and pain. The air smelled of gunpowder, and, though perhaps she imagined it, the iron tang of blood.

The enemy forces retreated, and a cheer arose from town of Ampang. Suan gave a whoop from her protected spot on the ridge. She got up, ready to run down to join her family and friends.

But a great shriek rent the air, not human, but like metal dragged over stone, the opening of the Gates of Hell. A creature came upon the field, wide and tall as an elephant, its length that of seven elephants lined up tail to trunk. Suan remembered what the miners had said about the naga and the sutra.

"Tai Lung," she whispered. King of the dragons.

•••

The dragon was sluggish, like a snake on a cold night, but it moved forward, always forward, towards the town. It screeched and yowled, a sound that turned Suan's spine to agar. It had no legs that she could see. People in Ampang, valiant defenders all, threw down their matchlocks and ran.

The dragon stopped and seemed to be deep in contemplation. Then, shaking its mighty head, the size of a fully grown bull elephant, it emitted a roar. Its mouth opened. Suan heard chugging noises as steam escaped the dragon's mouth. The chugging increased in volume. A pause.

The dragon coughed.

White flame roared forth, so bright in the nighttime that it left pinpricks of pain in Suan's closed eyes. The town caught fire.

Attap and corrugated tin roofs alike exploded. Buildings were aflame, halfway to ashes.

Pa could fight with guns and swords but not a destructive fire like that, thought Suan. He could only run away, as he had with her when she was a small girl. She could run away now – go, and survive. After all, she was going to do that just a short while ago, wasn't she? Pa would want her to be safe.

Oh! Pa. Where are you?

Suan shook her head. What a silly question. Of course he had stayed in town. He did not know where she was and was probably looking for her.

How does one fight a dragon? Did the dragon's presence mean that mythical creatures truly existed? Her eyes seemed to prove that it did. What then, about the ox in the ground that was said to be the spirit of the tin ore? Did she, as the pawang believed, bring this ill-luck amongst her people by acting like an arrogant fool?

The chugging from the dragon began, as though dragon-fire needed to be built up, like Suan's fire at the forge.

Chugging. Like bellows at the forge.

Suan squinted at the dragon. It did not seem to be doing much. In the light of the fire from the burning town, she saw that the dragon did indeed have legs. It had a multitude of legs. Thin, human legs.

You cannot fight a myth, thought Suan, but there are many things you can fight.

"Hold on, Pa, I'm coming!" shouted Suan. "Just stay safe."

She leaped on to the oto-gajah and maneuvered to the lake to pick up water with the trunk. Once the tank was full, she charged down the hill towards the dragon, still lying at the edge of town.

Something about the charging tin elephant must have seemed a threat, because the dragon shifted in the time it took for Suan to cross the clearing. Now the dragon faced the oto-gajah. Not good, but not bad, either. At least it wasn't facing Ampang.

The chugging built to a crescendo as the oto-gajah surged forward.

Suan screamed out loud, "Let it work, let it work, please, let it work!"

The dragon coughed.

Suan flipped a toggle switch and crouched. The oto-gajah's ears fanned out. Fire spattered on the shield. The dragon-fire seemed to go on forever, surging around her oto-gajah. She hoped, prayed, that the tin would not melt.

All of a sudden, the dragon-fire stopped.

Tentatively, she peeked out over the oto-gajah's dome. The fire had spread in Ampang. Residents were shouting, screaming for buckets and pumps and hoses, but wherever water touched, the flames leapt twice as high.

Water feeds the dragon-fire, thought Suan.

The chugging began and built in volume. Suan recognized the pattern. She thought she knew what to do about it. She hoped and prayed that it would work.

Ha! So that was what Pa meant about holding onto superstitions. It was all people could do in certain situations when everything else was out of their control. She was ready to accord him that win.

She curled the oto-gajah's trunk upwards in what some people referred to as the "ready to bestow fortune" position.

That cough again, the precursor to destruction. Suan hit a lever. A jet of water gushed from the oto-gajah's trunk into the dragon's mouth.

A series of pops emanated from the dragon. Smoke billowed from the head, thick and black and oily, smelling of brimstone, hugging the ground like a waterfall of thunderclouds.

The dragon screamed with the voices of many men.

●●●

Some said later that the explosion could be heard all the way in Klang, Sungai Ujong and Malacca. The next morning, villagers in Sumatra talked about the bright light that had lit up the Malayan shores like a premature dawn.

Suan crawled out of the crumpled oto-gajah, which had been thrown head over heels in the blast. The surrounding field was flat, shrubs burnt away, charred twigs now sparkling with fiery fruits.

She stumbled to the town, her ears – nay, her head – ringing like the inside of a bell. A group of men resolutely wasted water on a crackling building. She grabbed the nearest soot-covered firefighter.

"Don't argue with me. Find an ax and break down these houses before the rest catch fire. Stop using water. We need sand. We need to go to the mine and get the oto-gajahs –"

"Ah Suan?" said the man. He dropped the bucket he was holding. "Ah Suan, you're alive."

"Pa?"

Suan's father embraced her.

•••

The ninth oto-gajah was rebuilt with help from a strange source, for the pawang knew a recipe for dragon-fire. The fire burned from an oily substance and grew when water was added to it. This type of burning gave more motive power and was more beneficial than gunpowder for the engine. Soon, oto-gajahs took over the work of the mine. Former miners became mahouts and begged for nothing.

Pa's second wife and sons were lost to the fire. Suan missed them as much as she missed her own mother and brothers.

A lady came to visit and offered a balm. "She's been to the Golden Hills, Pa. She's been to places so hot the ground is sunburned. She's been to places where the water is frozen, even from the sky. She's spoken to everyone and seen everything. She's so brave for a woman."

"Brave for a man, too. Ah Suan, you will make her a good companion."

"Oh. I never thought of leaving."

The lady left, and in her wake Suan bubbled with ideas too large for the town she had grown up in and saved.

One dewy morning, Suan climbed the dragon-fire-fueled oto-gajah and took leave of her father.

"I'll be back, Pa," she said.

"Go slowly," said her father, with an easy smile and a wave. In his heart, he knew that Suan would never come home. His daughter would grow, in body, mind and soul, away from his eyes. She would be replaced by a stranger. In his heart, Suan's father cursed the luckless tin elephant.

# The Sugimori Sisters and the Time Machine Conflict

## Brigid Collins

*Brigid Collins is a fantasy and science fiction writer living in Michigan. Her short stories have appeared in* Fiction River, The 2015 Young Explorer's Adventure Guide, *and The* MCB Quarterly. *Books one and two of her fantasy series,* Songbird River Chronicles, *are available in print and electronic versions on Amazon and Kobo. You can sign up for her newsletter at tinyletter.com/HarmonicStories.*

Bright sunlight came through the large square windows to the left of the student desks. It glinted off the bookshelf under the window, bounced from the blue and green globe in the corner by the teacher's desk, slid past the poster of the Declaration of Independence tacked to the white wall, and fell in a big splotch on the chalkboard at the front of the classroom, turning the middle of the board lime green and highlighting the neatly written words: "History paper final draft due Friday".

Despite the fact history was not Ellen Sugimori's favorite class, excitement ran through her. The teacher would hand back their rough drafts at the end of class today, with her comments attached. Ellen couldn't wait to see how much Ms. Haley loved her paper on the Japanese tea ceremony.

While Ellen's classmates shared nervous glances, all worried about the extra work they would clearly have to do to polish *their* papers to a perfect final draft, Ellen smiled at her own genius.

Being of Japanese descent, Ellen went to Japanese school

every Saturday. After an exciting adventure with Little Sister last summer, Ellen had done a project about the Japanese tea ceremony. Everyone at Japanese school had loved it, and the teacher called it the best project of the lesson.

When Ms. Haley announced the History paper two weeks ago, Ellen only had to tweak her project a little and write the presentation into a paper. It was the easiest paper Ellen had written all year, and she never even needed to step foot in the school's creepy, haunted library. She was dying to read Ms. Haley's praise.

"All right, class," Ms. Haley said, scooping up the pile of papers. "Once you've got your rough draft, you're free to go. Please read the comments carefully and work hard on your final drafts."

Ellen held her breath as Ms. Haley moved up and down the rows. *Finally*, the teacher reached her desk. Ellen grinned and reached for her paper. Ms. Haley smiled back, but in a funny way, with her lips very thin.

Ellen looked at her rough draft.

At the very top of the page, in red ink, read the words "Please do more research. This paper does not properly discuss the history involved."

Ellen's jaw dropped. She flipped through the pages to find them covered in more red notes.

By now, her classmates had filtered out into the hallway, and Ellen was alone with Ms. Haley.

"Did you have any questions for me, Ellen?" Ms. Haley asked. She smiled that thin-lipped smile again.

Ellen swallowed and turned back to the first page of her paper. "I don't understand. Everyone at Japanese school liked this project."

"It's a very good project, Ellen, and I know you're excited about the tea ceremony," Ms. Haley said, "but you didn't include any of the history. Why don't you go down to the library and do some research? I bet you'd find that period of Japan's history fascinating."

Ellen gulped and tried to ignore how her hands trembled at the mention of the library.

Unable to speak around the burn of misery in her throat, Ellen nodded and shuffled out of the classroom, her rough draft crumpled in her hand.

Laughter echoed in the halls as Ellen trudged through the crowd of students. It was the sixth graders' lunch period, but Ellen couldn't join in with her classmates' jokes. She wasn't even hungry anymore, though at the beginning of class she'd been dreaming of the bento box her mom had packed her.

Ellen grimaced. Even thinking of the onigiri, usually her favorite Japanese food, made her stomach do flip-flops.

The route to the cafeteria carried the students past the school library, and Ellen glanced at the heavy-looking doors as she came up to them. A shiver went down her spine at the sight of their dark wood. They didn't even have the little windows all the classroom doors had.

Casting one look down to the cafeteria, Ellen sighed and squeezed her rough draft. Her lunch was ruined anyway.

The cool metal handle of the left-hand door tingled against her palm, but the door itself was not as heavy as it looked, and it swung open easily when Ellen pulled. When she stepped inside, the door closed again with a soft click. Silence descended as if the library door were some magical barrier against the noise of the sixth graders beyond it.

The air was so still and musty inside the library that Ellen thought she must be the only person here. The librarian's desk stood abandoned when she turned to look. Still, Ellen found herself tiptoeing past the desk and to the shelves.

Just because the librarian wasn't there to yell at her didn't mean she wanted anyone, or any*thing,* else to hear her. Was it her imagination, or were the dim lights flickering?

Ellen shivered and crept into the history section to search for books on Japan. She'd find her books and get out of here before the ghosts could catch her.

She was reaching for a book, her fingers about to brush the stiff spine, when she heard a sound.

A soft thump and the hiss of paper sliding on paper slithered from the shelves behind Ellen.

Ellen gasped and snatched her hand back. She turned towards the sound, keeping her back pressed against the bookshelf. If a library ghost was coming for her, she wouldn't let it jump on her from behind.

She held her breath and strained her ears, listening into the silence.

The papery sound came again. It was closer this time.

Ellen's heart pounded, and when she heard footsteps coming nearer, she couldn't stop the tiny whimper that escaped her.

The footsteps picked up at her sound. Ellen tensed to run, ready to abandon her research to save herself. What was a bad grade on a paper compared to being caught by a ghost?

But just as she leapt out from the Japanese History section, someone else came from around the other side of the shelf. The two of them collided painfully, and Ellen fell to the floor, her rough draft fluttering out of her hands.

"Owwww! Why don't you watch where you're going?" said the other person.

Ellen gasped. "Little Sister? What are you doing here?"

Sprawled beside her on the stiff, floral-patterned carpet was Risako, a scowl on her face and papers scattered around her.

"I'm doing research, what does it look like?" Risako said. She gathered her papers into a neat bundle, tapping them on the floor to straighten them out.

Ellen glanced around for the ghost she'd heard, but she soon determined that there had been no ghost. This time.

"You scared me, Little Sister," she said finally, pushing herself to her feet. "I thought you were one of the library ghosts."

Little Sister snorted. "There's no scientific evidence to say that ghosts exist. You can be scared of them if you want, but I prefer to stick to scientific fact."

Ellen rolled her eyes and kept glancing over her shoulders. She didn't see any harm in being careful.

"What are you researching?" Ellen asked, finally satisfied that no ghosts were hanging around.

Risako scowled at her notes. "I'm looking for information on Galileo's findings on the moons of Jupiter for the first-grader science fair, but the school library doesn't have the sources I need."

"What do you need to know?" Ellen asked.

"I want his thought process, what observations he made each night, what sort of materials he used to make his telescope. I don't think I'm using the right brand of paper towel tubes."

Ellen kept herself from rolling her eyes. Little Sister was smart for a first grader, but sometimes Ellen wondered if she had a firm grasp on reality.

"Sounds like you really just want to talk to him, then," Ellen said, thinking suddenly of her own research. How cool would it be to discuss the tea ceremony with an ancient Japanese emperor?

Oblivious to Ellen's daydreaming, Little Sister turned back to the book shelves. "Well, I was hoping to have my time machine out of the prototype stage before testing it, but I might have to risk it if I can't find what I need for my science project."

Ellen snapped out of her thoughts of *kimono* and *samurai* and whirled to follow Little Sister. "A time machine? I thought you were getting your spaceship ready for another flight?" Ellen knew she had seen Little Sister tinkering around her cardboard monstrosity in the back yard last weekend. Ellen still couldn't believe it had actually taken them to Mars.

"Oh, I am," Little Sister said, digging around in her backpack. "The time machine is a side project. I'm trying to keep this machine compact."

She held out her favorite yellow wristwatch. A bundle of red and blue pipe cleaners was tangled around the band on either side of the face, and a small cardboard circle hung on the end of one pipe cleaner. Ellen saw scribbles in black crayon on the circle, but she couldn't make out what they might mean.

Ellen looked up to meet Little Sister's gaze. "That's a time machine?"

"Like I said, it's a prototype."

"But it can take us back in time?"

Little Sister fiddled with the arrangement of the pipe cleaners and twisted the dial on the side of the watch. "It can, but it's only strong enough right now for one trip and the return." Little Sister sighed. "I planned to test it out by going back to two days ago and keeping Mom from having *natto* at dinner, but my science project is more important."

Ellen and Little Sister shared a grimace at the memory of the sticky, stinky, slimy mess of soy beans they'd had to choke down. Little Sister obviously hadn't tested her time machine yet if Ellen still remembered their unfortunate dinner.

Little Sister shook her head as if to get rid of the memory and fiddled with the watch dial again. "Do you want to come with me to meet Galileo?"

Ellen chewed her lip, considering. "I really need to fix my history paper. We should go back to the invention of the tea ceremony."

"What? No, I'm visiting Galileo for my science fair project. We can go see the tea ceremony once I've got the machine out of the prototype stage."

Ellen grabbed at the time machine. "My paper is due next week, I can't wait for the next version. We're going to feudal Japan!"

Little Sister squirmed out of Ellen's reach, clutching the watch against her chest. "My science project is due next week, too! It's my machine, so you'll have to wait."

"I'm older than you," Ellen countered, reaching out again. "Give me that machine!"

"Make your own!"

With a growl like their neighbor's dog, Ellen lunged across the aisle to crash into Little Sister, knocking them both against the shelf of Asian history books. She ignored the books tumbling to the floor around her and grabbed at the yellow watch.

As her finger brushed against the cardboard circle, a sickening jolt tugged somewhere behind her belly button. Colors swirled around her, and the bookshelves melted together into a twirling vortex. Wind roared past Ellen's ears, and the strong scent of copper overwhelmed her. She couldn't feel the library's stiff carpet under her knees anymore.

Lying beside her, Little Sister glared up at Ellen. "What are you doing? Did you even set the time destination?"

"No," Ellen said. "I didn't do anything! How do you work this thing?"

"Let go of it, I'll fix it!"

"No way," Ellen said. "You'll take us to see Galileo. Just tell me how to set it."

As the colors danced around them and the noise rose to the roar of a freight train, Ellen and Little Sister grappled over the yellow wristwatch. Little Sister tugged on the band, and for a moment, Ellen thought she'd lost control of it. With a sharp jerk, she pulled the watch back.

The machine slid out of Little Sister's hands, and the vortex of colors stopped. Heavy heat descended on them, and a sticky-sweet scent rose up from the canopy of green, leafy trees below them.

Ellen screamed. The trees rushed up to meet them, and Ellen braced herself for impact.

Branches and broad leaves whipped at her as she tumbled through them. The snap and crack of breaking branches came like a typhoon. If she made it to the ground with any of her bones unbroken, it would be a miracle.

Finally, the wild descent came to a halt. Her head spun, and it took her a moment to realize she had reached the ground. In fact, she was lying in something cool and wet. She felt it seeping into her hair and school clothes. Ooh, Mom was going to throw a fit.

"Ellen!" Little Sister called from somewhere above her.

Ellen struggled to keep from sinking into the sucking mud and sat up. Her whole body ached, and scratches stung on her arms and legs, but she didn't think any bones were broken. A miracle, after all!

"Ellen, help!" Little Sister cried.

Ellen looked up and found Little Sister dangling from a

branch, the back of her school blouse snagged on the end of it. The tree looked odd, with its long, pointy leaves and gray bark, yet Ellen thought she'd seen a picture of something like it before.

Ellen stood and stepped away from the mud puddle. It stank, and the thick heat settling over her made her want to gag. She moved into the huge ferns at the base of Little Sister's tree and hoped the big fronds would scrape some of the mud from her clothes. Instead, the yellow spores hiding on the curled undersides stuck to her skin. Ellen grimaced. She looked like she had a bad, yellow case of the chicken pox.

"Get me down from here," Little Sister said, swinging her legs.

Ellen scowled up at her. "Serves you right. Where are we? *When* are we? This isn't feudal Japan."

"I have no idea! You never even let me look at the time machine. Get me down."

Ellen trudged over to the tree trunk and wrinkled her nose at the long, amber trails of sap oozing all over the rough gray bark. "Ugh, get yourself down. I'm not touching that tree. And if you had just worked with me instead of trying to take us to see Galileo, we wouldn't be in this swamp... jungle... thing."

"You're already all messy," Little Sister pointed out. "You landed in the mud. Look, you got my time machine dirty."

Ellen glanced back at the mud puddle. The yellow wristband flashed out of the muck, the red and blue pipe cleaners looking like they'd been through a particularly clogged pipe.

Ellen tromped back into the sloppy ground, trying not to breathe, and scooped up the watch.

"Maybe I'll just go back home myself," she said, not looking at Little Sister. Risako could always tell when Ellen was lying.

This time was no different. "You can't work the time machine without me. Besides, Mom will ground you for a million years if you leave me in a tree in... whenever this is. Get me down, and I'll figure out when we are."

Ellen sighed. The mud was drying on her skin and clothes, and sweat dripped down her entire body. She was oozing just like that tree, and the unforgiving heat of this place mixed with the stink of the mud puddle made breathing near impossible. She was tired of fighting with Little Sister. They'd both lost their chance at visiting someone in the past. It was time to go home.

"Ellen!" Little Sister screamed.

"I'm coming, I'm coming," Ellen said, turning back.

But Little Sister kept screaming, her eyes bugged out and her arms and legs windmilling like she was trying to backstroke.

The leaves behind Ellen rustled, and she whirled just in time to see a huge, rust-orange creature fly out of the canopy, swooping towards the branch where Little Sister dangled.

Leathery bat-wings sent the humid air swirling, and a long, pointed beak full of tiny teeth opened as the pterodactyl stretched its taloned feet towards Little Sister.

Ellen suddenly remembered the books about prehistoric periods where she'd seen pictures of these strange trees before.

"Risako!" Ellen cried. She stumbled forward, reaching for the tree. She didn't even think of the oozy sap as she wrapped her arms around the trunk.

The pterodactyl screeched, Little Sister shrieked, and Ellen twisted her head up to see the monster flapping up and through the canopy.

Little Sister hung from its claws, her yells growing fainter as the pterodactyl carried her away.

•••

Ellen dropped back down to the muddy ground, tears blurring her vision. She was hot, dirty, her arms and legs stung from a million scrapes, and her sister was about to be a dinosaur's lunch.

*Pterodactyls aren't dinosaurs*, Little Sister would have said in her know-it-all scientist voice. But Ellen didn't care about the correct classification of the monster that was going to eat her sister.

A huge, prickly insect crawled up Ellen's leg, and she batted it away with a strangled yell. The thing opened its way-too-huge wings and buzzed away with a deep drone. It flew in the same direction the pterodactyl had gone.

Ellen dashed her tears away. Sitting in a stinky mud puddle and crying wasn't going to save Little Sister, and it certainly wasn't going to get her out of the Cretaceous Period and back to the school library.

Brushing what mud she could from herself, she set off through the thick ferns, following the pterodactyl. She tried not to think about how she was following the big insect, too.

What was she going to do? She had no idea where the pterodactyl had gone, and it was certainly flying faster than she was clawing her way through these ferns. Even if she managed to find it again, she had no way of fighting it off of Little Sister.

The time machine's wristband dug into her palm, and she stopped to look at it again. How did it work? It was just an old watch and some pipe cleaners. The hands were unmoving, stuck on 12:00. The cardboard disk hung limply from its pipe cleaner hook, damp from the mud. It had stopped working as soon as it was out of Little Sister's hands. Ellen couldn't fathom how to get it to work again, and she was afraid to try. She didn't actually want to leave Little Sister behind here.

Even though that's what she'd said. It didn't matter that Little Sister had known she was lying. The last thing she'd said to Little Sister was that she wanted to leave her behind in this horrible place, right before she'd been scooped up by a big not-dinosaur.

Tears pricked at her eyes again, but Ellen blinked them away. She'd apologize to Little Sister as soon as she'd rescued her. Then they'd go back home. She tucked the time machine into her skirt pocket.

She struggled against the underbrush until her stomach let out a long, uncomfortable growl. Lunch period had come and gone, and Ellen had skipped it to go to the library.

She found a small patch of open ground and stopped to open her backpack. The bento her mom had packed her sat right on top of her books, and Ellen pulled it out and snapped the plastic lid open. The salty aroma of the seaweed and rice and the faint undertone of the salmon and mayonnaise filling had her stomach growling again. Her favorite. She pulled the first one out and took a big bite.

She finished that one in record time just to make her stomach stop growling. As she picked up the second onigiri, she realized that her stomach wasn't the only thing growling nearby.

Something lurked in the clump of ferns to Ellen's left. Something that sounded big and hungry.

Ellen held herself still despite every instinct screaming at her to bolt. Weren't dinosaurs dependent on sight to hunt? She remembered that from somewhere. Then again, she'd never really kept up with dinosaur research.

The fronds rustled, and a snout like a curved parrot's beak poked out. The scaly nostrils flared, and a whuffling sound filled the tiny clearing.

Ellen clutched her plastic bento box in trembling hands as a big triceratops stepped out of the ferns. Its frill was as big as the chalkboard in Ms. Haley's classroom, and just as green. The three horns curved upwards to end in sharp points. The dinosaur walked right for Ellen.

Ellen squeezed her eyes shut. *Triceratops ate plants*, she chanted to herself. *It doesn't want to eat me.*

Still, the bento box rattled in her hands when the triceratops stopped right in front of her. A musty smell wafted off its scaly hide, and it reminded Ellen of old books.

The triceratops sniffed at the bento box with deep breaths that dragged at Ellen's school clothes and smelled like it really needed to brush its teeth. Then it butted at her with its beak.

Ellen screamed and fell over, but she managed to keep ahold of her bento box. The triceratops took a single step to follow her, and she found herself looking up at its neck and chin.

Maybe the triceratops didn't want to eat her, but that wouldn't stop it from stepping on her!

Luckily, the dinosaur backed up and stuck its beak right into Ellen's face. It nudged at her hands and the bento box.

"What, do you want a snack?" Ellen asked. "You want my

onigiri?" Maybe triceratopses liked seaweed and rice and salmon.

An idea formed in Ellen's head. The triceratops didn't have any trouble barreling through the underbrush, unlike her. And she had something he obviously wanted to eat.

A quick scan of the area showed Ellen a supply of branches littering the ground, as well as vines crawling up the wide trunks of the prehistoric trees.

The triceratops nudged at her again, reminding her that he wanted his treat. Ellen fumbled at the lid of her bento while she figured out the rest of her plan. This certainly wasn't the first time she'd shared Japanese food with a strange companion in order to save her own life.

She dug one of the two remaining onigiri out of the bento box and tossed it a little ways away from her. It landed in the dirt with a soft thump.

The triceratops stepped over to it, crushing a fern on the way, and lowered his head to eat.

With her new friend distracted, Ellen rushed to get a sturdy branch, and then she moved to the nearest tree trunk. She wrapped her fingers around a vine and tugged on it. It was just like playing tug-of-war in gym class, right down to the burn of the rope as it slid against her hands, but more was riding on her winning this match than a grade in gym.

Finally, Ellen freed the vine from the tree. While the triceratops finished off his snack, Ellen wrestled the vine, branch, and bento box with the remaining onigiri into a lure.

Her lure finished, Ellen clambered onto the triceratops's back before he could stand back up. She was surprised at how leathery the dinosaur's skin was. She'd thought they had scales like the pet lizards in her science classroom did.

The triceratops stood with a lurch, and Ellen nearly dropped her branch lure. The huge frill rotated away as her new friend tried to look over his shoulder at her. Ellen regained her balance and giggled at the few grains of white rice stuck to the triceratops's beak.

"Okay, 'Tops. You want this other onigiri? You gotta help me rescue Little Sister first."

Ellen slid forward and dangled her bento lure in front of 'Tops's face. Just as she'd hoped, the dangling box and the remaining onigiri drew his attention immediately. Ellen swung the branch in the direction of the pterodactyl's flight.

'Tops bulldozed through the underbrush, while Ellen held onto his frill with one hand and directed him with the lure in the other. She kept her eyes on the canopy of leaves ahead of them, hoping to get some hint of where the pterodactyl had taken Little Sister.

After a while, Ellen pulled the lure up, and 'Tops came to a stop. There'd been no sign of Little Sister or the pterodactyl, and Ellen was afraid they'd lost the trail long ago.

What was she thinking, trying to use a land-bound dinosaur to track a flying kidnapper? And now she was sitting here, hot and stinky, and sleepy, with her skirt pocket vibrating and her only companion a hungry triceratops.

Ellen snapped awake. Her skirt pocket was vibrating! She dug into it and pulled the time machine out. The pipe cleaners were twitching, the cardboard circle was swaying, and the hands of the watch were pointing to Ellen's right. When she twisted that way, the hands swung like a compass needle.

Ellen peered through the dense foliage over that way and thought she could make out a craggy rock face a ways out.

'Tops set off as soon as she dropped the lure before his beak again, and they covered the distance in the time it took Ellen to question her trust of a broken wristwatch. Then again, Little Sister's devices did seem to work best when she was around them.

As they neared the tree line, Ellen spotted a cave high up on the cliff face. A pterodactyl sat there, spreading its giant bat-wings.

A splash of blue and white the exact shades of their school uniforms waved like a flag as the pterodactyl herded Little Sister into its nest.

A surge of victory rushed through Ellen, and she urged 'Tops on faster.

They were just about to break out of the trees when 'Tops came to a shuddering halt. He refused to budge another step, no matter how much Ellen waved the bento box.

"Fine, you lazy bum," she grumbled, sliding off his back. "You couldn't climb those cliffs, anyway. At least I got full marks on the climbing wall in gym."

Ellen set off into the open area, dry dirt and rocks crunching under her school shoes. The area was silent, but at least the air tasted fresh out here. Ellen took a deep, appreciative breath.

Now that she looked at the cliff face from the ground instead of perched on 'Tops's back, it looked really high. Climbing up there would take hours, and while the open space let a breeze ruffle her hair, the hot sun still beat down relentlessly. She might pass out before she got halfway up!

Unless she got a ride up there.

"Hey, ptero-brain!" Ellen shouted, cupping her hands around her mouth. "My sister's not a big enough snack for you. Come get me, too!"

High above her, the pterodactyl poked its long beak out of its cave.

Ellen waved her arms and shouted some more, but the pterodactyl didn't come any closer.

Exhausted, Ellen slumped forward and panted. Stupid pterodactyl. No wonder they were extinct.

Maybe she could still find a use for 'Tops. There had to be a path she could ride him up. She turned around to walk back to the trees.

Something towered between Ellen and the trees, its mouth open to display its sharp teeth and its cruel talons tearing up the dirt. Its head was tilted so one cantaloupe-sized, yellow eye peered down at her. The crimson feathers along its head, back, and even on its disproportionately tiny arms, didn't look quite the way Ellen remembered from the drawings in her school books, but she still knew the T. rex on sight.

Ellen couldn't help herself. She screamed and dropped her

bento box lure as she tore off towards the cliffs at her top speed.

Her feet slapped against the hard ground, sending puffs of dust flying, and her chest heaved as she dragged breath after breath into her lungs.

Behind her, the T. rex followed, its footsteps shaking the earth. It let out a screech that filled Ellen's mind with images of birds of prey swooping in on her. Its hot breath brushed the back of her neck.

Ellen put on another burst of speed and flung herself into the rocks at the cliff bottom. She ducked under a rocky ledge when she felt the snap of massive jaws closing behind her ear.

Pressed against the cliff wall and shaking with fear, Ellen watched the T. rex shuffling around, trying to poke its snout under the ledge.

Finally, the T. rex roared loud enough to rattle every rock in the area and stomped a few paces away to wait for Ellen to come back out.

Ellen scanned her tiny sanctuary for anything she could use. All she found were rocks and more dirt. At least it was cool and dry here in the shade. She'd catch her breath for a moment and figure something out.

The time machine buzzed in her skirt pocket again. She pulled it out to see the hands spinning rapidly. Did that mean Little Sister was directly above her now? Ellen couldn't get any closer without going where the T. rex could catch her.

Ellen scowled and sat down. It would be nice if Little Sister would help out some. Couldn't she find a way to climb down here on her own? Surely she'd seen Ellen come out of the jungle.

A wave of anger washed over her, even though she knew it wasn't fair of her. This was all Little Sister's fault! Ellen wished she could tackle her into the cliff wall like she did at the bookshelves back in the library. Falling rocks would hurt more than falling books, but...

Ellen jerked to her feet. She *could* bring Little Sister down to her! She'd just have to be quick. Very quick.

Ellen stepped out from her little rock ledge and waved her arms at the T. rex.

"Come and eat me, you overgrown chicken!" Ellen shouted.

The T. rex came towards her with thundering steps and gaping jaws. The only thing faster than the reptile was its nasty meat-breath.

Ellen forced herself to stay where she was until the T. rex was close enough to bite her in two. As its toothy maw descended like a screaming missile, she scrambled back to her rock ledge and cowered with her arms over her head.

The impact of the massive T. rex into the cliff face sent tremors through the rocks and Ellen. Cracks appeared in the wall, but it wasn't quite enough yet. Ellen saw the dinosaur back up, shaking its head. It turned to walk away.

"No!" Ellen cried. She grabbed up a rock and hurled it after the retreating T. rex.

It howled and swung back around, its yellow eyes rolling in fury. Crimson feathers flew as it charged forward again.

A loud crack reverberated at the second impact, and Ellen ran to avoid the rockslide as the cliff face came crashing down.

"Little Sister!" Ellen yelled once the echoes faded.

Someone coughed in the rubble. Ellen rushed to dig her out, tossing rocks haphazardly until she uncovered Little Sister. A bruise was forming on her cheek, but she didn't look any worse for her tumble from the pterodactyl's cave.

"Wow, what a ride!" Little Sister said. "Nice thinking."

"Take the time machine and get us out of here," Ellen said. She shoved the time machine into Little Sister's hands, and Little Sister tweaked the pipe cleaners and spun the watch dial.

The rocks to their left flew upwards as the T. rex clawed out of them with an earth-shattering roar. It wriggled towards them, moving like it hadn't just been crushed in a rockslide.

Ellen screamed again, and she and Little Sister grabbed each other. They wouldn't be able to move away in time.

A screech pierced out of the sky, and the pterodactyl shot down into the rubble, flapping its wings and jabbing its beak at the T. rex. It screeched again in challenge, then whipped around to face the girls, talons grasping.

Ellen punched at the talon approaching Little Sister. This stupid not-a-dinosaur wouldn't take her sister again.

The pterodactyl rolled around her punch and reached for Ellen instead.

The claws closed around Ellen's shoulders and she was pulled out of the rocks. Little Sister's hand slipped away.

"Take the time machine back home, Risako," Ellen yelled. "Save yourself!"

At least Mom couldn't ground her for a million years if she became ptero-lunch.

The world dropped away below Ellen in a reverse of their arrival in this time, and she swallowed against the urge to scream again. She squeezed her eyes shut.

Her arm jerked hard, and she opened her eyes to find Little Sister dangling from her hand. She'd jumped up at the last moment!

"We're both going home right now," Little Sister called up to her.

"What if we bring the pterodactyl back?" Ellen asked. Just imagine *that* in the library!

"We don't have a choice now. Hold on."

Little Sister fiddled with the time machine and clicked the dial back into place. Something yanked inside Ellen's stomach, and the swirling vortex of colors replaced the blue of the sky. The scent of copper returned, and Ellen no longer saw the ground miles below her. The pterodactyl's grip on her shoulders faded.

The vortex disappeared, and Ellen and Little Sister fell to the floral-patterned library carpet. Something crashed to the floor beside them, and a flat wing blocked the dim light from the ceiling.

"We made it!" Little Sister said, sitting up. Ellen sat up, too, shoving the big papier-mâché model of a pterodactyl off herself. They must have knocked it down upon their arrival.

"What on Earth is going on back here?" a woman cried. The

librarian appeared from the bookshelves, her eyes squinty with anger and her fingers twitching for her detention pad like a cowboy at a shootout.

"Sorry, ma'am," Ellen mumbled, grabbing Little Sister's hand and dragging her into the hallway.

The bell rang to signal the end of lunch period. Students poured out of the cafeteria, groaning about the return to class.

Ellen looked at herself and Little Sister. They weren't as dirty as she'd thought, though they were both streaked with dust and small scratches that could be explained away as paper cuts.

"I'm sorry about ruining your prototype test," Ellen said. "And for the things I said back there."

Little Sister shook her head. "It was a pretty good test, anyway. I'll just have to do my science project research the old-fashioned way."

"Yeah, I guess so," Ellen said, thinking of her own history paper.

Little Sister waved goodbye and headed down the first-grader hallway.

Ellen sighed. She needed to head to class, too. Shrugging her backpack onto a shoulder, she glanced back at the library.

For some reason, the heavy doors didn't look so intimidating anymore. What were silly library ghosts compared to facing down a T. rex?

Although Mom might ground her for a million years for leaving her bento box in the Cretaceous Period!

# Alien Gifts
## Sherry D. Ramsey

*Sherry D. Ramsey is a Canadian speculative fiction writer, editor, publisher, creativity addict and self-confessed Internet geek. Her debut novel,* One's Aspect to the Sun, *was published by Tyche Books in late 2013 and was awarded the Book Publishers of Alberta Book of the Year Award for Speculative Fiction. The sequel,* Dark Beneath the Moon, *came out from Tyche in 2015, and Sherry's first middle grade novel,* The Seventh Crow, *was published by Dreaming Robot Press also in 2015.*

Shallie woke, remembered what day it was, kicked off the thin microfiber sheets and rolled out of bed. Through the sleep pod's skylight, a sulky trickle of orange sunlight outlined the silent computer and the metal footlocker holding Shallie's clothes. Those things and the bed just about filled the pod. She flicked on the computer and set the screen to mirror mode so she could scrape her dark hair into a neat topknot. She pulled a clean excursion overall out of the footlocker and slipped it on, practically dancing with anticipation.

Today was the day she'd finally get to meet the aliens.

Her parents had already emerged from their own sleep pod and sat at the tiny table in the middle of the living pod, eating breakfast. The inflated pod walls undulated slightly, giving under what must be a brisk wind outside on the planet's surface. The place seemed prone to wind and dust storms. They didn't last long, but this part of the planet was covered with such deep dust—regolith, her mother called it—that sometimes the landscape could change dramatically during a storm. Shallie hoped nothing big would blow in today.

"Breakfast is ready," Shallie's father said with a smile, squeezing food paste from three different tubes onto Shallie's plate and adding a few spoonfuls of water. He passed it under the heating lamp and the paste squirmed and reconfigured itself into more solid-looking mounds of nourishment. Some people liked to watch while their meal went through this transformation, but Shallie didn't. The long wriggles of paste reminded her of colorful worms.

It had been a long time since Shallie had actually seen a worm, back home on Earth—a hundred and six years, in fact. Of course, she'd spent a hundred and five of those years in cold sleep, so it really felt like less than a year. Ten months on the ship, two weeks on the planet, preparing. Still, even a year was a long time, and there was something about just *knowing* it had been more than a hundred years, even if she hadn't experienced them, that made it feel indescribably long.

"Is everyone else ready?" she asked her mother, spooning a bite of "waffle" into her mouth. It tasted a little like waffles, Shallie thought, but mostly not.

Shallie's mother didn't look up from her screen—probably reading another report. Sometimes Shallie wondered how there could possibly be so many topics requiring reports, but her mother was the mission leader, so Shallie guessed she had to know about absolutely everything.

"Reports look good," her mother said. "The rest of the team is on track, and word from the Others says they're ready, too."

"Will I be able to talk to any of the kids?" Shallie asked.

Her father chuckled. "I don't know about *talking*," he said, stirring more sugar powder into what he called his almost-coffee. "None of us are doing more than very basic communicating with the Others yet. But you should have a chance to interact with Other children, yes." He reached out and tweaked her topknot. "That's why we brought you a hundred years from home, right?"

She grinned. "Right." She opened her screen and brought up the rudimentary communication symbols they'd worked out with the Others, even though she was certain she had them memorized. For today, she had to be sure.

•••

Tlik'chik woke, remembered what day it was, detached from the sleeping-mesh and tumbled out of the darknest. She blinked in the orange sunlight pouring in through the bignest's light panels and padded to the wash chamber, where her parents lingered over their morning wash. Joining them in the thin trickle of water, barely enough to wet her feathers, Tlik'chik shivered in the cold as the family preened and washed each other. Then Tlik'chik's father braided her hair and curled it around her head in his own special way, pinning it tightly, while her mother heated foodpods in the warmer. Finally Tlik'chik scooted away from her father's fussing, snatched up a couple of foodpods and took them to the biggest window with a view of the planet's surface. She squirted breakfast into her mouth, barely tasting it.

Today was the day she'd finally get to meet the aliens.

Tlik'chik dialed down the opacity of the light panel so she could look outside without squinting. Even after quite a few cycles on this planet, the orange sun's light always felt a little too bright, a little too strange, and sometimes it made her head ache. She wondered if the aliens found it uncomfortable, too. She'd read all the data about their home planet, so she knew their own sun was even brighter, hotter and yellower than this one. Tlik'chik took another squirt of breakfast and tried to imagine it, but failed. She wondered what the aliens would think of her own planet's sun, its beautiful dark-red glow so much gentler than this one. A strong wind had picked up outside, swirling tall cones of pale dust into the air and sending them dancing around the bignests of the rest of the duty clan.

"Are you ready to meet the aliens?" Tlik'chik's mother chirped, her short fingers flying over the touchscreen, checking the data. The pads on her fingers made soft bumping noises in the quiet bignest.

Tlik'chik turned from the window and threw the empty foodpod into the recycler, dropping the other one into her pocket. Tlik'chik's father was fastening his honor tabs onto the front of his uniform. She felt a sudden surge of pride that he'd been selected to lead the contact mission.

"Definitely! I want to know what their kids are like. Do you think they'll want to play itri-sticks with me?"

Her mother looked up from the touchscreen and smiled. "It might take a while to teach them how to play, since we don't have much of a common language yet," she said, "But that's why we're here, after all. I think itri-sticks would be a great idea."

Tlik'chik rummaged in her bag of belongings until she found the long box of polished, brightly-colored wooden sticks, and slipped it into her pocket. She might play itri-sticks with an alien! It was going to be an amazing day.

•••

Halfway between the human camp and the alien one, a weirdly-twisting tree thrust gnarled branches toward the planet's greenish sky. The tree bore a full, rustling cover of pale yellow leaves, and beneath its canopy was the spot where the two missions had decided to meet. Until now, they'd communicated only by simple messages, each trying to learn as much as possible about the other side. Shallie had seen a picture of the meeting place, taken by an observation flyer, but she hadn't been there herself—no one had, yet. Secretly, Shallie wondered why they didn't just get together from the beginning—surely it couldn't be any more difficult than learning a new language on Earth, which lots of people did every day.

But, no, her mother said. This was so much more important than just learning a language; the very first meeting with beings from another planet. And although it seemed both sides wanted only friendship, they had to be very careful. If they didn't know enough about the other culture, someone could make a terrible mistake by accident—make a rude gesture without realizing it, or use a word in an offensive way, and then who knew what might happen?

Shallie thought the grown-ups were probably being too careful—grown-ups often did that—but there wasn't anything she could do about it. She'd made a point of learning everything she could for herself, though. If anyone was going to make a terrible mistake today, it wasn't going to be her.

The pod walls swayed to one side and then snapped upright again. A small hissing, almost like rain but with a harder edge, filled the pod as dust peppered the outside.

"The wind's really picking up out there," her mother said, worry evident in her voice. "I wonder if we should try to postpone the meeting?"

"No!" Shallie almost shouted. She'd been waiting for this moment. "If I have to wait another day to meet the aliens, I think I'll *die*!"

Her father smiled indulgently at her. "I don't think it will be quite that serious," he said. He went to one of the pod windows and peered out. "It's windy, and there's some dust blowing around, but I doubt it's going to get any worse than this. If we wait for a day with no wind, we'll never meet them!"

"Let's see what Tomaso thinks," her mother muttered, and pulled out her communicator. She held a low-voiced conversation with her second-in-command as Shallie gathered up the drawings she'd sketched as a gift for the alien children. They were all scenes of Earth as she remembered it; their house, her school, the park where they liked to camp. Dogs, cats, horses, other earth animals. Flowers, trees, cars and airplanes. Shallie had carefully printed the names of everything at the bottom of the pictures. She hoped they'd like them as she put them carefully into the envelope she'd brought along, and slid some blank pages and coloring sticks into the envelope, too. If she could manage it, she'd ask them to draw her some things from their world.

"Okay, we're going ahead," her mother announced, slipping her communicator back into her pocket. "Inspection outside in ten minutes."

Shallie stood by the door, tapping her foot impatiently as her parents gathered up the things they were taking as meeting-gifts and finally led them outside the pod. Nearby stood three more pods, identical to theirs, where the rest of the mission crew lived. There should have been four, but one family had not come out of the cold sleep when the rest of them had awoken. It had been the other family with a child; all three had died sometime during the voyage, which Shallie thought privately was actually just as well. The deaths hit everyone else in the mission hard, but she thought it would have been worse if only one or two had not awoken. Imagine being the one left? She shook her head. She didn't want to think sad thoughts now. They were actually going to meet the aliens!

The other mission members emerged and drifted toward them, chatting nervously and checking equipment as they walked.

A gust of wind scudded into her, and tiny bits of dust and sand stung her cheeks. The envelope twisted in her hand, almost flying out of her grasp. She blinked, turning away. "Ow!"

Her father was at her side, shielding her from the wind. "Here, walk beside me," he said, and she took his hand as they turned their steps toward the meeting place.

•••

Tlik'chik and her family and the rest of the duty clan arrived at the meeting place just a little ahead of the aliens. She was happy about that—it would be so exciting to watch the aliens come into view, walking on their long, skinny legs. One of the first things both sides had done, long ago when communication had been established, was to exchange pictures so each would know what the others looked like. Tlik'chik had studied them diligently, wondering over the aliens' flat, bare faces, lack of feathers, and long, thin limbs. They weren't ugly, she'd decided long ago, although some of the duty clan thought they were. They were just different in an interesting way. She liked that they had hair on their heads, like her people did. It made them a little less strange.

Tlik'chik's mother leaned close. "Are you excited? Not frightened, are you?"

Tlik'chik held up three fingers and shook them, *no*. "Of course I'm not afraid! This is the most exciting thing ever!"

Her mother smiled and rested a hand on her shoulder for a moment. "Good girl."

The wind whistled and snapped the leaves of the tree over their heads, whipping even taller cones of dancing dust to life. Tlik'chik reluctantly closed her inner eyelid to protect her vision, hating the way it made the scene before her a little unfocused. Still, she'd see even less with her eyes full of dust.

*And here they came!*

The aliens crested the top of a low rise, all dressed in similar, one-piece clothing of different colors. They did not seem to march in any ceremonial way but formed a loose group. One smaller alien detached itself from a taller one as they came into view. Tlik'chik thought the shorter one must be the alien child—there was only one among them, just as she was the only one in her duty clan. She fingered the itri-sticks in her tunic pocket nervously, her mouth suddenly gone dry. She hoped the alien child wouldn't think they were stupid.

As the aliens grew closer, Tlik'chik was relieved to see they weren't all *that* much taller than her people. Her father stepped forward and held up a hand in the traditional greeting.

One of the alien females—Tlik'chik knew how to distinguish them, from the pictures—stepped forward and mimicked the gesture, then made one of her own, holding out her hand for Tlik'chik's father to grasp. Although both sides had prepared the other for what would happen, Tlik'chik felt as if all her feathers were sticking straight out from her body. They touched! They clasped hands! For the first time, two entirely different peoples had come together. Tlik'chik grinned widely and hugged herself.

The leaders began a laborious process of communicating their prepared messages, and Tlik'chik quickly lost interest in what the adults were saying. Her eyes sought and found the alien child—a girl, she realized—who had her eyes fixed on Tlik'chik. The alien girl smiled and pointed to a thin packet she held, then pointed to Tlik'chik.

*This is for you*, Tlik'chik understood the gesture to mean.

Her heart felt like a stone in her chest. She hadn't brought a gift for the alien girl! Her hand went automatically to her pocket, and she realized, over a tiny pang of regret, that it would be all right. She'd give her the itri-sticks, not just teach her to play the game! Her father would understand, and he'd help her make a new set.

Tlik'chik glanced at her father and the other adults—they were entirely engrossed with the aliens, just as the alien adults seemed to be with them. The initial greetings were over, and the two groups moved closer together, exchanging ceremonial items and trying out their halting knowledge of each other's language. Tlik'chik looked back to the alien girl, who jerked her head to the side. *Let's go over there*, she seemed to be saying. Tlik'chik inclined her head forward, which she'd learned, for the aliens, meant *agreement* or *yes*.

Together they sidled away from the adults, unnoticed, and stopped under another nearby tree, shorter and less impressive but still whipped by the wind. The alien girl had small eyes, the color of bingi flowers. She stood about a head taller than Tlik'chik. She tapped herself on the chest and said, "Shallie."

This wasn't a word in the agreed-upon communication exchange, so Tlik'chik thought it must be the girl's name. She tapped herself likewise and said, "Tlik'chik."

The other girl's eyes opened wider and she tried it out. It didn't sound quite right, but close enough, Tlik'chik decided. She inclined her head again and then tried out the girl's name. It didn't sound right to her own ears, but Shallie smiled, so it must have been acceptable.

The tree above them shuddered in a huge gust of wind, its dark-leaved branches creaking. Shallie squealed and put her arms up to cover her head against the harsh peppering of dust the wind lashed into them. When she did, the thin packet whipped out of her fingers and sailed away from them on the gale.

Instinctively, Tlik'chik jumped to catch the packet, and she felt the wind sweep her up and away.

•••

Shallie flailed her arms after the envelope, trying to catch it, even though she knew it was already too far away. She felt a burst of hope when the alien girl leapt for it—but hope quickly turned to fear as she saw the rising wind sweep Tlik'chik off her feet and carry her away.

*They must have very light bones, like birds*, Shallie heard the scientific side of her mind think. Then after only a brief, startled moment, she ran after the helpless alien. The wind had knocked Tlik'chik down and was tumbling her over the ground like a discarded toy. Even as Shallie ran, the wind whipped and tugged at her coverall with frenzied strength. They hadn't seen a windstorm this strong since they'd been on the planet, and none had blown in so quickly. A gust pounded against her back and almost sent her stumbling, just as Tlik'chik squealed and coughed, clutching at the ground in an effort to halt her momentum. The alien girl rolled through the swirling dust a couple of times—

—and disappeared.

"No!" Shallie gasped, almost choking on the dust-filled air. Behind her, she heard faint shouts. She glanced over her shoulder and gasped. A towering red-grey wall of wind-whipped dust bore down on her parents and the others. It looked like a monster, tumbling and swirling, about to swallow them up. She saw her mother, hands cupped around her mouth to call after Shallie, disappear into the dust-monster.

Shocked and stumbling, Shallie sensed the drop-off before she saw it. But not in time to stop her feet from pounding over the edge into nothingness...

It seemed a long time later when Shallie opened her eyes to dim, filtered light. Reddish-grey dust danced and drifted in the sparse beams. She pushed herself to a sitting position, wincing at the pain in her shoulder and hip. She coughed reflexively, feeling half-choked on the dust.

"Oh!" said a voice nearby, and Shallie startled at the dark, hunched shape to her left. She tried to scramble to her feet but fell sideways, her head spinning.

"Tlik'chik! Tlik'chik!" the voice said, and the alien crept over to her, putting one small hand gently on her arm. "Shallie?"

Shallie could have cried with relief. She nodded and patted the alien girl's hand. "I'm okay, I think," she said, then realized the girl probably didn't understand. She met Tlik'chik's eyes and smiled and nodded, patting her own chest. "Okay."

Tlik'chik held up a finger and flicked it up and down, which Shallie knew meant *yes* for the aliens. The Tlik'chik held out Shallie's envelope, now slightly crinkled and smudged with dust. "Okay!" she said, beaming.

Shallie took it. It must have blown over the same drop-off she and Tlik'chik had tumbled into, and the alien girl had found it. Carefully, slowly, Shallie stood up and looked around. This seemed to be a natural cavern, but the light came from a long way above them. It looked like hundreds of dust storms had drifted piles of soft sand and dust into the pit, so neither of them had been seriously injured in the fall.

Unfortunately, the mounds of dust didn't reach nearly high enough for them to be able to climb out.

They stared up at the opening. The distant roar of the wind and the dust still sifting down through the air told them the storm continued to rage on the planet's surface, even though the cavern lay quiet and still. Shallie wasn't sure how far she'd run before she fell into the pit. Would their parents be able to find any trace of their footprints? Or even tell which way they'd gone? How bad would the storm become? It had descended so fast and fiercely—she imagined their tents being torn to shreds. She pulled her mind quickly away from that thought.

Tlik'chik tapped her on the arm, and when Shallie turned to her, the alien girl motioned a thin limb around them. She said something Shallie didn't understand, but she thought she knew what the girl was saying. They should look around the cavern, see if there was another way out, or anything to help them. Shallie nodded and pointed to the left.

"I'll look over here."

Tlik'chik nodded and pointed to the right. They moved in opposite directions, stepping carefully in the faint illumination from above.

It didn't take long. The cavern was probably thirty feet long and a bit wider, starting from the end where they'd fallen in. A few fist-sized rocks were scattered randomly on the floor, along with a rare dead tree branch or two and a few odd tangles of twigs that reminded Shallie of tumbleweeds. She and Tlik'chik met at the far end of the cavern, where a narrow opening in the stone suggested a dark passageway beyond. The girls looked at it together. It wasn't wide enough for either girl to fit through. Without speaking, both turned and walked back to the slightly brighter end of the cavern. They didn't need words to understand there was no way out.

Shallie sat on the floor with her back against a wall of cool stone. Tlik'chik joined her. Shallie passed the envelope to the alien girl. "This was for you, anyway," she said. "You might as well have it."

Although it was obviously a struggle, Tlik'chik forced a smile as she accepted the envelope. Then she dug into a pocket in her tunic and pulled out a long, narrow box. She handed it to Shallie, gesturing for her to open it. Inside lay what looked like a handful of chopsticks tied into a bundle with a silky red cord.

"*Itri,*" Tlik'chik said. "*Wol-ken.* Shallie."

Shallie accepted the sticks and examined them. Although they were polished smooth like chopsticks, they varied in lengths and had different colors painted on each end. They were very pretty, but she had no idea what they were for. She smiled at Tlik'chik anyway. "Thank you! I love them."

Tlik'chik set her envelope down on the dusty floor of the cavern and motioned for Shallie to put the sticks down on it. When Shallie did, the alien girl untied the cord and proceeded to lay out the sticks in a complicated pattern, chattering to herself a little as she did so. Shallie didn't understand a word, but she concentrated on the lilting sound of the girl's voice anyway. It was better than worrying about the howl of the wind far above them outside.

•••

Although she knew the alien girl couldn't understand the instructions for playing itri-sticks, Tlik'chik kept talking to distract herself from their predicament. And once the sticks were laid out, it wasn't too difficult to explain the game through gestures and examples. Shallie seemed to catch on quickly, apparently intrigued by the intricacies of color-matching and strategic placement that made itri-sticks both complex and fun.

As they played, they taught each other the names of the colors. *Do-ta* was *red, chok* was *yellow, bek-ta* was *blue.* Tlik'chik knew there was no way she would remember all the alien words, but she was determined to learn them at least as well as the other girl learned the names unfamiliar to her. Tlik'chik won the first three games, but clapped her hands in surprise and delight when Shallie won the fourth.

Shallie smiled and gathered the sticks together, binding them carefully with the cord. "Thang-gue," she said, but Tlik'chik didn't know the word. Hoping it would be all right, she smiled back and nodded. She picked up the packet Shallie had given her earlier and looked at the alien girl with a question. Perhaps she'd show Tlik'chik what was inside now. As Shallie nodded and took back the packet,

Tlik'chik couldn't stop herself from glancing up toward the opening high above them. Dust still drifted in, dancing and whirling madly as it rode the air currents down into the cavern that had become their prison.

•••

Shallie showed the alien girl the opening in one end of the envelope and Tlik'chik slid the papers out. Even in the dim light, bright colors lit up the pages. Tlik'chik's smile spread as she examined Shallie's drawings.

"Here's a dog," Shallie said, pointing. "We keep them as pets, sometimes. Cats, too, like this one. *Cat*," she said, tapping the picture.

"Cat," Tlik'chik repeated.

"House," Shallie went on. "It's where we live. We go inside," she told the alien girl, pointing to some people she'd drawn and walking her fingers over to the house.

"Inside!" Tlik'chik agreed with obvious delight.

Shallie handed her one of the drawing sticks she'd included in the envelope. "You draw one," she urged.

Tlik'chik frowned, then took the drawing stick and turned one of the sheets of paper to the blank back. With quick, sure strokes, she sketched an odd-looking tree with a round sort of hut nestled in its branches. On the ground she drew what might have been herself. She tapped the figure and then the hut. "Inside! *Tou'lach*."

"Tou'lach," Shallie said, wondering if it was the word for "inside" or "house." Mentally she shook her head. It didn't matter. As long as she and Tlik'chik could distract themselves with the pictures, the way they'd done with the stick game, at least they weren't panicking.

But she couldn't help thinking the bellow of the wind above their heads sounded even louder. She strained to hear her parents' voices calling for her, but they just weren't there.

They went back to the pictures. "Present," Shallie said, tapping a wrapped gift she'd drawn with a birthday cake. She tapped the envelope and the papers, and then Tlik'chik's arm. "Present. For Tlik'chik."

The alien girl's face lit up. "Present," she repeated. "*Wol-ken*. For Shallie!" She pointed to the sticks they'd played with, and then tapped Shallie's arm. They really did seem to be making progress.

Shallie smiled back at her, but as Tlik'chik bent over the next page, she saw the alien girl dart a quick, concerned look up. Listening for her own parents' calls, Shallie wondered? Far overhead, the wind continued to howl like an angry beast.

●●●

Tlik'chik was worried. Even though she was enjoying this little game of language with Shallie, the sounds of the storm far above them continued to rage. The scouring wind would have erased their tracks almost instantly, and the swirling dust would make it impossible to see. Had anyone even noticed which way they'd gone?

By the time they'd looked at all the pictures and Tlik'chik had drawn more for Shallie, they'd both learned a few new words. But what would they do next? Go back to itri-sticks? Tlik'chik felt her stomach grumble, and she remembered the foodpod in her pocket, left over from breakfast. Glad of the distraction, she pulled it out and opened it, then offered it to Shallie.

The alien girl looked uncertain. Tlik'chik squirted some of the smooth paste into her own mouth, then held it out to Shallie again. Hesitantly, Shallie took it and dabbed a tiny amount onto one finger, then tasted it. Her eyes watered and she blinked, passing the foodpod back to Tlik'chik. Shallie smiled slightly and held up three fingers, shaking them *no*.

Despite her hunger, Tlik'chik slipped the foodpod back into her pocket. If Shallie couldn't eat, she didn't want to, either. At least not yet. But now she felt the chill that had descended on the cavern without her noticing, and she realized food was not the most urgent of their problems. Beside her, Shallie shivered. And the light from above had dimmed even further. It was almost gone. Tlik'chik imagined the planet's short day drawing to a close, the bright orange sun fading. The cavern would soon be dark, and cold. Maybe very cold. They needed to think about the coming night.

Taking up one of the drawing sticks, Tlik'chik sketched a fire on the back of one of the pages. Surely Shallie would recognize it?

Shallie nodded at the drawing and glanced around the cavern. She crawled forward from where they'd been sitting, and came back with one of the dead tree parts littering the floor. Tlik'chik nodded, and together they scoured the cavern for things that might burn. This time they didn't separate but by unspoken agreement stayed close to one another.

The pile they assembled was woefully small. Tlik'chik squeezed one of the branches between her fingers and thought it felt damp. Would it even burn? And if it did, what they'd gathered would be consumed quickly. It might provide a bit of heat and light, but not much.

Shallie must have been thinking the same thing. Above the pile, she held two stones she'd picked up and struck them quickly together. No spark. Tlik'chik could barely make out the alien girl's face in the smudge of light left to them. She looked grim but determined.

The next attempt brought a spark, but the twigs didn't ignite. A second spark landed on the twigs and a tendril of smoke wisped up for an instant, but disappeared as the spark went out.

Tlik'chik looked around again, although they'd been over every bit of the cavern. Then she saw the envelope. It, and the papers inside it, would burn—but how could she suggest sacrificing the other girl's gift? If Shallie was angry at the idea, it could cause a rift between their people before they'd even started to get to know each other.

Of course, it would only become a problem if they were ever found.

●●●

Shallie blinked back tears of frustration. They needed to get this fire going, to give them some warmth and light. She was almost afraid to hope, but it sounded like the storm on the planet's surface might be quieting down. Maybe their parents and the others would be able to begin searching for them, even though she knew the day must be almost over.

She saw Tlik'chik's eyes land on the envelope of papers and knew immediately what the other girl must be thinking. They would burn. But could she suggest burning them? Shallie caught her eyes and nodded. "It's okay," she said, holding up a finger and flicking it the way Tlik'chik had done to mean *yes*. "I'll draw you some more."

Kneeling, Tlik'chik slowly pulled the drawings from the envelope and crumpled them up almost reverently, as if performing a ritual. She placed the crumpled balls of paper under and around the twigs.

It still looked like it would make only a brief, sad, fire.

The itri sticks bumped in Shallie's pocket as she leaned forward to strike the rocks again. *Wood.* They were wood, too! Shallie's hand moved toward her pocket but stopped. They were so beautiful, and such an elegant gift! Could she possibly suggest burning them?

But Tlik'chik seemed to have realized Shallie's thoughts, as well. She nodded. "O-kay," she said carefully, and pointed to the pile of paper and twigs. "Okay, Shallie."

Shallie passed Tlik'chik the itri-sticks, and again, with careful precision, the alien girl added the sticks to the pile. She met Shallie's eyes and nodded. Shallie struck the rocks together. Nothing. Again. Spark. Again. *Spark.*

Tlik'chik leaned over and gently blew on the sparks. One went out, but one flared and caught the paper it had landed on. The edges curled and blackened as a growing flame licked across Tlik'chik's picture of a fire. Smoke curled up from the end of an itri-stick as flames flickered around it.

Shallie set down the rocks she'd used to make the sparks, and scooted around the fire, close to Tlik'chik. As more and more of their tinder caught and smoke rose toward the hole far above them, Shallie felt the alien girl put an arm around her shoulders.

"Okay," Tlik'chik said.

Shallie nodded as the fire pushed back the cavern's chill.

"Okay," she agreed. "We'll be okay."

She hoped they were right.

•••

Tlik'chik dreamed she heard her father calling her name. He seemed to be far away, and as so often happens in dreams, she couldn't open her mouth to answer him. Other voices joined her father's, some strange and speaking a language she didn't understand. But she did recognize one word. Shallie.

She jolted awake just as Shallie did the same. They'd fallen asleep with their backs against the cavern wall, arms around each other to preserve the warmth their fire had lent them. It had burned down to embers now, but tendrils of smoke still wafted up toward the sky, escaping into the sunlight. The cavern had lightened again, and the dust had stopped falling; the opening high above them was a bright hole in the darkness. The roar of the storm was gone. There were only the voices.

Beside her, Shallie jumped to her feet, shouting up to the hole. Tlik'chik joined her.

"Here! We're down here!" she called. Tlik'chik knew Shallie was yelling the same thing in her own language.

Shadows appeared at the opening.

"Tlik'chik! Are you all right?"

"Yes! We're fine!"

"Shallie!"

"We're here!"

"We're lowering a rope for you!"

A rope snaked down from above. Shallie turned to Tlik'chik with bright eyes. "Okay!" she said, pointing to the smoke rising from the embers. "We did it!"

Tlik'chik nodded. The searchers must have seen the smoke rising from the hole and knew where to find them, even though the massive storm would have erased all traces of their footprints. She saw Shallie glance down at the remains of the fire, and their gifts to each other. She looked up and caught Tlik'chik's eye, smiling sadly.

"Itri-sticks," she said. "I liked."

Tlik'chik nodded. "Draw-ings," she said. "Shallie make more?"

Shallie agreed with a smile and threw her arms around Tlik'chik in a tight hug. Tlik'chik hugged her back and smiled. The real gift was still right there.

# View from Above
## Jeanne Kramer-Smyth

*Jeanne Kramer-Smyth has been writing since she first got her hands on a typewriter at age nine. Since then she has worked as a software developer, traveled the world, and written poetry. She is currently an archivist by day and a writer, glass artist and fan of board games by night. She has studied fiction writing with both Judith Tarr and Mary Robinette Kowal. She especially enjoys fantasy, science fiction, YA, and historical fiction. She lives in Maryland with her husband, son, sister-in-law, and cat. You can find her online at www.jeannekramersmyth.com*

Kendree completed the final checklist and pushed the ignition button. It always unnerved her that there was no sound to confirm that the engines were cycled up. The lights on the control panel paraded past agreeably, just as they had every time her father had taken her out for practice. Mother said she was too young. Father said anyone who lived on a spaceship needed to know how to fly a shuttle. In case of an emergency.

This was an emergency.

The spacesuit crinkled as she swiveled to the launch panel on her right, taking deep breaths of the fake lemon scented air from the refresher. Bracing herself for the alarm that she was 90% sure she had disabled, Kendree flipped the launch trigger. The shuttle lifted gently from the docking bay floor. No bells clanged. The lights outside the cockpit didn't suddenly flash red and orange. The bay door slid smoothly open, revealing a wide swath of dark space and stars and the edge of the planet below.

Kendree checked the coordinates one more time, then initiated the autopilot. Her heart raced and she held her breath until the small shuttle was clear of the doors and had turned toward the planet. The navigation display projected a total travel time of 18 minutes.

She switched the side screen to replay the last few minutes of her friend's video message. Elissa's eyes were puffy and red, but she wasn't crying. Her voice shook a little as she explained that her parents were evacuating her and her sisters. They were being sent to hide out on their family property a few hours away from the city and the battlefields that had formed around it. Elissa looked over her shoulder at some noise outside her door before turning back to say "Sorry, I have to go. I'll try to send another message soon, but the country house doesn't have an uplink to the satellite. I'll miss talking to you." She ended the transmission before Kendree had even been able to tell her to be safe.

Kendree had been nervous about the war brewing on the surface for weeks. It was all some awful drama left over from when different Earth factions had settled the planet generations ago. Her parents swore her friend would be okay. They kept saying that Elissa's parents were scientists. They weren't soldiers. They would evacuate to somewhere safe before it was too late.

She and Elissa had never met in person, but it was lonely up on the spaceship with just her parents. They had been in geostationary orbit over Elissa's home city for over a year as Kendree's parents did their Space Archaeology work. Her mother had met Elissa's mother through the university in the city below and thought the two girls might enjoy meeting each other - at least over the video channel.

It was hard to be alone on the ship for so long with just her parents for company. She and Elissa had rapidly progressed from awkward "my mom says I have to talk to you" acquaintances to best friends who told each other everything. They loved the same books. They played each other their favorite music. Elissa told her that it was the best to have a friend who wasn't part of the social scene down on the planet - she could tell Kendree anything. And she did.

The idea of not talking to Elissa for more than a day, let alone for some unknown long amount of time, made her heart ache. The idea that she might be in danger -- that she could be hurt as politicians and their soldiers fought over who was in charge? That made her skin crawl.

The sun was just cresting the horizon, flooding the planet below with a warm arc of light. The autopilot was handling everything, but that didn't mean it wasn't a bumpy ride dropping down through the atmosphere. This shuttle wasn't big enough to absorb and suppress the vibrations. The cabin slowly ratcheted the pressure up to prepare her for the increased gravity on the planet surface. Kendree had watched instructional videos about this, but she had never felt it herself.

She had asked Elissa for the coordinates of the country house a few months ago when Elissa had first mentioned it. Kendree had accessed the maps her father used for his remote sensing studies and imagined visiting Elissa there. The maps were based on satellite imaging and were used to search for promising archaeological sites, but they worked just as well to view the terrain on the surface.

"Kendree, what are you doing?" Her mother's voice burst through, loud and frantic over the ship-to-ship comm-link. She was grateful there was no video. Kendree considered just ignoring it, but her mother wasn't going to give up.

"I'm just going down to pick up Elissa. I'll be back in a few hours."

"You can't do that. Turn that shuttle around. It's too dangerous."

"I'm not turning around. In fifteen minutes I'll be on planet at their summer house. I bet they won't even have unpacked yet."

"You can't! Kendree... it isn't safe." She faintly heard her mother calling for her father, her head probably turned away from the microphone.

"You said that they were in a safe place. So it will be safe for me too."

"There are reasons we don't go down to the surface of this planet, Kendree. Your body has no immunity to their illnesses.

And you already have enough to deal with without getting sick."

Kendree didn't respond. She was watching the planet below speed toward her. To the east were the battlefields. So many soldiers in battle armor that glinted in the rising sun. Had they been marching all night to get into position?

The shuttle turned and she got close enough to see some of the large battle machines on the ground. Huge, hulking, and dark, they towered well above the heads of the troops. The largest one lumbered forward, jostling soldiers who clambered on its surface adjusting things she couldn't see. She hadn't realized how close to the battle zone the auto-piloted route would take her.

"Its going to be fine." She wasn't sure if she was telling herself or her mom.

"You can't open the doors when you land. You have to just relaunch. I am so sorry."

"No. Mom, that isn't an option." The shuttle was now flying over the heart of the capital city. She could see the rolling countryside coming up fast.

"Kendree?" Her father was now on the line too. "Honey, I know you don't want to hear this, but you could be a danger to your friend too. She might not be immune to everything you've been exposed to."

"Dad, we've been here for almost a year. That is a long enough quarantine for anything we might have brought with us. Or should I say brought with you. You never let me get exposed to anything."

"There is a reason for that, dear." Her mother sounded sad. Kendree knew that the life of isolation they led was to keep her immune system from being challenged. "I'm sorry." She added quietly.

"I know you are. But I'm twelve. I'm not a little girl. Don't worry, I have a good plan."

And with that she shut the communication link down and watched the woodlands and fields unfolding below her. The shuttle cast a moving shadow as she flew west away from the rising sun.

She braced herself for what turned out to be a gentle landing on a fairly flat patch of grass.

Kendree reached down and disengaged the latches that had held her chair in place. With practiced deftness, she rotated 180 degrees and guided the motorized chair to the storage compartment where she had stashed her helmet and gloves. She hadn't wanted to wear them for the flight down because they restricted her movement and sight lines, but she knew her parents were right. She was convinced she was no danger to her friends - but she knew that her immune system was compromised enough that they were a very real danger to her.

It had been hard getting into the suit without her parents' help - but she had managed. She had only cursed once, and that time under her breath so she didn't wake her parents before she had effected her escape.

They had had her suit custom made, her legs resting together inside the bottom half of the suit. There was no need for separate legs in a suit for someone whose legs didn't work. For someone who couldn't walk. When she put it on the first time, she had felt like a mermaid. She pulled on her gloves now, hating the loss of dexterity and sensation.

It was awkward getting her helmet on with her gloves in the way, but she managed it. She engaged the helmet lock and felt cool, sweet air begin to flow from the pack mounted on the back of her chair. Inside her mermaid space suit she was safe. She planned to keep herself quarantined in her room on the ship as long as the girls stayed with them.

Kendree opened the shuttle door and rolled down the ramp to the grass outside the small house. She approached the door to the small wood house slowly. The sun was up, but it was still early. The ground in front of the building was covered in gravel. She turned on the sound feed in her helmet to hear it crunch as she drove the chair across.

There was no sign of activity inside. She looked for some sort of intercom or button and saw none.

She was able to get close enough to the door to knock with her gloved hand, but there was no answer. She knocked again, this time as hard as she could. She waited, but still no answer. The doorknob didn't turn. Of course it was locked. They were hiding and trying to be safe.

Kendree backed away from the door and surveyed the building more carefully. It was two stories, with two broad windows on the lower floor and four smaller windows spaced evenly across the upper level. She imagined that the girls bedrooms were upstairs. The windows were covered by curtains, but the window all the way to the left had a small plant balanced between the curtain and the windowpane. Elissa was obsessed with growing things. She would have brought her latest project with her and scouted out the window with the best sun in her room.

She needed some way to get her attention. The gravel at her feet was ideal, but it might as well have been a mile away. Her suit was not designed for picking up small objects on the ground. Luckily she remembered the grabber she always kept strapped to the side of her chair. She managed to use it to transfer a small pile of the rough grey stones into her lap. Her first try at throwing them was an utter failure. Gravity was weird. If she had been on the ship, with the gravity turned super low so it was easy for her to maneuver without using much leg strength, she could have tossed them the entire length of the ship's central hallway. Here they landed barely beyond her feet.

Her second throw was no more successful. She stared thoughtfully at the tool leaning against her leg. She lifted it and put a few rocks in the scoop and carefully rotated it over her shoulder. Holding as tight as she could with both hands, she snapped the rod forward. The rocks went flying. They clunked against the wide wood door and fell onto the doormat. It took four more tries before she got the rocks to clatter on the window on the second floor. After her second hit, the curtain moved and there was her friends face. Kendree waved, then worried that she was just frightening Elissa. The curtain fell back in place quickly.

Kendree held her breath until the door opened.

Elissa was shorter than Kendree had pictured. Getting to know someone just from their torso on a screen would do that she guessed.

"Elissa." Kendree suddenly realized Elissa couldn't hear her. She toggled on the speaker in her helmet and called out again quickly. "It's me! Kendree!" She hoped that Elissa could see her smile through the helmet from her spot shifting from foot to foot in the doorway. "I'm here to rescue you." She gestured to the shuttle behind her.

"What?" Elissa peered out at the driveway and up at the sky before stepping out the door. She had fuzzy slippers on her feet and a red nightgown covered in yellow stars. "How did you get here?"

"I flew the shuttle." Kendree sat up a bit taller. "I've been taking lessons for more than a year now. And the autopilot did most of it." she admitted. "Get your stuff, we can't stay long."

"I can't go with you." She didn't sound so sure. Elissa looked past Kendree's chair at the shuttle. "How many people can fit in there at once?"

"There are seats for six." Kendree waved her forward. "Come look."

"I can't believe you are here." Elissa's skin was olive and her long black braid glinted in the morning sun as she picked her way across the gravel in her slippers. She stopped right in front of Kendree's chair looking thoughtful. Kendree had never told her about being confined to chairs in gravity, but Elissa didn't seem surprised. "Can I hug you through that?"

"I think so." Kendree leaned forward a bit and Elissa wrapped her slender arms around the bulky suit. Kendree couldn't feel anything, but her friend so close and holding her suddenly made her eyes feel leaky. She couldn't cry. No way to wipe tears in here and she had to see to get them back to the ship safely. When Elissa stood up, Kendree took a deep breath and let it out slowly before speaking. "Is it just you and your sisters here?"

"Yes." Elissa looked back over her shoulder toward the house.

"I don't know if we can talk them into going with us."

"Sure we can." Kendree smiled at the 'us'. At least Elissa had decided to come with her. "Wake them up and get everyone dressed. We have to go fast. I think that some of the soldiers on the battlefield might have spotted me on my way in."

"Oh." Panic flashed in her friend's dark eyes. "Okay. Wait here." she said needlessly before turning to run back into the dim foyer.

Kendree waited. She watched birds wheeling in the sky overhead. The sky was so wide and blue. The trees so tall, taller than the house and shading it with their leaves. Kendree spent a lot of time looking at photos and watching videos of things she couldn't easily get to in the real world - but the perspective of looking up was strange and unsettling. And kind of magical. She had spent most of her life looking down. Down from hospital windows. Down from the ship's viewports.

Elissa reappeared dressed in a grey jumpsuit and carrying two dark bags. Her sisters, one older and one younger, were with her.

"Kendree," she started out formally, "this is my older sister, Ruth, and my little sister, Vali." They both shared Elissa's coloring, though Ruth's hair was cropped short and Vali's hair was down to her shoulders and loose, waving in the morning breeze. Kendree wished she could feel the wind against her skin.

Ruth stood tall and looked almost grown up. Kendree remembered she was supposed to start at the city University in the fall to study linguistics. Vali hid behind Ruth's legs. She was eight, four years younger than Elissa. They wore the same style grey jumpsuit.

"Are you ready to depart?" Kendree tried to sound formal and serious, even though she was bubbling over with joy inside. It was going to work!

"I can't talk her out of it." said Ruth bluntly, gesturing at Elissa with her chin. She kept a hand on Vali's shoulder. "I'm not letting her go alone. And I can't leave Vali here without us. So I guess we're all going." She hauled a huge backpack onto her back and grabbed another smaller bag with her right hand. She held out her left hand to Vali and then headed toward the shuttle with the smaller girl in tow.

"Okay." Kendree turned her chair and accelerated to catch up. "Come on Elissa!" She called out, hoping her friend was right behind her.

The chair reached the ramp at the same time Ruth and Vali did. Ruth stepped back to let Kendree maneuver up and into the shuttle. In moments they were all aboard and figuring out how to strap down their bags at Kendree's direction.

As soon as everyone was safely strapped in, Kendree closed the door and went through the pre-launch checklist again. She felt everyone watching her every move. Her mouth felt dry. She wished for a way to drink some water, but the helmet had to stay or she might as well not have bothered with it in the first place.

And then they were lifting off. The auto-route back to the ship was the default navigation program.

The shuttle wheeled back to the west toward the city.

"We shouldn't be flying this way," said Ruth, "Can't you re-route us?"

"Umm.." Kendree took a deep breath. "I haven't learned that yet. I'm sorry."

They watched the city grow large before them. The shuttle gained altitude. Then they could see the battlefield.

"Are we going to fly right over them?" Elissa asked nervously.

Ruth started to murmur something. Kendree thought it might be a prayer, or some sort of private little song. Vali was silent, but Kendree was afraid to look at her tiny face.

"When I flew in they ignored me." Kendree tried to sound bright and confident. "It's going to be okay."

"I'm sure it will be." Elissa backed her up, reaching across the space between them to put her hand on the arm of Kendree's suit.

They could do nothing but watch. The field was even more full than when Kendree had flown in at dawn. Less than an hour had passed, but now the sun was at full strength, glinting off of armoured suits and large war machines.

The shuttle rose and now all they could see was sky. Kendree had started to relax when the loud blaring of an alarm filled the small cabin.

"What does that mean?" Ruth shouted over the noise.

"I think..." Kendree clumsily flipped through the alert screens. "I think someone fired something at us from the ground." She found the switch to change the view shown on the large main screen. Now they were watching the battlefield receding quickly behind them. In the center of the screen was something glowing, round, and getting closer to them as they watched.

"What do we do?" whispered Elissa.

"We go faster." Kendree swiveled her chair and realized that she couldn't type on the keyboard with her gloves on. "Elissa, I need your help." Kendree rotated the pilot's keyboard toward her friend. "I can't type with these," she waved her heavy gloved hands, "but I can tell you what to do."

"Hurry it up." Ruth said, still watching the screen.

Kendree talked Elissa through the menus as fast as she could. The shuttle began to accelerate, pushing them all back in their seats and slowly, so slowly, pulling them further ahead of whatever the soldiers had shot at them. Moments after their shuttle broke through the atmosphere, the missile exploded in a bright burst of yellow and gold.

"That was too close." said Elissa, "I can't believe it didn't catch us."

"Switch us back to autopilot." Kendree sighed. She wanted to laugh or cry or hug someone, but she was still in her mermaid suit and strapped to her motorized chair. "We'll be at the ship in just a few minutes." She flipped the view screen back using the big switch, one of the few things she could manage with her gloves on. The sky changed from the blue of atmosphere to the darker background of space, with the ship already growing larger on the display.

The girls from the planet watched the ship open its hatch for them, gaping at the machinery and the wide reach of space beyond until they were swallowed by the dark docking bay.

The final step of the autopilot sequence disengaged the door and lowered the ramp. Kendree's parents stood just outside.

"I told you she was wearing it!" her father elbowed her mother and pointed at Kendree's space suit. "Well done!" he called to her.

"Kendree...." her mother choked out before she ran to her side, taking one of her bulky gloves in her hands.

"I'm sorry." was all Kendree could manage before her face was wet with tears. "I couldn't leave Elissa down there. I knew I could go get them."

"We understand." her mother responded gently. She took a deep breath and turned to their guests. "Welcome to our home, the TIRS-OLI." Kendree had explained months ago to Elissa that her parents had named the ship for old Landsat satellites technology that was first used to map Earth from space, but from the confused look on Elissa's face, her friend had forgotten, or maybe was just too worried to remember.

"Our parents..." Ruth began.

"Not to worry." Kendree's father reassured her "We sent them a message the moment you cleared the atmosphere." He turned to Kendree. "A little close there at the end, wasn't it?"

"Yes." she nodded, tears now dripping off her chin and pooling in the bottom of her faceplate. "I told Elissa how to speed us up. I couldn't with these." She waved her glove-encased hands before clumsily disengaging her chair lock and moving to her father's side. He put his broad arm around her shoulders. "I'm sorry." she said again.

"Let's get everyone settled." her mother said cheerfully. "Girls, right this way."

"Kendree, come with me." said her father. "We need to get you into quarantine."

"Quarantine?" asked Elissa, "Can't she take all that off now that she is off the planet?"

"Her immune system is very poor, Elissa," Kendree's mother explained, "I know you and your sisters don't seem sick, but just being in contact with you could make Kendree very ill. She is going to have to stay in her own zone for most of your stay. Besides," she added more sharply, "That's as close as we can get to grounding her on this ship."

Elissa ran to Kendree, looking a little surprised at how light on her feet she was in the reduced gravity. Leaning down she put her forehead against the top of Kendree's faceplate. "Once you are out of that thing, I'll have them show me how I can talk to you." she placed her hand on the glass over Kendree's cheek, "Thank you for rescuing us, you crazy person."

"You're welcome." Kendree smiled, the skin of her cheeks crackling from her dried tears. "Wait until you see the view!"

# Cap'n Harry and the Pirates
## Austin Hackney

*Austin Hackney worked for two decades in children's theater and television before dedicating himself to writing. His fiction, for both young people and adults, has been published under his own name in* Aquila Magazine for Children, Dark Tales, Scribble, The Criminal Class Review, Unsettling Wonder, Stupefying Stories, *and* Quarter Reads. *He divides his time between homes in Northumberland, England and Tuscany, Italy. He has two children and when not writing or reading, is a keen field ornithologist involved in conservation work in the UK. Austin's Twitter handle is @AGHackney, He also blogs at austinhackney.co.uk.*

Harriet Howland – the freebooting aviator and Cap'n of *The Redoubtable,* an enviably fast old style Skyship that she'd obtained on her first adventure across the Dark Sea to the Moon - was preparing to celebrate her birthday in style.

"Now listen up good an' proper you lot!" she said to the gathered band of rag-tag skyfarers who were comrades, crew and family to her. "We done right well to get that treasure an' bring it back safe an' sound from the Outer Archipelago. The Ancient Seal of the City, no less! I'm dead proud of us all, ain't I just. An' I've 'ad notice that the Lord Mayor of Lundoon 'isself is comin' aboard this very after' to collect the blessed thing. Frankly, I'll be glad to get it off me 'ands. While we've got it aboard, we ain't none of us safe. We all know there's other interests that wouldn't stop short o' bloodshed to get their piratical 'ands on it."

Harriet paused a moment in her oratory as a general murmur

passed among the assembly.

"'owever," she continued, beaming, "As it's me bloomin' birthday, I reckon we should 'ave a fine and fancy feast to celebrate our safe return. Whaddya reckon lads an' lasses?"

Caps flew into the air, borne up above the general cheers and whistles of approval. "Three cheers for Cap'n Harry!" cried a voice, and soon they all took up the cry, "Pip-pip-hooray!" followed by a hearty if somewhat tuneless rendition of "for she's a jolly good fellow."

"I thank you all, from the bottom of me 'eart. Now, then – even a feast don't make 'isself, so let's look lively – we'll be wantin' ale and grub and a space clearin' for music an' dancin'. Let's be about it!"

While the crew set about their preparations, Harriet went down to her cabin and locked the door. Sibelius, the one-time Secrets Trader, member of the Monkey Nation, and now Harriet's best friend and First Mate aboard *The Redoubtable*, was waiting for her.

He sat by the latticed window, looking out over the expanse of Dark Sea that still lay between them and the curvature of the Earth. Beyond the Earth the distant suns of the Outer Archipelago glittered and twinkled like Christmas fairy lights.

"That's them lot busy, at any rate," said Harriet.

The sky-monkey turned and nodded, smiling, showing a golden tooth. His leather cap was pushed back on his head, a tarnished silver ring pierced his ear, and his brass goggles hung about his neck. With one hand he brushed some invisible dust off his jerkin and breeches and then, reaching up a muscular, hairy arm, swung himself down onto the ground.

"They're still there," he said. "And, je crois, they come more close."

"D'you think they're onto us, then?"

"Perhaps, mon amie, perhaps. But I do not think they can know of the treasure. It is possible that they want to find me. After what happened before …"

"Yeah," said Harriet, adjusting the eyepiece on the electroscope and flicking the brass switch so that the device popped and crackled into life as she bent down to look into it, "well they ain't 'avin' you and that's an end to it. You might 've given them Pirates the run around, but you saved all our skins."

"Even so, mademoiselle, I would not like to put you or the crew in danger."

"I reckon we're already in danger enough until we shift this treasure, Sibelius." She adjusted a knob on the side of the electroscope. "Looks like they've come to a standstill. I wonder why they don't come no closer? Mayhap it's 'cos they know we're expectin' the Lord Mayor's ship up from Lundoon? No, wait a minute ... They've launched a shuttle – an' it's headin' towards us!"

As she finished speaking, a quiet bell tinkled from the communications device atop her Captain's desk.

Harriet pushed aside the charts and star maps that were spread out over it so she could reach the winding handle. A few vigorous turns and a small cylinder popped out a tube at the top of the machine. Harriet caught it, and fingered out a typed scroll. Her eyes scanned the script.

"The Mayor's on 'is way now," she frowned. "That's bad timin' and no mistake."

Sibelius rubbed a leathery hand over his hairy chin. "The shuttle, she gets closer," he said. "But it seems she changes course, towards the Earth ... "

"Maybe they're goin' to try an' intercept the Mayor?"

"But why, if he does not have the treasure?"

"I don't know. You keep an eye on them pirates an' we'll prepare to repel boarders if we 'ave to. It's too late to warn the Mayor now 'es on 'is way."

Harriet opened the oak box which held the treasure and withdrew a circle of embossed gold and silver; the Seal of the City of Lundoon. She slipped it into the leather pouch hanging from her belt and headed back up on deck.

The deck had been swept and swabbed, colored flags were festooned between the rigging, delicious smells wafted up from the galley, and the crew were already busy laying out trestle tables and rolling barrels of ale ready for tapping.

Harriet stood on the hind deck and looked out through her handscope. Above her the huge gas balloon that kept the ship afloat swelled and swayed, the steel cables that bound it to the body of the ship twanging and humming in the cosmic wind. The Dark Sea stretched out around her in all directions, the islands and stars near and far aglow with colored radiance.

The pirate shuttle sped through the inky darkness, like a flash of white flame in the night. But its course, as Sibelius had said, had changed. *What are they up to?* she thought. *We should move The Redoubtable closer to port. If we're in sight of the Skywatch they're less likely to attack.*

"Cap'n! Come quick!" The cry was urgent, almost panicked.

Harriet ran down to the main deck. A little huddle of crewmen stood by the open door of her cabin.

"It's Sibelius!" one of them cried. "They've kidnapped 'im!"

"Who 'ave?" said Harriet, blanching as she pushed through the little crowd and into her cabin.

"The pirates!"

"But they're miles … " The words dried on her lips. The window where Sibelius had been sitting was smashed, shards of glass and papers scattered over the floor, a chair knocked over. Beyond the broken glass a small, silent windcraft, boldly flying the pirate insignia, sped away into the dark.

"Sibelius," said Harriet quietly, her heart pounding. *The shuttle was just a decoy – and I fell for it!* Then she was all action. "Right, you lot – get this mess cleared up and the window fixed. Davy, Sam, you follow me."

Up on deck, she rang the clanging alarm bell. "I don't want to spoil the party," she announced to the crew. "But there's been pirates on our tail since we left the Inner Reach. We was keepin' an eye on 'em, but it seems they tricked us good an' proper. They sneaked up in a windcraft. They've 'knapped Sibelius."

The crew gasped and the gasp was quickly followed by loud and angry shouts. "Let's go after 'em, blow 'em out the sky!"

"Aye, aye. But wait," said Harriet. "They'll see us comin' a mile off, an' this ol' girl, fast as she is, ain't no match for the speed of a windcraft. 'Sides, we've the Mayor on 'is way to collect the treasure."

"We've got to save Sibelius!"

"'Course we 'ave," said Harriet. Her heart was suddenly thumping. A prickle of sweat broke out at the back of her neck. How long could she wait? She couldn't. She'd have to offend the Mayor. *He'll think I've stolen it*, she thought. Then said, "Meself, Davy an' Sam are headin' out now to give chase. Fire up the steamrocket! And look lively!"

Once in the pilot's seat, with Davy and Sam strapped in behind her, Harriet pulled down her goggles, checked the pressure gauge and yanked back the contact lever. The steamrocket roared into life, a jet of hot steam shooting out from behind. Harriet released the brake and the thing shot forward, rising from the foredeck and soaring into the dark.

The cosmic winds blew and buffeted the little craft and Harriet strained to hold a steady course.

"Full throttle, Cap'n!" shouted Davy over the noise of the engine and rushing air.

"It is full throttle," Harriet shouted over her shoulder. "But we're losing ground on the windship."

"If we don't catch them before they get back to their ship, what then?" chimed in Sam.

"Then we board 'er," said Harriet, her face grim.

The others said nothing then. To board the pirate ship, just the three of them, was about as dangerous a thing as they could possibly do.

Even as they ripped through the Dark Sea as fast as the steamrocket could manage, Harriet knew, watching the windship whooshing ever faster into the distance, that they had no chance of catching up.

Once she'd seen the windship moor alongside the pirate vessel and lock on, she swerved away and flew the rocket in a broad arc, out over the top of the ship and round back toward *The Redoubtable*. It was an unnecessary manoeuvre, but she needed time to think.

*I gotta rescue Sibelius, no question,* she thought. *But I can't risk the lives of Davy and Sam, to do it.*

"Davy," she said as she cranked the rocket into cruise speed and tripped the gyroscopic autobalance mechanism on. "I'm goin' down. I'll take the batwings. You keep the rocket circling slow an' out of reach of fire. I'll signal you when I've got Sibelius."

"You can't go in on your own, Cap'n! It's too dangerous."

"It's more dangerous to try an' land this thing," she said. "If I go down on the wings, there's a chance that I can get aboard without 'em seein' me. We'll play 'em at their own game. You make out that you're heading back home an' while they're watching you, I'll sneak aboard."

"But Cap'n …"

"It's an order."

"Aye-aye, Cap'n."

A moment later and Davy had taken the controls.

Harriet was sitting on the edge of a lateral rocket fin, pulling a stiff leather pack onto her back and tightening the straps around her waist and over her shoulders. She reached behind her and wound the crank handle on the side of the pack, listening to the *clickety-clack* as the clockwork mechanism wound tight. She pulled down her goggles, leaned into the wind - and jumped.

For a few seconds she fell through the dark emptiness, then she pulled the rip cord and the batwings, oiled leather stretched over a wooden framework, sprang out from the pack. She was in full, flapping flight, the mechanism clattering steadily behind her back.

She kept high at first, out of sight, as the steamrocket arced round, banked, and headed back towards *The Redoubtable*. Then she spiralled down towards the pirate ship.

Batwings were only meant for bailing out in emergencies. The mechanism would wind down and leave her stranded, at the mercy of the cosmic winds and the infinite vastness of the Dark Sea, if she didn't reach a landing point soon.

Harriet circled down above the pirate ship. It was much larger than her own and clad in heavy steel plates. The menacing skull and crossed bones flag fluttered from its turret.

*Funny thing is*, Harriet thought as she came closer, *it looks like there's no-one about. Place is deserted.*

Imagining the pirates all below deck gloating over their latest prize, her confidence grew. She steered herself between the iron and steel chimneys and over the blackened deck, searching for a place to land.

Then she saw Sibelius.

He was locked in a cage on the main deck. The cage itself was secured to posts by chains. *They're right full o' themselves these blinkin' pirates*, thought Harriet. *Thinking they can get away with this without even placin' a guard!* Even so, she had no idea, looking at the chunky padlock, how she was going to get him out of there before somebody *did* show up.

Harriet landed as lightly as she could, a soft thud. *"Sibelius!"* she hissed as she unbuckled the belt and shrugged the straps from her shoulders, leaving the batwings to clatter unceremoniously to the floor.

It was only when she reached the bars of the cage she noticed the expression on the sky-monkey's face, the rapid shaking of his head and the anxiety in his eyes.

But by then it was too late.

Pirates appeared from everywhere. They popped up from behind barrels, through doorways, dropped down from the rigging and emerged through trapdoors. Cutlasses flashed and the barrels of pistols all pointed her way.

*It's a trap!* Harriet looked left and right and all around, but there was no way of escape. *You're losin' your touch, Cap'n Harry,* she thought to herself. *That's the second time in one day that these lousy pirates have got the better of you.*

"Welcome to my parlour, said the spider to the fly." Harriet spun round to face the speaker. It was the pirate captain, her old enemy and would-be nemesis. He grinned at her even as Harriet felt her own brow knot up in consternation. "How kind of you to … drop by."

The pirates sniggered.

"What do you want Sibelius for?"

"Sibelius? Oh, the ape. Only as bait for the more important prize."

"Me?"

"You!" the pirate snorted. "Hardly you! You flatter yourself, my dear. It is the Seal that I want. Your job is very easy. Give it to me."

"I ain't got it. It's back on me ship."

The Captain sighed and took a few paces towards Harriet. She tensed and backed off, but her arms were suddenly held fast by two rough looking coves whose skin was blotched and dirty and who stank of sweat and stale rum.

Suddenly the pirate Captain was right in front of her, his peppermint breath cool on her cheeks. "You shouldn't lie to me," he said quietly. Then his hand moved like lightning and a thin, curved blade flashed a malicious smile. Its treacherous kiss cut her belt and the pouch containing the Seal fell at his feet with a heavy thud. Without taking his eyes from Harriet, he lowered his boot onto it lightly and smiled. "Thank you," he said.

Harriet struggled to free herself from the grip of the pirates but they held her fast. The pirate Captain picked up the Seal then turned his back and walked away. With a dismissive gesture of his hand he said, "Take them away!"

•••

It was gloomy and cold in the bowels of the pirate ship, where Harriet and Sibelius were locked in a holding cell. A feint glimmer of sickly light spilled in through the grimy glass of a tiny porthole above them. Cobwebs hung thick in the corners and an occasional spider scuttled through the shadows.

"I'm dead sorry, Sibelius," said Harriet. "I come 'ere to rescue you and just got us both into worse bother than before – an' I lost the blinkin' treasure. I'm a fool an' no mistake."

Sibelius sighed. "No, mademoiselle, I do not think you are a fool. You are brave and perhaps a little *foolhardy*, but not a fool."

"The question is, 'ow the blazes are we goin' to get out o' this pretty mess? 'Seems our adventurin' days may be over."

"Listen!"

Heavy footfalls sounded on the other side of the door. Both Harriet and Sibelius stood up and edged closer, stepping over the scuttling spiders that cleared out of their way. They both listened intently.

The footfall stopped. "Oh this is a fine job!" said a gruff voice. "Stuck down here in the grimy hold to keep these little wretches under lock and key."

"They say the monkey can talk."

"Bewitched, I'll wager. That girl may fancy herself the cap'n of a ship, but my money's on her being nothing more'n a witch, if the truth is known."

"I'd rather have her as my cap'n than that miserable fellow up top, witch or no witch."

"You keep your voice down, mate, or it'll be you that's hanging from a hempen rope today and not these two here."

Harriet gulped. Sibelius rubbed his hairy hand around his neck.

"They say the Captain is scared of spiders, you know. Makes out he's brave and bold, but he's scared of spiders!"

"Good job he don't come down here, then, mate! Place is riddled with 'em."

Harriet and Sibelius exchanged glances and then looked around at their cobweb infested prison.

"I saw him once, the Captain, up on a chair and simpering like a tearful toddler, because there was a spider in the corner of his chambers!"

With silent understanding, Harriet nodded to Sibelius and a moment later they were busy catching every spider they could lay their hands on. They shoved them into their pockets, into their shirts, anywhere they could find. There were hundreds to be had.

"Mademoiselle, régarde!" said Sibelius suddenly, a hint of excitement in his voice.

Harriet came over to look. Tucked in the corner of the cell was a thick white bundle of gossamer web, packed loosely around the softness of thousands of spider eggs. Harriet grinned. Sibelius lifted the nest carefully away from the wall and put it into his pouch.

A horn sounded. The guards shuffled and grumbled and then the bolt squealed back and the door opened. The guards stood with their long-barrelled flintlocks pointing at Harriet and Sibelius.

"Right then," said the one with the gruff voice. "No funny moves or I've orders to shoot you down on the spot, understand?"

One behind each of them, the guards led them along a corridor, up some steps and out onto the deck. Harriet's heart skipped a beat when she saw the ropes and the nooses hanging from the bar. *Four of 'em. One for me*, she thought, *one for Sibelius and...* Her heart nearly stopped altogether.

The steamrocket rested on the aft deck. Sam and Davy were tied up to masts next to the improvised gallows.

*Oh blimey. 'Ow did that 'appen?* She thought. *Now we're doomed for sure.* But she caught their eyes and gave them an encouraging wink, although in her heart she felt that she had betrayed them all.

"This," said the pirate captain, from his carved wooden seat that had been set out on the deck together with a table bearing a cup and jug of wine and a cushion on which was nestled the Seal of the City, "will be our last meeting, I think."

Harriet said nothing, but held her head up high. Inside she felt like screaming. She was breaking out into a sweat. But she wouldn't show fear to the pirates. She wouldn't give them that victory, too. And besides, it was her duty to encourage her crew and show them a good example, even to the last.

The pirate Captain smiled. "I shall enjoy watching you … dance."

Something tickled Harriet's wrist. She glanced down to see a couple of hairy spider legs tapping out from her sleeve. She quickly pushed them back in.

"Take them up!" said the pirate Captain, pouring himself a glass of wine.

"Now!" said Harriet. She ducked down beneath the gun barrel and tripped her guard by the legs, sending him crashing to the deck. Sibelius had did the same. In the moment of surprised confusion which followed, she and Sibelius tore off their jackets, releasing dozens of spiders, which jumped and scuttled all over the deck.

The Captain screamed, spilling his wine like blood down his front. Harriet rolled and jumped, taking down another pirate and wresting his cutlass from his hand. She swung up into the rigging as a gunshot splintered the wood next to her head. But she was fast and not an easy target.

"Never mind the flies!" screamed the Pirate Captain. ""Get rid of these sp-sp-spiders! Get them off me! Get them off me!"

As Harriet reached the higher rigging, she looked down and saw Sibelius opening his pouch. In that moment, the nest burst and a cloud of thousands of tiny spiders exploded into the air below.

Spiders were everywhere. They were crawling on the deck, over the masts, rigging and sails, and on the clothes and faces of the pirates.

In the chaos that ensued, Harriet untied a halyard and swung through the air to the other side of the ship, landing expertly next to Davy and Sam. She cut their bonds with a single stroke of the cutlass.

"To the rocket" she said. "Fire her up!"

As the boys headed back to the steamrocket, Harriet fought her way to the captain's table. It had been knocked over as his crew had rushed forward to try and get the spiders off him. The Seal of the City of Lundoon lay at her feet. She was just about to pick it up, when she felt the sharp stab of an elbow in her side, and another hand snatched it up. The hand belonged to a grim and dangerous looking fellow if ever there was one. "Not so easy, little witch," he snarled. He pulled out his flintlock and raised the barrel only inches from Harriet's face.

*It's over*, thought Harriet and closed her eyes ready her for the shot. But the shot never came. Her eyes snapped open again. The thug stumbled backwards, dropping his gun as he struggled to wrestle free from the hairy, muscular arm that had tightened about his neck. "Sibelius!"

The thug passed out on the boards and the sky-monkey tipped his leather cap at his Cap'n, the Seal safe in his simian grip.

"Quick! To the rocket!"

As they reached the rocket's hatchway, they heard the pirate captain, who was now free of spiders, shouting the order, "Stop them! Don't let them get away!"

Harriet kicked back, knocking a pirate from her as she scrambled into the rocket after Sibelius. The steel door swung shut and she bolted it down. Bullets pinged and ricocheted from the metallic surface as Harriet threw herself into the pilot's seat.

"She's not up to steam yet, Cap'n!" said Davy, an edge of panic in his voice. "I don't think we'll have enough power!"

Harriet yanked back the brake release and engaged the engines. Steam shot from the jets at the back of the rocket, but it was not enough to get them airborne. She pushed hard on the throttle and the steamrocket jolted forward, careering in a crazy zig-zig across the deck, sending pirates leaping to the left and the right of them.

"Hold on tight!" she called and shunted the thrusters into full power as they smashed through the balustrade at the ship's edge and dropped into empty space.

The rocket spiralled through the Dark Sea at a dizzying rate. "We'll 'ave to freefall while she gets up steam!"

"She's there Cap'n, she's there!"

Harriet saw the pressure needle climb, re-engaged the engines and the rocket shot forward. Harriet lifted it and stabilised their flight path, getting her bearings and heading back to *The Redoubtable*. She could see the Mayorial Vessel, accompanied by a fleet of fast-flying, armed guard ships, had already docked.

"I think we done it," she said, grinning. "I think we bloomin' done it!"

•••

Harriet stood on the foredeck of *The Redoubtable* watching the captured pirate ship being escorted by an armed City Guard down towards the Earth and the gaols of Lundoon. The treasure, the great Seal of the City, she had returned to the Mayor, whose gratitude extended further than expected as he promised her and her crew a plentiful reward for their part in the capture of one of the most notorious pirate gangs of recent times.

"It would seem, mademoiselle that our adventuring days are not over after all."

Harriet turned about to look at Sibelius.

He was grinning, his golden tooth twinkling. "The crew are awaiting their orders, Cap'n."

Harriet looked down and saw the crew assembled on the deck amidst the bunting and the burgeoning tables. *Blimey,* she thought. *I'd clean forgot.*

"Now then, lads and lasses," she called. "As I was sayin' before we was so rudely int'rupted, 'ow about a feast to celebrate me blinkin' birthday?"

As the crew cheered and the band struck up a tune, Harriet felt Sibelius, her best friend and First Mate, come and stand next to her.

"Happy birthday," he said.

"Yeah," said Harriet. "Ain't it just!"

# Where You Want To Be
## Jeannie Warner

*Jeannie Warner spent her formative years in Southern California and Colorado, and is not afraid to abandon the most luxurious environs for a chance to travel anywhere. She has a useless degree in musicology, a checkered career in computer security, and aspirations of world domination. Her writing credits include blogs of random musings, thriller novel manuscripts, stories in* Tightbeam *online magazine,* KnightBridge's Rom Zom Com *anthology, the* Mad Scientist's Journal, *several police statements, and a collection of snarky notes to a former upstairs neighbor. She lives in the San Francisco Bay area near several of her best friends whom she refers to as "minions."*

Ollie sat back in the pilot's chair with a happy sigh. The chair was too large for her slender fourteen year-old frame; the seat was originally built to the specifications of an adult raised planetside, so it gave her room to sit cross-legged as she worked. The instrument panel in front of her blinked green thanks to the past few hours she'd spent with the manual and a surreptitious kick to the underside of the console. Reaching to one side, she flipped a switch. "All sorted, Dodger! Our course is laid in and logged."

"That's Cap'n Dodger," came the crackling reply after a moment, and Ollie grinned. Ever since the previous Captain Sykes got himself nicked by dirt-side authorities doing one of his "trades" with stolen goods a few cycles back, Dodger had taken over command their cargo ship. Since joining up a couple years before, Ollie knew being captain was all Dodger ever wanted to do, and he'd wasted no time after the arrest donning Sykes' uniform jacket to wear it constantly even though it was too large. Dodge wore it with the sleeves rolled up and held his chin very high.

"Captain Dodger," Ollie repeated dutifully, though her smile was in her voice.

"I best come up and check it," he said. "Since it's yer first an' all."

Ollie rolled her eyes. "Okay. Excited much?"

There was no reply to that beyond a dismissive snort, and Ollie laughed as she thumbed off the intercom. He might act casual, but she knew Dodger was excited about the prospect of seeing his sister again. They had both been in the FAGN program since early childhood, but weren't assigned together. The Federal Association for Generational Navy  was a well-intentioned program to find something useful to do with all the children born in space whose parents either couldn't (by virtue of being dead) or wouldn't (by virtue of lacking the ability) take responsibility. As far as work programs and vocational training go, it was moderately effective - if you got on a good ship, with good contracts. The Federation provided subsistence, so luxuries were a bonus you won for yourself.

Dodger hadn't talked much about his sister when Ollie joined the crew two years ago as a stowaway. Their ship did mostly salvage ops – there was a lot of wreckage in and around asteroid and ring mining. Captain Sykes had started gravitating toward less than legal jobs, but once he was gone between Dodger and Ollie, they had figured out how to make more money running supplies and doing a little ring mining. That is, ice and water. There is never enough water in space. Ollie had a head for figures that helped them make a profit on their jobs, keeping them on the only-slightly-illegal side of operations. There was supposed to be a duly appointed FAGN officer in charge of the ship. Dodger was still three months shy of the age for full citizenship status, so they couldn't get his self-promotion legitimized.

A thumping on the stairs and a creak of the cockpit door opening heralded Dodger's arrival, and Ollie swiveled in the chair to wave hello. Dodger was a hand span taller than she, with a shock of dark brown hair and matching brown skin with the indeterminate bones of a space mutt. He wore the captain's coat, and below that the same grey overalls as Ollie herself. He was scowling, but Ollie's grin never wavered. She could see the excitement dancing in his eyes.

"Callie oughta be signaling us soon here," he muttered, checking over Ollie's programming in the console. "She said she would when they cleared the gas giant. I reckon today. Maybe even this shift."

"Do you want to take the shift from me?" Ollie asked with a fake innocent look that didn't fool Dodger for a moment.

"Nah. I'll just hang out a bit. You know. See how you do with comms." She knew that her work on communications was calm and professional. Ollie had taken it over as one of her ship's duties months ago, for all official waves. But she also knew nerves when she saw them.

"Okay, Dodge. Captain Dodger," she said, as he shot her a look all over again.

They sat there in companionable silence while Ollie pulled up charts on the current mining operations in the new system. Outside the stars barely seemed to move even with the engines at three-quarter burn. "When did you last see her in person?" Ollie looked back toward Dodger, who was starting to fidget with a lucky credit chip he'd won in an unsavory poker game back near the Pleidies.

"We was nine an' eleven," he said. "We'd asked to be on a ship together, but there was only two berths open. I went with Bill 'cause I didn't like how he looked at Callie."

"You think he woulda…" Ollie didn't want to finish the question, and Dodger shrugged.

"Maybe not. I was supposed to look after her, though. Mum said. Even though she was older. She's an officer now, I hear." There was justifiable pride in his tone. "Gonna have her own ship soon. Not as good as mine, 'course."

"Of course."

A green light flashed on the console, and Dodger lunged forward to slap his palm down and open the channel. "FAGN ship *New London* here."

The connection wasn't good, and the sound crackled. "Dodge? Is that you? We're being boarded!" A well-groomed young woman appeared on the screen, dark hair pulled back neatly into a bun at the back of her neck. Her face was a match for Dodger's, but more feminine with subtly rounder eyes that were darker in the moment. She wore a jacket like Dodger's that was tailored to her frame and size. "I don't know why. This isn't according to protocol at all."

Behind her, the door to the bridge opened and white man with dark, curling hair with a neat moustache appeared. This one was perhaps thirty, dressed in formal Federation uniform, scarlet jacket and trousers tucked into shiny black boots. Everything about his appearance gleamed. The one mar on his otherwise handsome face was a scar that stretched from his eyebrow down to his cheek, leaving the eye behind it milky white with a crease in the lid. His voice was loud and slightly braying as he reached forward and laid a hand on Callie's shoulder. "I am Captain Jazz Hook. On behalf of the Federal Association of Interstellar Systems, this ship is being decommissioned as an FAGN vessel, re-appropriated by my staff, and will be sent to Stargazer Station effective immediately. All crews will report to the same station for a new assignment either on the station or within the administrative ranks. Those under thirteen will immediately be enrolled in the education system to receive proper training for a future productive role in society."

Dodger's breath caught with Ollie's as they watched Callie struggling in the man's grip, which tightened on her as she tried to move away. He didn't seem aware that the camera was on, or that a channel was open and broadcasting. "What? Why? Captain Hook, we are operating precisely according to orders and within budget." Budget was usually the magic word in the Federation. If you didn't cost money or make waves, you did as you pleased.

"That is not my concern. The FAGN program is ended, effective two standard days ago Federation surface time." His tone went from officious to patronizing, which was almost worse. "Special interest groups, they passed new legislation. It's not right for children to be forced to run about in space without supervision. It's for your own good. And don't worry, your rank will be translated into the new bands of a proper Federation corporate position. I'm sure you'll make a very fine administrative assistant."

Callie tried to push off the older man's hand. "Don't you 'central supervision' me, mister! You can't just end the FAGN program. Captain Richards and I are duly approved and appointed ship's managers. I'm sure if you'll review our record--"

"All the FAGN records have been reviewed by appropriate personnel." Hook beckoned. In the doorway, two more officers appeared and took hold of Callie on either side. They lifted her out of her chair to face him. "Your lack of immediate compliance with my authority only demonstrates the general laxity and disobedience that has characterized the FAGN program recently." His tone turned vaguely conciliatory. "Look, we all realize that the program was a mistake. Children need close adult supervision at all times to protect them, and help them be productive adults one day. It's a very dangerous universe, little lady, and while I'm sure it wasn't *your* ship involved in heists this last year, it doesn't mean we can allow this kind of activity to occur with a program under our insignia. Men, arrest her for insubordination. And you - go along now, there's a good girl."

Callie continued to protest as the two red-clad goons hustled her out. Dodger stood beside Ollie in stillness, a hand clapped over his mouth to stifle words that threatened to pour out of him. Thoughtfully, Ollie reached out to turn off the two-way communication, leaving incoming signal only. Standing alone on the screen, Hook's unguarded expression turned to one of vague disgust. "Revolting," he muttered, and pulled a small jump drive from his pocket to insert into the ship's console. "The sooner all these space rats are rounded up and dumped for re-programming the better." He drew back his fingers after plugging in. "It's sticky? Stars preserve us, the whole place is sticky. The…" His voice trailed off as his eyes focused on the screen, seeming to look directly through the screen. "Hello, what's this? Is there someone there? Can you hear-"

Callie and Dodger's hands collided as they flipped off the communications switch, and in the silence that followed they stared at one another with wide eyes. Then Dodger's face scrunched up, torn between tears and anger. "I'll spend a year in a sanitation tank afore I'll let them take my ship away. We worked too hard. We all done good jobs." He leaned back against the entryway and slid down to sit on the deck panels, scrubbing at his face and hair with his hands. "But they got guns, Ollie."

"Guns ain't everything in space. I mean, I reckon we can get a paint job to cover our insignia, an' maybe a new transponder back at Midway Station. It'll cost, but with the last ice transport we have extra." Ollie's mind started racing, coming up with the plans needed to strike out as independents, away from the whole FAGN system. Hadn't they been on their own for the last twelvemonth? "Our ship mighta been lost. We ain't checked in officially for a long time anyway, right?"

"They got Callie though," Dodger said, lifting his chin again to stare at the now-blank screen. "You hear what he said? They're gonna "re-program" her, turn her into some kinda office drone that ain't never gonna ship out again." He took a breath, then flashed an echo of his earlier proud smile. "Didja see her uniform? She looked good, eh?"

"Real good, Dodge." Ollie stood to attention beside her chair. "So you reckon she'd make a good first mate here, on the *New London*?"

Dodger stared at her for a moment, then a smile crept across his face. "That's Captain Dodger. She better 'member it, too."

"You best tell her that in person. Let's figure out how." Ollie held out a hand, and Dodger shook it solemnly. Letting go, Ollie beckoned him to sit on the chair with her. She punched up new nav charts. "Stargazer Station. That's two star systems away, nearly a full night's travel. If we burn hard, we could be there by morning."

"They'll have guns and locks and cameras," Dodger pointed out.

"We got a Paris," Ollie retorted, referring to their most studious, technical-minded crew member.

Dodger grinned. "That we do! An' one brilliant Captain." He slapped the open-ship comms button. "All hands on deck! We got us an emergency here!" With that he stood up, and draped an arm about the girl's shoulders. "Come on. We got us some heroic rescuin' to go plan." He paused, then looked sideways at her. "We got a plan, right?"

"We will," Ollie nibbled on her lip, thinking fast as she let him lead her out.

Down in the hold, the crew assembled in the area normally reserved for ball games. Ollie remembered when she first arrived on ship, when the collective of oddly-shaped youths unnerved her. No longer. They were all family now, this crew of mostly space-born mutts. Dodger and Ollie were the only planet-born of the lot, but Dodger spent enough of his childhood in space that his bones never grew out all the way, leaving him below average in height for his age. Tiny and Mouse were both under four feet, Tiny because his legs were spindly and near useless, and Mouse because his legs were missing below the knees. The engineer, Paris, had the darkest skin and hair of anyone, though when he grinned it was a flash of white that brightened his whole face. He didn't have a straight line in his body, but he never forgot a wiring diagram he looked at. Bongo had easily the longest arms of the group, and an easy way about him that made friends with everyone for all that he was the prankster of the crew. Mattie was the oldest at nearly twenty years old; looking at her she was mostly torso and curving, muscular arms; she could move tons of cargo in zero-gee like she was dancing with it. Mattie preferred playing net ball to reading and figuring, save for her stash of space-opera novels she scavenged. She wore her black hair in a tight braid that wrapped in a spiral on the back of her head, and had become like an older sister to Ollie in their time together.

Out in space protein was scarce, gravity was rare, and accidents twisted the body; it was a combination that resulted in a wide variety in body shapes. You grew how you grew, and the children of the stars were no two alike.

Dodger semi-floated down the stairs in the ship's partial gee to stand in front of the crew, who arrayed in a semi-circle in front of him. Ollie settled herself on the stairs, wrapping her arms around her knees and propping her chin to ponder as their captain caught them up on current events. As usual, he didn't mince words much. "Folks, we got us a situation here. Seems the Federation thinks they can take away our ship an' turn us into station-bound idiots doin' something "productive" for our corporate masters. I'm gettin' the idea that's working sanitation, food service, and bein' some officer's secretary." A mutter passed through the ranks, and Dodger half-grinned at Paris. "You might end up some kinda engineer, maybe. You got the smarts for it. But what do I got? An' Ollie here, we all remembers how she wants to stay away from the arms of her lovin' family."

"You got leadership skills, Cap'n Dodger!" Mouse saluted with a cheeky grin. Beside him, Tiny cheered with a woo and a fist pump.

"Yeah, but that ain't gonna get me anything but re-programming in the Federation system, and a future herdin' garbage, given my age and size," Dodger pointed out. "Plus, there's this complication. They took Callie's ship, an' her with it." Smiles disappeared at that. For all that their diminutive captain was devoted to this ship-born family, they all knew his loyalty included his distant sister.

"So we're gonna get her back," Ollie spoke into the sudden silence. "I been thinking. You know, it'll really let their guard down if we come in voluntary-like."

Dodger turned and looked back incredulously. "Are you freakin' *kiddin'* me?"

Ollie raised a hand. "Hear me out. They dragged off Callie. Like as not her crew, too, if they're loyal like us. I mean, we'd all fight for you, right?" There was a mutter of assent around the bay. "Right. So she's under guard. I reckon they're all going to be guarded. But volunteers? What if we, poor orphan souls, saw the wisdom of the Federation?" She stood, placing her hand over her heart to look solemn. "I, for one, want to be schooled in how to be a proper citizen. I want a real job, something really productive for society. In fact, I think it's my destiny to be a secretary to some high-ranked Federation official. Mattie, don't you want to work in laundry?" Mattie looked startled, then started to chuckle wickedly, catching the drift of Ollie's thoughts.

As her plan formed in her head, Ollie started pointing around the floor. "Tiny and Mouse, you two would be great cleaning and recycling. Paris, I bet if you volunteered for maintenance or even decommission duty, you'd know that space station and dock like the back of your hand inside a day. You know, pick the really dirty jobs with fuel lines an' propulsion systems, an' other stuff that would help get one ship ready while makin' it real hard for others to follow. Is somethin' like that possible?"

"Possible? Easy. It would be…fun." Paris's normally serious face broke into a smile that danced in his dark eyes.

One by one as they were named the gang looked thoughtful, considering their parts. "Yeah, what about me?" Dodger demanded, a trifle cross that he hadn't been the one to come up with a plan, but not so angry as to sabotage it outright. "What do ya think I'd be good at?"

"Why, being bad of course," Ollie grinned at him. "And real pissed off that we rebelled against your oh-so-wise leadership. Maybe you'll get put in the holding cells so that you can find Callie and let the others in there know the plan. I ain't never seen anyone pick a pocket or pilfer stuff like you. Surely you could get a couple door keys on your way in, and save 'em until they're needed? Someone gotta fetch out Callie."

Dodger's chin lifted, and he planted his fists on his hips. "That's right. I *am* the best." And that was that. Ollie left the crew planning their performances, and went up to chart a course of surrender and compliance.

It was a full sleeping cycle to get the New London to Stargazer Station, and Paris was at the helm as they opened up a hail with Ollie beside him. "Stargazer Station, this is the newly decommissioned FAGN ship *New London*, reporting in as ordered." He winked at the girl standing by the chair, then added, "Our Captain was a little sulky about it all, so we had to lock him in his cabin. Could you send some officers to, ah, help him disembark?"

"Of course, *New London*," came the reply. "And thank you for your cooperation. You'll find the orientation complex to your right immediately as you dock."

"I'm sure we will, Stargazer. *New London* out." Paris turned off the comms and winked at Ollie, who was nervously biting her nails behind him. "So far so good. You know they're going to have full grav on the station. That'll make it harder on some of us." Full gravity was hard to walk in, for those without long, straight legs.

"I know," Ollie said. "But ya know something? If we believe in each other, we can do a lot more than if we worry about the hard stuff. The odds ain't great as it is."

Paris nodded. "It's a good plan, though." And with that solemn approval, he turned his attention to docking.

Just as anticipated, there was very little trouble getting Dodger marched off under arrest, protesting loudly all the way. He was even sporting a darkening eye by the time they wrestled him to the bottom of the gangplank. "I got rights! I'm a Captain, doncha know? Hey!" He wriggled and shoved, and winked once back at a sober-faced Ollie to confirm that he'd taken care of his first acquisition.

For the rest of the crew, there was paperwork. Lots and lots of paperwork, and endless aptitude tests. Ollie noted that wherever they went, there were indeed armed adults and cameras constantly, hovering over them. As she had anticipated, Paris did indeed get shuffled off to maintenance and engineering, for his clear knowledge and experience keeping the *New London* in the sky. The rest of the crew adjusted their answers to all the questions as Ollie had directed, finding their ways into the innocuous but useful tasks the Federation assigned.

Two days later, Ollie was sitting at her post as a very junior secretary to the station's command staff, performing yet another system mock-backup training drill according to the manual, sighing over the tedium of it. She'd done much harder programming on board the ship, and the strain of pretending to be a wide-eyed, enthusiastic Federation drone was starting to wear on her. Additionally, the constant adult supervision made her tense – it was easier to keep your head down and do a very uncreative job than to improvise or improve the routine. She was sure it was well-intentioned. But there were no ball games, no yelling, no exploring of the station, no hide and seek or other games at all. To be sure, the adults were all very solicitious, and quick to find all of her mistakes for her. "Now, you must be more careful, Olivia." Ollie was deathly tired of being called Olivia. "What if this was not a drill? Anything could happen."

Ollie wasn't buying it. She'd made mistakes before. She'd nearly died once in the black, with only the quick-thinking Dodger saving her. The consequences of failure before ranged from death to a cuff across the head from Captain Bill or, after he was gone, a lot of flashing lights and warning sirens from the ship's computer, followed by pointing and laughing from the rest of the crew. Ollie never made the same mistakes twice, because the consequences were either dangerous or embarrassing. The consequences here were lighter, and therefore taught her nothing. She was waiting for a sign. Or rather, a set of signs that her plan might be ready.

Tiny and Mouse brought the first, when they came to dump her waste paper basket. Tiny winked. "Didja hear, Ollie? That rotten ol' Captain Dodger got hisself dumped into a cell with some girl named Callie. He went through a bunch-a other cell mates, but she's the only one that calms him down. Ain't that a shocker?"

"I'm shocked all right. Shocked it only took 'em twelve days to find someone that calmed that reprobate." Ollie nodded back. "When's th' regular day cycle where y'all take out the garbage?"

"Tomorrow," Mouse averred. He rode on the cart where his lack of legs wasn't an issue, and manhandled the larger refuse cans with ease from his perch. "We dumps all these carts behind the kitchen ports, an' sort it all into recycling vs. what gets dumped into orbit."

Ollie nodded. "Tomorrow, huh? Okay. If you guys see Mattie, tell her that she should do all the delicates in tomorrow's wash."

"Sure thing, Ollie!" Tiny offered a cheeky little mock salute and turned to start pushing the cart and his mate out of the office. They passed a frowning Officer Hook, and immediately lost their smiles and ducked their heads. Everyone did, when Hook was around.

Ollie, too, bent to her task as Hook came up to stand over her. "You're planet-born, aren't you girl?"

"Yessir," she offered in a small voice. But no more. She knew never to volunteer anything.

Hook's dark gaze swept over her, marking her blond hair and pale eyes, her straight-limbed delicate beauty, and his fingers tapped along the synth-leather of his belt. "You'll do. You look better than the other children. We need an interview done tomorrow with a passing news broadcast crew; they've announced their intention to dock at oh-four-thirty in the second cycle." He sniffed. "See if you can get someone to do your hair, and make sure you wear a clean uniform. You're going to represent the face of the new Federation orphans initiative." His smile was dark, and a little oily. "We must show we're raising future generations. If you do a good job, you might even become a celebrity. We'll need to keep you, at least, for when the inspections come."

"Me at least?" Ollie swallowed hard.

"The others represent too high an impact on our protein allotment, and other resources. We'll be shipping the rest of the leftovers off to work in the water reclamation facilities on one of Saturn's rings in the old Earth system. The Federation needs ice."

"Water is life," Ollie whispered, going a little pale. It was also well known that life expectancies were short for anyone stuck as an ice miner.

"Just so, just so. I'll see you tomorrow, Miss Olivia." Hook turned to stalk out. "Miss Olivia. Yes, that's what we'll call you. Little Miss Orphan Olivia— " the rest of his soliloquy was lost as the door shut behind him.

Ollie's voice was shaky as she stabbed the IT comms button. "'Scuse me. Maintenance? This is Ollie in the officers' cube area. Can y'all send someone to look at our speakers? They've gone mighty crackly."

Paris's calmer voice echoed back. "Roger that, Ollie. I'll be there shortly." And true to his word, appeared two minutes later. "What's up? You look upset."

"It's gotta be tonight," Ollie whispered low, darting looks all around. "There's a news crew coming, and Hook's gonna ship out kids to the rings for ice mining. Betcha they'll pick the troublemakers first."

The young man frowned. "No bet. Today, then. I'll pass the word - let's go at dinner." He paused, then grinned whitely. "I got new keys today; I can cut grav to parts of the station at six bells in the dog's watch. Reckon that'll give us an advantage with the Feds at dinner. The *New London* is in berth twenty-two."

"I'll let Mattie know – it's laundry day and she can tell everyone," Ollie's spirits rose, and for the first time since landing on the space station, she went back to her bunk humming.

Her room was only six feet square, with a bed that slid in and out of the wall and a small sink with a can that popped out of the floor in the corner when you stepped on a lever. The walls were metallic, and the floor a composite of ground space dust and polymer. Ollie smoothed out her sheet, and started putting her very few personals into the center. A few minutes later, "Laundry!" came the familiar cry outside her door, and Ollie opened it to see Mattie there with her hamper on wheels.

"Thanks," Ollie offered up her only spare uniform and towel. Her explanation was mindful of the bugs they expected to find in all their sleeping quarters. "Twenty-two, and flying practice tonight, six bells in the dog. Haven't you always wanted to fly?

Tell people to pack snacks if they can."

Mattie grinned, twirling the laundry cart easily over her head and down again so that Ollie could dump her load in. "Who don't love flyin'? Twenty-two. Dinnertime for officers, snacks for us. Gotcha." The long-armed girl turned and limped off with the cart, swooshing it from side to side as she went (complete with the appropriate whooshing sound effects), to go warn the rest of the crew in their various tasks.

The next two hours passed, and Ollie's stomach knotted back up. She chewed two cuticles ragged, and repacked her very few personals three times into a small bundle tied in a sheet. As six bells sounded through the station she ventured out into the corridor, heading toward the docking bays. Halfway there, she felt abruptly lighter. Anticipating what was to come, she grabbed at a doorway and waited another second. Her feet came off the floor as a klaxon sounded, and she pushed hard to float the rest of the way toward the next doorway. *"Alert. Alert. Please remain calm and in your berths. Maintenance to the control rooms. Repeat—"*

In the distance, she could hear voices raised as officers yelled back and forth. Ollie continued her quick, weightless navigation of the hallways with the ease of one used to zero-gravity, meeting up with the crew as she went. Mattie joined her first, the older girl floating a bulging laundry sack behind her. She was graceful in motion without gravity, like a dancer without the need for legs or feet. "Tiny an' Mouse are seein' the garbage out from the prison level," Mattie yelled into the other girl's ear, until the klaxon abruptly went quiet. In a more normal tone, "Bongo's already on board. Got a bunch of kids from there. Dodger an' Callie are arguin' about something, stowed in the garbage cans. Let's go warm up the ship."

The two girls reached the cavernous main hangar, looking through the numbered slots to spot their own ship. Mattie saw the *New London* first, and launched toward it like an eagle striking through the air until she caught herself on the landing struts. Ollie followed, a trifle more seagull-like in her path, and tossed her small bundle up the gangplank. The two girls worked in tandem, unhooking the manual clips holding the *London's* landing gear onto the tarmac.

Paris appeared next, and launched himself at the ship next to the *London*, a similar FAGN-style cargo ship with *Indian Princess* painted on the hull.  He had his own bundle with him that he lobbed unerringly toward the *London's* hatch. "Callie's ship," he gasped, a touch out of breath. "I heard she an' Dodge are fightin'. Just in case." His grin transformed a somber face into a handsome one. "We got maybe ten minutes before they get the grav controls sorted out. Best be prepared for anything."

Ollie nodded, ignoring the faint twinge in her chest region at his smile. The three quickly unlocked the two ships, and Paris disappeared inside the *Princess* to warm up the engines while Mattie did the same on the *London*. Ollie pulled a pry bar from the toolkit and waited at the bottom of the gangplank.

Tiny and Mouse appeared at the doorway pushing a long garbage barge loaded with six 200-liter cans, followed close behind by three Federation non-comms in uniform. "Stop! You can't be in here!" The boys wrenched the barge sideways to dump the bins just in front of the entry way. The contents floated out in a cloud, including piles of refuse and six youths that scrabbled out of the mess.

"Scatter!" Tiny shouted at them. With the ease of the space-born, the unknown children pushed off unerringly toward the *Indian Princess*. TIny then grabbed Mouse's pack and launched himself across the void toward Ollie. The two caught free hands, and with an elbow locked around the hydraulic strut controlling the gangplank, Ollie flung the boy and his packs up into the hold. "More's comin'! We just gotta hold 'em off!" Tiny said as he continued on to his station.

Behind him, Mouse turned with a grin to face down the adults that grabbed for him. Despite his diminutive size, the boy's ease in weightlessness offset the advantages of the two women and a man grabbing for him. "Stop! Oof—!" the man and women collided, with the third grabbing for Mouse's shirt. He twisted out of it, leaving her holding fabric as he reversed his position with his back to the doorframe and shoved at the woman with both feet and a heave of his shoulders. Without gravity, the momentum sent her cartwheeling across the hangar toward the ceiling on the far side.

Turning mid-air, Mouse grabbed the pair clinging to the each other and heaved them off in yet another direction. "They're coming!" he yelled, and gathered himself to push off for the *New London* gangplank as voices sounded from behind him. As he landed beside Ollie with a handhold on the edge of the hull, he eyed the prybar in her hand and winked. "That's the spirit." With a pat on her shoulder, Mouse pushed up past her.

From the entry point, there came a rush of youths in the plain grey overalls from the holding cells. Yelling and whooping, they rushed the *Indian Princess* as well as two more ships in the decommission line, easily overwhelming the three uniformed officers to cuff them to the fuel pumps. But no Dodger and Callie. Ollie grew anxious.

"Ready to depart, Ollie. Any sign of Dodge?" Mattie's head poked out.

"Not yet. He—" Ollie was interrupted by yelling from the entrance.

"Dark and stuffy rules lawyer! Defend yourself!" came a familiar voice echoing through the hangar.

"Idiot! Just get rid of him!" Callie appeared first in advance of her brother, and shoved herself through the entryway. She looked around a touch wildly until her gaze landed on her own ship, and she launched herself toward the *Indian Princess*.

Dodger appeared in the doorway, hooking one foot on the edge as the rest of his body dangled sideways back into the long hallway he'd just vacated.

"The prisoners will return to their holding cells. You are irresponsible and unfit for citizenship in the Federation, let alone command as an officer." Hook's voice boomed after him, echoing through the hangar as if he addressed all those escaping. The man himself appeared a moment later, catching Dodger around the waist as the two of them went flying together in a tangle of arms and legs across the open space.

"I know you are, but what am I?" taunted Dodger in return. As if all his fierce, irrepressible nature needed to exert itself at once, he was a flurry of fists and feet and knees and elbows, striking at Hook as well as any surface they encountered as the two bounced about like a pair of rubber balloons held together by static.

Ollie sucked in a breath as she watched, hand tightening on the steel bar. The two were surprisingly well matched in the struggle. Hook was clearly more experienced with combat and causing bodily harm, but Dodger's ability to manoeuver in zero-gee and upper arm strength served him well, and he made sure Hook bore the brunt of each impact even as the boy's face took a pounding.

The return of full gravity, when it happened, was helpful to neither. The two were perhaps four meters up a wall, where Hook had Dodger pinned, when weightlessness ended and the two fell to the ground in an awkward heap. The older man rose first, a sneer twisting his lips. "That's it, boy. You're mine now." He grabbed Dodger up from the deck with a hand around the boy's neck.

Ollie let go the hydraulics once her feet were on the ground, and launched herself across the distance to close in silence. Hook's hand cocked back in a fist as Dodger struggled in his grip, the boy's fingers struggling to pull the older man's hand loose. He made choking noises, body writhing against the wall behind him. Hook leaned in close, his face close enough as he nearly spit in the lad's face. "You are nothing but a little space rat, and you'll be a space rat until the day you die, which will be soon if I have anything to say about it."

"But you don't," grunted Ollie as she swung her pry bar at the back of Hook's head. He staggered, then dropped like a puppet with his strings cut as Dodger threw himself sideways. The boy lay on his hands and knees for a moment, sucking in breaths as he rubbed at his throat. Ollie leaned down to listen at Hook's lips.

"Is he dead?" Dodger asked hopefully.

Straightening, Ollie shook her head. "Nope. Good thing, too. We don't need a murder rap chasin' either one of us." She offered Dodger a hand, which he ignored as he struggled to his feet.

"I didn't need no help," Dodger muttered.

"Reckon not," Ollie nodded, trying for a straight expression. "Your ship is ready fer takeoff, Cap'n Dodger. Your sister?" They both looked to the *Princess*, whose gangplank was closing as the engines started to gow.

"She's goin' alone," Dodger sighed, and grabbed Ollie's hand as the two turned to run across the tarmac to the *New London*, whose engines were starting their low whine that presaged the thunder to come. "Apparently we both got us a powerful need to be in charge. I couldn't reason with 'er."

"Girls are like that," Ollie grinned as the pair dashed up the gangplank. She hit the closing controls, letting go of his hand when they were together in the belly of their ship.

Dodger lifted his voice to yell, "All clear, Paris! Get us outta here!"

"Aye aye, Cap'n!" came the response, and the *London* lifted to head out of the space station. A few moments later, they were on full burn out of the system with Dodger and Ollie on the bridge as Paris left to go check on his beloved engines.

"You mind if I send a private message?" Dodger looked to Ollie, who smiled and shook her head.

"You go on."

"Thanks. And Ollie?"

"Yeah?"

"That was a great plan."

# The Hope of Astraea
## Wendy Lambert

*Wendy Lambert writes speculative fiction and is a graduate of the Odyssey Writing Workshop. Her stories appear in* Necrology Shorts, In the Shimmering, *and the* 2015 Young Explorer's Adventure Guide. *She works as a school librarian and lives in Utah with her husband and children.*

"Is that the graveyard?" Cordelia pointed at the dots scattered across the navigation screen.

"Yes," Cordelia's dad replied. "We'll reach it within the hour." He tapped on the control panel, redirecting the massive solar sail by less than half a degree to avoid the drifting wreckage of ships from a long forgotten war. "Now, I need to concentrate – did you finish your schoolwork?"

"Yes." Cordelia squirmed her way onto his knee. "How close will we get to the graveyard?"

"Too close, if you don't leave your dad alone." Captain Alex stood up from her console and arched her back in a stretch.

"Captain's right. I need to concentrate. Besides," he shifted Cordelia off his knee, "at eleven, you're far too old to be sitting on my knee, don't you think? Why don't you go help Gran in the garden? I hear the strawberries are ready."

Cordelia scowled. She didn't want to pick strawberries. Her place was on the bridge of the Hope of Astraea – the starship she'd command when Captain Alex, her aunt, retired someday. She'd carry on the tradition of the past eighty years, bringing precious food and water, medicine and supplies to the farthest reaches of the system – a mining colony on the ship's namesake, the moon of Astraea.

When she was captain, she'd be able boss everyone about, keeping the Hope of Astraea running smoothly. But she wasn't captain yet, and it had been a very long time since she'd had fresh strawberries. Besides, Gran could tell her more about the ship graveyard. It'd been nearly four years since they'd last looped past it, and she didn't remember it very well.

"Okay, I'll help Gran," Cordelia said.

"What, no argument? You must not be feeling well." Cordelia's dad pressed the back of his hand to her forehead.

Cordelia batted his hand away. "Dad."

"That ship wasn't there last time. It's not on any of the charts," Captain Alex said, pointing at a dot in the upper right quadrant of the screen.

Cordelia moved in for a peek, but her Dad shooed her towards the bridge door. She slapped her hand against the button. The door opened with a whoosh. Milo, her very annoying little cousin, sat in the corridor. He'd been banned from the bridge since he'd let his silvery cyborg hand loose, and it'd caused all sorts of mischief before shorting out a console.

"Well?" Milo said.

"Well, what?"

"The graveyard. Are we almost there?"

"That's my business. And the captain's!"

"Is not."

Cordelia sighed and rolled her eyes.  She edged past Milo and broke into a run down the hall, her bare feet slapping against the worn wood planks.  She couldn't help but slow to look out the porthole as she passed.

"We are close," Milo said in knowing satisfaction.

"I never said –"

"But you're looking out like you're going to see something."

If she ran fast enough and took a detour through engineering, maybe she'd lose him, at least for a while. She rounded a corner, glancing back to see if she'd lost Milo when she ran smack into Uncle Joe.

"Whoa, slow down there," Uncle Joe said. He was dressed in his spacesuit, his helmet clamped under one arm and a deactivated fixer-bot under the other.

Cordelia grinned sheepishly. "Hi, how is she?"

"She's in tip-top shape, Captain Cordelia." He saluted her just like he did the real captain. "At least after I caught this malfunctioning fixer-bot that was punching more holes in the sail than it was fixing."

"Very good. Carry on, sir." Cordelia scrambled around him, expecting to see Milo at any second. Cordelia thundered down the steps into engineering. She zig-zagged around humming machines and computers.

A greasy hand shot up from above a machine and waved. "Slow down, Cordelia."

She skidded to a fast walk. "Good morning, Aunt Syrina. How's everything running today?"

"Output's a little low. I'm making a few adjustments."

"Very good," she said.

Cordelia raced up the stairs on the opposite end of engineering, taking them all the way to the top of the ship, to the garden. Its massive windowed dome gave the best views of inky space and distant stars. The heavy aroma of dirt mingled with the sweet scent of strawberries. She hadn't outsmarted Milo at all. He knelt next to Gran over the strawberry patch.

"Gently now," Gran said to Milo.

Milo moved his cyborg hand towards the tiny stem of a strawberry.

"That's it . . . hello, Cordelia," Gran said without taking her eyes off Milo.

Milo lifted the strawberry and dangled it above the basket. "Can I eat it?"

Gran smiled. "Sure, just this one." She plucked a strawberry and held it out to Cordelia. "For you, my dear."

Cordelia took the strawberry and bit into it, savoring the sweetness.

"Now that we've satisfied our taste buds, shall we?" Gran handed Cordelia a small basket. Gran had outdone herself this year. The plants bowed with all the berries. "How's the Hope of Astraea today?" Gran asked.

"Fine. We're approaching the graveyard, and Uncle Joe brought in a broken fixer-bot. Engineering reports a slight decrease in output, but they're making the necessary adjustments."

"And our course?"

"On schedule for the drop."

Milo cleared his throat. "I heard there are dead bodies floating around in the graveyard." His eyes were wide, and he crushed a strawberry in his cyborg fingers. Cordelia shook her head and frowned.

"Now where did you hear something like that?" Gran asked.

He pointed at Cordelia.

Gran laughed. "She's just trying to scare you. There's only the wreckage of ships floating about. Now, tell me Cordelia, what's the most dangerous part?"

"Making sure the sail doesn't hit large debris. We need to maintain our speed and course so we make our drop on time."

Gran's eyes sparkled with approval. "You'll make a fine captain someday. It's important to remember all those details." She tapped at her head, covered in soft gray curls, edged in black. "And what happens if we are off by even a quarter of degree?"

"We'll miss our drop, and the miners will starve. And we won't make our turn in time, and then we risk starving, too," Cordelia said.

"That's right," Gran said.

Cordelia's basket was nearly full. There would be plenty of strawberries for pies and shortcake.

The peace was shattered as an alarm shrieked in rhythm with a pulsing red light. Cordelia had never heard nor seen that alarm before. Gran's soft eyes turned hard, and she straightened her back, looking just like the faint memory Cordelia had of her when she was still captain.

The ship jolted suddenly to the right, knocking them all to the floor. A shadow darkened the dome momentarily as a starship passed overhead.

Gran grabbed both their shoulders, pushing them through the flowerbed, past the cherry tree towards a vent. "In there now. No matter what happens, you stay put. You hide. Do you understand?"

"What's that alarm? Gran, what's happening?" Cordelia asked. Milo whimpered.

"Cordelia, you stay hidden. You keep Milo safe. Promise me."

"I promise." Cordelia climbed into the vent behind Milo.

The ship pitched hard to the right again, and then she felt it slow down. That wasn't good. Milo clamped his cyborg hand too tightly around her arm. Cordelia worked her fingers under the hand and pulled it free.

"It's going to be okay," she whispered to Milo.

Gran raced from the gardens, leaving Cordelia with the sound of her own thumping heart matching the rhythm of the alarm, continuing even after the sound abruptly stopped. She strained to hear the muffled voices, recognizing some as her aunts, uncles and older cousins. Some were definitely not her family.

The stillness of the garden broke as a man in ragged clothes and unkempt beard barreled into the garden, holding a gun – a pirate! He circled the garden, pushing aside branches, peering into the shadows and stopping for a time right in front of their vent.

Cordelia was certain he could see them between the slits in the vent, could hear her thumping heart. But he didn't say a word. He paused at the strawberry patch and popped a berry into his mouth. He took her basket of strawberries and left. For a long time they sat there in silence, waiting for Gran to return.

"Do you think it's safe?" Milo whispered.

"No," Cordelia said. "If it was, someone would've come back for us."

"What do we do?"

"Well," Cordelia said, having had all this time to think on it, "we need to see what's going on."

"But Gran said not to leave the vent."

"Who said anything about leaving the vent?"

Milo grinned.

•••

From behind the vent cover and between rows of crates, they could see the entire family – aunts, uncles, cousins, her dad, and Gran – with hands and legs bound, crammed in the corner of the cargo hold. They looked okay, except for Uncle Joe, who sported a nasty bruise and cut on his face.

It hadn't been easy snaking their way through the ducts. The hardest part proved crawling quietly, and it didn't help that Milo had a metal hand and an endless number of questions.

"Are you sure they're pirates? They don't have eye patches or parrots. I haven't heard any of them say *argh* even once," Milo said.

"They're not like pirates on water, but they boarded our ship. They're holding our family hostage and taking our stuff – they're space pirates," Cordelia whispered. She then raised her finger to hush any more questions.

The six pirates had carried crate after crate of food and supplies meant for the miners of Astraea out of the cargo hold and loaded them onto their ship. They'd stolen a dozen crates before they gave in to their hunger.

Cordelia hadn't noticed how skinny the pirates were until they cracked open one of the crates and began devouring the food inside. They even ate her juicy strawberries. The pirates had set their weapons on the crate beside the door, just feet away from the vent, where she and Milo gently nudged each other back and forth to see out. The pirates were focused on the food and watching her family, leaving their backs to the two children.

"How's your hand?" Cordelia whispered to Milo.

"What?"

"Do you think you could get those?"

Milo's eyes went wide. "What're you thinking?"

"Those weapons are dangerous. The pirates aren't watching. We need to get rid of them so that nobody gets hurt."

Milo grinned and wrenched his cyborg hand free of his arm. Cordelia carefully pushed the hinged vent cover up and gave Milo a nod. His cyborg hand crawled out of the vent and gripped the edge of the wooden crate.

It always amazed Cordelia how a cyborg hand could do what hers couldn't. The fingers crawled upward, scaling the crate in seconds. Milo was concentrating so hard that his tongue wagged at the corner of his mouth.

Cordelia glanced back and forth between the hand and the pirates wolfing down her strawberries. Milo's hand gripped the handle of a knife between its thumb and index finger and then skillfully backed down the crate to the vent. Cordelia snatched the knife and set it down beside her.

Milo went to work again. His tongue whipped around his lips as the hand crawled back up the crate and grasped a length of metal pipe. The hand inched back down, the pipe clenched between the thumb and index finger but beginning to wobble. Cordelia stretched out her hand too late. The pipe slipped from his fingers and clanged to the floor. She grabbed Milo's hand and shut the vent cover tight just as the munching pirates spun around.

Milo clung with both hands to her arm in a breathless moment of terror as one of the pirates, a wild and mean-looking one, investigated the sound. He bent down, eyeing the area suspiciously and grabbing the pipe. He set it back on the pile of weapons.

The pirates continued devouring their ill-gotten feast. Cordelia peered from the slits of the vent cover. Her dad stared past the pirates, between the stacks of crates; he looked right at her and winked.

Cordelia gasped. "Try again. Be careful."

Milo nodded, and his cyborg hand once again inched out the vent and up the side of the crate.

"I see most of the jackets you're wearing have the Zancor logo on them. Are you from the Astraea mining colony?" Cordelia's dad called out to the pirates. Even with their backs to her and Milo, she could see them fidget uncomfortably.

"What do you care?" one pirate shouted back.

"It's just that we're bringing the food and supplies to you. All this is meant to supply your colony for the next four years. It seems that –"

"It seems that it's none of your business," the ragged pirate with the scraggly beard, the one who had searched the gardens, chimed in. Of all of them, he seemed to be the man in charge, the pirate captain.

"I'm not trying to pry . . . just want to understand." Her dad's voice was sugary sweet. Far more than these pirates deserved, she thought. But the distraction was good. Milo had successfully retrieved the pipe and was now bringing down a small pistol.

"Is there some problem with the colony? We're not within communication range, so we haven't had any updates in quite some time," Cordelia's dad asked.

The pirates looked at each other, all with guilty expressions, like they'd just been caught with their hands in the cookie jar. The pirate captain spat at the ground. "All is not well, sir, and hasn't been for quite some time. Miners are mistreated. Conditions have . . . shall we say –deteriorated."

"I see," said Cordelia's dad.

Milo's tongue wagged like a fast-spinning merry-go-round while he fixed his concentration on the last weapon, a long-barreled gun. It was trickiest of all. Cordelia was grateful her dad kept talking.

"I'm sorry for your troubles. Surely we can come to some sort of agreement. You all look hungry – I get how desperate you must be feeling, out here in empty space, so far from your families."

Milo inched the gun down the side of the crate, holding it carefully above the floor. Cordelia looked each of the pirates up and down. They were so focused on her dad that they weren't watching their weapons disappear into the duct. Cordelia reached out and snatched the gun from Milo's grip. His hand crawled back in.

"I can't agree," the pirate captain said.

"Come on." Milo tugged on her arm.

She wanted to hear her dad out. If anyone could convince them to give up their pirating ways, it was him.

Each carrying half of the weapons, the two children crawled towards airlock number two, far away from the tethered pirate ship and the cargo bays.

"It's clear," Cordelia said and poked the hinged vent cover outward. She climbed out, still cradling half the weapons in her arm. Milo poked his head out, looking both ways down the hall before crawling out.

They both knew they weren't supposed to jettison stuff into space. Cluttered it up unnecessarily, Gran always said, but this was a special circumstance. Besides, this part of space was already cluttered up with those torn-apart ships. By the look of things, they were in the middle of the graveyard, far too close to the scarred, endlessly floating hulks.

Cordelia and Milo tossed the weapons into the airlock.

"Maybe we should just keep the one?" Milo protested. "I could shoot the pirates."

"No," Cordelia said decisively. There was as much chance they or their family would get hurt if he tried that.

She closed the airlock door and hit the button. Moments later the weapons soundlessly rocketed into space, joining the graveyard of the forgotten war.

"Now to catch us some pirates," Cordelia said.

•••

In a rush of whispered words, they'd come up with the plan. Cordelia knew that catching the pirates wouldn't be as easy as stealing their weapons had been. They decided to lure the pirates into one of the empty cargo bays and lock them inside. It was the luring that troubled her. She knew from the dropped pipe that the men would come running at a sound, but what if they didn't follow? What if she and Milo got caught instead?

She hoped Cousin Liza, the head cook, would forgive her for any dents to her pots, but the noise had to be loud enough to attract the pirates' attention. With a last deep breath, she threw the stack of pots to the floor and made herself wait so the pirates could see her.

"My gun – our weapons!" a pirate cried.

Two angry-looking pirates tore out of the cargo bay and gave chase. Cordelia led them down the hall and turned the corner. Their legs were longer, and they were gaining, but she was a step ahead. She grinned. The plan was working. She half-turned around to see them racing after her, and as she turned forward again, she pelted hard into the pirate captain.

Where had he come from?

He grabbed her. "Got ya!" he said triumphantly.

Cordelia kicked and wriggled, but his hands gripped tighter and tighter.

"Well, well, well," one of the other pirates said. "Looks like we got a rat."

"Let me go!" Cordelia shouted.

The pirate captain laughed. "Not on your life. What'd you do with our weapons?" The pirate lifted her off the ground.

Cordelia kicked her legs. "I won't tell you."

"Then I'm afraid something bad is going to happen to your family. I don't need a gun to hurt them, you see."

Cordelia gulped. She could see it in his eyes. He would hurt them, all of them. "Over there." She pointed down the hall. "Cargo bay four."

The pirate dragged her down the hall with the other two pirates following close behind. Cargo bay four was filled with empty crates.

The pirate captain held her tight. "Where are they?"

"Over there." Cordelia pointed to the far corner stacked tall with crates.

The two pirates glanced doubtfully at Cordelia, but with a nod from the pirate captain, they made for the corner. They tossed crate after crate aside, smashing them against the floor.

"They're not here," the pirate called.

"Where –"

The door to the bay whooshed closed. The pirate jerked around at the sound, loosening but not releasing his grip on Cordelia. Cordelia kicked his shin as hard as she could, just like she did when playing soccer with Milo in cargo bay six.

The pirate grunted and let go. Cordelia darted away squeezing between two stacks of crates to the vent access. She threw up the hinged cover and wriggled inside. She heard the crates being shoved aside as the pirates clawed their way to her. One grabbed her foot; she kicked up hard, smacking him in the face. He recoiled, letting go of her foot. She scrambled away as fast as she could, hoping none of them were skinny enough to fit in after her.

Cordelia crawled through the duct and stopped just outside the opening in the hall, listening for sounds of trouble. It was quiet.

A hand reached for the vent cover. Cordelia scooted back before she realized it was Milo's. The silvery hand slipped under the vent and gave an enthusiastic thumbs-up.

"You okay?" Milo whispered.

Cordelia crawled out of the vent. "Yeah. You sure it's locked well?"

Milo grinned and nodded. Cordelia checked the door lock, just in case. The pirates inside talked in low voices. One started pounding on the door.

"That's three. Just three more to go," Cordelia said.

An alarm blared at the same moment that blue warning lights began to whirl.

Cordelia and Milo gaped at each other.

"What does it mean?" he asked.

"Nothing good. You hide, okay?" She ran in the direction of the bridge, hoping the sound didn't bring the other pirates out.

Cordelia reached the bridge and slid into the captain's chair. The view-screen in front of her and every other on the bridge displayed the same scene – the Hope of Astraea hurtling towards a massive piece of a wrecked battleship at the edge of the graveyard. When the pirate ship had tethered itself to the Hope, it'd thrown her dangerously off course. The battleship would hit and damage the Hope's miles-wide solar sail that caught the sun's radiation and pushed them through space.

The warning alarm was clear. There wasn't time for the ship to change course. The defensive laser array that normally blasted away pieces of space debris, ice, asteroids and meteors wouldn't fire automatically on a ship. The computer didn't know that this ship had long ago been abandoned. It needed a human to give the command.

Cordelia tapped at the screen, giving the command to fire on the battleship and blast it to smithereens. Within seconds, the central laser cannon sent bursts of brilliant purple beams towards the ship. The ship seemed to absorb the beams, but soon it began to glow from the inside before it exploded in a million fiery pieces.

The laser array lit up again, targeting one piece of wreckage after another, blowing them into tiny bits that would inflict minimal damage to the sail. Cordelia couldn't help but hold her breath as the Hope sailed into the debris-filled space where the battleship had once been.

Sensors beeped as pieces of the battleship rained through the bottom center of the sail and engulfed the Hope of Astraea, sounding like sand hitting windows. Uncle Joe and his fixer-bots would have to spacewalk several times to fix the sail, but it would've been a thousand times worse if they'd plowed through the battleship, risking not only the sail but the whole of the Hope.

Cordelia let out a deep breath in relief. She brought up the navigation screen. The pirate ship had pulled the Hope of Astraea a fraction off course. It was enough, though, that if they continued on their present course for much longer, they would miss the drop point entirely, leaving the miners to hunt empty space for their food and supplies.

She'd watched her Dad make course corrections hundreds of times before. She tapped the command, altering course to match the computer-suggested path.

A hand gripped her shoulder.

The pirates. How could she have forgotten about the pirates?

Cordelia whipped around.

Her dad beamed down at her.

"Dad!" Cordelia jumped up and threw her arms around his neck.

He hugged her for a long time. "You okay?"

"Yes, but what about the pirates?"

Her dad chuckled. "Well, I'd hardly call them pirates . . . more like starving runaway miners. The last three surrendered. They lost their nerve when the alarm went off and their buddies never returned."

"Your dad's being modest," Captain Alex plopped down into her chair. "He'd nearly talked them into surrendering before the alarm."

"We almost had 'em," Cordelia said.

"We really did," Milo called from the edge of the bridge.

The captain waved him forward. "That was quite the *handiwork*, Milo," she said.

Cordelia couldn't help but giggle.

Milo grinned. "Thanks, Mom . . . I mean, Captain." He saluted her with his cyborg hand.

She saluted back and turned to Cordelia. "You saved us. And by the look of things, you got us back on course."

"Just keeping my . . . the Hope of Astraea safe, Aunt . . . Captain Alex. It's my duty."

"Not just yet. I'm not quite ready to retire."

Cordelia blushed.

"But thank you for keeping her and us safe. And I'm sure there's a whole colony of miners who will be grateful when they hear of your heroics."

"Why don't you and Milo go talk to Gran?" Cordelia's Dad suggested. "She said something about needing to pick more strawberries for a celebration."

"Beat you there," Milo said.

"Oh no, you won't!" Cordelia lighted past Milo, racing for the gardens and Gran.

Proof